D0338333

Practical Demonology

Practical Demonology

CLARE REES

AMULET BOOKS • NEW YORK

Cataloging-in-Publication Data has been applied for and may be obtained from the Library of Congress.

ISBN 978-1-4197-4558-4

Printed and bound in U.S.A.
10 9 8 7 6 5 4 3 2 1

Amulet Books are available at special discounts when purchased in quantity for premiums and promotions as well as fundraising or educational use. Special editions can also be created to specification. For details, contact specialsales@abramsbooks.com or the address below.

Amulet Books® is a registered trademark of Harry N. Abrams, Inc.

ABRAMS The Art of Books
195 Broadway, New York, NY 10007
abramsbooks.com

To Maggie and John

Chapter 1

"Plague! Plague!"

A new voice cried the announcement this morning. Last night the crier had called the warning through the citadel streets until their voice went hoarse, and then bells had been rung until the early hours. Surely there was nobody now who didn't know?

Non listened for the voice as it moved through the different passageways and alleys, trying to work out where it was, how far away now, whose house it was outside. Apart from the crier, the street was eerily silent. There were none of the normal morning noises—that undertone of life you didn't notice until it wasn't there. The emptiness felt oppressive, more jarring than any noise would have been.

She lined the bottles up in front of her. She'd already pasted the labels on, and the first batch of medicine was cool enough now to go in. The second was bubbling on the stove. Another five minutes, no more. The smell was filling the room, acrid, sharp, so that it collected at the back of her throat. But she liked it—that part-chemical, part-herby smoke that was so strong it was almost a taste.

One wall of the room was lined with books—half were science and medicine, but the others were stories and tales of people's lives.

Some were made up and some were true, but Non didn't always feel there was much difference. Some of the true stories, the experiences people had lived, were so fantastical and bizarre that they didn't seem to be so different from the fairy tales. There were enough different worlds and life stories of extraordinary people in the room that you didn't need to leave.

It was the medical books she meant to read, of course, so she could go on and become a doctor, just like her dad. It was a great career choice—sensible, useful, helping others, respected. Absolutely a great decision. And she was really glad she'd made that decision. There hadn't been another one to make that would be as sensible as that.

It's just that the medical books weren't always as interesting as the others; even when she'd read them, sometimes she couldn't remember what they'd been about. It was fine, though; when that happened, she just switched off whatever her daydream had been—those unofficial, unexpected thoughts that kept seeping in—and read the page again until it all made sense. It was all fine, and she liked staying here, in safety, inside the walls of the house—living other people's lives, hearing other people's stories, experiencing more than you ever could outside in the world by yourself.

There was a gap on one of the shelves, the blank space there important. Even when her dad bought new books, and though there was a stack overflowing onto his desk right now, they were never put on the shelf to fill that gap. It was a gap that, Non estimated, would fit maybe four reasonably sized books or notebooks. She didn't wonder about it much other than to notice it, though it had obviously been where her mum's books went. Her dad didn't comment either. It was just one of those many things they didn't want to discuss and didn't need to discuss.

On the other walls, there were rows of bottles and jars. Most Non knew the names of, at least, and could identify, but not all. Some were dusty each time she cleaned them—still untouched and unused since the last time. She knew what some of them did—what they cured—and how the careful combination of two powders could change the properties of the medicine into something quite different. It was interesting, sort of, but it sometimes felt more like the witchcraft in those fairy stories than science. The medicine books were not that different from how she imagined witches' potion books to be. Especially now, when they didn't have a cure—when they didn't know what the plague actually was.

She hadn't entirely made the medicine up. It was all sensible ingredients. A pinch of this to stop the diarrhea, a pinch of that to ease stomach cramps, a pinch of this to help with the nausea. It would help those suffering from the mysterious illness anyway. There were notes in the back of the medical books—things people had tried before, the last time the plague had struck. One interesting thing they'd noted was that there appeared to be two different types of plague—similar symptoms, but one more serious than the other. That bit had been underlined. The problem with plague, though, was that when it struck, nobody had time for exploring interesting things, so that crucial detail didn't seem to have been researched further. It was too early to tell which strain it was yet, but she hoped it would be the milder form. She'd used the notes as a guide in making the medicine anyway, but in a more sensible ratio, and had added in mint and sugar to help with the taste.

She wrote her own notes in now—and a date. Two different hands had made the earlier notes, and the ink was faded. She wondered how long ago they had written their findings down. This century? Last? And she wondered how many people had died those times. It was different when you didn't know the people—it was just an abstract concept then, the number of deaths. She didn't let herself think about how many there would be this time. They'd learned from the mistakes of the past, and they were ready. Like everything in the citadel, the plague was predictable, and there were procedures to follow, all written down neatly in the council rules. It's only that the outcome of the plague was unpredictable, that's all.

"Oh, Non, don't worry about all this." Her father's voice made her jump. As he came in, she could see his face was already lined with tiredness, his shirt crumpled. He must have slept in it—even though she'd left out another three, clean and ironed, ready for him to change into. "Thanks for doing it, but you'll be late."

"I don't think I should go," she said. "I think I should stay and help you here."

"You won't help me by being here."

"But I can make the medicine and make sure you eat."

"And I can do those things too. You'll be more of a worry to me if you're here. I'll be worrying about you catching it."

"But what if *you* catch it?"

He paused. "Then we'll figure that out if it happens." He paused again, looking at her through the steam. She busied herself taking the bubbling medicine off the stove.

"This one is done now too," she said. "And the bottles are ready. You just need to pour it in when it's cooled. I've left everything ready for you."

"I know you're scared, Non, but you are going to have to leave."

Non didn't flinch, because she was already so tense she could barely breathe. "I got as much food in for you as I could," she said. "But it was difficult to get everything I wanted."

"I'll be all right, Non. I know what I'm doing."

"And I know what I'm doing too. I'm not a child!" she snapped. And then wished she hadn't. She felt whiny, pathetic, and immature just using that line—like it undermined everything she'd already said and done, as well as any of the arguments she was going to make.

"No. You're not." He sighed, and she knew she was keeping him from those who needed him. "So you understand the dangers. And the fact is, right now it's more dangerous for you to stay."

She smiled grimly and closed the books, putting them back in their correct places on the shelves.

"You'll be a worry to me if you stay."

"Fine."

"Have you got your own things packed?"

She checked through her bag. She'd thrown everything in last night, when the quarantine had been announced. But she'd packed badly. Even as she was doing it, she knew she hadn't wanted to go.

"I still think I should stay," she said. "I could even just stay indoors here and not go out. That would be almost like going to quarantine."

"No, staying in a plague-ridden citadel is not as effective as going somewhere that has no infection at all." He paused. "You *will* be fine, Non. Just like I'll be fine. Stay inside the castle walls and you'll be safe. Keep up with your studies and then maybe you can help next time there's a crisis. It'll only be a couple of weeks anyway. Treat it like a holiday."

She grimaced. "Worst holiday ever."

He laughed. "I love you, darling, and so will everybody else—if you only give them a chance to get to know you. Maybe just try that?" He gave her a long look, then added, "Look, just stay inside those castle walls. Keep yourself safe. It's only a short journey to get there, and then you'll be out of harm's way. It'll be fine, Non."

She reached over and hugged him tightly. "I love you, Dad."

He hugged her back before peeling her arms away and pushing her toward the door. "I love you too. But you've still got to go."

Chapter 2

There was no one on the streets that morning—most of the shutters were still closed. Although they lived close to the gate, in this part of the citadel the houses were built very close together, the passages so narrow that at some points Non had to walk sideways so her shoulders didn't brush against the walls. On this bright morning, the sun did break through in places, squeezing between the roofs and awnings and washing lines of the houses, revealing peeling paint, trails of green fungus, and crumbling mortar. But it never made it down to the cobbled pathways. They remained permanently in shadow and were often mysteriously dirty, slippery with mud and things Non didn't want to think too much about. She walked slowly here and then had to loop round, because the streets didn't go straight and none of the paths led directly to anything; there was always a complicated diversion that made the citadel feel larger than it was. It could have been described as a maze of streets, except that a maze suggests an answer—some sort of plan. There was nothing like that here. The streets were just a mess.

If she hadn't been so anxious, she knew she'd have cried, so she was grateful for that, at least. She felt completely tense with it all, her shoulders tight, the muscles sore, the start of a headache at the base of her neck. She deliberately tried not to think about anything—not about people dying, about her father maybe getting ill, about going to live with strangers, about leaving the citadel walls. She thought very hard about not thinking—and it was with a sort of success. She focused on walking, and breathing, and trying to relax her shoulders.

As she reached the gate, everything opened out, the area around it clear—in case troops had to gather urgently, or in case of emergency evacuation from the fortified farmsteads. The cobbles here were arranged in neat rows of evenly cut stone, gleaming and welcoming; the guardhouses lining the square were freshly painted, the walls sturdy and secure; the armor of the soldiers was polished and new; and two pots of blue and purple flowers bloomed on either side of the portcullis.

Twenty or so students had already gathered. Not everybody had come. Some were ill already, perhaps, or some had stayed to look after family members. Still more were sure they'd be fine if they just stayed indoors for a few days.

Non joined the back of the group, but Meg spotted her and waved.

"Non! Non!" She grabbed Non's hand and pulled her right into the center of the students.

"I've decided this is going to be great, isn't it?" said Meg. "Who's up for a party?" Her long blond hair bounced on her shoulders every time she moved, the ends swaying back and forth just above her waist. It was tied at the top with a red ribbon, but the ribbon was more of a gesture to convention than something that served a purpose. It seemed to just make the waves in Meg's hair more obvious, and they spilled out anyway, shining every time they caught the light—which was often, because Meg flicked her hair as she talked. Her eyes were a bright green, and the combination made her look pretty and sweet. But her eyes saw more than people thought, and behind her easy laughter there was a determination not everybody spotted. And anybody who didn't spot it was in trouble.

"It's the plague, Meg. We're going to quarantine," said Non.

"Party!" said Meg, grinning.

"Plague!" said Non, shaking her head.

"Quarantine party!" said Meg, nodding.

"Meg! We're being sent away because they're trying to protect us."

". . . which also means nobody is supervising us."

"It might be serious."

Meg pulled a face. "It won't be, though, will it? My mum's definitely overreacting. Half the people supposed to be going haven't even bothered turning up. I'm just going to make the most of no school before they change their minds and bring us back. Let's at least try and have some fun, Non."

Non normally liked to let Meg do most of the talking for her. It wasn't that she didn't have things to say—it's more that they weren't always worth saying. And sometimes the conversations she had with herself, inside her own head, were more interesting than what other people talked about, anyway. Meg always made her laugh, though, even if Non didn't always listen to absolutely everything she said. You didn't have to with Meg; she'd repeat the important bits if Non didn't reply. Always being next to Meg meant that she didn't get looked at much either. It was like when somebody stood in front of a fire.

You could see they were there, but they were in shadow, surrounded by all that brightness and warmth. Non had always seen this as an advantage, so far.

"I wonder if there're going to be any hot boys from the other evacuated castles," said Meg. "What do you reckon?"

"Doesn't matter if they're hot or not. You'll just convince yourself they are, anyway."

"Yes, well, I like to look for the positive in anyone . . ."

"No, you don't."

". . . and particularly in men. I think there is normally something nice about them if you look for it, and also I think that I want to make sure that I've tested out a range of men. I'd hate for my future husband to be more experienced than me."

"Unlikely."

"Hopefully not. How embarrassing would that be?"

Non undid the strap on her bag and looked inside. She checked her underwear, hairbrush, notebook, and other bits. She knew there was something she was forgetting, but maybe that was just a sign of anxiety? Because there was nothing obvious. "I don't think you should be kissing anybody at the moment though," she said. "What about the plague? It probably spreads through human contact."

"I'm not *planning* anything," said Meg. "And I won't kiss them if they're bleeding from the ears or have giant growths under their arm or anything. But if a nice opportunity comes up, I might take it."

One of the boys, Chris, sniggered. "Comes. Up," he said.

Meg stared at him blankly. "What do you mean?" she said, her head tilted to one side and her eyes wide.

"Oh. You know," he laughed.

"No?" Meg frowned delicately. "Maybe you could explain it to me?"

He flushed and looked away.

"Idiot," she muttered to Non. "The boys from this citadel are such losers. I bet the ones from the other castles will be way nicer."

There was a hush and several soldiers walked under the portcullis. They were led by Commander Edwards, one of the citadel's military leaders. As he saw the students, he moved his mouth into a smile shape, but the rest of his face remained still, so his stretched lips looked more like he'd just eaten something bad than was giving a friendly greeting. His face was covered in scars, which reached across one side of his face entirely. There was a sizable gouge out of the back of his head, and the spiderweb of scar tissue that covered it seemed almost to glisten in the early-morning sun. He kept his hair short instead of growing it to cover the scars, and the stubble was patchy and dark, which added depth to the layers of his injury, highlighting them with shadow.

His eyes moved over the courtyard, and he seemed to both focus on nothing and see everything.

"Out." He gestured across the drawbridge. "Get on the carts, some of you. Others, walk. All of you get your weapons out. Any questions?"

He turned and walked back across the drawbridge without waiting to see. A few people did put their hands up, but there was nobody to answer their questions, so their hands wavered in midair for a few seconds before they put them down again.

Non unslung her crossbow and put her bag across her shoulders instead. She felt for the spear hooked onto her belt and checked her arrows, lifting them, stroking her fingers across the feathered ends as she walked through the gate. She tensed slightly as she always did when they passed underneath the portcullis, but its chains were still coiled up and the soldiers were relaxed. The noise as it fell every evening, that groaning screech of metal sliding against metal, was something that always made her flinch.

The air outside was immediately cooler, and it somehow felt bigger too, so that each breath seemed to fill Non's lungs more easily that the air inside the citadel. It all felt too open, like there was too much of the world out there. The walls of the citadel were still at their backs, but the feeling of not being enclosed made everything seem blurry—the distances and size hard to gauge.

Non looked over at the line of trees beyond the field and the river running between them. For a moment all that open space seemed to spin together, the sky above and the trees and the grass a swirl of colors, but she blinked and took a deep breath and the lines became sharper again. It was only a short journey to the castle. She didn't need to worry. She scanned the trees and the grass again, but it was fine. Absolutely fine. She gripped her bow more firmly, though, just in case it wasn't.

"Get on the cart," shouted a soldier. "Move!"

Those nearest clambered on. Non put her bag on the cart but then stepped away so she could walk next to it. She felt twitchy now, restless. The stress of the plague and the lack of sleep were making her feel funny, and she thought the rocking motion of the cart probably wouldn't be a good thing. She also wanted to be able to run if she needed to, be able to get away from danger more quickly than she could if she was sitting on a cart.

The students were unusually quiet—whether from nerves at leaving their families, anxiety about plague, or the more normal worry about demons and gormads. The soldiers spread out around them, surrounding the vehicles, and a group of boys joined them too, holding their weapons out and swaggering with importance. They looked around gravely, as though they were ready to fight anything that would come their way. And some of them would be good in a fight, probably. But most of them looked like what they were: young men in their last few years of school who might go on to join the military, but who might also become lawyers, farmers, teachers, shopkeepers, or any of those other jobs that didn't normally involve killing.

Meg leaned back on the cart and tossed her hair; several of the boys flinched, as though those blond waves were a whip. Their weapons drooped as they stared at her, and there was a slight smile on her lips, which meant she was going to enjoy herself on this trip.

The cart set off along the wide track through the fields, and they moved out from beneath the shadow of the citadel. The sun was suddenly blinding, and Non turned to walk backward for a moment, looking at the gate. She didn't remember having looked at it properly before. *Really* looked. The citadel was so obviously unnatural, with its straight, smooth lines and massive size. The walls were thick and towered over the valley, with its softness and the gentle curves of nature. The dull gray of the stone was dotted here and there with trails of white limestone, which seemed to waterfall down to the ground, getting wider as they neared the grass. The battlements above were precise and neat, from down here more like a decoration than a defense, the crenellations crimping at the edge of a card. But guards walked back and forth along them slowly, their eyes trained on the fields and valley, watchful and steady. In the guard towers, helmeted archers stood, their crossbows resting on the walls, the arrows ready for use.

From out here, there was no sign of the mess inside the walls, the hundreds of people jammed in together. All looked orderly and organized. The red kites circled over the citadel as they always did, perching on the castle towers, lining the battlements, their feathers shivering in the breeze but their eyes focused, their beaks razor-sharp. Sometimes they'd fight overhead, flying in to attack each other, their calls eerie and echoing around the valley. But mostly they just circled the citadel, watching and waiting.

A few of them flew lazily over the carts this morning, following the students on their journey. Non hoped it was just boredom, and not that they'd spotted anything down on the track. The birds followed death: the already dead, and the promise of death.

"So how bad is the plague, Non?" asked Ellie.

Most of the students, and some of the soldiers too, turned to Non with interest. She felt her cheeks getting hot at their glances and hoped she wasn't blushing.

"There are a few confirmed cases, but Dad thinks it's been caught early. He hopes there won't be many problems."

"Is it worse in the other two castles?"

"I don't know. Maybe."

Her answers weren't as scandalous or interesting as they'd

sounded like they might be, and most people turned away again. In truth, her father hadn't had time to tell her much about the plague. He and the other medics had been too busy trying to help those struck down with the illness. But he wouldn't have told her anyway. Being the doctor's daughter had never meant that she'd had access to all the intriguing medical secrets people always assumed. It just meant cleaning the surgery a lot, plus sorting out all the medicines and bills. That never stopped people from asking her questions, though.

Meg leaned over to Non and Ellie. "You do realize we can do whatever we want for the next few weeks. Nobody will ever know what we get up to," she whispered. "And I'm going to get up to every-thing. *Everything.*"

Ellie laughed, then covered her mouth with her hand as though she was shy. She wasn't shy.

"What about you two?" Meg whispered. "We'll have nobody watching us, nobody telling us what to do, and nobody'll care what we get up to, because there's much worse things going on in the world right now."

"But people might tell on us when the plague is over and we go back to the citadel," whispered Ellie.

"Then we just deny it," said Meg. "But also, why would they tell, when they'll be behaving badly too?" She raised her eyebrows.

"Meg, no," said Non. "Don't drag everybody else down with you."

"Oh, I don't think I'll really have to drag anybody. I think a lot of people are already thinking the same."

They looked at the others. Those people they'd known all their lives. When she thought of them outside of school, Non still pictured some of them the way they'd been as young children and not as they were now. It was hard to remember that they'd grown up.

"I'm up for having some fun," Ellie whispered, then giggled, covering her mouth again as though to conceal what she'd said but also drawing more attention to the fact that their discussion was secret.

"Me too," said Non. "Of course." Though—was she? She couldn't really think of anything bad she wanted to do now that she was away from her dad and anybody who might judge.

What would she want to do with all this freedom? For a moment, all the possibilities and all that choice felt almost like they were crushing her, like the requirement to behave badly was just another set of expectations to smother her. She liked the certainty of her life in the citadel, the rules, the plans, the way her life was going to be—training as a doctor, becoming a doctor, taking over her dad's business, marrying some as-yet-unidentified citadel boy and having children. It was safe, secure, comfortable. Predictable. She liked being judged, and she liked meeting the expectations of anybody judging her. She also liked blending in, being part of a background that nobody noticed. She didn't see it as shyness, exactly, more just that she didn't see any benefit to being at the center of the attention. So clearly she'd have to behave moderately badly just to blend in, but not too badly or she'd stand out. It would be a challenging balance, and already she wished she'd stayed inside the citadel with the plague.

But Ellie giggled, and Meg sat up straighter on the cart, facing toward the front once more.

Up ahead, Commander Edwards seemed to have disappeared. Non hadn't noticed him leaving the path, but she couldn't see him among the trees on either side of them or in the fields across the river. The rest of the soldiers remained, still watchful, their hands on their weapons, ready for an attack at any moment. But Non could see that all the boys had relaxed now. They seemed to have forgotten they were in danger and were just strolling along looking round at the trees. A couple were resting their arms on the carts, chatting or thinking about climbing on. Most of them had put their crossbows back over their shoulders, and those with swords or spears were either using them as walking sticks or were swinging them back and forth casually. Was nobody else worried? How was nobody else worried? Non checked her arrows again, slid her crossbow down her arm. But then she slung it back up again. She should try to relax too. She knew that.

And it was a beautiful day for a walk. The birds were singing in the trees, flitting back and forth above their heads. The leaves were new, fresh and green, some still unfurling at the edges or growing out of their dark branches—blooming, exciting, alive. A tunnel of mottled, shifting light swayed above them, the gaps in the trees exposing the bright blue of the sky. To the sides, small mouse-monkeys skipped through the dry leaves, and the creeping, twisting shoots of brambles were starting to emerge from the undergrowth. Through the trees, here and there, they had a glimpse of the glistening river, the water brown and swirling as it flowed down the valley. Every so often a shadow moved across the track—just one of the gliding red kites high above the valley—but it was always fleeting, just a flicker of darkness in the light filtering through the trees. Some people chatted quietly, but others were more silent than they would normally have been.

Still thinking about what they'd left behind, or what might happen without them being at home.

After another hour, Cirtop Castle appeared, hazy and stark, suddenly just there above the trees. With its jagged edges, it was clearly ruined, but the walls of the castle seemed to blend in with the rock of the cliff face beneath, making it seem as though it had grown out of the very hillside and giving it an appearance of permanence beyond that of mere human houses. It was rugged and gray, built for defense, not beauty, so that even the attempts to destroy it and use it for building materials elsewhere had failed. Red kites were circling above it too, slow and majestic, floating on pillars of air.

"Ugh," said Ellie. "It does not look nice."

"Definitely a good thing I didn't bother bringing my party dress," said Meg.

"It's probably better from the other side," said Non. "That must be where the main gate is, so the best houses are probably there." She let her voice get quieter toward the end of the sentence, though, because it was obvious the battlements weren't even finished. Instead, wooden planks had been placed precariously over one part of the cliffs to allow the guards to walk along the perimeter of the castle. They were probably secured safely from up above. It's just that against the scale of the cliff, they looked like nothing more than a haphazard birds' nest.

They were almost there, safe, in the shade cast by the castle's cliff, when Non saw the demon. She saw the person it was chasing first, a sudden movement among the gently swaying bushes beyond the river. She had time to look round and see that the soldiers were facing the wrong way, their eyes ahead on the castle and safety. She had time to look up at the battlements and see that the guards there were looking at the cart and the students instead. The conditions were perfect: low wind, visibility good, the person it was chasing clear of her firing line. Non had time to center her crossbow and take careful aim before she released the arrow, and then it cut straight through the air, so sleek and fast she could barely hear it.

The demon was gaining on its prey, its running too smooth to be human, too elegant, too fast. Suddenly others saw it too, and Non could hear the panicked shouts from those on the cart around her and from the wall above, but when the arrow hit, there was a split second of silence. The demon held its hands up and opened its mouth into an O of exaggerated surprise that was almost comical. The arrow hit it directly in the chest, and it teetered there before the explosion of blood came. Something inside the demon burst, and blood sprayed across its chest and face, darkening those too-bright eyes and sending a red cloud of droplets onto the surrounding grass—a neat halo of glistening darkness.

It fell, and even in death that fall was graceful. It seemed to slide toward the ground, its legs bending neatly, and its back and arms merely relaxing downward so that it landed with a slow unfurling, a dance of death.

Almost instantly, the circling red kites above were swooping down to pick at it, pulling at the flesh and jumping on its limbs so that an impression of movement, life, remained. One of the birds hopped onto its calf, pulling at the muscles and sinews there, clawing and pecking at the meat, its beak already wetly red with the blood. Every so often, it would pull on something that made the demon's toes twitch, and Non stared at those feet, waiting for the next movement just to check whether it was alive. It wasn't, of course—the birds were always the first to know when demons were properly dead. They were always ready to feast, the winners in any battle.

"Good shot," said Commander Edwards, suddenly at her elbow. Non flinched in surprise, then shrugged casually, but she gripped her crossbow harder so that her hands wouldn't shake.

"Get somebody to clean that up, though. We don't want it lying round. It might attract vermin."

"Oh. Who should . . . ?" asked Non.

"Somebody," said Commander Edwards, looking directly at her. He walked slowly around the side of the cart. Each of the soldiers kept their eyes on him rather than looking for demons. Their weapons were drawn and ready, their bodies tense.

"It's you," whispered Meg. "He means you. You've got to get rid of it."

"I can't! I can't even lift it!" said Non.

"What about the rest of you, though?" asked Commander Edwards, his voice casual, relaxed, but with a sharp undertone that would cut diamonds. "She managed to kill it. But why was hers the only arrow? What were the rest of you doing? Without her, some of you would be dead."

None of them looked at him or at each other. They kept their eyes on the ground, or on their weapons, or on the cart wheels. Non felt her face flush again, in embarrassment or guilt. Why had she been the one to fire? She almost wished she hadn't bothered now. She stared round at the valley instead of looking at the others. Was anybody else looking for demons? She felt for her other arrows. Where had that one come from? Would there be others?

"You!" said Commander Edwards suddenly. Several people flinched. "You! Get rid of the body!"

He wasn't looking at anyone in particular, but Non stood up. It had to be her he meant. She pulled on Meg's arm.

"Come on," she whispered.

"No way!"

"Please!"

The carts started to move again. Commander Edwards walked ahead of them, giving his spear a twirl so that a couple of nearby students had to duck out of the way.

"I would so love it if somebody big and strong would just get rid of this dead body for me. I'd be very, very grateful," sighed Meg. She didn't say it loudly, but several of the boys paused. A couple of the soldiers looked her way too. They started to turn uncertainly in her direction.

"Everybody keep going toward the castle. Except you and you." This time Commander Edwards pointed clearly at Non and then Meg. "*You*, get rid of that body." His voice was a low growl, and there was almost an emotion on his face.

For a split second, Meg looked like she might be about to toss back her hair and smile at him, but then she decided against it.

"This area is clear," a soldier called to them, running past. "Body pit is over there."

Chapter 3

The dead demon was now visible only because of the twitching, flapping birds jostling on it. They covered every inch of its body, a moving, writhing coat of feathers hiding the death beneath. And the thought of touching those dead arms made Non's stomach clench. Would the birds follow as they pulled it across the bridge? They were getting lazier, more relaxed, swooping down lower than she remembered in the past, like they knew the humans weren't going to harm them. Or maybe the birds felt the humans were almost dead. Not quite—but almost. It was just a matter of biding their time, and then the red kites could have their biggest feast ever.

"Let's go now," said Non. Up on the battlements, there were several guards looking down at them. Their crossbows were trained on the valley, and they were scanning back and forth. If anything came, they were protected for the time being.

"I swear this is the most disgusting thing I've ever had to do," said Meg. "That thing is going to make me throw up." She gagged in an exaggerated move. But then she gagged again, less dramatically and more real this time. She looked away and took a couple of deep breaths. "What if there are more demons down here?" she whispered.

Non looked around, but the trees were sparse and the low bushes along the river that had concealed the demon were not moving. The grass was barely even swaying in the breeze.

"Come on," said Non, nodding toward the riverbank. "Let's get this out of the way before we get too scared. I don't know if the people from the other two castles have arrived yet."

"You mean they might be watching?" asked Meg. She pulled her hair over one shoulder and glanced up at Cirtop. "Let's do this quick, then." There was no way to look good while also trying to dispose of a monster's dead body. Non really didn't want her first introduction to new people to be while she was covered in demon blood.

They both started to jog. As they got closer, the birds flew away reluctantly. Some hopped only a few feet from the body until Non ran at them, and then they flew away majestically, huffily, some settling on the tops of the nearest trees, but mostly they returned to the skies and circled round again, gliding. Their heads faced away, but Non knew that if they left, the birds would swoop down again immediately, pulling at the body.

Close up, the demon was disgusting, truly repugnant. It was more like a biological model of a human than a real thing, a painting of a mammal rather than something that had lived and, supposedly, breathed. The veins and sinews and muscles were all visible, carefully overlapping and wound together, clinging to the white-yellow bones beneath. Here and there, spots of blood oozed through in beak-size holes, dark clots straining against their surface tension but still holding. There was a loose muddle of muscle and veins between its legs, which probably showed it was male. But then, weren't they all male?

The grass around it was wet with gore and gobbets of flesh left by the birds, and its lidless eyes stared upward, the complex threads of nerves and cartilage still visible in the darkness of the sockets behind them. Yet there was a strange beauty in the naked, skinless demon. The perfection and machinery of the body was its own sort of magic, like the creatures were human, really, just peeled-away versions of somebody in the citadel, maybe. For a few minutes, both Meg and Non stood staring, marveling at the monster and their closeness to it. It felt intimate, intrusive even, to be looking at the demon in death when in life they would have been running from it. There was a moment when Non almost started to feel sorry for it, but then she reached the mouth, with its double rows of pointed, sharp teeth, and the fingers, with the thick, curved claws—more like knives than fingernails. She felt proud of her kill then.

"I really do not want to have to touch that," said Meg. "Let's just move it quickly, but don't walk too fast, because I don't want to get any goo on my trousers."

"Shall we take it over the bridge, then? I'll grab its arms and you its legs?"

"I feel sick. But yes. And don't touch its claws or teeth."

"No."

Non took off her scarf and wrapped it round the creature's claws, covering them. Then she grabbed the arms and pulled. They weren't slippery with blood, as they'd appeared. They felt almost sticky but not unpleasantly so. Smooth and a little warm—though maybe that was from the heat of the birds or the morning sun rather than any remaining memory of life. The demon was heavy, though, and she didn't manage to drag it far by herself.

"Come on, Meg." She smiled exaggeratedly, in case anyone in the castle was watching. "I can't do this myself." She gave a loud laugh and Meg looked up, startled. "Make it look like we're having a great time!"

Meg laughed loudly, but then she laughed properly so that Non started too as well. It was now ridiculously funny.

"I love carrying dead demons!" said Non. "Look at me. This is just a normal day, touching a naked monster. It's fine! Everything's fine!"

Meg gagged again. "Oh my God, there was a little bit of vomit that time. Quickly—I don't want to have new people seeing me spew everywhere. I'll never get a man then."

"Do you want just one?"

"Oh my God, are we discussing my love life *now*?"

Meg snorted and shook with laughter as they lifted it together. Or, rather, they lifted the limbs and then dragged the torso along the ground, leaving a trail of flattened grass behind them. The arrow, still protruding from the chest, swung back and forth as they moved, and it felt like an insult to leave it in the body. An indignity. But at the same time, Non didn't want it back, and she didn't fancy wrestling it out of the flesh, so it stayed there, swinging. *Sorry I've lost my arrow—it got lodged in the torso of a demon I killed* would be a pretty good excuse for getting a new one.

"Your love life is the main thing we discuss," said Non. "I don't see why we shouldn't do it now."

"Mm-hmm," said Meg, her mouth clamped shut. She did look

pale, and her eyes were watering. "Definitely let's never speak about this thing again, though."

They were both breathless by the time they reached the bridge, and Non's arms were starting to ache from the weight, but she didn't want to stop, because if she put the demon down on the ground, she wasn't sure she'd ever pick it up again. There was sweat on Meg's forehead too, but she still had her hair tucked over one shoulder and was trying hard not to show the strain.

"It feels like you should be able to squeeze the blood out of the flesh, doesn't it? With it all exposed like this. Like when you're squeezing out a flannel," said Non.

"Please don't try to do that," said Meg, holding the demon as far away from her as she could. "My clothes aren't dirty at the moment, and I can still come back from this." She swallowed. "We can make this a funny story, Non, something we laugh about. But I can't laugh about it if I'm covered in demon goo. There would be nothing funny about that at all."

Non narrowed her eyes. "Do you think the body is duller than when we picked it up? Less shiny?"

"Maybe, a bit."

"Like a film is growing over it?" Non peered in at one of the arms she was carrying.

"Not going to look. Don't care," said Meg. "But I don't think so. That would be a type of skin, wouldn't it? I thought the whole point of them was that that's not going to happen, so I guess the blood is just hardening inside. All clotting or something."

Suddenly Non felt a bit sick, not like she was going to throw up, but her stomach was churning unpleasantly. She looked back up at the castle instead. There was a line of heads along the battlements, but she couldn't tell if they were watching her and Meg, if they were soldiers just doing their job, or even if they were facing the valley or not.

The body pit was down a little-used track, a path that had been made by people wearing the grass away through walking back and forth. Non backed down it, the demon's body sliding a little as they went down the slight slope. "I need to drop it for a minute," said Meg.

Non put the arms of the demon down gently. Already they felt a little stiffer, less graceful.

"It's just over there," she said. "The pit. We're almost there."

Meg nodded. "It's just really heavy."

They both looked around as they caught their breath, but there was still nothing moving down here. Non was grateful she had her crossbow slung over her shoulder, though.

"If others are in the castle already," said Meg, "we can make a glamorous late entrance. We can wash in the moat on the way past and then sort out our hair before going up. We'll be known as the ones who arrive late, looking gorgeous. Not the ones who were getting rid of a dead body. This'll be fine."

"My hands aren't even dirty," pointed out Non. "There's nothing on them."

"They're all demony, Non. You have to wash them."

"Yeah, I will, obviously. Come on, let's move this again." She bent down, and they picked up the body once more. "I'm just pointing it out. I'd have expected to be covered in blood because of it not having any skin. And we're not. It's interesting that something is holding its blood in place."

The pit was partly covered with slats of wood. Non kicked a couple of the slats to one side, looking in just enough to check that this was the right place, but not enough to take in the full horror of what was down there. She glimpsed a couple of charred arms, clawed and stiff but recognizably demon. They dragged the body to the edge and rolled it in. It hit the bottom of the pit with a dry crunch, like when you stepped on a pile of leaves in the autumn.

Suddenly Non wanted to get out of there immediately, like those demons in the pit might come back to life, climb out, and grab her while she wasn't looking, like anything might jump out from behind one of the far trees, like there were things everywhere, ready to get her with their claws and teeth just now at her back. Again the world felt too open, too big, the air too fresh, too full of places for demons to hide. She took a deep breath and clenched her hands round her weapons.

"Your scarf is still round its claws. Do you want it back?" said Meg.

"No. Let's just go now. Please."

"Are you sure? It's a nice one." Meg leaned over the pit with a grin as though she was going to reach in and get it, even though Non knew she obviously wasn't going to.

"Stop wasting time. Help me put those slats back!"

Non bent down and grabbed her end of the slats, trying not to look beneath them as they pulled the wood back over the pit. The air above it was warm and smelled thick with decay—but earthy and wet, like mold or mushrooms. It was a smell you'd associate not with dead flesh but dead vegetation.

"Let's go," said Non.

"Not too quickly," said Meg. "Walk like we're not bothered."

"I am bothered, though. I'm really, really bothered, and I want to get inside somewhere with a thick gate and a giant portcullis that we can close." But Non did walk more slowly, and she steadied her breathing. A couple of the soldiers on the tower above them waved, and Non felt herself relax, like they were returning heroes. She felt her stomach starting to settle.

"Does my hair look a mess?" asked Meg.

"No. It looks fine. They'll love you—you know they will."

Meg laughed uneasily and wiped her eyes on her sleeve.

They reached the edge of the cliff, and here the outer wall began, the roughly cut blocks joining the stone of the hillside. The walls were much lower than in their citadel. Much lower, barely twice the height of a person. They were still thick and strong, but they didn't have the decorative battlements or carvings of their castle. Moss grew over some of the stone, and the blocks were uneven, so that the parapet above was not completely straight.

They washed their hands in the moat, scrubbing and scrubbing, even though their skin wasn't broken and they hadn't touched the demon's claws. It was murky and cold, but at least it was fresher than the stagnant pools of the citadel. Meg washed her face too and wiped it on her sleeve again. She laughed. "This is the most ridiculous thing. I swear you owe me big-time."

"At least you now know where to put other dead demons. Useful."

"I would have been happy to never know that information. How do I look?"

"Fine. All the boys will definitely fancy you."

"Boys?" said Meg. "What? Who even cares about them? They won't notice anything. The girls are the ones who really matter."

Chapter 4

The castles were built to keep out the Northerners, and before them the Southerners. But there were island pirates before the Northerners, barbarians before the island pirates, and marauding tribes before the barbarians. Castles were built to keep all of them out too.

The castles had always been built strong, and they'd always been built tall. They were high up, so that from the top of the towers you could see down the full length of the valley. Inside, the people had always clustered together underneath the walls, cramped and miserable and grateful for the protection from whatever scared them.

Because before the Northerners and barbarians and Southerners and island pirates, there had been the wild beasts—the gormads and dragonites who roamed the deep forests, the lynx too, and the more unknown creatures, only a shimmer in the darkness, something strange that might be hiding in there. Just a shifting shadow, maybe.

And every so often, sometimes so infrequently that it felt like legend, a story to tell round the firesides, the demons had attacked. Some centuries it was a few missing people, a warning to children not to stay out too late by themselves, but when it felt like everybody had forgotten and the only danger was from weak, tangible human enemies, the demons would return.

Non had grown up with them. It wasn't because they surrounded her or because she always saw them. No, it was their absence that haunted her. When they were mentioned, there was a hush, a cloud of quiet and significant looks, a silence that stayed with her everywhere she went. Non didn't leave the citadel, but she felt the demons with her anyway, the weight of their presence on her shoulders.

She didn't remember the family the demons had killed, couldn't remember the mother she'd once had, but she felt her every time somebody tilted their head to one side sympathetically when they looked at her, or every time somebody was extra kind to her because she was motherless. So she was never rid of those mysterious deaths that nobody talked about, and she could never forget about the demons. Sometimes it was hard to separate the demons from her dead mother—the killers and the victims stuck together, mingling, wrapped around each other in her thoughts. Colorless, see-through, vague, the memories of others—not hers.

So it wasn't that Non wanted to get revenge on the demons for killing the person in the life she could have had; it was more that she was sick of them still always being associated with her, always being something that people thought about when they saw her. And she thought of them always too. With fear, of course, but also with a growing anger, maybe even a fascination. Had killing one just now changed that? Even as she walked through the gate behind Meg, she knew she felt differently toward them in some way. Was it because it had been so easy to kill? Was it because it had looked so interesting in death? She felt proud of having killed it, she knew she did, even if that wasn't something she'd admit publicly. It had surprised even her that she had been the one to do it, and it was hard to stop herself from grinning at the thought that she had actually managed to kill a monster! She never, ever would have thought she'd have been capable. But she'd never been that close to one either, and she'd have liked to get another look at it, to stare at it, to see it properly, to learn more about it. It was weird to feel that, though. She knew that. Definitely weird. All the same, she glanced back at the plain as they walked through the gate, just in case there were more of them.

As the gate guard tested them for plague—taking their temperature, searching for the rash—she remembered what she'd forgotten. It wasn't too big a deal; it was just her anatomy books. But it did mean she wouldn't be able to do the studying she'd said she'd do and that she had honestly intended to work on. Because where better to read something a little dull than on a hillside where there was nothing else to do? The guard nodded at them both, and they walked through the gate and into the unpaved, open grass behind the ramparts.

"Meg, did you bring any books or anything?"

"Ha-ha! As if!"

"What are you going to do in the evenings?"

"I'm going to lounge. I might also laze, or perhaps slack off. Although, looking at this, I might be spending a lot of time trying to keep warm."

They'd known the castle was unfinished, but from inside the walls, it looked barely started. The outer walls were solid and strong, but the inner walls were little more than earth ramparts with a few stones on top of them. They would be easy to defend and were definitely practical, but in comparison to the citadel, they were very rustic. Nothing was mud at the citadel: All was decorated, neat, hard-wearing stone. The influence of nature was clear here, though, and where stone from the hillside could be used, it had been left so that rocky outcrops remained among the mud and grass, which was being nibbled at by sheep. Even the well had a couple of hens perched precariously on its walls, pecking at seed or insects lodged in among the stones. At home, nature was something to be pruned, shaped, or cleaned away; no live animals entered the citadel apart from the rats and the cats that kept them at bay.

Double-story guard towers were built into the outer walls of the castle. They had wooden roofs and looked warm, at least, but from this angle, no other buildings appeared to have any roofs. In fact, most of them barely had walls. Higher up the hill, near the top of the cliff, the ruined keep of the castle stood, jagged and tall. From this side, you could clearly see that none of the rooms were completed and, though there were low walls here and there, which might provide shelter from the wind, none of them had doors or windows.

"I guess everybody must be up at the top," said Non. "In those buildings."

"Maybe it looks better from up there. Because it looks like a complete dump from down here."

"At least we won't die in here."

"Yeah. That's a bonus, I suppose."

They walked up the rough, twisting stone pathway—though

most of the hillside was open, so they could have cut across the grass to reach the castle courtyard more quickly. Between the ramparts and the castle, there were only piles of stones here and there, the outlines of buildings that had once existed. On some of them, grass had grown right over those walls so that they were little more than strangely regular humps in the ground. For a moment, Non tried to picture this as the alive, bustling castle it must once have been—like their own citadel. But it looked too much like a windswept, rolling hillside. It was difficult to imagine anything living here apart from sheep.

When they reached the top of the hill, the rest of the students were sitting around in the castle courtyard, crouching on mats or lying on the hard stone. Here, at least, the surface had been kept clear of weeds and had been recently swept. The courtyard was sunken, and while the walls were rough and low, it looked like somebody had recently started to rebuild them. The mortar was fresh, and the stones were not coated in moss.

"Oh my God, that was amazing, Non," said Ellie. Everybody was looking at her. She took a step to the side so that she was slightly behind Meg again and looked down at the floor as though she was having to concentrate on the uneven stones. "Get rid of that demon OK?"

"No, we brought it with us," said Meg. A couple of people peered behind her as though she genuinely might have done. Meg laughed. "Is it only people from our castle here so far?"

"Yeah. This place is awful, isn't it?" said Ellie.

Nobody replied. Ellie lived in one of the bigger citadel houses, near the top of the hill by their castle. Her house had real stained glass in its many windows and a view overlooking the whole valley. Most of the citadel was awful in comparison to where she lived.

"What do you actually do in quarantine?" Meg turned to Non.

"Try not to die," said Non.

"No, I know," she laughed. "But are we really just going to sit around here, plague-free, and hang out with the other people who've been evacuated?"

"We're supposed to be studying, I think," said Non. "That's what Dad said. Because it's the schools that are evacuated, we're supposed to be having lessons."

"Has anybody brought any books?" called Meg.

A couple of people replied that they had, but most shook their heads or ignored her.

There were twenty or so students sitting around, all familiar to Non from the citadel, even if they weren't in her year at school. The youngest was around fourteen years old, and all of them were wearing trousers and sturdy, practical boots. A few had accessorized their outfits with a colorful hat or bright top, but generally they looked like they had dressed to spend a few weeks on an abandoned hillside. There was no sign of anybody in charge—Commander Edwards had disappeared again—and no sign of anybody who had any sort of plan.

Non lay back against one of the walls. What was she going to do without her books? Sit around and *talk* to people?

Chapter 5

A horn sounded from the battlements. "Castle Goch are here!" came a call. Most of the students sat up or started to rearrange their clothing. Non grabbed Meg's hand.

"Come on," she said. "Let's go up and look."

There was only a ladder up to the parapet here, but Non climbed it quickly. There were two watchers on the castle ramparts. One of them was surveying the surroundings carefully as normal, but the other one was focused on something in the distance, shielding her eyes from the sun. It was she who was holding the horn, and as Non watched, she raised it to her lips again and gave another loud signal call.

Non and Meg carefully edged along the wall. There were no battlements on this section, and the cliff dropped away sharply beneath them. Non looked in the direction the watcher was facing. It took her a few minutes to see movement and then longer to work out what she was looking at.

There were ten of them, and they were jogging in formation, keeping to a steady pace despite the boggy ground they were running across. The outer students were holding bows clasped loosely in their left hands, but the others had theirs still strapped to their backs. None of them appeared to have spears at all, which was surprising, as Non had thought those were standard weapons. She wondered what they did in close combat.

As the joggers got nearer, Non could see that there were three girls among the group. Their hair was tied up, plaited securely, and coiled in buns. They seemed to have a sort of uniform, so that they looked militaristic, together, and . . . just organized, really. They were all wearing skintight clothes: She noticed the girls particularly—they wore greeny-brown camouflage trousers and brown tops with utility belts, and the colors blended in almost exactly with the surrounding vegetation so that at times it was difficult to see them. They were all thin, toned, gorgeous, and lithe. Non could see that from this distance. It was possible that she was exaggerating it a bit, but she thought she could see the six-packs of the boys rippling through the material of their tight shirts as they ran.

"Oh dear." She blew air out of her cheeks and turned to Meg.

Meg looked at her, wide-eyed. "Have they not come with any soldiers? Have they come by themselves!"

"It doesn't exactly look like they need anybody to protect them."

"Wow. It's double the distance we came, isn't it? I bet they walked most of the way and then just started to run when they got close so that they looked good."

"Nah, that's what we'd have done. I have a bad feeling they've run the whole way."

The pace of the students was very steady, very practiced. They seemed perfectly in tune with each other, and when they turned to run round the cliff toward the gate, it was seemingly without any signal. They also remained evenly spaced, a regulation arrow length apart, even though those on the outside were having to run faster in order to keep up as they turned the corner. If a group of students from the citadel had tried to do that, there would have been arguments about which way to turn when they hit the cliff, and they'd have been out of breath by the time they reached the moat.

Non exhaled loudly. She hoped the quarantine was going to be short. Forgetting her books was one thing, but sharing a hillside with these people didn't look like it would be loads of fun.

"They look nice!" said Meg.

"Nice?"

"Yes. Nice people."

"Nice, nice. Or just *nice*?"

"Like I said. Nice." Meg laughed and clambered down the ladder.

Non sat on the wall for a little longer, this time facing the castle and looking down. From here, she was at the highest point in this part of the valley. She could see the whole of the hillside and all the people on it. The top of the hillside had been flattened out, probably many centuries ago, by the long-dead people who'd built here first. It wasn't as bad as it had looked from down below. There were a few other ruined buildings up here aside from the castle courtyard. The walls of those still stood, and in some of them, cloth roofs had been slung across as temporary shelter. Inside, people would be protected from the wind for a while, but rain would leak through, would seep into the cloth quickly and onto anybody sheltering in there.

There were a few other scattered hummocks and artificial pits in the ground between here and the ramparts on the other side—more than she'd realized. If the grass covering them was cleared away, some of them might . . . be something. It could be livable, this castle. Non wondered why nobody lived here permanently.

Down the valley, the river wound through meadows and low shrublands, the trees and thickly wooded hills rising up on either side. Here and there were the jagged remains of ruined houses, but those were mostly obscured by greenery growing over them. It was good to be able to see out. It was good to be able to see the world beyond the walls without having to be out there. The way they'd come, the river meandered up the valley, twisting round behind a distant hillside, which concealed the citadel and the other castles too. Cirtop was the castle closest to the sea and the coast. Right now, Non was the farthest she had ever been from home.

A red kite called overhead. Down at the gate, the new arrivals had been allowed in but were lined up in an orderly fashion by one of the buttresses, waiting for their plague checks. They were still standing to attention, their weapons still combat-ready. Non couldn't see whether they were out of breath or not from this distance, but they didn't seem to need to lie down, have a little cry, or drink loads of water, as anybody from the citadel would have done if they'd run that distance. It was as bad as she feared.

The horn sounded again, and Non turned back to look at the valley. This time it was more obvious. She could see the next arrivals—who must be the Kintaborel Castle students—by the red kites circling above. A large open cart, drawn by six horses, was trundling along the track. It was coming the same way they had traveled earlier, and it must have gone right past the citadel. It took Non a few minutes to work out what was weird about the image, because she was watching for other movements, for things hiding in the trees, perhaps. But as the cart cleared the tree line and rounded the last bend, Non could see that it was only the girls who were sitting in the cart, and around them the boys were walking, their weapons ready. As the cart passed beneath her, Non could see that all the girls were wearing long skirts, mostly down to their ankles, though the boys were wearing completely normal trousers and boots. What made it really odd, though, was that none of the girls had weapons. It wasn't just that they weren't wearing them at that moment, it's that there were no weapons belts on their outfits: no spear hooks, no sword sheaths, no arrow pouches. She searched the cart in case the girls, all of them, had taken off their weapons for a bit to relax. But there was nothing anywhere that they could use to defend themselves if demons attacked.

Commander Edwards was leading the Castle Goch students up the track now, the soft cadence of his voice somehow cutting through all the other sounds on the hillside. Where had he come from? Non couldn't see into any of the four guard towers, so maybe he had been in one of those, sitting quietly by himself. She couldn't imagine what he did when he was by himself. Didn't *want* to imagine.

Non climbed down the ladder, ready to meet the new people. The citadel students were still concealed by the brow of the hill and were arranging themselves into relaxed positions again, as though they would be caught unawares by the new arrivals.

"Good morning, everybody," said Commander Edwards to the hillside in general. "Here are some new students. Make them . . . welcome. Your sleeping quarters are behind these walls. One of them is for the boys. One for the girls. I don't know which one is which. But sleep separately." He waved vaguely in the air and then sauntered off down the hill with his hands in his pockets, leaving the ten new arrivals standing uncertainly in his wake, shielding their eyes from the glare of the sun.

Nobody was quite sure what to do. The Castle Goch students stood, shuffling, looking uncertainly around, as though he'd pointed somewhere real. The citadel students remained frozen in their fake-casual lounging positions, as though interrupted in the middle of something important.

"There's one building over there," said Ellie, pointing. "And a smaller one over there. Maybe the girls go in that one."

Non climbed over the wall, which seemed the best way in. The room Ellie had chosen for the girls had a dirt floor rather than grass, so the cloth roof must have been there longer than it looked. It was rectangular and large, but there were outcrops of sharp stone layers along one side of the floor, so the area in which they'd be able to sleep was limited. There were already bedding rolls stacked up there, and some of the girls wandered over to move them in order to claim the spots where they'd be sleeping.

The taller of the three Castle Goch girls took the hairband out of her ponytail and casually shook out her long, glossy red hair so that it slid down her shoulders. She tilted her head to one side implacably and then slowly peeled her skintight top over her head, revealing another top beneath, which was so narrow that it really did cover little more than her breasts. She had a gloriously smooth, lightly tanned stomach. Non held her breath, but she thought she heard a few gasps. This was one of the most gorgeous, perfect human beings she had ever seen. The girl cast her top into the opposite corner of the tent, and with a flick of her beautiful hair, she threw her bag down next to it.

"I'm Jane," she said without smiling, "and this is Becky and Chantelle." She gestured to the two equally gorgeous girls behind her. Becky also peeled off her top, revealing a similarly tiny top beneath. She had tan lines on her shoulders, showing that she had, on occasion, worn other similarly revealing tops. Was this what they wore every day? Non suspected she knew the answer. Nobody had seen Non's stomach for years, except by unfortunate accident. She'd barely seen her own stomach, except when she ran past the mirror on her way to grab something to speedily cover all that pasty flesh. It wasn't too bad, or anything—it wasn't too wobbly and looked all right if she stood upright and breathed in . . . but she wasn't ready to parade it, exposed, in public. Non definitely felt right now that had she known, some of that time she'd wasted this spring in studying could have been better spent sunbathing and doing sit-ups.

All the girls paused, looking silently around, sizing up the space and the position of the bedding rolls, as well as Jane's discarded top. It was an important question of tent etiquette and, of course, so much more than that. Where should they put their things? Should they carefully arrange the sleeping rolls and put them next to their friends'? Or should they leave it until later in the evening, thus showing that they were friendly but before knowing whether they *wanted* to be friendly . . .

Or should the citadel girls choose the opposite end of the room from Jane's top, thus showing that they wanted to keep their distance (metaphorically as well as literally) and leaving a gap for the unknown Kintaborel Castle girls in between? Certainly, this opening move would show whether they were willing to be easy friends or not.

"Put your stuff down next to mine, Chantelle and Becky," said Jane. Silently, both girls walked over and laid their things down.

"It's lovely to meet you all," said Meg.

"Yeah," said Jane, looking around and still not smiling. She seemed to look more at the walls and the earth than she did at the people. "Yeah."

One of the other girls, Becky, did smile at everybody, but it was guarded.

"Well, this is *nice*, isn't it?" said Meg.

Non frowned at her.

Outside, there was the low muttering of other people arriving, and all the girls looked up at the wall. But the Kintaborel Castle girls had obviously been directed to the door, a narrow gap in the wall beyond the stone outcrops. They arrived, six of them, laughing as they chatted to one other. They held on to each other's arms as they stepped over the uneven stone, as though they were uncertain of their footing even here. Their shoes were delicate—strapless and beautiful—the leather thin and perfectly shaped around their feet. Some of the shoes had engravings on them, or patterns of flowers; they were like nothing Non had ever seen before. But some of their skirts were so tight and long they could barely walk, their steps limited by the silken material.

"Oh, we're so pleased to meet you all!" said one of them, a tall girl with her hair tied back under an embroidered veil. Her smile was so genuine and so happy that everybody smiled back, laughing at each other in relief. "We've been so excited to meet new people, and I know we're here under tragic circumstances. But I thank God for bringing us together."

She held out her arms in welcome to all. "Let us pray in thankfulness for our safe arrival."

Chapter 6

"It's too easy," said Meg. "I don't think I can be bothered."

"What?" asked Non.

"The male-female ratio. There's just way more boys than girls. It means I hardly have to do anything and they'll all be interested anyway."

"OK."

Meg sighed. "The only thing is, I didn't bring anything else to do."

"You were honestly just going to spend your whole time getting boys to chase after you?"

Meg shrugged. "What were *you* going to do? It's more interesting than math or whatever."

"You've just done some interesting math."

"What?"

"Nothing. Don't worry."

Meg arranged her hair so that it was draped artfully over her shoulders. They were back in the castle courtyard sitting on the ground, and she leaned back so that her face was tilted up toward the sun. The light fell on her so that her cheekbones were highlighted.

She pouted and parted her lips slightly. There was a sigh from the group of citadel boys sitting against the wall.

Non rolled her eyes. "You can't help yourself, can you?"

Meg held her position for another couple of seconds before spluttering with laughter, flecks of saliva suddenly bursting from her mouth and ruining the image of beauty.

The courtyard was starting to fill up—all the evacuated students from the castles squeezing into the space; as each of them climbed over the wall or entered through the door gap, for a moment their hair flew up in the wind. The air was warm and there was a closeness to it that felt like the promise of rain, but the sky was cloudy in that muggy, summery, nonspecific way that meant anything could happen. The wind was probably the lightest it would ever be, but already, after just a few hours, Non could feel a harshness to her skin from its constant blasting. The hillside was very exposed, and the whole valley seemed to act as a funnel for the wind, squeezing it between its steep sides, so that it focused all its energy on brushing past Cirtop. It would be brutal here in the winter.

Although people were chatting to each other, or smiling, they were all sitting in their castle groups. There was a relaxed feeling—still almost a party atmosphere. Here, everybody was away from the structure of their days and the demands of their ordinary lives. They were doing something different and had no responsibilities. The plague wasn't severe, so there wasn't even much worry about the people left at home.

The chatter died down as three commanders entered the courtyard. The first was a woman, with her thick hair tied back in a ponytail so tight it seemed to pull her cheeks and lips back with it. Her face was very tanned and was scattered with uneven patches of sunburn or some sort of rash, a combination of features that unfortunately made her cheeks look bloodstained and dirty; there were also those creases around her eyes that on other people were often called laughter lines, but looking at her facial expression now, Non thought it was more likely that in her case they were from squinting into the sun or lots of grimacing at things. She urged the students along, shuffling them around on the stone so that there was room for everybody. "Sit down, those of you at the front, so the others can see." A few of the students looked round confusedly, unsure as to whether she meant them. Everybody squirmed around uncertainly in the too-small space. She made an exasperated tutting noise. "You, you, you, you. Sit." She pointed fiercely at four girls at the front. They sat immediately. "You, move. You, move." She pointed at two others, who obeyed her instantly. "You, you, you." She pointed at several other students, clicked her fingers and then gestured to the floor. They all sat, though one boy Non didn't know took a split second longer than the others, either out of clumsy stupidity or to hint at possible rebellion. The woman gave him a long look.

"I'm Commander Rogers," she said, introducing herself brusquely, and almost reluctantly. "You can call me Dog. I'm in charge of this castle, which means I'm in charge of you while you're here." She didn't look thrilled at the prospect, and Non wondered whether she'd been given a choice to accept the evacuees during the quarantine process or not. "You're not just going to be sitting around. You're going to be having some lessons. You're also going to be working . . ."

There was a flurry as she said this. Whispering, people looking at one another.

". . . if you want food," she added. "You can choose to sit around if you want, but this castle is providing you with food. If you want some, you will work in return."

Commander Edwards stepped forward lazily, nodding politely to Dog as he passed. "Good evening, everybody. I do so hope you had a good journey.

"The main things you're going to be doing are getting this castle livable. There will be military tasks—securing the areas and so forth. There will also be some light building work to repair the castle."

He smiled amiably despite his words, making it sound as though, somehow, this would be like a relaxing holiday.

"Light building work," whispered Meg. "Really?"

Non looked round the courtyard with its unfinished walls and incomplete rooms. She started to laugh.

"We start tomorrow morning," he said. "Are there any questions?" He immediately turned toward the door gap and started to walk away.

"Yes," somebody called. Commander Edwards continued to walk out. Dog turned toward the speaker. "I have a question, Commander," the voice repeated.

Commander Edwards paused and slowly turned back to face the courtyard. The citadel students gasped. His face wore a jovial smile, but his eyes were ice. He looked directly at the speaker.

Non moved round so that she could see the speaker too. He was sitting in among the Castle Goch boys—a group of young men so perfect in looks that Non hadn't been able to let herself look at them properly before. Collectively, they were muscular, tanned, clear-skinned, and just beautiful examples of human beings. They were also all tall, powerful, and confident in their bodies. Even their hair seemed to move differently from everybody else's in the wind, giving them a fun, slightly ruffled look, rather than the disheveled, tangled mess it seemed to create in everyone else. They were the same age ranges as the boys from the other castles, but even their youngest boys, the fourteen-year-olds, looked strong and tall, rather than gangly and awkward like the ones from the citadel.

Non was going to look at them properly as individuals, absolutely. It's just that they were so beautiful it made her confused. She couldn't quite remember how to arrange her face and didn't want to make it look like she was staring at any of them for too long. Next to her, Meg was fiddling with her shoelace and staring at the wall.

"I know we haven't been lied to, sir. But we weren't told we would be doing hard labor when we were instructed to go here."

The speaker was one of the shorter of the young men—though that didn't mean much, given that it felt like they towered over Non. He was crouching rather than sitting, and he leaned back against the wall, giving the impression that he was relaxed. But Non could see that he was gripping one of the stones beside him, and his other hand was tapping against his leg.

"Feel free to leave at any time," said Commander Edwards. "You can go whenever you wish." He smiled properly then, like the thought of somebody walking home to a plague-ridden castle through demon-infested woods pleased him. And he turned back toward the door gap, walking out, followed by Dog.

There was a cough, and the third of the commanders stepped forward. His stomach bulged over his trousers, and his black military uniform looked like it had been assigned to him when he was a much thinner man. His head was largely bald, apart from a few wisps of gray hair that seemed as though they might have grown there by mistake. But he had a neatly trimmed beard and a mustache that curled upward, outlining his smile. And he was smiling encouragingly at the speaker.

"I'm Commander Daffy, and I've come from Kintaborel. For public health reasons, it's very good that you are here. You're safer; the public is safer without you at home. You can be spared. It makes sense to have fewer people around when the communities are tightly packed, as ours are at home. Moving you is a sensible decision."

"Well, what about our younger brothers and sisters, then?" asked the boy.

"Do they need looking after?" replied Commander Daffy.

"I could look after them," he said.

"So they do need looking after, then," said Commander Daffy.

The boy shrugged.

"I'm sorry you couldn't bring them, but we took only those who were able to look after themselves and who weren't needed at home. That's you lot. A younger child wouldn't be much use in a demon attack, would they? Or if we have to ask them to cook or build?"

"Well, why are we building, sir?"

"Public service. This castle has really only been used as a military base for centuries. Our castles are overcrowded now, so it might be a good idea to think about moving some people out here."

"Are we starting this tomorrow, then?" asked somebody else.

The commander turned to the new speaker, but Non kept watching the first one, the Castle Goch boy. He was frowning into midair. Not at Commander Daffy, exactly, but at the air beyond him. He was idly throwing the stone back and forth between his hands, and Non couldn't tell if it was a frown of concentration or anger. But he seemed full of pent-up energy, despite their long run to get here. He looked like he could easily run all the way home again and then do some sort of other athletic activity afterward. Whatever it was fit people did.

"Tomorrow . . . ah," said Commander Daffy, "I think we've got a couple of tasks for you. We would like to send some of you round to scout out the local area, just to see if there's anything useful out there beyond the normal roads and tracks. You'll be mapping it, essentially. And the rest of you—most of you, probably—will be building up these dormitories. The choice will be up to you, though."

Most people turned to chat to those next to them at this point, though Commander Daffy remained standing in the middle of the courtyard, waiting in case of further questions.

"You're going to want to stay in here and build stuff, aren't you?" whispered Meg. "I know you are."

"Definitely," said Non. "I'm not going anywhere dangerous." Although even as she said it, she wondered whether that was entirely what she wanted.

"Well, I helped you get rid of that stupid dead demon that we're never talking about ever again. Now all I'm asking you to do is leave this castle with me."

"I only had to kill that demon because we left our castle walls. If we'd been inside, it would never have happened."

"I'm not building something," said Meg. "That sounds like much harder work than walking round the hillsides."

"I promised Dad I'd stay inside."

"But your dad's not here, is he?"

Non did want to stay inside. She liked the safety of the walls. And it would definitely be the most sensible thing to do. She looked back at that boy again. It felt like he had so much energy, it was actually spreading through the room toward her, and suddenly she did feel like she needed to run, or walk, or stretch, or something. It wasn't that she found him attractive—those gorgeous specimens lounging around him were much more good-looking, definitely. It's that there was something about him that made her want to keep checking what he looked like. His features were difficult to remember, so she felt like she needed to look again.

"Go on, Non. When do we ever get the chance to do anything like this? We *never* left the citadel. It'd be amazing to see what's out there."

Dog reappeared at the door gap and mouthed something at Commander Daffy. He nodded and bowed his head, almost as though she was his boss, but Non hadn't thought the commanders had a hierarchy, so that was unlikely. There was something unusual about the relationship between the three commanders, though it was possibly just that each of them seemed so unusual as people. She somehow couldn't imagine them sitting down together to plan the running of this castle, even though that was what must have happened.

"When's supper?" called somebody.

"I'll see if we can rustle something up for you," said Commander Daffy. "You must be hungry after your journey here."

"No. There isn't anything. You haven't done any work yet," said Dog. "So there's no food for you. Unless you happened to bring some yourselves?"

Chapter 7

The next morning, Non and Meg were in the group that met down at the drawbridge—just as it was inevitable they were going to be. It was partly because of Meg's whinging. Non knew she would just keep on and on until they went, so getting it out of the way early would give her the moral authority to demand that Meg stay in the castle with her for the rest of their time at Cirtop.

But there was also that slightly pathetic worry that Meg might just go without her anyway, leaving Non alone with all these new people. Not to mention the old ones. The possibility of spending a whole day in awkward conversation felt scarier than leaving the security of the castle for the possibility of facing demons.

And there was also, a bit, the hope that the boy from Castle Goch might be going. He hadn't looked like he would want to be kept inside and build walls. Non didn't let that be her official, main reason for wanting to go, and she'd deliberately thought really hard about other things whenever that idea came into her head. But she had taken extra care with her appearance that morning anyway.

There were only about ten of them who met at the drawbridge, all the others from Castle Goch. They were all chatting and joking with each other as Meg and Non arrived, and although several looked over, nobody acknowledged them. He wasn't there. Non felt immediately disappointed, as she'd known she would. She also knew that was ridiculous and was cross with herself for making up this whole stupid scenario. And because she'd made it up, she was now going to have to wander round the hillside being exposed to nature and danger. Today was *not* going to be a good day.

"Good day!" Commander Edwards appeared behind them. Both Non and Meg took a step forward so that they wouldn't be too close to him. "There's a nice number of you, and a few more to arrive."

He looked at each of the students slowly.

"Right. You can go in two groups. You can take a different side of the valley each. Don't go—"

"Sorry we're late, Commander." Two figures ran up to the drawbridge—from the other side of it. They had clearly been outside the castle by themselves, something that Non hadn't known was an option, or that anybody would even want to be an option. But one of them was the boy.

Non had to stare at the ground to stop herself from smiling. It was ridiculous.

"Just sorting out some stuff. Sorry," he said, a little out of breath.

"Yes, I know. It's fine," said Commander Edwards. Meg nudged Non's thigh with her hand gently. *It's fine.* The commander had never spoken to anybody from their castle like that. They'd have had some sniffy threat if they'd been late—though none of them would have ever dared to be.

Non grabbed Meg's hand and, just casually, as though she was moving to make space for the others to hear what the commander was saying, she edged over so that they were standing closer to the boy and his friend—halfway across the drawbridge.

"So you'll all take your weapons—crossbows *and* spears, please—and you'll be scouting an assigned area. All you're looking for are areas of interest. We want to know exactly what's out there, and we're deciding if there's anything we want to look at more carefully. We know the areas around the other castles really well. This one is not as familiar, so we'd like you to check it out. You're going away from the paths and tracks to look at places we haven't been for a while. Don't do anything stupid. If you see something suspicious, don't check it out. Just remember where it is so you can tell us, and we'll send an armed unit up. Questions?"

Commander Edwards remained standing, looking at the students.

"Can you give us examples of what an area of interest might be? What sort of things do you want us looking for?" asked one of the girls. Non recognized her as Becky, Jane's friend.

"Yes. Human buildings would be useful. They'll all be ruined, but if you can detail how ruined, that would be helpful. We're looking for places we could hide or that could be fortified as outposts. Places demons could hide, or where there might be suspicious activity, would also be good. Don't go in if you find any, obviously. Areas of thick vegetation that we should cut back. Areas of food, either fruit trees, roots, berries, or animals—you know the sort of thing.

"Take a note of it all. You can have some paper and draw us a rough map. We don't expect you to cover all of the area today. Everything understood?"

They nodded. It was pretty clear, in a vague sort of way.

"Obviously, we don't expect any trouble, or you wouldn't be going out. But if you do encounter any demons, then run, don't engage. Get yourselves away from the situation and don't fight unless you absolutely need to.

"You two, you, Non, and Non's friend, go up that side of the valley. There are a few abandoned buildings. Check them all out. You're expected back midafternoon." He had gestured to the two boys from the other side of the drawbridge, as Non had hoped he would. She felt a flush of excitement, which she immediately tried to hide. She checked her crossbow and the arrows. They were all loose and pulled out smoothly as she ran them through her fingers. They'd be easy to access if she needed them. Their group set off across the drawbridge.

"Non's friend?" Meg mouthed. "Non's friend!" Non smiled. It was the first time anybody had ever seen their friendship that way round, and Meg's irritation was almost funny enough to cancel out the worrying fact of Commander Edwards knowing who she was.

"Hi," said Meg out loud to the boys. "This is Non. Obviously, you know that, because *she's* been introduced. But I'm Meg."

"Hi, Meg."

"Hi."

Both the boys smiled at Meg, and for a moment Non felt annoyed. It wasn't jealousy. It just felt like this was quite a boring pattern, like she was getting tired of watching other people watching Meg.

"I'm Paul," said the taller of the two boys. He was blond, tanned, and absurdly good-looking. He almost didn't seem real; his features were so even and perfect they were like a doll's—the doll that would be the prince in any child's game. He kept his eyes on Meg.

"I'm Sam," said the boy from last night. Even as he was standing there, his feet weren't still. He was tapping them back and forth on the grass, kicking at a small stone. He did look at Meg, of course he did, but he nodded at Non too. She wasn't ready for him to notice her, and afterward she couldn't remember what expression she'd had on her face. She hoped that it was a greeting, but she worried it might still have been annoyance at Meg or surprise at him looking her way. He didn't keep looking at her anyway.

"Hey." Becky came up behind them. "Shall we get going?" Today she was wearing a short cropped top and very tight trousers. Her weapons belt sat neatly on her stomach muscles, accentuating their slight curve. Practical, yet also sexy.

They set off across the flat floodplain at a jog, and straight away Non felt a jolt of fear. After yesterday, and killing the demon, that fear felt real, but it also felt a bit exciting: both danger and thrill mixed together. She was scared—of course she was—but it felt a little like she wanted to test that fear again. To just give it a little prod and see what happened.

The area around the castle had been mostly cleared of anything apart from low shrubs, so that there were no hiding places, but the rest of the valley was thick woodland. Ancient, undisturbed, though following the winter, the brambles and ferns had mainly died back, so there were ways through, and even standing in the woods you could mostly see a fair distance. After a few minutes, and just out of sight of the castle, their pace slowed to a walk. Even still, Non found herself puffing and panting a bit. She excused herself with the thought that exercise had been difficult in the citadel because of the lack of space, but walking around until midafternoon was feeling like quite a big task right now.

Carrying their weapons was already tiring. Becky was using her spear as a walking stick, Meg was trailing hers along the ground behind her, and Non had put hers back over her shoulder.

"Your weapons are supposed to be combat-ready," said Paul.

"If I see something coming, I'll hold it up again," said Meg.

"But that's the point," said Paul. "By the time you see them coming, you need to already have your weapon out, because there isn't time."

"There is time. I can see there's nothing for ages." Meg turned to Non and whispered, "I think he might be a bit annoying, actually." It wasn't a very quiet whisper, and Becky smiled too.

"Well, there's trees over there," said Paul. "Can you see behind the trees?"

"No. But I'd see any demons running from the trees. Why don't *you* go and check if there's something behind them?"

"Don't be stupid."

"Then don't be a prick."

Becky coughed into her arm and looked away. Paul looked shocked.

"Look, why don't you keep your sword out and then you can defend us all," said Meg. She smiled at him sweetly. "You're so strong and lovely, and I know you will be able to protect us with your big muscles." She flicked her hair back.

Paul opened his mouth to reply, but then he shut it again and looked away. His face was flushed, but he held his sword up again.

Everybody was quiet for a while. Sam walked in the front, which gave Non time to watch him and the way he moved. She did also keep an eye out for demons and for things that might be of interest. But mainly she looked at his back, and the way his shoulders moved underneath his shirt, and the curls of his dark hair against his neck. Also, she was out of breath as they started climbing up the hillside, and she was glad the others didn't have to see that.

They headed straight for the buildings Commander Edwards had pointed out. Although an old road had been visible from the bottom of the valley—its shape still clear because of the absence of trees—they had avoided it, climbing straight up the valley through the woods. A few times they lost sight of the buildings, when trees or a steep section of the hill obscured the view, but they were large and unnatural, and so they were easy to find again.

Sam stopped in a clearing. The grass was low here, and through the trees, the first of the houses was in sight, only a few paces away.

"Rabbits," he said, pointing to some holes below the trees.

Becky marked something on their paper.

"Rabbits?" whispered Meg. "Are we sure?"

"Don't know," whispered Non. "But I'm not saying anything."

Rabbits in the citadel arrived already dead for the market. They were usually skinned too. Although Non had known they came from somewhere, it had never occurred to her to wonder where.

"There're lots of droppings," nodded Paul. "So this warren is still being used. They must have run away when they heard us coming."

Meg peered in at the droppings and nodded too, a serious frown on her face. "Definitely note this down, Becky. There's lots of them." She winked at Non.

Non smiled, but she felt suddenly spooked. The ruin of that house, with its sunken roof and sagging walls, made her feel uncomfortable. Maybe the people who lived here before had eaten rabbits from this clearing. Maybe that's why the house was there.

"Imagine wanting to live out here," she said to Meg.

"I know. Weird. All this space. I wouldn't like it at all."

"What do you think happened to them?"

"The people? Nothing. Probably just moved into one of the castles."

They walked right around the house, but plants had grown over the roof and trees were growing inside, their roots pushing through cracks in the walls. There was no room for anything to hide in there—human or demon—and though they marked the building on Becky's paper, they knew it wasn't useful. It would barely even be worth hiding behind.

They passed other buildings, but they were in a similar state. A few of them had the remains of old furniture inside, long rotted and falling apart; one of them even had a large blackberry bush growing right in the middle of it, thousands of little blackberries forming behind the white blossoms, tiny and green. Becky marked that house on the map especially. Otherwise, though, there was nothing of interest.

"Why do you think they left their furniture behind?" asked Non.

"Too big to carry. And a bit rubbish," said Meg. "Don't make a drama out of it, Non. There's no personal things left here, are there?"

"No."

"So, that means everybody took them with them. The people didn't die. They just chose to leave."

Non didn't say anything, because she didn't want to be annoying—and she also didn't really want to have Meg agree with her. But she did wonder if the walls and roofs were so decayed whether anything inside the houses might not have decayed too. If, perhaps, over the years, the wind might have blown away any papers or paintings and animals may have chewed at clothes; toys and plates may have rotted, been covered over by creepers, or crumbled into the mud. No, she didn't want Meg to agree with her or for them to stop and look inside the houses too closely.

They reached another clearing. They were almost at the brow of the hill, and from here they had a good view of the castle. They could see the tiny dots of the soldiers creeping along the battlements and looking out over the empty floodplain. There were ten or so red kites in the air, drifting on the gusts of air blowing along the valley, their wings barely moving at all. There were another three low buildings here, their walls so crumbled that anything hiding inside would have to be almost lying down. But there was also a church. A completely intact, well-made, solid church. Not only were its stone walls still standing, but its door was still closed, the roof slates were still neatly attached, and the windows mostly still contained their glass.

"Let's have a look at the church," said Paul, pushing open the gate to the graveyard.

Chapter 8

The church reminded Non of the citadel. The stone was smooth, well cut, and made to last. The tower had battlements on it—for decoration probably. She knew that. But it was decoration that could be useful. It felt like an echo of Cirtop down in the valley, a smaller, child's version of a castle, as though you could play at battle here with toy swords and shields and nobody would get hurt. The tympanum above the door had decorative stone carvings on it, regular repeating patterns, and once-painted statues looked out across the valley, their eyes now blank and dead.

The heavy wooden door was studded with large metal bolts, and a trail of rust wept from each hole, running down the pitted, ancient wood. Sam tried opening it, then Paul, then Meg, but it was firmly locked. There was no way they were getting in there.

"Let's walk round," said Paul. But Sam was already leading the way. Non checked her hair. She'd plaited it this morning, and now a few strands were coming loose round her forehead. She smoothed them back as they walked.

The church was surrounded by a thick, chest-high wall, which hemmed in the graveyard. Things could be hiding behind that, of course, but then they'd have to clamber in, which would delay an attack. The wall was another defensive advantage. The grass was not as thick in the graveyard as it should be, which probably meant an animal of some sort was grazing it, and there was a sort of trail cutting through it—maybe from wild sheep or something. Non didn't say that, though. She somehow couldn't work out how to put the words into a proper sentence, but she looked around for any signs of the animal so they could write it on the map.

They walked almost the whole way round before they found another door. They all saw it at the same time. And they all realized it was odd. The door was nailed shut. Wooden planks were firmly placed against it, securing it, even though it was also clearly locked. Words had been painted on it in black. Although faded, those words were still legible. They had been written very clearly in capitals, and the brushstrokes showed that they'd been traced over several times. They said DO NOT ENTER. Around the frame of the door there was a pattern of neatly spaced circles. Still bright with paint even after all these years, each circle was filled with intricate decorations—looping spirals, dots, curls, hidden animal faces—but the center of each circle was clear and blank so that the wood of the door showed through in the shape of a cross. They were beautiful—but strange. Each one was different but so regular in shape that they must surely have been printed, or maybe drawn with a stencil. The gap for the cross in the middle felt surprising, like the absence of the main purpose. Normally the cross was the main feature of any art or drawings Non had seen in churches, not the stuff around it. She would have liked to have a closer look, but she also didn't want to go too close to that door by herself.

"What does it say?" asked Becky.

"What do you mean, what does it say?" replied Meg.

"It's OK. I can read it. It's fine," said Becky. She squinted at the door, her lips moving slowly.

"It says, DO NOT ENTER," said Meg, watching her.

Sam had turned his back to the door and was looking round the area. But there was nothing moving. Nowhere close by that anything could be hiding. Non unhooked her spear.

"What have you been writing on the map?" asked Meg.

"What I've written on the map is fine, OK?" said Becky. "It's fine."

"Let me see."

With a sigh, Becky thrust the sheet of paper at her.

"It's only got drawings on it," said Meg.

"Does it need words? You can see what everything is supposed to be."

"Is this supposed to be a rabbit? Because if I'm honest, it's not very clear."

"You don't need to be honest, Meg," whispered Non. "You really don't."

"What shall we do now?" asked Sam.

"Well, I don't think we should enter," said Paul.

"No." Sam frowned. "Definitely not."

They all stood there silently for a few seconds. Non suddenly wanted to go back to the castle very badly. But looking at it from here, she was aware of how far away it was down there in the valley, how long it would take them to get there. The trees were a thick cover of rippling greens and browns, always moving, and masking a hundred possibilities—most of them bad. The church, on the other hand, was stable, unchanging, secure, and she could touch it. It even had arrow slits on the tower, in a curved style that matched those of the citadel. They *were* in the shape of a cross, so they were suitable for a church, like it was fine if anything was killed through them—still a Christian death.

This time, she deliberately didn't think before she spoke. "One of the windows on the other side is broken," she said. "And there's a ledge beneath to stand on. We could maybe have a look."

Everybody turned to her, and for a minute she wished she hadn't said anything. But then Sam smiled at her. Non smiled back at him.

"I don't think we should," said Paul. "I mean, it's probably not good if the door is locking something in, is it?"

"Come on, I'll boost you up to have a look," said Sam to Non. "You're the smallest. If you just check it out and then we go, we'll have something definite to tell Commander Edwards."

Non nodded, and she smiled again. They started walking back round to the other side of the church. Meg looked at her, then looked at Sam. "It's interesting that we're here, Non," she whispered.

"Shh," said Non, pushing her away.

"It's just—" Meg leaned in farther and whispered so that only Non could hear, "It's just that I was a bit surprised you agreed to leave the castle. I thought you'd argue a bit more. Interesting."

"Shh," repeated Non, walking more quickly so that she was ahead of Meg.

There was a narrow decorative ridge of brick poking out from beneath the trails of ivy that covered the side of the church.

"Here," said Sam. He put his cupped hand down for Non to step in, though he didn't need to. The ivy was strong and the vines thick. There were several footholds she could have used. She put her foot in his hand anyway but pulled on the jutting, crumbly brickwork to take her weight. She clambered up and steadied herself before peering in. The window here was streaked with lines of dirt and dust on the inside, but through all the murk she could make out a large hall containing a number of overturned benches and the scattered debris of books and clothing. Ripped pages of the books were strewn evenly across the room in a confetti of destruction, the paper now curling with age and damp. There were bodies on the floor, decayed beyond the stage of being smelly, but some of them were wearing clothes, which could often bind the skeleton together, making them seem weirdly recent. A couple of strands of ivy had crept in through cracks in the window frames, splaying out to partially conceal this scene of death with a shroud of green, new life. Leaves had grown over the faces of the victims, and shoots encircled fibulae and tibiae. Nothing had moved in here for a long time.

"I can't see properly," she said. "There are at least five dead bodies. It looks like there's been a fight."

"I think we should go in," said Sam.

"I definitely don't," said Paul. "The sign on the door says not to, and Commander Edwards also said not to."

"The sign on the door is probably a century old. Whatever it's about is dead. Very dead," said Sam.

"And this place is really easy to defend," said Non. "The windows are too high for anything to get through without ladders or help. And it would take a lot of pressure to get that door open."

"What if there is something inside?" asked Becky.

"Like what?" replied Sam.

"Well, what's the sign on the door for then?" said Paul.

"Plague?" said Sam. "Something like that? Non's right . . ."

Non turned her face back into the church and grinned.

". . . it's worth checking out because it's so easy to defend. We'd be stupid not to check it out."

Non shuffled along the ledge to the broken window. Using her spear, she pushed the few remaining shards of spiky glass into the church. They fell with a clatter, and it was a loud noise in the stillness, false and unnatural.

"Nothing's moving inside. I think." There was a quiver of movement from the far corner, the shuffling, shifting noise of papers blowing in a light spring breeze, not the jerky, sudden stumbling awakening of a demon. Non pulled herself onto the windowsill and clambered down onto a bench beneath. She could hear the others already climbing up behind her.

"Ugh!" said Meg, pulling a face and brushing aside a cobweb. "This is properly creepy. Becky, you should draw some skeletons on your map. These need burying."

Becky climbed over. She scowled at the paper, but she did mark something on it.

Non pointed over to the corner. Nothing was moving now, but she could see that one of the fronds of ivy had been twisted round.

"There was something over there," she said, hugging her arms to her chest, "just something small. Maybe a rat?" Non looked beneath her bench. There was nothing under there that she could see at all. It was in shadow, and obviously the sun never reached this part of the church, because the ivy hadn't grown here. She could see the stone of the floor beneath her. It was clear.

The others were all in the church now, standing on the two benches nearest the window. Non peered at the back of the church, where the tower was, but the whole place seemed to be clear. It wasn't obvious what had happened here at all.

"I don't want to step on the floor," said Meg. "Non thinks there's rats."

Becky pulled a face.

"We'll just walk along the benches," said Paul. "We can get the whole way round the church just walking on those. And we can poke at the ivy with our spears to check there's nothing in it."

"Add rats to your map, Becky," said Meg.

Becky scowled again, but again she wrote something down.

This time there was definitely movement from the corner, a slow, turning, yawning twitch, a pull of the ivy clinging to one of the skulls. It tugged at the jawbone so that the mouth suddenly gaped open in a soundless scream, like a repellent, dusty puppet.

"I'll go and have a look," said Sam. He crept along the bench toward the movement, then he took a step onto another overturned bench. It wobbled slightly under his weight, and he steadied himself with his spear.

"I can't see anything else moving," said Meg tentatively.

Non crouched down so that she could see below the benches. There was nothing obvious.

Sam's bench gave a bigger wobble, and he paused again, steadying himself, then he turned round to the others and grinned. "It's like an assault course," he said. "We should all do this. See who can get round the church the fastest without falling onto the floor."

They all smiled. Non thought that, after he'd checked it all out, she might be up for doing that. So long as it was all definitely safe.

There was the altar at the front, a couple of the benches grouped together so that you couldn't see what was behind them, and the staircase that led up to the tower was in shadow. But that was it. And she'd been able to see, when up on the window ledge, that there was nothing hiding in any of those places. No, the real problem was the ivy. It clung to everything on the other side of the church, covering anything that was on the floor, including parts of each of the bodies, so it wasn't clear what was under there.

Sam reached the corner of the church. "Oh," he said, peering in, "I think it's . . . demon eggs! This is amazing!"

Meg glanced at Non.

"Yeah. I think that must be what this is. That's what happened. So there should be at least five eggs, then," said Paul.

Non deliberately didn't look at Meg. Meg grabbed her arm. "I think we should leave this and go back to the castle," she said.

"We might as well just check them out now, since we're here," said Paul. "The bodies are long dead, so it'll only be the eggs."

"No, I really think we should go back now. Now."

"It's fine," said Paul.

"You're being a prick again," she said. "What happened to all the obeying the rules stuff now? I want to go." Meg suddenly sounded really panicky. Emotional, like she was about to cry.

"What's the matter?" whispered Non.

"I really think we should go. Are you OK?"

"Yes. I'm fine. *You*?"

"Yes. But . . ." Meg's voice trailed off. Non could feel Meg's eyes watching her, and she deliberately made herself look relaxed, though her legs suddenly felt shaky.

Sam was standing on the floor now, next to a thick clump of ivy. There was a partially concealed skeleton in front of him, and he was prodding at it idly while he waited for the others to climb along the benches.

"I want to see. It's not dangerous," said Non.

Meg held her arm. "Please."

Non shook Meg's arm off and moved away from her.

"I think the egg is definitely dead," said Sam.

"How long do the eggs normally take to hatch?" asked Becky.

"I don't know," said Paul. "But it's when they've absorbed most of the nutrients from their host, so the person is normally dead, I think. Not this dead, though." He laughed but then stopped himself and looked round the room. Nothing was funny in here, and suddenly Non felt sadness for the skeletons who had once been people.

"So, I guess," said Sam. "I guess these people must have got infected, and then the villagers must have locked them in here."

"Maybe when the eggs got near hatching?" offered Becky.

"Maybe."

Meg squeezed Non's arm. "I'm sorry," she whispered. "I love you. But I don't think you should look."

Non took a step away from her again and kept her eyes on Paul and Sam.

"I'm going to smash the eggs," said Paul.

Sam shrugged. "Are you? Careful with the skeleton, then. I think these people need to be buried properly. They were very brave."

Paul raised his spear above his head, then he brought it down hard. Splintered fragments of something flew against his boots, and the ivy around the skeleton collapsed to the floor as whatever had been holding it up crumpled. Dark juice seeped slowly toward Paul's boots, and he took a step backward.

"So satisfying!" he said.

And then, as he turned to grin at everyone, there came a pulling and a shifting under the ivy. From behind there was a shuffling and a rolling. There was a split second of calm, a pause, what felt like a slow, indrawn breath of fear, as though all the oxygen was being sucked from the room. And then it came from the altar: "Scrrrrreeeeeeee."

Then another from under a bench: "Scrrrrreeeeeee."

Then another from a pile of hymnbooks: "Scrrrrreeee."

More haunting than when they'd heard them from the citadel. The calls were amplified, like a horn, louder than any human voice. Like a jarring, cacophonous choir, the cries came, rising and falling notes in a melody of death and hell. Harmonizing in polyphony without breath. Non shook the sound out of her mind, blocking it from taking over. *Remember to breathe. Stop the noise. Stop the noise.*

"We've got to stop it!" she screamed, though she wasn't sure anybody else could hear her words. Non pulled at Meg. "Stop it!" she repeated. Meg nodded, her face pale.

"I'll get the one behind the altar," she screamed, gesturing toward it with her spear. Sam's face was a frown, and his shoulders were hunched. He ran to the pile of hymnbooks and smashed his spear down. He missed in his hurry and smashed it again. One of the calls stopped.

Non ran through the ivy, straight down what remained of the aisle—there was nothing big moving there, and anything that wasn't completely dead would definitely be awake by now. But it was so difficult to think or to focus on anything. Her brain felt foggy and full with the noise, the endless, endless "Sccccccrrrrrrreeeeeeeeeee." *Must stop the noise. Must stop the noise.*

It was perched, teetering on the edge of the altar, no longer inside the body that had once been leaning there. The skeleton sagged to the floor now, still held together with its faded blue dress.

Non raised up her spear and bashed it down hard, the eggshell crumbling like rotten wood beneath the force of her blow, releasing mucus inside. Immediately it stopped its deathly shriek, and immediately the fog started to clear from her head.

As each of the eggs was smashed, the pain and fear emptied from her body, leaving her shaking and weak. The church was no longer a good place. They needed to get out.

"Is everybody OK?" Non said, looking around. Tears were still running down Meg's cheeks, and everybody looked shocked and subdued. "Let's get up that tower quickly and look around. Then we need to leave. Come on."

Chapter 9

The red kites swooped low over them as they stood at the top of the tower, the air singing as the birds' wings cut through it. The birds hovered, every so often diving down but then swerving away at the last moment to rise up again.

For the first few minutes nobody spoke; they each looked down over a different section of the miles of matted shrublands and trees that surrounded them. All the castles could be seen from up here: the citadel spilling out from behind the hillside where it nestled; Castle Goch a craggy outcrop, spiky and regular in the distance; Kintaborel Castle beyond, just a line of gray above the trees. Each one of them an eye over the valley, a place of safety, guarding the river. But they were looking for more than just the castles now.

Cirtop was close, big, secure, those walls welcoming and well defended, but the soldiers were still moving slowly along the ramparts. No flags were raised. Nobody was charging across the plain with their swords out. No rescue unit was coming. Though Non could still feel the screaming of those eggs vibrating unpleasantly inside her, the noise didn't seem to have reached the castle. She hoped nothing else had noticed either.

"The best way is down the old road," said Sam.

"But the way we came is quicker," said Paul.

"It's not quicker if we break an ankle falling down the steep bits."

"The old road, then."

"Do we need to go?" said Becky. "If we stay here, won't the soldiers come and find us?"

"Yes," said Paul. They all looked at each other. The church somehow felt safer than going back out in the woods. They would just be stuck in here with a pile of dead bodies, that's all.

"We can't," said Sam. "We really can't. It'll take a few hours after we're due back before they realize we got into trouble, so they'll be sending a search party out just as it's getting dark. If there is trouble . . . that's when it'll strike, an ambush, and they'll be running straight into it."

"So we need to get out of here quickly, don't we?" said Meg quietly. "They must have been calling . . . mustn't they . . . for demons?"

"Can anybody see anything moving yet?" said Sam.

"No."

"No."

"No."

Without noticing she'd unfastened it, somehow Non's crossbow was now in her hands, armed and ready. But there wasn't even a rabbit down in the graveyard.

"So we're clear for now. What do you think? Road or straight down the hillside? Bearing in mind there probably are some coming," said Sam.

"I think road," said Paul. Becky nodded in agreement.

"Non?" said Meg.

"Yes. Road," said Non. "Let's just go now, then, and get it over with." But she didn't know what was scarier: running through a hillside with hidden, angry demons, or going back into that church again.

— ∘ —

They set off along the old road at a jog. Non put her crossbow back over her shoulder, but she kept an arrow out, clasped in her hand as she ran. Nobody spoke this time, and as they went back past those ruined houses, it did feel like something could be hiding behind them now. Every shadow that shifted, every low wall, was now somewhere a demon could be crouching; Non jumped at every creak of the branches, started at every falling acorn, flinched at every bird call. They knew what they were waiting for, and they knew it would come.

As they ran through the clearing with the rabbit holes, the pace picked up. Next to her, Meg still looked drawn and shaken, but she was clearly determined to get back to the castle before they were attacked, and she was running faster than Non had ever seen her move before. They wouldn't be able to keep going like that for long, and Non was already feeling her lungs hot and large in her chest, but she was also glad to be putting as much distance between them and the church as possible.

The road was not so overhung with bushes here, but the trees and bushes were thick higher up the hill and offered cover for demons, hordes of them. The tree canopy overhead also blocked the castle from view so that they had no idea of the distance they were traveling or how far there still was to go. Every so often the shadow of a red kite flickered across the path in front of them, slicing through the dappled patterns of the leaves. Non felt encircled by trees, hidden from the sky and world by layers of leaves and branches. Despite what the trees could be hiding, they offered a false feeling of protection, of safety. A bubble of false calm.

Sam slowed suddenly and stopped, pointing up the hill, through the wood. They all paused, listening, and then it came: "Scrreeeeeeee." A distant screech. It seemed to be behind them.

"Where is it?" whispered Meg.

"I thought the one I heard came from the top of the hill," whispered Sam, so quietly that they all had to lean in.

"Do you think it's more than one?" asked Becky.

"No. I think the sound is probably just bouncing around the valley," he said. "It might be a group of them, but it's probably just one." Non leaned over, putting her hands on her knees and trying to ease her breathing for when they started moving again.

"Scccccrrreeeeeee," the call came again, even more distant this time but impossible to pinpoint. Maybe they were going away? Heading toward the citadel?

"Come on." Sam started off this time at a trot. They had to keep moving.

There was no sound but the pounding of their boots on the wrinkled mud and the skittering of small stones over the track as their feet kicked them out of the way. The road was straight for another couple hundred feet, so they could see that the way was still clear until then.

Non could hear the screeches calling back and forth, the sound seeming to come from different locations each time. There was definitely more than one demon, and they were definitely communicating with each other. It was impossible to avoid the feeling of being hunted.

They jogged on and on. Non had a stitch in her right side, and her body kept trying to get her to stop: Her legs were starting to stagger with tiredness, and breathing was getting difficult. She didn't know how much farther she would be able to go.

But it was Meg who stopped first, panting. She shook her head and held up her hand. "Have to slow down," she gasped out. They gathered around, catching their breath. They could allow themselves seconds at the most.

"They're getting closer, aren't they?" said Paul. "Why are they shouting?" Nobody answered; each tried desperately to rest so they could run again. But they'd never been told about this sort of behavior from demons. It definitely felt as though they were prey.

"The commander said we shouldn't fight them, right? That we should just run," Sam checked.

"God, I'm not doing anything else," Meg said emphatically, and a little desperately. "Let's go faster."

"But we'll be leading them right to the castle and the others," said Sam.

"That's exactly where I want to lead them," said Meg. "To a unit of trained soldiers who can deal with it."

"Come on," said Non, standing up again. She was exhausted, but she also didn't want to die.

They moved on again, and up ahead the trees were thinning out, opening up to the sky and letting the afternoon sunlight through in harsh bursts. The feeling of safety was already going; when they were out of the trees, they'd be totally exposed.

As they reached the edge of the woods, the trees gave way to a large area of boggy shrubland across which Non could see the castle again. Now that they were closer, she could make out a single red flag draped over the side of the battlements: Demons had been spotted in the area. There was a watcher standing above it looking across the shrublands, and they spotted the students immediately. They started signaling across, and a horn was sounded from somewhere within the castle.

Sam, Becky, and Paul all stopped and stared.

"What is it?" asked Meg, coming up behind. Paul held up his hand, and they panted for breath as the watcher spelled out the message with their flags.

"They say," said Becky, "demons are behind us . . . and in front of us to the right. Come straight across."

"Did they say how many?" asked Non.

"No." Meg looked at Becky for a second, as though she was going to say something about what she *could* read. But she didn't. Because it wasn't important, was it?

Non stepped straight off the road, into the thick undergrowth; it was the fastest way to the castle, but it was going to be treacherous. There was no path, no tracks, just places where the shrubs were thinner than others. There was no way they could see what was concealed beneath the bushes, see whether there were holes that could twist an ankle or tree roots that could trip them up. Either would kill.

Non ran, pushing through what bushes she could and jumping over the patches of thicker vegetation. They had spread out this time, each running, desperately, their own route, and Non could see the others out of the corners of her eyes at a distance of several feet.

And then she smelled it. The sweet, earthy, fungus smell of the demons. It wafted toward them in waves as the gusts of wind blew the stench hotly over the shrublands.

"Quick!" Non screamed, "they're here." Somehow her crossbow had slid down so that it was hooked around her elbow now, and an arrow was in her other hand; she ran quicker, swerving away from the trees on her right that obscured the view.

They emerged suddenly and swiftly, breaking through the center of a knot of bushes. There were three of them, the closest one with its claws already raised and ready to grab. Its lidless eyes swiveled, wide and brightly white. Its rows of teeth glistened with saliva as it bared its mouth as though in a joyless smile; Non could see its muscles moving as it ran, each ribbon strand of the pectorals rising and falling as it swung its arms back and forth, tense with power.

Meg screamed loudly.

"Run faster," Non shouted.

"We're not going to make it. We'll have to fight," shouted Sam.

"Just keep going. There's only three of them," Non shouted, bashing through more of the bushes, the branches swiping back onto her face.

But the demons were freakishly fast. They seemed to move at an impossible speed, finding all the easiest routes through the undergrowth, never tripping or catching on the branches. They were comfortably keeping pace with the students, were only feet behind them. Non didn't know if they were going to make it.

The castle was getting closer now. Non was having to concentrate on each next running step as she sped over roots and briars, but she could see the safety of the dark stronghold looming up in front of them, the shadow of the cliff falling across the plain. She ran, her back arched away from those grasping claws reaching out behind her. She could feel her heart pounding in every part of her body—it was hurting her chest now. But they needed to keep running.

The moat appeared in front of them. But she didn't stop. If anything was in the water, then at least she couldn't see it, unlike the demons she could smell only just behind. She jumped straight in, making it almost to the middle of the swirling murk before she lost momentum. The water came up to her chest, and she splashed wildly, trying to keep on running, desperately trying to get away but finding herself slowed by the drag of the river.

Non turned, raised her crossbow and shot, the face of the closest demon only a few feet away. The arrow hit it straight in the eye, freezing its face in its killing snarl. It fell immediately, crumpling by the side of the moat. She reached for another arrow, but then overhead there was the familiar whoosh of others, flying from behind her.

"Come on quickly and steadily—we've got you covered," a deep, confident voice shouted across from the opposite bank. Commander Edwards and Dog were crouching, combat-ready; Dog was holding a black crossbow that she was still pointing at the demons, already steadying her aim. As Non waded through the water, Dog released the first arrow. Then, pausing only momentarily to check her positioning, she swiftly shot another and then another.

Commander Edwards leaned forward and grabbed Non's hand, hoisting her up firmly. As she turned to look back over at the other side, she saw the dead demon lying sprawled on the edge of the moat with its claw just resting on the surface of the water, the lapping flow catching and dragging at it. The arrow she'd shot was still sticking out of its head, and a trickle of blood was dripping steadily down that and into the water now, a dark stain at the edge of the moat.

Behind her, there were two arrows in the other demons. One of them was no longer moving, finally dead. But the leg of the third was still twitching, desperately twisting at a warped angle, as if it was trying to stand up again and walk.

"Two out of three's not bad," said Commander Edwards with a grin.

"Couldn't get a clear shot," said Dog, squinting over the moat. "The kids were in the way."

Commander Edwards unhooked his spear, weighing it in his hands, turning it around a couple of times as he frowned in concentration. He pulled his arm back, holding the spear halfway down the shaft, and threw it hard across the river, twisting his body with the power of the throw. It hit the demon's head with a loud crunch. The leg stopped twitching.

"Well." He turned to the five students. Meg had scrambled up too and was lying facedown on the grass, but Sam, Paul, and Becky were still standing in the moat, dripping and pale. "I see you might have found something of interest, then."

Chapter 10

Dog marched them, still dripping, straight through the castle gate and into the nearest guard tower. A few Kintaborel Castle girls were getting water from the well, and they turned to watch curiously as the wet students passed. Non's legs felt wobbly and weak from all the running, and maybe the fear, but she managed to stand tall as she passed, though her hands wouldn't stop shaking.

"So we need to debrief you," said Dog. "Tell us what happened."

A rough map of the valley was drawn on the walls of the guard tower. Non recognized some of the features on one of the walls: the church, a few of the houses, a clearing, the road. But there were a lot of missing details. The map on the opposite wall of the room was similarly sparse, though there were some dark areas of shading, and she wondered what instructions the other group of students had been given that morning after they'd set off to climb the valley. She wondered if they were back yet.

Sam started to speak. "We didn't see much. Everything looked fine. An ordinary abandoned village . . ." His voice was clear and confident. Non was glad that he was speaking, because she didn't think she could. He looked pale, though, and one of his hands was clasping his sword, his fingers tapping on the handle.

"Where? Draw on the houses."

Becky stood up and started drawing the buildings and places she'd noted onto the wall. Sam kept talking as she did so. At some point Commander Daffy came into the room, though he stayed at the back, watching everything and hunching slightly from the weight of the books he was carrying and that he seemed reluctant to put down. A soldier appeared and passed round water and freshly buttered bread. The bread was still warm and soft, the butter melting in oozing trickles, and Non didn't think she'd ever tasted anything so good. With every bite she felt herself relaxing, releasing the tiredness in her body.

". . . the church looks like a secure stronghold. It could easily be fortified. Non said that."

Everybody turned to her for a second, but she'd just taken an extra-large bite of the bread and her mouth was so full she couldn't speak. She covered her mouth with her hands and concentrated on the wall.

"When we went to check on it, we realized that it had five corpses in it. All had been infected by the demons."

Non swallowed. Meg moved over and grabbed her hand.

"Do you want to go outside?" whispered Meg.

"No."

"I think you should go. You don't have to put a brave face on it."

Non didn't answer, but she shook Meg's arm away. Dog looked over with a frown, but Non sat very still. She suddenly didn't feel hungry anymore.

"That is interesting," said Commander Edwards. "So the infected people hadn't actually gone to find the demons?"

"No. They'd been locked into the church, though. And somebody had written 'Do Not Enter' on the door."

Commander Edwards nodded slowly.

"We'll send a team tomorrow. How did they die? Any clues? Were they killed by the villagers?"

Sam looked at the others for help. Becky and Paul shrugged. Non didn't know what to do, so she took another bite of that bread. Her throat was very dry now, and chewing it was difficult. It was scratchy and hard in her mouth as she swallowed.

"OK. We'll investigate tomorrow."

Somehow Meg's hand was in hers as Sam told about smashing the eggs and the sound they'd made, and then about running and that feeling of being hunted. But as soon as the students were dismissed, Non let go and sped out the door.

"Non," Meg called. But Non carried on down the steps. She could feel the tension in her again, like she needed to run, like it was the demons after her and not Meg.

"Non!" She carried on walking toward the castle courtyard, but it was full of people building up the wall. She stopped for a second, uncertain where to go.

"Why are you so cross?" asked Meg. "You don't have to be OK, you know. You don't have to pretend. Seeing what was in the church was horrible for everybody. But not everybody's mum died like that—so it's worse for you. I feel really sad for you."

"It's not your business to be sad for me, though, is it? Because it's not your sadness. It's mine."

"I know," said Meg. "It is yours. But it is sad."

Meg's voice trailed away as she spoke, and Non felt a touch of sympathy for her then. But that didn't stop her being cross.

Non bit her fingernails. She didn't know what to do or say next.

Meg opened her mouth as though she was going to say something, but then she closed it again.

"What!"

"Nothing. I'm sorry. I'm just really, really sorry."

Non looked at her.

"I'll do whatever you want."

"Leave me alone, then."

"OK."

Meg stood at the castle entrance, her face creased like she was going to cry. Non turned away and stormed off toward the wall, with a purpose and as though that's where she'd definitely planned to go. But where she really wanted to be was in one of those dips in the hillside, those grass-covered pits in the earth that had once been something or other but were now just sheltered holes. Places where you could be enclosed by the grass and the castle and the earth and just feel the safety on all sides. But there were people all over the hillside, ripping away the grass to uncover ancient walls, removing stone from some places and piling it up in others, stirring mortar, shouting to each other, laughing. Cirtop was crawling with people everywhere. There was nowhere safe from their eyes.

So she found herself on the battlements again, edging along that narrow parapet with the cliff falling away beneath. There was nobody up here apart from the soldiers and the watchers, and at the moment there was nobody on this section of the walls—just a watcher on each of the towers.

She didn't feel sad. She felt angry. Really, really angry—her fists balled up uselessly with rage. It did make her think of her mother, yes—that person she couldn't remember. She'd always known the parasite had infected her, had thought before about those demon creatures growing slowly inside her, using her body, the cells multiplying in her blood, the egg developing in some cavity. She'd half pictured the changes, thought vaguely about how she'd have looked—but it had never been real. It had only ever been the polite, carefully worded explanations of others and a hazy picture in her head. But now she had the reality to remember—and she knew she wouldn't have to imagine it again, because the memory of those screaming eggs and those sad, wasted skeletons was going to stay with her. She felt really angry with Meg too, and everybody else. She knew it wasn't their fault, and she knew Meg was just trying to be nice. But she didn't feel like she wanted nice right now. It felt like, in some way, everybody had lied to her. Like the whole world was against her. She glanced around, and nobody was watching her, so she let a few hot, angry tears leak out. But her body was too tense for more, and she wasn't going to sit there trying to cry.

The plain was empty now, the grass and shrubs lightly rippling in the breeze. Sheep were grazing there, chewing slowly, moving from one patch of lush grass to another. There were no red kites circling above, though a few perched on the battlements, flying away whenever one of the soldiers got too close. The other birds must have gone to the citadel or somewhere where there was more guarantee of death. And those dead demon bodies had already been cleared away. Who had moved them, she wondered? When had that happened?

Below her, the targets had been set up for the soldiers' crossbow practice, but the range was empty at the moment, the soldiers maybe out and busy with shooting real targets. The cliff here was not as sheer as it looked; at points there was space for grass to grow, clinging into crevices in the rock. Non could see birds' nests in a few places, and little birds, ones whose names she didn't know, the small brown sort, flew back and forth with tiny pieces of leaf or twigs clasped in their beaks. She liked that thrill of leaning over to look, that feeling of the world spinning slightly as though she might fall. And she held on, knowing that she wasn't going to.

Round the corner, a figure appeared, running fast around the outer walls of the castle. She knew it would be Sam before she saw his face for definite, and then she watched as he ran out of view on the other side. The way his legs moved, the way his top brushed against his chest, the way he clutched his spear in his hand. She waited until he came round again, running more slowly now, steadier, and she watched him again.

Non walked down along the wall, round the edge of the hillside. That way, she would avoid talking to people. Several times, she knew people were looking at her, perhaps to wave, or perhaps to ask if she was OK, but she deliberately kept her face turned away so that she could pretend she hadn't noticed them.

When she reached the gate, she climbed down, and before she could think about it too much, she walked through it, to the outside of the castle. Today, just this once, it felt better being out there. She stayed between the castle walls and the moat as she walked round to the bottom of the cliff, but it felt like she could breathe more easily out here, let her shoulders relax, let her head clear.

Sam ran past her, on his way round again. "Hey," he said.

"Hey," she said back. But she focused on the targets, unhooked her crossbow, and got her arrows out for practice.

Chapter 11

When Non returned from shooting at things, she felt much better. She still didn't want to be stuck on a hillside with a group of people she didn't know, or the group of people she did know, but she was more ready to deal with it now. She hadn't spoken to Sam, though he'd run past a couple more times. But she'd had to watch him carefully as he passed—just so she didn't accidentally shoot him. No other reason. And they had smiled at each other each time.

When she went back into the castle, most people were lying around, exhausted. The other scouting group had mapped their part of the valley thoroughly but had not encountered any demons or anything unusual. And the majority of students, those who'd stayed inside the castle, had found that carrying heavy stone up a hillside and then laying walls hadn't felt very much like *light* building work at all. But the walls were higher in the castle courtyard and the dormitories. Almost so high that if you stood up, you couldn't see over. Almost, but not quite.

There was no sign of Meg among the group of students lying around in the courtyard, so Non spent the evening writing a letter to her dad. It took her a while, because the first couple she wrote she also ripped up. She felt better when she'd done that, and her third letter was calmer, thoughtful, and more logical. She could admit on paper, to him, what she couldn't put into words otherwise and certainly would never have said to his face: She wanted to know more about the people in the church. She wanted to know what had happened to them, what it had been like, why they were there. She didn't mention her mother, but she knew that's what she was also thinking about, or maybe trying hard not to think about. She dropped the letter down to the guardhouse so it could be delivered to the citadel in the next supply cart, but she still couldn't see Meg anywhere on the hillside. She didn't want to go looking for her either, because she didn't know what sort of situation she might find her in. Non had had enough of finding unexpected things today.

Supper came, a thick stew, and most people ate in silence, wincing as they swallowed chunks of boiling potato and pausing only to blow on the surface of the stew in half-hearted attempts at cooling it before panting as they bit into mouthfuls of melting, lava-hot carrot. It burned her throat, Non gulped it down so fast, but she still felt restless and hurried, like she couldn't settle to anything. There was too much leftover adrenaline from the day.

The only people from the citadel who were up here were talking to each other and didn't look like they'd want her interrupting, so Non got out her notebook again. She didn't have anything to do, but she didn't want to have to talk to anybody or look weird by *not* talking to anybody.

She found herself sketching the scene in the church. Just drawing out what they'd seen. She wasn't great at drawing, so it was mainly labels. But she put down where the eggs had been, where the people had been. And she drew the eggs then, what they'd looked like and what had been inside. She tried writing a description of the noise, but it was hard to capture in human words, to try and explain it in syllables, phonemes, graphemes. There was just too much of the animal in it—or maybe not animals at all. Maybe it's that it felt unnatural, not part of the valley.

She tried to remember exactly what had happened when Paul smashed the egg, and then when she'd smashed one too to make the noise stop—but her ideas were confused, and it was difficult to picture it clearly. The memory of that noise made her stomach turn and her head go fuzzy, as though it was constricting her brain.

On a new page, she started noting down what she knew about the demons needing human hosts to grow their eggs. But apart from that exact fact, she didn't know much—she didn't know the details and had never felt like she could have, or wanted to have, a conversation with her dad about it.

The sun was starting to go down, and although it was still bright enough to write, it was getting cold, so Non went into the dormitory for a jumper. The Kintaborel Castle girls were sitting on mats in the center. They were still wearing their silken slippers, and underneath their headscarves their hair was plaited in intricate designs. They were replaiting it now, weaving in beads and ribbons to add to the beauty. Against all the odds, they did look lovely, in the middle of this hillside. There were clues that they'd been working today—a couple of them had chipped nails, and there were smears of dirt on the long, tight skirts, but they still looked more like they were ready to go to a glamorous party than spend the night lying in a half-built room on a mud floor.

They smiled at Non as she went in, and she decided to stay.

"Hi, Non. I'm Callie, and this is Cath and Mary," said one of the girls. "We heard about you seeing those dead bodies in the church. Was it horrible? You poor thing."

Non shrugged in a way that she hoped would show she was both friendly but didn't want to talk. It didn't work.

"What was it like?" the girl asked.

"Um. Horrible."

"Really?" The girls gasped.

"It wasn't the bodies that were bad—it was the eggs inside them."

The girls looked at her expectantly. And then Non realized they didn't know why she might not want to talk about it. They didn't know her background. There was absolutely no feeling of awkwardness from them about what her reaction might be, which meant she also didn't need to worry about having the right reaction to meet their expectations. Other people's confused sympathy had always meant in the past that she'd needed to make it look like she needed their sympathy, or that she was grateful for it, when, in fact, it had usually been a pain. Her grief for her mother was a feeling of an absence, but other people's uncertainty about how to mention it usually meant it was easier to deal with anything surrounding her mother's death by just avoiding talking about it. So suddenly Non felt like she wanted to talk about the people in the church a lot, and she wanted to hear what these girls knew about demons.

"At least they were in a church when they died," said Mary. "That must have been a comfort."

"What did you get told about how the eggs are made?" asked Non. "I'm just wondering . . ."

"I think . . ." said Callie. The girls looked at each other with a frown. "They think it's a parasite, don't they?"

"Uh-huh," said Non, in a way that could be both agreeing or disagreeing, or even just a random noise.

"I know you get it from contact with the demons. Their claws or their teeth. I think they have to break your skin for the parasite to be released into your bloodstream."

"Yeah." The girls nodded.

"And then a few weeks later, the egg starts to grow in your stomach or your intestine or somewhere. And then eventually the infected person goes a bit nuts and decides they love demons and walks off to find them. When they do, the demon egg is normally ready to hatch."

So far, it was roughly what she already knew. But it was very rough. Was it their claws or their teeth that released the parasite? Or both? How did nobody seem to know this information?

"Where do the infected people go?" asked Non. "How do they know where to go?"

"I don't think anybody knows, do they? Just a demon place?"

And how did they not know this either? Did nobody follow the infected people? Had nobody followed her mum?

The girls were mainly doing each other's hair again now, and Non started adding this information into her notebook. It was more, but there were still a lot of gaps in her knowledge. She wrote a list of the questions she had at the back of the book, and there were definitely more of those than there were answers.

"Commander Daffy might know," said Callie suddenly, smiling over at her. "He's in this demon club. The Order of the Valley Guardians? So he might know more?"

The other girls laughed. "No, he won't," said Cath. "Non, it's just a club where the older men go. I think they just get dressed up a bit and drink cider. Is Commander Daffy definitely really in it?"

"A *demon* club?" asked Non.

"I think so. At least, they have shields and banners with a picture of demons on them," said Callie. "And I think it's supposed to be the demons they're named after—the guardians in the title. He is in it, Cath, I've seen him in their parades, and the men must know something about demons if that's what the club's supposed to be about, mustn't they?"

"They might," said Cath. "But I think they know more about different types of cider. I don't know if they do much about demons at all. It might be a monkey on their banners, actually—the symbol's not very clear."

"It isn't a monkey. You wouldn't call a monkey a guardian of the valley," said Callie.

"Would you call a demon one either, though?" asked Cath.

"No. But it's silly anyway. It's a club for men to show that they're really important. They like to wear these nice costumes and talk loudly," said Callie.

"Callie!" said Mary.

Callie grinned. "Sorry. That was mean. But there's no women allowed anyway, so I don't know what I'm talking about. And it's a secret club—though they're not very secret if we all know about it. And my mum says that's just so they can be secret about how much real ale they're drinking."

"They're all very nice men, though," said Mary sternly.

"Yes. Absolutely. Of course," muttered Callie.

Non didn't bother noting that information down, but she did decide it might be worth asking Commander Daffy sometime if he knew anything about the demons, and maybe she might note down what he said.

When they settled down to go to sleep that night, Meg still wasn't back. Non made sure her blankets were laid out for her anyway, and she lay down close to them, intending to wait up for her. But she must have fallen asleep, because the moon was up when Meg crawled in and nudged her awake.

"Where have you been?" whispered Non.

"Talking to me now, are you?" whispered Meg, noisily rearranging her blankets.

"Sorry for getting cross. I just needed to be by myself."

"OK." Meg leaned over and gave her a hug.

"Have you been by yourself too?"

"No."

"Who were you with?"

"Paul."

Non groaned. "Really? I thought you said he was a prick."

"I didn't let him speak. It was fine."

"Oh, Meg! Is he in love with you now?"

"No. It's fine."

"Really?"

"He was maybe a bit clingy. I had to send him away. But it'll be fine. He's strong."

"He's strong? Oh, no." Non sighed. "Meg, we're stuck in this tiny castle with him for weeks."

Chapter 12

Non kept her eyes shut, hoping and hoping that when she opened them she'd find herself in her comfortable bed at home, waking up slowly and chuckling to herself about her crazy dream. Possibly with a cup of merrol tea on the side because, hey, it was a fantasy, after all. But through her mist of happiness, the grumpy reality just kept oozing on through; she could sense the breathing of the other people nearby and could feel the hard, slight dampness of the earth beneath her, clues that things were not quite as she'd like. She nuzzled into her blankets, turning away from the intrusive brightness of the sun; it felt early, but the awning above them seemed to suck any heat and light out of the air and squeeze it out into the room below, so it was already ridiculously stifling.

A hand bell started ringing somewhere nearby. "Breakfast in ten minutes," came a shout.

"Oh, shut up!" groaned somebody.

But the Kintaborel Castle girls got up, arranged themselves into a circle, held hands and started to pray. The Castle Goch girls raised their eyes at each other, and Jane smirked.

"Hi, Becky," said Meg. "Did you sleep well?"

"Fine, thanks," said Becky quietly, but she looked at Jane as she spoke, not Meg. And she made it clear she didn't want to continue the conversation.

Jane ignored them.

"Is my hair straight?" Jane asked Becky.

"Yeah. It looks great."

"I think I might go and see Paul," said Jane. "See if he's missed me."

Meg suddenly started getting ready, brushing her hair and tying it up again. Non looked at her and raised her eyebrows. The Kintaborel Castle girls started to sing, quietly, still holding hands. This time their faces were all raised up to the sky, and they still had their eyes closed.

Non got changed very quickly, with her back to the rest of the room. She tried to make it look as though her blanket was merely draped around her shoulders for reasons of warmth, but actually, keeping it balanced casually around her shoulders while she wriggled into her clothes had taken some pretty crazy maneuvers. They'd then had to carry on as normal while the Castle Goch girls glided gracefully around the dormitory in their underwear. Nobody had really relaxed with each other yet, but she'd definitely seen Cath roll her eyes at Mary when Jane walked around for a full five minutes brushing her long hair while wearing just her knickers.

———— o ————

"You're going for a quick run before breakfast," said Dog. "We've got to improve your fitness. Girls first, then boys. Boys, you can sort out the weapons for the day while you're waiting."

Most people in the courtyard groaned, but Dog ignored them.

"Girls, you'll be running as a group. Jane will take the lead." Jane remained expressionless, as though this news meant nothing to her: There was no flicker of surprise, no pride, not even boredom. She slid a hairband off her wrist and, twisting her hair round into a shining, snaking bun, wrapped it firmly up on the top of her head.

"Why are we running with just girls?" asked Becky. "No offense, but wouldn't it be better to run in our castle groups? I think we probably have different . . . running styles."

"What's your running style, Non?" whispered Meg. "Mine is only when necessary."

Dog didn't look at Becky as she spoke, but at the Kintaborel girls. "There's too many of you to all go out at the same time, and splitting you up by dormitory is just an easy way of dividing you. You all need to aim to match the pace of the fastest, and the fastest people might not be from your own castle."

Becky and Jane gave each other a look.

"Shall we do a warm-up?" asked Ellie.

Dog shrugged. "Can if you want. Don't think you normally get the chance when you're running away from death."

"Yeah. True . . ." said Ellie. Did this mean that they should do a warm-up or not? Ellie seemed uncertain. She looked around. There were a few shrugs and raised eyebrows. Meg smiled encouragingly. "OK. Stretch your right leg like this." Ellie held her right leg out to one side and leaned over to the other. She then quickly swapped to the other leg and repeated her movements. Most of the group copied, half-heartedly sticking legs or arms out at a series of twisted angles according to their level of enthusiasm. Dog stared off into the distance, squinting with a keen concentration as though she could see something of great importance.

"Right," Dog said when Ellie stopped their warm-up. "You will be carrying your weapon with you. Whatever you normally carry." Dog sounded bored now. "Not because you're going to be attacked, but because you need to get used to the weight." She eyed the Kintaborel Castle girls particularly as she said this. Non tightened the strap on her spear, pulling it up firmly behind her head. She didn't want it rubbing against her while she was running. They'd gone for spears rather than crossbows this time, because they seemed more useful at close range. She looked round the group surreptitiously. Only the citadel girls had spears. The Castle Goch girls appeared to have long sheathed knives strapped horizontally to the front and back of their weapons belts. The Kintaborel Castle girls appeared to have . . . nothing. They were wearing their long skirts, though, so there was a chance they had something concealed up there.

They set off at a steady pace out of the castle, heading toward the sun. The flags were black today, showing that all the demons had been cleared from the immediate area, but Non no longer trusted that, and she looked round the plain suspiciously. The other girls obviously felt the same; too wary for chatting, they jogged for the first few minutes in silence, getting their bearings and anxiously scanning the surroundings for movement.

By the time they had lapped round the castle once and reached the tree line, the girls had predictably divided into their three distinct castle groups. Castle Goch were taking the lead, obviously, moving effortlessly over the countryside and appearing unfazed by changes in the terrain so that they moved just as smoothly over grass and bumps as along the pitted gravel road through the trees.

Non was grateful to be in the middle. While they were already out of breath and feeling a bit tired, it was heartening to hear the occasional muffled screech from the Kintaborel Castle girls behind as somebody stumbled over a rock or as a branch flew back into a face. The incompetence of Mary, Cath, and their group in their long skirts made Non feel speedy and brave, spurring her on to, if not run faster, at least make sure she was trying to move her arms like Jane, Becky, and the girls up in front.

There was also that whole thing about the feeling of safety that came from being in the middle. It felt like they were partly enclosed, if not by an actual wall, then by a human barrier of other girls. If demons did attack, they were surely more likely to attack the girls in front or behind, so providing a kind of human buffer zone for Non and the citadel students. She tried not to imagine anybody being dragged away, obviously, but there were a couple of the Kintaborel Castle girls who were a little on the plump side, so they'd probably delay the slavering demons for a good while.

They were onto another track now, one Non hadn't been down before. The land was open on their right, a shaggy, overgrown patch of bog that Non could see across for maybe half a mile. A heron was standing, statue still, staring down at something in one of the streams. She knew the bird wouldn't be there if there were predators nearby, but she didn't like the openness of that land. They were exposed. The air on that side of the track felt colder. There was woodland on their left, with high shrubs between the tall trees, and yes, there were many, many hiding places there, so the view was limited. But somehow that side made Non feel less anxious.

Non's group was jogging in tight formation. Very tight. Those on the outside of the group were supposed to have their weapons out, ready, while the ones on the inside were supposed to be able to rest a little, with their spears tied up on their backs so that the heavy, awkward metal was no longer weighing down their arms. They would then swap around positions every so often on the signal from the lead runner. It was all supposed to be so structured and carefully planned, just as they'd been taught at home. The thing was, they'd never actually done it . . . and it was all a bit scary being outside a castle in the reality of things. Nobody really wanted to be on the outside, so the group kept on edging closer and closer together, making it actually very hazardous to jog properly when it was your turn on the inside, having to avoid the tripping legs and the vigorously moving arms and weapons. Non had narrowly avoided being poked by Meg's spear on a couple of occasions, and it was starting to get silly.

But then there was a muffled screech from behind them, louder than before. The noises changed.

"Help, oh, help!" came the strangled call.

"Run!" somebody screamed.

There were sobs and startled, wordless shouts. Meg and Non sprinted immediately onward, breaking formation. Non felt a grabbing hand on her shirt, pulling at it fiercely, but she knew that it was just somebody behind; she could hear the breathing of something human and scared.

She could see the world now only in small, panicked chunks,

could see a tree, now the running feet ahead of her, now the road. Everything else was fuzz.

The screams came again from behind. Two voices this time.

Non grabbed Meg's wrist, pulling her forward in desperation. She tried to focus, but her eyes were still watery and hazy at the edges. It was still difficult to see everything in one go. Somewhere in the corner of her vision, she saw the smooth flight of the heron as it raised itself into the air.

She turned from side to side, ignoring the breathless pain in her chest. There was nothing else. She could see nothing up ahead. There was no movement in the trees. The attack was behind her. Between them all and the castle. In order to make it back, they would either have to run round for at least another mile to complete a circuit or fight the things and get past them.

They would never make it. She would never make it round. They would have to fight them. There was nothing for it.

Up ahead, the Castle Goch girls seemed unconcerned. A couple of them were jogging backward, looking behind them, but otherwise they seemed to be treating things exactly as they were before . . . except that the pace was perhaps a little quicker.

"Come on, run faster," called Jane. "Come on!"

Non risked a glance behind her. The Kintaborel Castle girls were running for their lives, expressions of cold terror on each of their faces: mouths open with gasping sobs, arms raised in panic. They had separated out now, and several of them were just behind Non.

The girls at the very back were stumbling and unsteady, only feet ahead of three grasping demons. It was obvious that they wouldn't make it. And they didn't have any means of defense.

"We'll have to fight. We'll have to," Non shouted. "We can do it if we all work together."

"No, just leave it. We'll get back OK if we keep running," Jane shouted, not even looking back.

"We've got to help them!" shouted Non, desperately looking around. There was a chorus of calls from behind her: pleas for help, pleas for life.

She reached up and unfastened her spear as she ran. She was going to have to do it. Meg gripped on harder, clawing at her. "No," Meg gasped, "No!" Non shrugged her off. She knew she had to help them.

"I'm not going to just leave them to die," Non screamed hopelessly at all the girls in front of her. She stopped still and turned, waiting. She steadied herself and raised her spear as the panicked runners sped past, focusing herself only on that moment of contact with flesh. She felt others move to stand next to her and saw three other raised spears out of the sides of her eyes.

The first demon seemed to come directly for her. She was ready to fight him. She prepared for a hit at his head, but he ran straight into her spear. It went right through his chest for a foot with a slow, wet squelch before he stopped, stuck. Neither moving forward nor backward, he seemed content to rest halfway along the hard metal pole, waving his arms vaguely in her direction and making a soft grumbling noise. His eyes stared directly at her, and blood bubbled out of his lipless mouth, trickling down his chest. It left a trail there, as though there was a surface, something to which liquid could stick. He gave a sigh and tilted his head.

To each side she could see demons being ineffectually batted at, or poked with spears, but at close range it seemed to be much more difficult to actually kill one than they'd been told. Non tried to shake her spear, to throw the demon off, but he moved only an inch, stepping to one side as she tugged at it. He was heavy, and each pull she made just seemed to drag him closer to her.

She toppled the demon over, her spear still sticking out of his chest. He fell against the other monsters so that they tumbled too, trapped underneath his weight. "Come on, let's get moving again," she called as the demons struggled to get free. It wasn't the best combat move she'd heard of, but it would at least delay the monsters.

———o———

The portcullis dropped behind them with a grating *thud*. Non pushed Meg forward up the path, but a number of the girls had just collapsed directly onto the ground and were now lying down panting, gasping, or just clutching aching, injured body parts.

Commander Edwards and Dog were standing to the side of the gate. Commander Edwards surveyed the gently sobbing group of exhausted girls with an air of detachment. "Not as bad as I'd expected," he announced loudly, making several of them jump in a panic. "Take half an hour for a break and then meet on the low field for weapons training." As Non watched, Meg feebly managed to muster her inner strength to raise her arm above her head and stick her finger up at his departing back.

Non's legs felt shaky, and she could almost feel little ripples of alternating cool and warm blood pumping through them as she tried to calm herself. She could hear the demons at the portcullis, pushing and scrabbling into it as they moved from side to side, searching for a way through. The frame was rocking back and forth on its hinges as they nudged at it, the light squeak and rattle of the chain locks audible even from here.

But it wasn't the threat of the demons that kept Non from relaxing. It was the reactions of the others: Commander Edwards's lack of interest; the failure of the gate sentries to make even an attempt at doing their job; the guilty hovering of the Castle Goch girls, who were now standing awkwardly around on the hillside looking vaguely concerned.

Non squinted across the backs of her resting companions and made eye contact with Jane, who quickly looked away, and then Becky. She forced her mouth into a smile; she'd been going for "carefree and happy" but suspected that her cheeks had shaped her expression into more of a "sarcastic and mean."

"How are things?" she said, trying to keep her tone neutral . . . or as neutral as you can when you're attempting a casual chat across a pile of sweating, traumatized teenage girls.

"They're just pacers," said Jane anxiously. "Don't you have them? You know. Their teeth and claws have been removed . . ." Her voice trailed off.

Non raised her eyebrows and gestured toward the rocking gate.

"The demons who followed us?" said Meg. "Those killers out there, you mean?"

"Yes." Becky looked uncertain. "We've had them for years. Quite a long time, actually, for demons. I don't think they die as quickly when they're pets. Or maybe they do. I don't know about these things." She gave a girlish little giggle. "These are the Castle Goch pacers. We brought them with us when we came down. I mean, you start running and they just follow along behind." Becky shrugged and looked to her friends for reassurance.

"They're falling apart a bit, actually," said Jane with a breezy tone, obviously deciding that she was going to make light of the situation. "We'll probably need to get some new ones quite soon. Though I'd be quite sad to have to bash in the head of Old Grumpy out there." She smiled.

"You've got names for them?" asked Meg.

Jane nodded.

"Do you keep them in the castle? Do you feed them?" asked Non.

"No!" said Jane, as though this was the bit that was shocking. "They fend for themselves mostly. Sometimes they go away for a couple of days, but they almost always come back again."

"Sometimes with a friend." Becky gave a shy smile.

"You own those demons?" Ellie sat upright. And other girls were sitting up now too, staring at the Castle Goch students in horror. "You brought them with you and didn't think to mention it? And then you let them attack us!"

"They weren't attacking," said Jane. "They were just playing."

"They really weren't just playing. It looked like they were trying to kill us."

"Well, they weren't," said Jane. "And if you had run faster, it wouldn't have been a problem."

"I can't believe you're trying to defend them," said Ellie, her eyes wide. "You're nuts. Really, nuts."

"I don't think we're the crazy ones here," said Jane, storming off up the hill. Behind, Becky and Chantelle followed more slowly.

"Well, what you *think* is also really nuts," said Ellie, but not loudly enough for Jane to hear.

Non was still shaking, her legs too wobbly to stand. She gripped onto Meg's hand as she watched the Castle Goch girls leaving. Outside the castle she could hear their pet demons—the pacers—pushing against the portcullis so that the chains rattled. Even that noise made her skin crawl—the idea of those monsters outside trying to get in was genuinely terrifying. There was no denying that they were killers, and that if they got the chance they would certainly infect or injure everybody in the castle. Close up they didn't feel so similar to humans—if anything, the fact that they looked almost like humans made them worse, like you should be able to negotiate with them or sit down and have a chat if you could only learn their language. But there was no way you could have a conversation with those creatures. And keep them as pets? Non couldn't think of anything less cuddly.

Chapter 13

Breakfast was an awkward affair. People sat in their castle groups again, the Castle Goch students loud and jokey, slapping each other on the back and laughing at things that weren't funny. It was as though they were making a big effort to show that everything was fine and it wasn't them who was weird, but everybody else. Keeping demons as pets was absolutely, definitely, completely normal.

Everybody else eyed them suspiciously and chatted in low voices.

Paul stared openly at Meg, his eyes rimmed with red. Non didn't see him eating. Meg's appetite was fine, though, and she laughed and joked with the other citadel students, reliving that morning's run and already turning it into a funny, exaggerated story. Paul seemed to slump lower against the wall every time she ran her fingers through her hair or casually put her hand on one of the citadel boys' arms.

"Why do we need to improve our fitness, exactly?" asked Non. "And why do we need to get used to the weight of our weapons?"

Meg shrugged. "It's just a general good thing, isn't it? And to be honest, we weren't very good, were we?" She laughed.

"True. And I would like to be more fit. It's just . . . It was weird the way Dog said it. Nobody ever worried about that much when we were in the citadel."

"No, but there were loads more people to defend us in the citadel," Meg pointed out.

"Do you mean like they might want us to defend *ourselves*?" chimed in Ellie.

"No!" said Meg, but she rolled her eyes to the others and they all smiled.

"Oh, don't laugh at me," said Ellie. "I'm not going to defend myself. You know I'd just be useless." She said it in a ditzy way and made her accent go particularly posh. But Non didn't know if she would be useless, actually. Ellie hadn't been one of the ones who'd fought the demons this morning, but she hadn't been one of the ones who had run away either. Non remembered her there, in the background, her spear unhooked and ready to fight.

They weren't given long to recover from their run. After a few minutes, Dog entered through the door gap, and a hush fell in the room.

"Right," she said. "You're all in the castle today. Doing some light building work. You're to stay in here so we know where you are. Or you can do some weapons training."

"Sounds like a fun day," whispered Meg.

"Light building work?" whispered Ellie. "Again?"

Non looked round the courtyard. There was enough heavy building work to keep fifty builders busy for years here.

"Somebody will be up to give you instructions in a minute. Stay here until then." Dog turned to go.

"Excuse me," Sam called after her. "Excuse me. Are you going back to that church now?"

"We have some work to do that doesn't concern you. You all stay in here and train with your weapons. Or you can do some light building work. If you prefer."

"I swear to God," whispered Meg. "If she says 'light building work' again . . ."

Dog didn't give the appearance of having heard her, but she paused and spoke to the room as a whole. "Remember you need to do something useful today—one of those options—*if* you want to eat." And then she looked at the students with a face that would curdle custard.

Sam carried on anyway. "If you're going to the church, do you want us to go with you to show you where it is?"

Dog frowned. "It's the great big church on top of that hillside. I think we can find it."

Non could see it even from where they were sitting. The tower of the church was clear above the battlements, tall and straight against the softer mass of the trees, still and stable against the slow-moving white clouds. She knew, looking at it, how much she wanted to go back. Not because Sam also wanted to go, but because she wanted to have another look. Just to see it again. It absolutely was morbid curiosity, and she knew it was her sick fascination wanting to look at those infected corpses and the smashed eggs. People would think she was weird for wanting to look, and she was. They would judge her—correctly.

But not going would bother her more. Staying inside today felt too small, like the walls were shrinking, squeezing the hillside together, suffocating her. She needed to be out, looking at the scene in the church again—even if it made her feel awful.

"Get to work!" said Dog. Students scrambled in every direction, some clambering over the courtyard walls into the dormitories, though it was more difficult to do that now that the walls were higher.

"I'd better go and hide for a bit," hissed Meg, ducking behind two of the Kintaborel Castle boys and weaving through the crowd to get out of the door gap. Paul stood up immediately, following behind, but his large, muscular frame meant that he was caught behind people and couldn't push through as quickly. His shoulders sagged.

"Hey, Paul," said Jane, putting her arm on his back.

"Hi," he said, moving to one side as he spotted a way through and letting her arm fall away.

Jane frowned.

Behind Non, Ellie and some of the others were complaining about the horrors of a day in which the treat was to do weapons training. Nobody was watching her. There was clearly going to be a few minutes of chaos, so that anybody could be anywhere. Non found herself following Dog down the hillside.

———o———

By the time she reached the castle gate, Sam was already standing there.

"Why are you here? What is it?" asked Dog.

"I want to train to be in the military," said Sam. "I'd love to gain experience from seeing this kind of expedition. Can I come?"

Dog gestured at several soldiers, waving them through the gate. They were already fully kitted out and most were carrying both swords and spears.

"Please?" said Sam.

Dog looked past him at Non. "And what do you want?" She grimaced. Sam turned round, seeing Non for the first time behind him.

"I want to go too," said Non. "If that's OK?"

Dog frowned and waved her hand in an impatient gesture.

"It's just, I drew diagrams of where everything was yesterday," Non said. "All the eggs and bodies. I thought it might be useful. Maybe?"

Dog narrowed her eyes. "You're the one who actually managed to kill a demon, aren't you?"

"Yes."

"Those diagrams might be useful. Can you draw more today?"

"Yes." Non was glad that Dog hadn't asked to see her crude sketches. *Diagram* was a very glamorous word for what was little more than labeled stick people.

"Fine. You can both come. Get your things. We leave in two minutes."

———o———

Somehow everything was different outside the castle. Not better, just different. She felt a jolt of fear again as soon as she stepped through the gate, her chest tightening, her heart beating faster. But she took deep breaths and focused on the church, letting the cool valley wind fill her lungs as she told herself she wasn't scared, that she was leaving the castle with a squad of armed soldiers. Somebody had shooed the pacers away, and there were no demons out there on the plain, only the slowly moving sheep on the other side of the moat, chewing and bleating, their tails flicking back and forth.

She also felt something else . . . a thrill. Nobody out here knew her or knew anything about her. They wouldn't question her wanting to go back to the church and look at the bodies again. She also liked that nobody was watching her with Sam. She could not talk to him if she pleased and no one would judge her, but no one would judge her if she did either. She took a deep breath again and relaxed her shoulders.

"What route did you take yesterday?" asked Dog.

"We went directly up the hillside," said Sam, "but when we returned we went down the old road. The road was better."

Dog nodded. She gave a signal, and ten or so soldiers set off at a jog toward the hillside. The rest of them set off toward the road. Sam and Non followed.

For a few minutes, they didn't speak as they walked across the plain next to each other, but then Sam grinned at Non, and it was the smile of togetherness—comradeship—of two people who were doing something they weren't supposed to be doing.

"Do you all think we're really strange for keeping demons?" he said.

Non opened her mouth. Searching for a polite thing to say was tricky in this situation. "It does mean you're all really fast runners."

"Yeah, it does. I definitely hated them getting near me when I was little," Sam laughed. "I suppose it is a bit odd. But you don't hate us?"

"No, of course not. Though . . . we are all wondering what other surprises you've packed. Perhaps some plague sandwiches? Demon parasite juice?"

He laughed again. "Plague sandwiches? What even would those be? Human flesh?"

"I don't know. I didn't think that one through. But since you're Castle Goch, I'm not surprised you have a suggestion for the sandwich ingredient."

Without anybody else watching, it felt easy talking with Sam. It was a bit like he was Meg and she could just relax with him. Even though she knew she was watching his face more than she did with Meg, the way his nose wrinkled as he laughed, the way his hair flickered in the breeze, the way his eyes were always searching the undergrowth and the hillside. Here, outside the castle, she could be a different person, one who didn't freeze as soon as other people spoke to her—one who was braver, less scared. And she barely even noticed she was out of breath this time. Going up the hill felt much easier today.

———o———

By the time they arrived at the church, the heavy door was open, the boards removed and stacked to one side. A heap of ivy was already piled up, and as they walked through the graveyard, a soldier emerged with another armful.

"Report," called Dog.

"The floor was obscured with weeds," he said. "We've removed most of those but have left the bodies and the rest of the church as it was."

"Anything of note so far?" she said.

"It's hard to tell. One of the windows was open, so the room has been exposed to the elements, which may have affected the position of things. And we don't know what the students touched yesterday."

"Nothing, I don't think?" said Sam, looking at Non. "We did smash the eggs, but we left the benches and everything else as they were."

"There was movement, though," said Non. "In the ivy. I'm not sure."

"Show me," said Dog, and they entered the room.

It felt like a different place from yesterday. Without the ivy, the church wasn't mysterious. It was dirty and dusty, the skeletons ragged and the mouse-monkey droppings in piles along the edges of the benches.

"Over there." Non pointed. The ivy covering the skeleton had been removed, apart from a couple of strands that had grown through the eye holes in the skull. They still protruded, the leaves delicate and dark, the fresh twisting green contrasting with the death beneath.

Where the stomach would have been, the egg lay smashed, that juice from inside still sticky and wet. It looked now as though the skeleton had had a last strange meal. There were a few shards of the egg remaining, and Non bent down to pick one up. Thicker than a hen's egg, it was rough like the weathered surface of granite, but it was sandy-colored, yellow brown. It felt heavier than it should, dense, and it definitely did not feel fragile. She put it in her pocket and bent in more closely to examine the smashed egg. The pieces there had mostly broken off in large chunks, so that it could be put back together as a jigsaw—if anybody wanted a demon egg jigsaw. It had broken neatly, not crumbled—so the shell had remained strong, even if it was decades old.

"Why didn't the demons grow?" she asked. "What's the juice?"

"I don't know," said Dog. "Just record all this information, and we'll send it back to Kintaborel Castle, where somebody can look at it. They're the ones who deal with this sort of thing."

One of the soldiers came up and whispered something to her. She nodded and went to the back of the church. Non took a piece of the ivy from the floor and prodded it at the egg juice. It was thick and viscous, the surface tension strong, so that when she pulled the ivy away, a strand of the juice pulled away with it, sticky and shiny.

"Over here too," said one of the soldiers behind her. Sam leaned over Non, turning the skull of the skeleton to one side. As he did so, a section of it fell away, delicate and neat like broken china, the skull thinner and finer than the eggshell.

"This one's been hit on the head too," said Sam. "They must have been killed before the eggs could hatch. That must be why the demons were never born."

Non looked up at the wall, away from the skeletons. Where the ivy had been pulled away, it was paler—free from dust. But there were traces of the paint that had been there before. Several places looked like they might once have had angels painted there, the ghosts of their human outline and what could have been wings still visible. Behind the altar there was a gruesome doom scene, the mouth of hell in the shape of a large monster with devils shoveling naked, weeping humans into its jaws. The artist hadn't been talented, and the paint was faded, but Non could see that the devils had been modeled on demons. Their eyes were staring straight out at the congregation, rather than at the puny humans on their spades, and they were large—their claws and two rows of sharp teeth exaggerated.

Non blocked out the noise around her of the soldiers examining the skeletons and she let herself, for a moment, imagine how it had been for the five people here—locked in, dying, and staring at that scene behind the altar. But although it was an unsettling thought, it felt unreal. The people were too dead. She couldn't picture it. She was just about to turn back when she saw another one of those circular patterns. And then another one. High up above the altar and the doom scene—so high that whoever put them there must have had a ladder. They were very faded, much more faded than the ones outside, so she could see there was no point going to look at them more closely, because there was no way she would be able to make out the details of the pattern. She thought there were other splotches too—places on the wall that hadn't been covered by the ivy and so had been bleached by the sun. They might have also been circular patterns, because just like around the door, the remains of the paint were evenly spaced. What she could see was the contrast between the two artists. Whoever had painted the circles was enormously more talented and professional than the person who had painted the demons beneath.

"Are you OK, Non?" asked Sam.

"Yes," she said. And it was easier to force her face into a smile than it would have been if he'd known anything about her. "I was just thinking, that's all." And with him looking at her, she found that the smile became real.

"It's odd, isn't it? What are your thoughts?"

"I don't know. I guess—why the church?" ventured Non. "Do you think it's important that they were kept in here?"

"I don't know. Maybe."

"Because Christianity defeats demons?"

"I don't think just religion works, does it? Holding up crosses and stuff. I know our Castle Goch pacers would ignore a crucifix completely. I think it's more that this is the biggest building the village had. And the one with the strongest door."

Non nodded. "I guess. It's just . . ."

"What?"

"Well, I still don't get why they were kept here at all. If it's just that this church had the strongest door, then why weren't they kept in the castle? It's so close by—surely the dungeons there would make more sense?"

"Yes . . . they would. Maybe the church is significant, then. Maybe they wanted these people to spend their last days somewhere nicer than the castle dungeons."

Non crouched down by the skeleton again. If she had her father's instruments, she could have a look at the goo and see what it was. But she didn't know what she was looking for, and she didn't know if it was dangerous. Maybe it still contained the parasites? She dropped her piece of ivy into it.

At the thought of her father and what he must have always known about her mother, she felt suddenly tearful, and she turned her head away. But the tears came anyway, and she stood up to go outside.

Sam followed, and when they reached the graveyard, her

shoulders were shaking with the sobs. He paused for a moment—she could sense him there behind her—but then he put his arms around her and stroked her back. She leaned into him and cried into his chest until all her thoughts were about his chest and not the dead people in the church.

Chapter 14

None of her friends had noticed Non was missing. And she got a thrill from that too. It should have been disappointment, or self-pity that she wasn't important enough to be missed. But she'd been with Sam, and the day had been exciting. So instead it felt good to have a secret, and she saved it all for herself, treasuring it, savoring all the details, asking others what they'd done with their day so that they'd talk and she didn't have to.

Meg seemed to have spent most of the day avoiding Paul, and also Jane. And the walls were now high enough in the dormitories that the students had needed to build platforms to stand on so they could reach the top.

As they were sitting round eating their stew, a shout came from below, and almost simultaneously Non realized that the watchers on the wall were signaling to somebody. A hush fell over the students, and they waited in near silence . . . and there it was: The signal horn was sounded. A supply cart had arrived!

"It's citadel," a watcher shouted down.

The citadel students ran quickly to the bottom of the hill, gleefully jumping over the little rabbit holes and uneven stone, and made it to the gate just as it was being opened for the two-horse cart. Only three soldiers were accompanying it, and they dismounted quickly, unstrapping their spears as they headed off to the guard towers.

Non vaguely recognized the driver. She didn't know his name, but she'd seen him around. It was his clothes that so reminded her of home. There was just something so "citadel" about them. Maybe the slightly tighter trousers? His short, spiked haircut? The neat beard? She couldn't quite put her finger on it, but you would just know that he'd come from their castle rather than the others.

The two horses were unbuckled and were led off to graze in the training ground field. A team of students already doing jobs for Dog were tasked with unloading the cart, each of them taking the bags and boxes up to the storage tents near the kitchen. The driver handed a two-liter bottle of something directly to Dog, and they stood for a few minutes ticking off items on her list and cross-checking it with his.

Finally the driver lifted a large wooden chest down from the cart. It was clearly heavy and overloaded with goodies. Ellie clapped her hands together in excitement. The driver opened up a notebook to take out his list.

"Chris . . ." He read the name out loud and then paused to riffle through the box. "Here." There were cheers and whoops. Chris beamed as he went down to collect his gift and letter, holding them up as though they were an award.

"Meg . . ." The driver riffled through his box again before pulling out a container. "Looks like somebody's been baking!" Again, there were cheers, with even a smattering of applause this time. Meg took a bow as she went to collect her box and the letters. She opened it immediately, stuffing a biscuit into her mouth and holding out another for Non. Then, with a smile, she passed the box round all the watching students. There were a few left, so she offered them to the soldiers and cart driver.

Most of the students on the hillside were standing around now. Nothing else was happening, and for a group of people who'd mainly been stuck inside the castle walls building . . . other walls, news from the outside world was exciting. As each student went up, there was a pause so that everyone could see what they'd been sent. It was mostly food, but some of the students received spare clothes or forgotten items and knives. Everybody received letters and cards, news of life back home.

By the time Non was handed her package, most of the group had already received something and were now distracted, reading their letters, eating their treats, and paying only cursory attention to the driver. Her parcel was wrapped up, messily, in brown cloth—and she struggled with the knots, as she always did with her father's presents. He was always careful to tie things up tightly, never using just one knot when he could use ten instead. So it took her a few minutes to open it, and by that time she'd already worked out it was books. But when she pulled back the cloth, she could see that two were notebooks, tattered and old. They were small and thin, but each of the pages was filled with drawings and messy notes. She didn't recognize the writing, and the notebooks weren't labeled with a name. The third book was thicker, neater, printed, and obviously brand-new. On the cover was written, *Daemonology: The Study of Daemons*. There was also a new set of pens.

Non opened the letter. It was short and scrawled in a rush. It didn't contain any mention of or sympathy for what she'd seen in the church, but Non wouldn't have expected that. It just said,

"Take care of yourself. Things very busy here. There aren't many books about demons, but here's the main one. It's funny that you're interested in them, because your mum had started thinking about researching them. I've included her notebooks with the information she'd started gathering. Look after them. Xxx."

The notebooks were suddenly very precious, and Non understood the importance of her father's letter, despite the casual way it had been written. She held them now as though they were gold leaf, the pages spiderweb delicate but weighty, heavy with knowledge. He must have kept them somewhere special, hidden away from view, and she didn't want to open them in front of everyone else now, so she wrapped them up again, folding that material over them carefully, her fingers clumsy and unsure.

Jane and Becky were standing right beside her now, nosily and silently looking on. Their gaze made her wish she'd asked for something more normal, like snacks or soap; she'd ask for that in the next supply cart, because some treats to remind her of home would be good. Non tied the string up again, this time in a bow, so it could be undone more easily. But she clutched the books firmly to her chest.

"Ellie," called the driver, and Ellie went up to receive her box. As she undid the lid, everybody watched, the citadel students knowing she'd have been sent something good. There were cakes on top, beautiful iced patterns on them, but underneath there was a layer of tissue paper, and she pulled out a pair of gray silk pajamas.

Jane gasped as Ellie held them up. The trousers were a plain, pale, smooth, shiny silk, but the top was very low-cut, with thin slivers for straps. It was trimmed with black lace and delicate little pink roses. What was Ellie's mum thinking? Ellie wrinkled her nose.

"I don't know if I like them," she said. Jane made a strangled noise and covered her mouth with her hand. "Hold them up for me, would you? So I can see?" She passed them to Meg, who held them up against herself and stood back so Ellie could look. But Meg was still carrying her empty biscuit box and her mouth was stuffed with biscuits, so it was awkward. She passed the top to Non.

Non held it up to herself and smiled at Ellie. She did a little twirl. The black lace of the top was itchy just against her fingers, and she knew it would be annoying to wear. The little pink roses would catch on things, and she knew if it belonged to her she'd spill something on it the first night and ruin it. But the silk was so smooth, and she ran her fingers down over the roses.

"Yeah. I suppose I'll probably wear it," said Ellie. "It won't be very warm, though. Probably not ideal for this castle."

Non looked up and saw Sam watching. He caught her eye. "It looks really nice," he said.

Non felt the redness of a blush rising into her cheeks, as she realized that she didn't know if he meant just the top, or the top against her. She bowed her head, letting her hair fall across her face to hide her confusion, and she passed the top back to Ellie.

Chapter 15

Despite its grand title, the actual information in *Daemonology: The Study of Daemons* could have been summarized in a single page. The introduction set out pretty much everything the book contained, but there were chapters too. Just reading their headings told Non everything she needed to know, but the writer had managed to fill pages with lots of unimportant, waffly details anyway. It was in large print, and there were lots of vague pictures, her favorite being the double-page spread in the center that was simply a diagram of a demon, with the label "no skin" pointing to its chest. And that demon didn't look much like any Non had ever seen, its arms and legs strangely proportioned, so that she wondered whether the artist had ever actually seen one.

Non was reading it on the wall, her feet dangling over the cliff. The early-evening air was cooler now, but it was pleasant against her skin, fresh gusts blowing through the valley, a reminder of the world out there. Meg was sitting next to her, cross-legged, farther in from the edge, and sketching in one of the pages from Non's notebook.

Non would have liked to be alone when she opened her mother's work, but there was no true solitude in Cirtop. This was as good as it got. Meg looked up and smiled at her as Non put *Daemonology* down, and she gave Non's leg a squeeze.

Below them, the Castle Goch students were out for a run—a proper run, not just a relaxed jog. Their pet demons were trailing behind them at a distance of several feet, and the students at the back of the group kept turning their heads to glance at the monsters. Now that Non knew the demons were pets, their fingernails and teeth removed, it was clear that they were different. They didn't seem to move in the same elegant way, their steps were more gangly than graceful, and their arms seemed to be permanently out to grab, rather than raising up just at the right moment. Was this the difference between dogs and wolves? Would they even attack the students if they stood still? Could they?

Sam was at the front of the group, next to Becky, and Non noticed how good Becky looked today, in her tight top and with her perfect body. They all ran beautifully together, had obviously spent many hours training alongside one another.

"Ugh, he does look sexy, though, doesn't he?" said Meg. For a moment Non was startled, but then she realized Meg was talking about Paul.

"Yeah. He's ridiculously good-looking. What's your plan?"

"I don't have one. It's a bit tricky. I think he might have been in a relationship with Jane. Oh, well. Never mind!" Meg pulled a face and went back to her sketching. "There's a couple of the Kintaborel Castle boys who are lovely too," she muttered. "They have a very respectful attitude toward women."

"Meg!"

Meg giggled. "Look, stop talking about me, and stop watching Castle Goch. Get on with it and open those notebooks!"

Non took a deep breath. The Castle Goch students had gone down the track now and were obscured by the trees. Up in the sky, a couple of red kites drifted, their wings still as the wind carried them across the plain. Others sat on the grass below, strange and ungainly on the ground, like oversize chickens, their bodies slow and plump.

Non opened the first of the notebooks. The writing was legible but messy, and she could see straight away that the book was just a selection of disordered ideas and observations. The pages weren't dated, and the ideas didn't seem to be in any particular order. In fact, sometimes it seemed that her mother had started on random pages and then worked backward. Most of the first book was on anatomy—so it appeared her mother must have been able to dissect a dead demon at some stage. Her recordings were such that, mostly, demon anatomy seemed to be very similar to human anatomy—a point that her mother made several times, scrawled in the margins or underlined. The reproductive organs seemed different, though, and the genitalia seemed to serve only for the release of urine. The demon penis, and here her mother had drawn a picture of one, seemed to resemble a cat penis more than that of a human. Her mother, and Non couldn't believe she was reading this, speculated that the penis probably couldn't become erect, due to lack of flaccid tissue. She had added a note underneath wondering whether, due to its angle, the demon penis might be used for spraying markers with scent, as a warning to other demons. Her mother wondered whether demons had territories, like animals did.

Non closed the first notebook. She thought she would have liked her mother very much. Very much indeed. But she also thought she might not discuss this particular section with her father.

She opened the second. This one was unfinished, and Non felt a twinge of sadness for the work that hadn't been completed. Most of the pages in this one were about the parasite, and her mother had sketched diagrams of the larvae and the blood at different stages of its life cycle. Non wondered how that had happened. Whose blood had it been? What had happened to them? Had they ended up killed, like the people in the church? How had they known they were infected? Were they worried? And when, exactly, had her mother left?

Non looked at all the diagrams—much more laboriously drawn than the hastily written notes next to them, neat and centered—even labeled with a scale to guide the understanding of the size. Was this a clue to her mother's personality? Non tried to imagine her writing these, but all she could picture was an arm writing in the notebooks, the rest of the image blurred and dark.

"You OK?" asked Meg.

"Yeah. Good. Really interesting."

Meg reached out for her hand. Non held it, but it was awkward turning the pages with just one hand, so she let go again. Some of the notes were short, not in complete sentences, like her mother had been rushing or had been so excited by her studies that her thoughts had been difficult to get down in words.

It was clear that her mother knew more than the writer of *Daemonology: The Study of Daemons* and that in comparison to her mother, the writer of that book had not really done much studying of demons at all. And also that if it was the main book on demons, humans hadn't spent much time studying them either.

The Castle Goch students were returning now, their steady pace still faster than Non's fastest sprint, and their pet demons still running along behind. One of them seemed to have a small branch caught on its head, which no one had removed, and Non wondered if the one she'd stabbed with her spear had recovered or whether these were different pets.

She took the piece of eggshell out of her pocket and looked at it again. She took out her own notebook and drew a diagram of the fragment, as clearly as she could, but then she labeled it in detail, her words making up for her lack of artistic talent.

On another page she made a couple of notes about the differences she'd noticed between the Castle Goch domesticated demons and the wild ones. She left space underneath so she could add some more notes there later.

Chapter 16

Non wasn't sure what it was that woke her, but she was suddenly aware of movement at the far end of the dormitory and the feeling of something being wrong. There was an edgy tension to the night, a stillness and a closeness that felt heavy, as though the darkness was pressing down upon her sleepy body. The air seemed warmer, somehow containing less oxygen than it should so that Non had to take deeper, more urgent breaths.

She lay soundlessly, listening for what it was that had woken her, checking the room for danger without moving her head. She could hear nothing untoward outside, none of the screams or alarm calls that usually signaled the arrival of demons . . . but none of the night noises you'd expect in a castle either: There were no low conversations from the patrols, no kettles boiling, no footfalls from passing guards. There were no human noises at all.

At the end of the room, there was a rustle, and a bulging, static dark shape relaxed. Silhouetted against the moonlit canvas awning above, Non had initially taken it for an untidy piece of furniture stacked up outside, but as it moved she could just see the outline of another woken statue, listening intently.

"What's going on?" she whispered toward it.

"Hey, who's that?" came a cautious murmur.

"Non," she whispered back.

"There're demons wailing in the hills. Listen and you'll hear them. They've been calling back and forth for a while."

Non sat up slowly, peeling her blanket off.

"I'm going out to see," Non whispered. "Want to come?" She crept quietly over the dim, dark shapes scattered across the grassy floor. Now that the stillness had been broken, the dormitory was suddenly alive again, and she could hear the gentle snores and soothing sleeping noises of the other girls. In their tiredness, they were angled awkwardly inside haphazard rolls of bedding so that she had to pause to feel a couple of times with her hands to make sure she wasn't about to stand on somebody.

She didn't wait. It didn't matter if the other listener came with her or not.

In the moonlight, the hillside had an ethereal, magical appearance. There were long pools of nothingness where elongated shadows concealed any number of terrors, but the grass shone silvery bright with a clear pathway for Non, leading up toward the castle and the ramparts above. Nothing moved, not even a slow, curling wisp of wind through the low grass, and the world seemed deadened, dulled, less dangerous . . . though Non knew this couldn't be the case.

There were soldiers leaning over the ramparts, looking through their binoculars across at the valley and woodlands beyond. Non clambered up to look over too, but though she strained her eyes to scan the sepia-tinted bogland below, she couldn't see or sense any unusual movement.

"There." One of the soldiers pointed to the left and adjusted her binoculars, focusing in on her target. "Do you see?"

The others turned to look in unison, insect-like in their tight black clothes and antennae-binoculars. Non climbed up higher, leaning over the uneven, unfinished wall to look in the same direction. A blast of cooler, fresher air brushed her face and hair as she pulled herself up to sit on the edge. But she couldn't see anything. The world below was one of dark, twisted shapes, of slow, wavering movements, of places where death could hide. Of places where a demon army could hide.

"Just underneath the overhanging oak tree?" said one of the soldiers softly.

"Yes," said the first soldier. "Facing this way."

They were silent again as they watched, unmoving and waiting.

Are they going to do anything? Non wondered. From this side of the castle, the nearest trees were outside the range of arrows. But maybe they'd go out and kill it by hand?

"Screeeeee," came a distant call, haunting and strange. It seemed to fit with the moonlight, belonging in this other world created from the shadows and darkness of the daytime. Non felt the familiar cold trickle of fear down her spine, but there was a thrill of excitement too. A challenge.

"Screeeeee," returned another call, closer and from their right this time.

"I'll keep locked on the oak tree target," said the first soldier. "Can anybody see the others?"

There was silence as the soldiers scanned slowly over the valley again, pausing every so often to focus in on objects concealed from Non's ordinary eyes.

There was a soft *gluck* from Non's right, and she turned away from the search. Commander Edwards was sitting a couple of feet from her, squinting intently down at the valley below, his pale face glowing a charmed, unearthly white in the moonlight. He lifted a small bottle to his lips again: *gluck*. Non suspected it probably wasn't water, but she'd thought drinking was forbidden when on watch.

"I thought you'd all be tired enough to sleep through this," he said to her without turning, sensing her glance.

"How many of them are there?" she asked.

"How many do we think?" Commander Edwards said conversationally to the soldiers. "Five?"

"At least," said one of the soldiers.

"I think I've counted five different voices, but we haven't seen that many. And obviously, they don't all need to use their voices, do they?"

"There're more each night. Each morning. They just . . . refresh overnight. Like a sort of evil mushroom. They just pop up." His tone was annoyingly cheerful, as though the new arrival of demons was an exciting zoological phenomenon akin to the swallows' migration or the journey of the salmon upriver. "And each morning we just kill them again. And again." He sounded a bit demented now. But it was all a bit fake, a bit exaggerated, as though he was acting a part. Non wondered if he was really drunk or just pretending to be.

"If you look up at the top of the valley . . ."

Non followed his hand. She watched for a moment—and then

realized what she'd initially taken for stars, or just a light from the moon, was moving. Slowly, so slowly, lights were edging through the trees on the brow of the hill, near the church. They'd go behind a tree for a few moments so that Non doubted she'd seen them, but then they'd emerge again, glimmering and flickering behind the darkness of the leaves. There was a bluish tinge to them, too bright, like they were sucking the light from everything around them. Non didn't need to ask if they were human, because the lights felt like the opposite of a cheery lamp people might use to brighten their way. They felt dead, dangerous, and even looking at them made her shiver.

"What are they?" she asked. "What is it?"

Commander Edwards laughed. "The story goes—you know the one, the children's tale—that they're lighting the way for a funeral. When you see them, it's a sign that somebody will die."

"But that's just a story." Non stared at the lights for a moment, then added, more quietly, "They say that about the calls too, don't they?"

"Yes. They do. I don't know what the calls really mean. But they are demon."

"What will happen then?" she asked. "Will you go out and get them?"

"Yes, just as we do every day. But not until tomorrow morning, when we can see properly." He took a final swig of his bottle, tipping his head back to get the last few drops. He tapped the base of the bottle with a determined and practiced dedication. There was a pause while he collected his thoughts again. "The watchers here will keep a lock on their locations and then signal to us when we head out at first light. It should be pretty simple at that point. Unless there're more than we can see, that is." He laughed mirthlessly, throwing the bottle down far into the valley below. There was no sound to indicate when it hit the bottom.

It made Non's stomach clench for a minute. The idea of demons standing, still and treelike in the woods, facing in the direction of the castle, was deeply unpleasant. Why didn't they attack? Why didn't they do something? What were they watching for, with their swiveling, white ball eyes? She didn't like the idea of their mindless, purposeless staring. It was a nightmarish thought.

How often did they do it? How often did they wander round at night calling back and forth across the valley? Was this normal? Had this always happened?

"Sir?" she asked. "Where do they go during the day? And . . . where have they come from?" Commander Edwards continued to stare straight ahead. She wondered if he'd heard. "Sir?" she asked again. He reached for the bottle that he'd just thrown over the edge, patting the wall next to him fruitlessly. There was a moment of that still, crushing calm again. The air felt suddenly dull and shrunken.

"I don't know, Non. We don't know," he said quietly. "We don't know anything."

He turned to her finally, and there was a sardonic smile this time. "We don't know anything," he repeated. In that emptiness, the calls came again, this time with a tone of sadness Non hadn't noticed before.

"Hullo!" came a sudden loud whisper beneath her, making her jump. Mary was standing at the bottom of the ramparts. Non had

forgotten that she'd invited somebody along. "What's going on? We haven't heard much shouting for a while. Are they still out there?"

Non nodded. Commander Edwards glared round and tutted loudly. "What are you girls doing up? You should all be in bed. Go, now. You, and you." He nodded at Non too. "Go to bed!"

Chapter 17

Non woke the next morning refreshed and strangely cheerful. Despite her lack of sleep and her new awareness of the dangers they faced, she felt different: more alert, more positive, more at home here.

The dormitory was the usual bustle of messy dressing and hair brushing, but Non saw things through new eyes this morning. She made eye contact with Mary and exchanged a knowing, quiet half smile.

It wasn't a surprise to her that when they went and sat in the courtyard for breakfast, they were told they were going to be staying around the castle today. Breakfast was yesterday's bread, or maybe the day before's. It was stale and hard. People frowned at it, but they all still ate it.

Commander Edwards and Dog were nowhere to be seen. In fact, most of the soldiers were nowhere to be seen. It was Commander Daffy who came and spoke to them this morning.

"So you're going to be having your first lesson today. Military theory." Most of the students slumped to get comfortable or shuffled closer to their friends. This, at least, was the opportunity to relax and have either a nice daydream or a chat. Military theory in the citadel was just that—theoretical. It didn't seem to relate to their lives at all—either because most of the students didn't see themselves going into a military career, or because even from what Non had seen, how people and demons behaved out in the valley was very different from how the chalk figures behaved on the blackboard.

"Right. This is important, because you'll have heard different ideas in your three castles, so we need to look at what you'll do here. I would strongly advise you to listen."

Almost nobody was listening. Most people were still politely facing the front and not talking, but their eyes were glazed over.

"Wake me up if he says anything interesting," whispered Ellie.

Non risked a glance at Sam. He was sitting up, his head angled slightly so he could get a better view. His hair was wet, the strands on the top drying fluffy and soft in the air, and Non wondered whether he'd been for a swim in the moat or whether he'd just washed by the well. He whispered something to one of the people sitting next to him, and Non turned back to Commander Daffy.

The commander was drawing something on the board now. There were crosses that were obviously supposed to represent people. Or possibly demons. Or maybe even castles. He was linking the crosses together with arrows, but there was also a range of other arrows going off in different directions.

"Is that clear?" said Commander Daffy.

"Yeah." Everybody who was listening, or pretending to listen, nodded their heads. Quite a few people didn't bother, though. A few even had their eyes shut.

"Right, we'll look at another scenario here."

"Sir," came Sam's voice. "Can I ask you a question?"

"You already are!" Commander Daffy stood back, chalk in his hand, his hands resting on his stomach. He beamed at Sam. "This might be a better way. Why don't you just all ask questions you can think of and we'll see how we can answer them?"

"Or," whispered Ellie, "we could all just promise to stay inside the castle and then there would be no need for military strategy at all?"

"Sir. You know the dead people we found in that church?" said Sam.

Every single one of the citadel students turned to look at Non, some moving round other people dramatically, so they could give her a sympathetic look. Non pretended she hadn't noticed and kept her eyes on Commander Daffy.

"Did you hear what we found?" Sam asked.

"I did."

"Well, what should we do if some of us get infected by demons? Should we do the same thing?"

"Lock your friends in a church?"

"Or a castle, or somewhere."

"I'm going to say yes. Yes, I think that was a good idea, overall, and our dungeons here would work well. We don't know all the details, but I guess those people must have been mauled by demons, so that the parasites were released into their bodies. What happened next is very unusual but has interesting military implications. For some reason, instead of making their way to the demons, as normal, the infected people must have locked themselves in the church while they were still able to think sensibly, or possibly their friends and families locked them in there to prevent them going to the demons."

"So if it happens, and somebody gets infected, should we bring them back here or to the church?"

Commander Daffy paused and frowned, pressing his lips together in thought. "I'll be honest, I don't know that there is a policy on this in any of the three castles. Sometimes we don't even know if people have been infected—or they don't even admit it to themselves. It's only when they disappear, leaving to go to the demons, that anybody notices there's a problem. But we do have comfortable dungeons here—so taking them back here would be a very good plan."

Non opened up her notebook. There was so much information here—and none of it had been in the official *Daemonology* book.

"I'd be really surprised if the people in the church didn't face a number of demon attacks as the parasites progressed through their life cycles. I find it difficult to believe that the demons would let their young grow in there without trying to rescue them. We don't know the details, but . . . well . . . I think it's worth noting that. That church is an easy walk from this castle and barely three hours from the citadel. It seems strange that we hadn't heard about a big attack or series of attacks there.

"We're wondering, in fact, if they were enclosed in the church at about the same time as the demon attacks on this castle, which was the time period when Cirtop was abandoned temporarily. That would certainly explain why we didn't know they were there."

Everybody was sitting up now. The story was too full of mystery and scandal to ignore.

"Wait," said Sam. "Sir, so this castle was abandoned because of demon attacks?"

"Yes. Not just that, of course. The other three castles were facing attacks from human forces, and it just wasn't sustainable to defend four castles in this valley. So this one was abandoned. Interestingly, we think it was actually used by demons for a time after that." Commander Daffy widened his eyes, knowing that that part of the story was going to get people interested. Ellie screwed up her face and looked around, as though the long-ago demons might have left some part of themselves behind.

"But we took it back, obviously, and used it as a guard post for a century. That would fit in with the timings, of course."

"Sir?" said Meg. "Why didn't any of the villagers—the ones who wrote the signs on the church and who locked them in—why didn't they come and get help?"

Commander Daffy smiled. It was a sympathetic smile, and Meg waited a couple of seconds before she answered her own question. "Oh, right, yeah. Because the demons killed them on their way."

"Probably, yes. Locking people infected with demon parasites in a church is a pretty good way of attracting other demons to you.

"Any other questions?" Commander Daffy asked. "Military questions?"

"Yes!" said Meg. "How do we know that this castle was used by demons?"

"Not a military question, and I don't know. I guess they left their droppings behind. Demon droppings are quite distinctive because of their meat-based diet."

Non was no longer writing in full sentences. There was more information here than she could get down in one go. She would have liked to ask more questions about their droppings, but she didn't want to be known as the girl who talked about demon poo.

"Was the castle cleaned after the demons were here and left their dirt everywhere?" asked Ellie.

"Also not a military question. And I'm sure it was."

Ellie looked around, with her nose wrinkled, as though some of that hundred-year-old poo might still be lying around.

"Any other military questions?"

"I honestly think I'd rather carry stone up the hill," said somebody. Most of the room laughed, but Commander Daffy didn't seem crushed.

"So useful. How helpful!" he said. "Getting ready for building work tomorrow. Yes! Do that."

Most people stood up, if not to go and carry stone up the hill, then at least to pretend that they were going to. Sam and a few of the other Castle Goch boys went forward to talk with Commander Daffy, and Non stayed to finish writing up her notes.

The boys and Commander Daffy talked quietly for a few minutes, Commander Daffy pointing to a few things on the board. But then, as Non was packing up to leave, she heard him saying, "I've got a few books you can look at, if you like?"

Sam nodded.

"Oh, but are you all Castle Goch?"

"Yeah."

"Will you be OK with that?"

Sam hesitated but then nodded.

"If you want to read them, you can sit in the guard tower instead of carrying stone."

Sam grinned and caught Non's eye. "Can Non come too, then? She's writing about the demons."

Chapter 18

Non didn't trust herself to speak as she followed Sam, his friends, and Commander Daffy down to the guardhouse. Mary and Callie were already climbing back up the hill again, carrying buckets of stone over their shoulders, their skirts hitched up slightly so that their ankles were on display. Meg was walking in front of three boys from Kintaborel, all of them carrying large loads and staring at her while she animatedly told them a funny story. She was carrying nothing. As Non passed, Meg let her mouth open wide in exaggerated shock, but Non just shrugged and smiled back at her. The hillside was full of people, though it wasn't clear exactly what most of them were doing.

Sam turned to her and whispered, "Another day we've got out of building work."

"Yeah," said Non. But it was tricky to even say that one word, and she knew she was blushing.

"I owed you a favor after yesterday." Sam smiled at her, and she felt herself relaxing.

"So now we're even?"

"Yeah." He wrinkled his nose. "But I really don't want to build any walls, so let's see if we can sign up for some mad mission tomorrow too."

"Or fake an interest in military theory?"

He laughed. "Anything. Although I do find it quite interesting."

They reached the guard tower, which was empty, and Commander Daffy ushered them up to the strategy room, with its large maps of the valley.

"We've got the official strategy documents for each of the three castles here," he said, holding up three large books. "We also have some other military history books here, if you want to have a look."

Sam took one of the books, as did his friends, and settled down at the table.

"And what's your name? Non, is it?" Commander Daffy lowered his head to speak to her and changed his voice so that it was softer, as though he was talking to a small child or a cute animal. She nodded. "Writing about the demons, are you?" She nodded again. "That sounds lovely. Lovely."

Non kept her expression neutral, even though it was honestly the least lovely thing she could imagine writing about.

"Well, I don't think I've ever read anything about the demons. Other than that we need to kill them, of course." He laughed, resting his hand on his belly as he did so. "There's probably something in the strategy books about them, but it's pretty similar to killing any enemy, I should have thought.

"So I'll leave you all here. But do come out and, ah, help the others when you've read enough."

He beamed at them.

Non got her notebook out. She didn't have anything new to write, but the information she had was all over the place and very messy, so she flicked through it, wondering if she could organize it more sensibly. Perhaps alongside her mother's notes and *Daemonology*. She didn't really need to be here, but it *was* better than carrying stone, and she was out of the wind. And she was with Sam.

One of Sam's friends was already leaning back, staring out the window, his book still open but the pages flicking slowly over, so that he'd have lost whatever he was reading. He also didn't seem to have started from the beginning of the book, as Non would have done—but then perhaps there was a particular aspect of military strategy that interested him. Sam and his other friend were bent over their books, and Sam was frowning in concentration. Non realized his lips were moving slightly as he read the words.

She leaned over to the middle of the table and picked up one of the military history books. It was old, the language antiquated, and there were no pictures at all. There were barely any paragraphs either, or headings, so Non found that after having read a couple of pages, she needed to start the section again because she couldn't remember what she'd just read. She flicked on ahead. It was, unsurprisingly, about a series of battles, sieges, escapes, and successes, all explored in extreme technical detail. The successes were much more boring than the failures, she found, because they were all about the options that could have been taken and why the chosen ones were correct. The failures, however, tended to be shorter, because the author clearly didn't like writing about them. They also just seemed to involve more drama. But even still, after twenty minutes or so, Non had had enough, deciding that one battle was very like another one—despite what the author of the book implied. She started to flick through, looking for mention of demons, but there wasn't very much. They were mentioned as a threat only in the same way as dragonites, gormads, or bandits could be considered a hazard to a marching army. In this time period, at least, the demons had not been a serious problem. Non looked at the date of the book. It spanned around seventy years of battles, two centuries ago. She put it back in the middle of the table.

Neither of Sam's friends was reading now. The one who had been staring out the window earlier had his head on the table and was having a nap, a trickle of drool at the corner of his open mouth. The other one had his book turned over to keep his page and was picking bits of dirt out of his fingernails. Sam was still reading, but his head was resting in his hand and he was frowning, his lips still moving, very slowly, as he stared at the page. As Non looked at him, he looked up and caught her eye.

"Find anything interesting?" he said, stretching his arms.

"No." She shrugged. "It's a bit boring, actually."

"Did you read that whole book?"

"I skimmed it. But it's just about loads of battles in the valley, and not much about demons."

"Oh, right." He reached out for his book again, as though he was going to go back to reading it. So Non spoke quickly.

"Did *you* find anything interesting?"

"Yeah." Non saw that he was still only a couple of pages into the book. He must have been reading even more slowly than she'd thought.

"What are you looking for?"

"I don't know. Just what to do in different situations. How the castles deal with the same problems differently, and why. We don't do much reading at Castle Goch, though, so it's quite slow."

"You don't do much reading? What do you do in school?"

"We've mostly finished school. We did learn to read and write. But we mainly learned to fight."

"I definitely prefer fighting. It's way more useful." Sam's friend—the one who hadn't fallen asleep—gave a stretch and a giant yawn. "Mate, I've had enough of this. I'm going out to move some stone around the hillside. Are you all right here?" He stood up to leave but paused for Sam first.

"Yeah," said Sam. "I'm going to stay a bit longer and try to figure more of this out."

Non didn't know how to react to Sam's comments. It didn't even feel like a confession; in the citadel, not being able to read properly would be something you'd want to hide, an indication that you were lesser as a person. But it obviously wasn't an issue at all in Castle Goch—or even a benefit. So did she think less of Sam? Was he now less intelligent or interesting to her? Or less attractive?

It did make him seem vulnerable, like he was no longer as perfect as she'd thought. And it did make him seem less attractive to her. Or maybe it didn't. It made him fascinating in a really different way. She let some of her hair fall over her face so that she could watch him through the strands without him knowing. He was so determined, staring at the pages. On his book, at least, the writing was arranged into separate bullet points and so must be easier to read than the one she'd looked at. He rested his tongue slightly on his lips, sometimes tapping it against his teeth, and his hair was sticking up on one side where he'd been leaning on it in his hands.

She wanted him to keep talking to her. "Sam?"

He looked up and grinned.

"You know what Commander Daffy said earlier? About the church?"

He nodded.

"I don't get it. I mean, I'm probably wrong." He shook his head at her and frowned, so she continued. "But there's things that don't make sense. Like, why weren't the people buried? Don't you think it's really weird? I don't see how they could have been there at all without this castle knowing about them. But if they were locked in there to stop them going to the demons, then all the villagers from those houses must have known about it. I get that maybe every single one of the villagers was killed by demons—but that door was nailed up from the outside by somebody. And then who killed the infected people?"

"Maybe they killed each other?"

"Yes. But then who killed the last one? I'd have thought it would be quite hard to bash your own head in."

"Actually, that's the bit that I thought was surprising . . ." He frowned. "Yeah. If I was going to kill somebody I loved, somebody who I knew was going to die because they were infected with the parasite—I don't know if I'd hit them over their head. It looked like quite a brutal way to die."

Non looked down at the page in front of her. She tried to focus on the words rather than the images in her head.

"Yeah. You're right," Sam whispered, "the whole thing is really odd. How come nobody's noticed them before? They've obviously been there at least a century, and they're very close to this castle. So how come nobody has gone up to check out the church before? It's not like it's exactly hidden, is it?"

Sam's friend sighed in his sleep, and Non jumped as though she was doing something she should be guilty about. She flicked through her notebook for a bit—but it was very disordered, the pieces of information all over the place. If she died, like her mum, people would look at her notebooks and think she was really messy. Just as she had thought about her mum. She vowed to ask her dad to send a new notebook in the next supply cart so that she could start putting it all together.

"Is there anything in any of the books?" asked Sam. "About what was going on in that time period in this castle? All that stuff Commander Daffy said about this castle being abandoned and then taken over by demons? That's got to be somewhere, hasn't it?"

Non nodded. She didn't fancy reading any more of the military history books—but at the same time, she did want to find out what had happened to the people in the church. Even their names. That information must be around somewhere, mustn't it?

There were another couple of shelves on the wall full of books. They didn't look dusty, so either somebody was cleaning the shelves regularly—unlike everything else in the castle—or they were being read. She couldn't imagine by who, though, apart from Commander Daffy—and he'd said he'd never read anything about demons. So did that mean there was nothing interesting in there? She thought about going through them—but then she reasoned Sam's books were also books she'd have to read at some point too, so why not now?

"You know the way you want to compare how they do things in each castle differently?" she said. "Well, wouldn't it be easier to look at the three strategy books together and compare them that way directly, rather than reading each book in turn?"

Sam looked up at her, startled, as though she was an absolute genius.

"Or maybe not. Whatever. Just an idea."

"No, it's a good idea. Maybe you could help, though? Because I think reading three books at once might be harder than just one." He grinned at her. "Never done it before, so I don't know. Standard Tuesday in the citadel, though, I imagine."

Non thought about pretending she would find it really hard, or perhaps making out that she was less intelligent than him. But he didn't seem bothered. His attitude toward her didn't seem to have changed. And honestly, just looking at the contents pages and then comparing three sets of bullet points did seem pretty easy.

"Can we look at what their policies are toward demons first, though?" she asked.

He nodded.

———o———

It was only much later, when she was lying under her blankets that night, that she wondered about Commander Daffy again. How did he know all that information about the demons in Cirtop if he'd never read anything about demons?

Chapter 19

They had to stay inside the castle for the next five days too, but they didn't see Commander Daffy, so they weren't able to get permission to go back and read in the guard tower again. And although Non kept meaning to wake up at night and go to look for those unearthly demon lights again, and listen for those chilling screams, she was so tired each evening that she fell straight to sleep instead. They saw Commander Edwards and Dog occasionally, but during the days both were missing, along with most of the soldiers from the castle. Non never saw them leaving or returning, and she couldn't bring herself to ask anybody else either, because she didn't want to make a big deal out of it.

The days had followed the same routine. Even though the castle now resembled an actual castle containing rooms with proper walls and floors, Non was utterly bored with light building work. Bringing stone up the hill, or mixing mortar, or placing stone on the walls—it was all more dull than it even sounded. Mostly she zoned out, each person slightly too far apart from the others to be able to speak much, so it wasn't even as though they'd had lots of relaxed chatting and the opportunity to get to know people better. And Non definitely hadn't been able to get to know Sam better. It had been mainly the Castle Goch students who'd volunteered to bring stone up the hill, and he'd been one of the ones running up and down the path, topless, his muscles rippling. The citadel students had generally volunteered to be the ones doing the standing-around or sitting tasks. A few times, Non had been able to coordinate it so that she was laying stones at the same time as Sam arrived with more. She'd always made sure that she was looking busy when he arrived, but he hadn't noticed her.

There had been this moment yesterday when she'd found a worm among the cement. She'd spent a couple of minutes watching the little swirls and patterns it made as it wriggled its way through it to the safety of the edge of the bucket. Non considered this to have been the highlight of her day. She found herself thinking about Sam a lot, but she didn't know if that's because she was enjoying making up a pleasant fantasy to make her rubbish life more interesting or if she actually was interested in him. She'd wiled away a niceish half an hour imagining kissing some of the other boys too, as a test. She found that she'd quite enjoyed that too.

"When do you think quarantine will be ending?" Ellie asked at breakfast that morning. "It's been going on for a while now, hasn't it?"

"I think we'll have at least another week," said somebody. "At least."

Meg raised her eyebrows at Non, and they both smiled. There was no way of knowing, except clues like the disappearance of the soldiers or the irregular arrival of supply carts. What exactly these meant, though, wasn't clear.

"Don't laugh at me," said Ellie. "I just want to know, OK?"

"I'm sorry. But I don't think anybody knows yet," said Meg.

"What do you think, Non?" asked Ellie. "Your dad's a doctor. Doesn't he know?"

"Um." Lots of people turned to her, and Non felt herself flushing. "Well, we don't know exactly how the plague spreads, and why it affects some people more than others. Probably not many people are going to die. But lots of people are probably going to get sick in all the castles. And they might get sick at different times, after some people have already recovered from it. So I guess we can't go home until everybody in our castle has been free of plague for a few days."

"So do you think that means we can go home soon?" asked Ellie.

"I don't know. I think maybe a few more weeks. Maybe."

Non could still feel her cheeks hot and her head full of clouds. Everybody was looking at her as though she actually knew what she was talking about, which she didn't, and that made it worse. She ate a piece of the breakfast bread and stared at the floor so that she couldn't talk anymore. This morning, the bread was so stale it was crunchy, and there was very little of it. The plate was not passed round so that the students could help themselves—instead a soldier handed out one piece each. There was also no butter, and Non needed a drink of water after every bite just to swallow it.

So for a number of reasons, when Dog appeared in the courtyard a few moments later, Non felt actually pleased to see her.

"We need some of you to go out this morning. Volunteers, please. There will be soldiers with you."

Almost everybody stood up, and Dog waved them down again. "We only need about half of you." She waved her hand carelessly over those nearest to her. "This half." It was only girls, because she was standing next to the girls' dormitory, and they all looked at each other excitedly. Just not doing building work for a morning felt like a holiday.

Non wasn't at the front of the horde stampeding down the hill, but she was near it. The Castle Goch girls went straight to the gate, but she and Meg walked down with Kintaborel Castle girls Callie and Mary. Their skirts had been creeping shorter and shorter every day, and their shoes were now so covered with mud that the embroidery was no longer obvious. But they still started every day with a prayer, and Non liked hearing them give thanks every evening.

Once they made it down to the gate, the group loaded into the cart with the guards and headed out to the valley. Sitting in the cart wasn't much faster than going on foot, what with all the potholes and the overhanging branches. Every so often they'd stop altogether and some of the guards would jump down to clear an object out of the way, while the others would stand farther along the track looking for danger. Non would have liked to walk; she felt too hemmed in. But it was so good to be out of the castle. The breeze against her hair felt different, softer, as it gently drifted across the grass of the valley and through the trees around them.

"We're going to a fortified farm," Dog called from the front. "It was secured after an attack . . ." She looked down at her notebook. ". . . two years ago, so there should still be edible food in there, and we should be safe once inside. But the soldiers will go in first to give it a check over anyway. Be vigilant.

"After checking it over, the soldiers will remain outside to watch the doors and defend you in the event of any attack. You will have no more than half an hour to get everything you can find. Get anything you can carry. Don't stop to read labels. We'll need food and clothes. Bedding, anything."

She turned back toward the road in front and didn't offer to answer any questions. Non suspected that avoiding them was why she'd turned away so quickly.

"What do you think's going on?" whispered Meg. And others were whispering too. Again, they were back in their castle groups, talking only to those they'd known the longest, suspicious of what the others might think and know. "If it was secured two years ago, the stuff there can't be that amazing if nobody's bothered going to get it before."

"Maybe it's not safe for the castles to deliver us food anymore?" ventured Non.

"Yeah. I guess. Hope they're not *all* ill, though."

"No." Though that hadn't been exactly what Non had meant. She wondered when the last supply cart had gotten through. She hadn't had the new notebook, snacks, or a letter from her dad, and she'd sent her request a few days ago. As she avoided the eyes of the citadel girls, she found herself looking at Mary. They both smiled at each other grimly. Non thought Mary might have started mouthing a prayer too, because her lips moved slightly.

———o———

A mess of carts and boxes blocked the route to the gate of the fortified farmhouse. They could climb round them, of course, but it would delay the unloading, and they could be used as hiding places. As the cart slowed, four soldiers leaped down and ran toward the debris.

"Get down and check the boxes. Salvage anything good. NOW!" Dog screamed at the waiting students.

Non jumped over the side, and behind her she heard the gentle thuds of others doing the same. The cart juddered off to turn, or perhaps kept moving because the driver didn't want it staying in one place for too long. She scanned the space warily, a gusting flurry of leaves catching her eye, but everything looked clear.

To her left, Jane moved silently forward toward the boxes, her spear already poised and ready. She glanced at Non and the others nearby before using her spear to signal that they should go around. Non nodded, changing direction as she jogged.

Ahead of them, the soldiers were moving the first of the boxes out of the way, pushing them up against the ramparts. A loose-limbed skeleton from behind the boxes sagged over to the floor, something—wasted muscle, remnants of flesh—still holding it together in the semblance of a humanoid shape, but its dangling, lolling head showed that there was no life there. Behind Non there were gasps as people saw it, but there weren't as many gasps as there should have been. Dog's attitude, and something about their whole situation, had made it feel predictable. Becky ran forward, glancing at the body. "It's demon," she said softly.

Non ran to another one of the boxes, one that was already pushed against the wall, though she checked behind it anyway. As she opened the lid, she could see immediately that the food inside would be almost all usable. It contained mainly bottled goods—preserved vegetables, chutneys, pickled grubs, and mysterious, colored liquids that looked like idleberry wine or spice spirits. Though the labels were now discolored and illegible, the dry goods it was loaded with were inside secure wrapping, so they might still be good. She pushed the box quickly to one side for loading onto the cart and gestured to others for help. She ran back to help lift a fallen ladder out of the way.

The sounds of breaking wood came from the cart across the entrance. A soldier was kicking the sides away, and Non saw that it was jammed into the gate, as though it had crashed there or perhaps had been put there to help block the way for intruders. As Non watched, a skull fell out, rolling across the floor. It was impossible to tell from here if it was demon, but Non assumed from the lack of reverence it wasn't human. As the soldier freed the sides, three other soldiers leaned over to immediately start pulling it away. This was a smooth, practiced military exercise. It was a choreographed and familiar routine. It was almost beautiful to see how they worked together, one running, one pulling, one passing objects, another leaping in. They seemed to be perfectly in balance with each other, a human machine, and Non wondered how many times they'd done something like this before.

"You, kids," a soldier called to them while another signaled to the cart driver. "Clear the rest of this exit. We're going in. Any trouble . . . run."

Jane caught Non's eye as she nodded in reply to the command. She too had the same look of awe. They exchanged half smiles before turning to clear more boxes.

The entrance to the farmstead was large and bright—there was room enough for a cart and the animals inside the high, wooden walls—but in the barn the light dimmed sharply, so that she could only make out about five almost-empty shelf units before the space merged into darkness. There was a pile of mainly headless bodies stacked on a pallet by the door, and a soldier wearing gloves emerged, dragging another highly decomposed body behind her. Non looked away so that she didn't have to notice whether they were human or demon, but right now, either seemed bad.

"There might be some more in there," the soldier said loudly, "so watch out. But we think we've got anything obvious. You two take a candle and go to the back." She pointed to Jane and Non with her free hand.

Meg and Ellie sped past with a loaded handcart.

"The building is now secured!" came a shout. "Team to cover the entrance. Call!"

"Secure!"

"Secure!"

Shouts came from within as Non lit the candle. Jane shielded it with her hand to help Non, though there was no wind.

"Now go!"

As they entered the barn properly, there was noise from all around them, from the yard outside, from the house, from the sheds. No demon could possibly be sleeping through this; they'd know by now if there was anything dangerous in here. Except it was impossible to shake the feeling that there was. As Non and Jane walked to the back of the barn, the light from the candle somehow seemed to work to make Non feel less safe, not more. It seemed to focus her sense of safety into one small, concentrated circle of brightness in front of her, somehow making the contrasting large mass of darkness surrounding them seem more terrible and terrifying and full of fear. Every time her candle moved, the shadows shifted with it, creating movement and a feeling of innumerable watching presences staring down, observing them from the concealed dark spaces on the shelves. Non found she had to keep moving her hand back and forth to search the shadows with the candle, and then to search again the shadows her movement had created.

"What can you see?" hissed Jane.

There was very little that hadn't been eaten by vermin. This aisle had held sacks of flour or maize, and maybe oats. There were trails of white dust and powder on the shelves and floor, but Non knew most of the contents would be useless now. All the sacks that she could see had large gnawed holes in their sides, and there were regular lines in the dust, which Non imagined to be pathways trodden over the years by mouse-monkeys and rats. There would be no point in carrying the sacks out.

"Move along a bit farther, away from these."

They edged along quickly, back to back, Non holding the candle up so they could see up to the shelves above them. There were a few places on the floor that were discolored or strangely rough. Non didn't hold the candle down to those, but she wondered which part of the barn the bodies had come from.

"Jars. Here," Jane hissed.

Non grabbed a handcart. There were four shelves, a few feet wide, stacked with an array of dark jars that glinted in the candlelight—jams and maybe honey. It was an impressive find, but they'd need two cartloads at least. Non already dreaded the thought of returning to this dark, threatening aisle. They pulled the jars straight into the cart, scooping them in quickly and climbing up to reach the ones right at the back. It would have been quicker if Non had been prepared to put down her candle, but there was no way she was letting go of that light. She could hear her own breathing, ragged and loud in her ears. She turned her head again, scanning and searching the darkness, but there was always that feeling of being watched. Every part of her felt exposed and at risk. The depth of the shelves left shadowy spaces for any number of things to hide, so there was no safe wall against which to put her back.

"Let's take it now," she said urgently. They could have fit a few more jars in, but she felt a need to check the escape route, to see the sunlight.

Wordlessly, Jane grabbed the front of the cart while Non pushed from the back. They skidded the length of the aisle.

Non felt a force of invisible things behind her, rushing to touch her and grab her with their dark, shadowy hands. A frenzy of panic urged her on, and she ran faster, pushing the cart at an angle to keep it straight.

"Steady," said Jane reassuringly. "It's OK."

"I know," said Non. And she did know. But she could still feel the fear at her back, even as they moved toward the safety of the light. She had to force herself to slow and to stop turning to look behind her.

Others were waiting for them at the entrance to the barn, and they handed over the loaded handcart for an empty one. Jane paused before they went back in, blowing air into her cheeks and holding it there before blowing it out again slowly.

"We can do this," she said.

Non nodded.

Chapter 20

They didn't see the demons until they'd almost stopped looking for them.

To leave the fortified farm without being attacked seemed so unlikely that Non felt on edge the whole way back. She could tell the soldiers were suspicious too as they whispered among themselves in hushed tones and didn't sheathe their weapons. The girls mostly didn't speak either, instead scanning the trees and shrublands anxiously.

But it wasn't until they were within sight of Cirtop that the monsters finally came into view. There were just three of them, on the track, walking steadily in the direction of the castle. Their heads were more upright, and they moved more effortlessly than a human, but initially Non would have taken them for an ordinary patrol out returning from a perimeter check.

"Sight," came the call, as the cart in front slowed. The demons stopped and then, like stringed puppets pulled by the same master, they turned in unison to face the carts, heads snapping up to stare at their prey with unblinking eyes. They were too far away for Non to make out the features, but they weren't all the same height. Seeing them next to each other made her wonder if they were all different, if, maybe, they had individual identities. They remained still, paused and expectantly waiting.

Dog called to the drivers. "Keep moving forward," she shouted. "Steadily. Run them over if you have to." She turned to the soldiers and the students. "Kids, stay on the carts. We need an archer on the front seat. The main goal is to clear them off the road.

"You and . . . you." Dog pointed at two of the girls. "Pick up the crossbows. Get in the front and get ready. The rest of you, get your spears out and move away from the edges of the carts. Do not engage with the enemy unless you have a clear strike. And whatever you do, do not get in the way of the soldiers."

The drivers slowed their horses, and the heavily loaded carts edged forward, barely at walking pace, as the soldiers ran ahead. The cart at the front contained some food but mainly the students; the cart behind was stacked high with goods. It had only the driver, but he was sitting on a platform and was protected by high, armored walls. The wheels of both carts dipped carefully in and out of each of the potholes, and the girls stood up, anxiously scanning the surroundings.

"What do you think?" asked Ellie.

"Should be straightforward," said Becky, squinting up ahead. "There are more soldiers than demons." She sat down again, but Non noticed that she kept her spear in her hand.

"Why do you think we don't just run them over?" wondered Jane.

The vision of whizzing into the demons, sending their smashed bodies to one side, was so unrealistic it was almost comical. Non could almost picture the bouncing, severed heads, the twitching, flying limbs, the squelching explosion of their stomachs, and the cheers of the girls as they hit each one in turn. But she could also see that it wouldn't work.

"The poor horses!" said Callie. "I don't think they'd like it."

"I think there are a lot of potholes where they are, so we couldn't go over that bit fast anyway," said Ellie.

"Yeah. 'Spose if they fell under the wheels, they'd make the road even bumpier," said Jane.

While none of this road was particularly good, the point at which the demons had stopped was unusually bad; the cart would never have been able to go fast through that section. And there was restricted visibility, with several thick bushes as potential hiding spaces. It would be the ideal place for an ambush, in fact, but of course demons didn't think like that.

Non toyed with her arrows, turning one round and round between her fingers with pent-up, nervous energy. There was nothing moving among the trees, but then again, they couldn't see more than a few feet to either side because of the thick undergrowth. She wouldn't have wanted to walk through this section on foot.

Their cart kept moving forward, the light shifting in the bushes to either side as they edged along the track. There didn't seem to be the normal woodland creatures skittering through the trees, and although she saw a few people glancing at the sky, there were no circling kites above them. But there was a light breeze, and sudden gusts pulled at the branches so that the leaves gave a shiver and ripples of energy ran through the woods.

Nobody spoke in her cart, and up ahead the demons seemed to have dodged the soldiers' arrows, so that they were now fighting them with spears. The soldiers' backs shielded the skirmish from Non's view, but it didn't seem as though the fight had been as easy as Becky had predicted. Maybe there were too many soldiers and they were all getting in the way of each other. Certainly, their maneuvers did not seem as practiced as when they'd been clearing boxes at the farm. Maybe having all the soldiers in one place wasn't a good idea.

And then suddenly, the first demons were there. There was a sick inevitability about it. One broke through from the undergrowth with no warning disturbance to the tree branches. And then there was another one. And another one. Somehow there were more of them in front. And then they were appearing from the bushes behind. Walking with a deadly focus, their graceful gait was no longer beautiful or magical but menacing and dangerous.

"Get ready," shouted Dog, spotting them at the same time. "Brace yourselves." Non checked her footing and raised her crossbow.

The first ones came fast, intent on their target, their claws already raised to grab. Non shot at one, but the arrow only glanced a shoulder. An arrow hit from elsewhere and a demon fell, but another appeared behind, walking over its body.

Non lunged forward with her spear, but from around her she could hear terrified screams. They were so tightly packed into the center of the cart that she couldn't move her arm far enough back to get momentum. She was more swatting at the demons uselessly than killing any and, as the first of the clawed fingers scrabbled at the sides of the cart, there were screams of fear from all around. Non glanced up.

The soldiers and Dog were surrounded, completely cut off from them by ten or more demons, all attacking at once. She could see both Becky and Jane standing by the cart driver methodically shooting arrows, but their supply couldn't last forever. Dog was crouching at the edge of the crowd of demons, and, as Non watched, she leaped into the army of monsters. Using her spear as a shield to push and knock over, she started trying to fight her way through to the girls.

They couldn't last for long. The carts had already come to a standstill; both the drivers were crouching at the front, trying to protect their horses. Somewhere in the woods, demons were wailing, and the noise was almost overpowering; Non could feel the sound starting to affect her thoughts, numbing her and taking over her mind with fear. There were too many demons . . .

She kicked at one with her foot, pushing its head back so she could stab it in the neck. It slid off her spear, crumpling against the edge of the cart, its head caught on the wood. She saw another one fall beside it. But behind her she could feel most of the girls crouching and crying. With a sudden clarity, she could see those pages of the three strategy books, could picture them next to each other. But there was no chapter in the book called "What to do if you're surrounded."

Another demon fell next to her, a spear sticking out of its torso. A few people were holding up sacks of goods to shield themselves, but the demon claws had already gouged thick tears in those, shredding them further with each new grab.

Non stabbed at another monster, scratching its head so that blood started to ooze down its skull. Its eyes swiveled toward her, and an arrow from somebody hit it in the arm. It growled in pain, stepping backward and holding its arm.

The soldiers weren't coming. Dog was still stuck, fighting. Non wondered if the reason the strategy books didn't mention this scenario was because nobody survived it. They were going to have to write their own guide.

"Who's got arrows?" she shouted. "If you've got arrows, pass them up to the front."

She glanced round at the others. They all looked pale and hunched. Some were shaking with their fear or crying. Very few were even holding their spears out anymore.

"Arrows," she repeated. "Arrows! If you've got them, pass them up to the front!" Several people turned their heads toward her, as though awakening from a trance. They fumbled slowly for their arrows, becoming faster and more focused as they did so. In turn, the others started moving slowly, reluctantly.

They were hugely outnumbered. There were at least fifty demons surrounding them, but what worried Non more was the number that could easily still be concealed in the surrounding thick undergrowth.

"We can't all fight," she said loudly. "There isn't room. Half of us need to crouch down to make space. Every other person, get down. Hold your spears out and try to keep the demons away from the cart. Get down!"

The students moved and crouched down: some quickly, but others tentatively, after looking to see whether they were needed.

"The rest of us have to kill. Aim for the head or the stomach. You don't need to rush. They can't get us here . . ." There was a forced calm to her tone, and she didn't need to add the last word—"yet." The danger was obvious to everybody; the cart was already swaying gently back and forth from the pressure of the demons desperately pushing against it. They clearly didn't have long.

"On my count . . ." She made eye contact with each of the students in turn. She could still see the fear in their eyes, but she could also see determination and survival. "One . . . two . . . three . . . GO!

Non aimed her crossbow at one of the demons. It looked straight at her and paused, almost making itself a better target. She released her arrow and it hit, straight through the eye. The demon fell immediately backward onto one of the others. Next to her, Ellie leaned forward and stabbed with her spear. It glanced off to the side of the first head, catching on the skull but jagging on the shoulder and getting caught in the flesh there. Ellie pulled her spear out again, but the demon grabbed it, its claws pulling on it with an unnatural strength so that Ellie nearly toppled over. Ellie let go, and Non handed her the crossbow.

Non took a deep breath and looked again at the swarming, deathly throng. In the corners of her eyes, she could see the first of the bodies crumpling to the ground as other people were successful. She raised her spear again. The demon in front of her seemed to pause and shake his head, his skull now gaping through his flesh, the brain visible and seeping out between the cracks somebody had made.

This creature wasn't a person, Non reminded herself. They weren't people. They had brains like animals. She remembered the dead bodies in the church.

She took another breath and pushed her spear down hard, right through the skull. It went through wetly, too easily, so that she almost lost her balance. The demon juddered there for a split second, eyeballs jiggling back and forth comically in the sockets, before falling slowly to the ground, withdrawing from her spear, so that sticky globules remained.

"Come on! We can do this!" came a shout from somebody.

She lifted up her spear again and brought it down hard onto another skinless head. And again, onto another gaping monster. And again, onto another bringer of death.

"This is not the end of the world! We will not die here," the voice came again. "Kill! Kill!"

Non felt the music of each kill, the rhythm of death. It wasn't pleasure, but it felt right. She felt more alive as the demons became truly dead.

She plunged her spear down until her arms ached and the already blurred faces of the demons became meaningless, featureless, fictional. *Kill, kill.*

"They're getting higher," came Meg's interrupting scream. "The demons."

Non stopped. Each successful kill was providing a body, a sort of platform, for the next demon to stand on, making it easier for them to reach the people in the middle of the cart.

"Stop killing!" shouted Non. "Stop!"

She paused and glanced round at the sweating, shaking students. Most of them were now speckled with blood or gore. Some of them still had their teeth bared in the ferocity of killing. But it had made no difference; there were still at least fifty demons surrounding them. For every one that they'd killed, another one had appeared. And there was no sign of the soldiers or of Dog.

Non called up to the Becky and Jane on the front of the carts, "Can we get this cart moving?"

"We're stuck. There are dead demon bodies in front of the cart. We can't go forward or back."

"Where is the best way of escape?"

"At the front. There are only three demons."

They only had one choice that Non could see. She sucked air into her cheeks and then blew it out again softly.

"Shoot those ones. I'm going to climb down in front of the cart and clear the bodies out of the way. Can you shoot . . . anything else that comes my way?"

"More arrows," called Jane. "Now!"

Non turned back to the rest of the students. "Create a distraction at the far end of the cart."

"I'm coming with you," said Ellie.

"And me," said Mary.

"Make sure there're no bodies under the wheels," Meg shouted to everybody else. "Use your spears!" She leaned over and scooped something to one side.

Non crouched on the edge of the cart, Ellie on the other side, and Mary behind.

"Are you ready?" she shouted behind her.

She could hear Becky and Jane already firing their arrows. It was now . . . or almost certainly never.

She jumped over the side and pulled a body away from in front of the wheel. It was much heavier than she'd thought, and she had to drag at it, but then she felt Mary beside her, and they lifted it together by the legs, avoiding those claws.

The horses were next to her, their tails flicking and their breath coming in terrified snorts.

Non ran forward, pushing another body out of the way. She grabbed two legs together and pulled, hauling them over to the side. She felt a head, or something fleshy and heavy, separate, a change in weight. There was no time to check. She dragged, heaved.

And as she pulled it out of the way of the horses, there was a warning call and she saw it: a wall of pulsating death speeding toward her, arms outreached, mouths already open. A seething, venomous mass of screeching evil.

"Run!" she screamed to Mary and Ellie. "Drive!" she screamed to the driver. She felt the horses start beside her.

She turned and fled toward the castle, the fear and horror making her, for a moment, almost blind in her running . . .

So that it took her a few seconds to register a platoon of heavily armed soldiers, led by Dog, running toward them from Cirtop.

———o———

Non slumped backward onto the food in the cart. She felt, rather than heard, the rustle of bags beneath her; her ears were still filled with the storming gale of her terror, so that the everyday noises of the world seemed filtered through a layer of felt. Her spear felt greasy with liquid, either the blood of the demons or her own sweat. And somewhere nearby, or maybe at a distance, she could hear sobbing:

the shaking, open-mouthed, convulsing sobs of somebody who doesn't care, of somebody angry at the world.

Beneath her, she felt the vibrations and gradient of the road change, to show that they were inside Cirtop, and, as the cart stopped, there was a moment of pure, perfect silence.

The quiet buzzed threateningly in her ears.

"You can rest for a moment," Dog's voice boomed out. "But this cart needs to be unloaded before lunch."

Non eased her aching body and sat up. Most of the students were still either lying back on the cart or staring vacantly into space. She looked over at Dog, who was intently examining her notebook. Dog turned a page slowly, with her usual air of stiff professionalism, but Non noticed a dark smudge running across the paper and thought that she detected a slight tremor to her hand.

"After lunch you will have an hour of target practice . . . and I think a few of you need to put a bit of work in, don't you?" Dog looked up sternly, but there was no reaction from the students.

Chapter 21

Nobody said anything for a few minutes. They just lay back on the cart. A few people were still crying, but they were doing it quietly, almost unconsciously. Dog had gone now, and there were no soldiers around at all. Non wondered where it was that they had gone. And where Commander Edwards was too. And when the supply carts from their home castles were coming.

Ellie was one of the first to sit up. "I can't believe we've got to unload this cart after . . . that," she said.

"It's better than clearing all those bodies off the track," said Meg. "What?"

"I don't think they can be left there, can they? They'd attract vermin." Then, with a smile, she added, "And they'd make the road really bumpy."

"Non, you were amazing, though!" said Ellie. And she did turn to look at Non as if she was amazed. Non looked away, feeling suddenly embarrassed, which, it turned out, was a stronger emotion than either fear or exhaustion.

"Non is always amazing," said Meg. "It's just she spends a lot of time trying to hide it." A few of the girls looked at Non as though they hadn't noticed her before, and here, inside the castle, Non didn't like the feeling of being seen. She started moving some of the sacks toward the edge of the cart so that they'd be easier to unload, and she'd have something to do. Slowly, others sat up or started to help Non, and there was activity again. Something to do. Something to focus on.

"Remind me again," Meg whispered to her, "why did we go to that farm? Why that one?"

Non shrugged. She wasn't ready to speak yet.

"Because, it looked like, I don't know if it was a surprise. They knew there were demons on the road, didn't they?" Meg added.

Non threw a couple of sacks down to waiting students.

"And what about that farm? What had happened there?"

"I don't know, Meg," she said. "I think I probably think the same as you."

"What is that?" asked Meg slowly. "What do I think?"

"I think. We think"—Non grimaced—"it's a lot worse than we've been told, isn't it? Demons are a bigger problem than we thought."

"Oh, is that what we think!" Meg laughed. Then she laughed so hard she had to bend over. A few other people smiled, just hearing her laughter. "It's just . . . it's just . . . I wondered. I wondered whether we were bait? Whether we were sent to that farm so we'd bring back demons for them to kill." She shook her hand at Non. "No, no, don't tell me otherwise. I'm glad it was all an accident." She kept on laughing, the sound genuine, as though it was properly funny.

And then there was an awkward jerking movement from the far end of the cart. Slowly, Jane sat up and turned to face the rest of them, her face screwed up with anger. "You killed our frigging pacer, you stupid bitches. Don't you ever look what you're doing? You stupid fucking . . . just . . . I can't believe . . ." She picked up a bottle and threw it into the middle of the cartload of food. Several people flinched or held their arms in front of their faces as it bounced off onto the grass, but nobody moved away. They were too stunned and confused. "What the fuck do you think you were frigging doing? Who did it? Who killed him?"

Non looked round at the others. Jane picked up another bottle.

"I don't think anybody knows," said Meg quickly. "We were all just really scared. I'm not sure anybody can tell the difference."

"What the FUCK! Aggghh!" Jane screamed the words and threw the bottle violently against the front of the cart. This time several students jumped down or shielded their heads in their hands. "You fucking . . . Agggghhhh! You shits make me so mad! I would NEVER do something like that to you. I will never forgive you for this." She gave a painful sob. "I . . ." Jane looked at them again for a long minute, her shoulders shaking with rage and grief, then she jumped down and ran off up the hill toward the dormitories.

"You should really look what you're doing, you know?" Becky said and slid off the cart, following Jane.

There was a moment of awkward silence.

"I think everybody reacts to fear in different ways, don't they?" said Mary, and a few people raised their eyebrows. "Sooo . . . were their pet demons in that crowd that were trying to kill us?"

"Must have been," replied Callie.

"Does anybody remember doing it?" asked Mary.

A few people shrugged. But there was no way they'd have been able to tell the difference. Non thought back, but it was just a blur of evil and panic. She could see demon faces, their teeth bared, their claws raised, and it was an uncomfortable feeling of death. She couldn't distinguish between the faces as she remembered fighting off the many creatures that were trying to kill her. All she could feel now was the threat, the terror, the adrenaline.

◦

Although Non still felt tense and her shoulders ached a bit, the attack had filled them all with a burst of anxious energy. That afternoon everything felt like a race against time. They ate their lunch while mixing cement; they did exercises while queuing for target practice. And they shot their arrows with ferocity and focus.

A few times, Non thought she heard calls from the hills again: either human or . . . maybe not. But each time she paused to listen, there was nothing more. Probably it was just her ears playing tricks on her, but the possibility that they weren't and the unreal, broken memories of this morning's attack left her working harder and harder. They needed to be ready for an attack at any time and, at the moment, the castle was still nowhere near ready to guarantee safety. Non felt like she wanted the walls bigger, and stronger, and higher. She wanted more weapons, more spears, more places to run to. They were all anxious and twitchy—even Jane. Maybe even especially Jane.

Non also felt the need to make sure that everybody was all right all the time, like a teacher counting her students on a class outing. Every few minutes she'd find herself looking around checking and just running through the tick list in her head: Meg, Ellie, Chris,

Sam, Jane, Callie, Mary, Becky. She had to climb on top of things a couple of times in order to see everybody, but they were never far away. Nobody strayed too far from the walls today.

It was only later on that day, toward the evening, that she saw Sam again, and it was the first time in a few days that she'd spoken to him. She was sitting on the wall, her feet overhanging the cliff, and, again, she had her notebook out, resting on her lap. It wasn't necessarily out so she could write in it. Mainly it was out as a barrier so she didn't have to talk to people and to calm herself. A way of controlling things. Because if they were on paper, they were facts—something that could be studied and ordered.

He walked straight along the wall and sat down beside her. They smiled at each other, but then they sat there for a few minutes without speaking. It didn't feel awkward. Non didn't feel like she needed to search for something to say with him; it felt like he just wanted to look at the outside too.

But then there was a sudden burst of laughter from the castle courtyard. They both looked back, but the walls surrounding it were too high now for them to see what was going on.

"Are you OK?" he said. "After what happened today?"

She shrugged. Because she wasn't really OK. None of them were. "I'm really sorry we killed your pacer," said Non. "We . . . couldn't tell the difference."

Sam sighed. "It's fine. It must have been terrifying, so I think we all understand. It's just Old Grumpy had been around for years, so I think we all got attached to him. We're just a bit sad, that's all."

"I'm sorry," she said again.

He nodded. The red kites were circling over the trees in the valley below. Non couldn't see whether there was anything down there or whether they were just flying around as they did sometimes. They swooped and turned, majestic and effortless, never seeming to move their wings.

"I remembered those military books, you know," said Non. "When we were out there being attacked."

"Did you?" He frowned. "I don't remember reading anything about what to do . . ."

"I know. That's what I remembered. There was nothing."

He was silent for a minute.

"So what are you saying?"

"I don't know. It's just weird, isn't it? Have you ever heard of demons behaving like that?"

"What, loads of them working together?"

"Yeah."

"No."

"But then I wondered if maybe that's because they do behave like that, just we don't hear about it. Because there are no survivors." She bit her nails and didn't look at him.

"It's possible," he said.

"The other thing that was weird was why we were sent there."

"I knew you'd say that," he laughed. "I think everybody's thinking the same thing! And why nobody had raided it before!"

"It's just . . . how come they knew about the farm, about the dead people inside and all the stuff in there? That farm was miles away from this castle—but they still knew about it."

"But yet nobody knew about the church that's literally over there." He pointed.

"Yeah." Non bit her nails again. The wind blew against her notebook, rustling the pages.

There was a scrabbling sound behind them, and a ladder appeared. Then Meg's face appeared as she climbed up it.

"All right," said Meg. "We've finished unloading the cart."

Non frowned. They'd finished unloading it several hours ago.

"There were quite a few bottles of spice spirits."

"Oh . . . right."

Meg winked at both Non and Sam. "We've taken them. They're in the girls' dormitory. Party tonight."

Chapter 22

"We are gathered here this evening," said Meg, "in solidarity for Castle Goch. We can't imagine your loss, and we don't understand it, but that doesn't mean we're not sorry. We are. And we do want to offer our sympathy to you." She spoke sincerely and sympathetically. A number of the Castle Goch students had their heads bowed or were holding hands. Jane sniffed and pursed her lips together in a half smile. Her eyes were red and puffy, but they were no longer filled with tears. Paul had his arm round her, and she rested her head on his shoulder. Paul didn't look at Meg.

There were students seated or crouched in every part of the girls' dormitory—even the uncomfortable stone outcrop in the middle had a couple of boys perching on it. Non looked around and couldn't see any faces missing. Most of them seemed to have made an effort with their appearance too—brushing their hair, even *washing* their hair. The Kintaborel Castle girls had taken their headscarves off, revealing the beautiful, intricate hair arrangements beneath. Only one girl still had her long skirt on, though it was ragged and caked in mud. The others had either ripped the torn material away at the knees, and one had borrowed a pair of trousers from somebody. Castle Goch were all still mainly wearing tight camouflage things, but they seemed to be cleaner tight camouflage things.

"Commander Daffy is in charge of the castle tonight," continued Meg, "because the others are off doing something important and mysterious. Saving our lives or whatever."

Chris started opening bottles and passing them round.

"I think that probably means we can do whatever we want and nobody'll notice." She gave a grin. "Party!" The room erupted into cheers.

"To quarantine!" she called.

"To quarantine!" everybody repeated, holding up their bottle if they had one, and just shouting if they didn't.

"And . . . to survival!" she said.

"To survival." People smiled more grimly for this one—but they still drank. Lots of people drank.

———— o ————

It was a brilliant night. It was probably the best Non had ever known. There was a magic to it, a feeling of desperate happiness, like everybody felt it was really important to have loads of fun. The most fun ever.

Somehow rules had been broken, or what they'd known had changed, so it was like they didn't need to obey anything anymore. It was like Cirtop was not in the same world as their normal lives—they were almost in a secret pocket of time, a hidden society.

Plus, they had alcohol.

Non spent the first part of the evening with Meg and Ellie. Later, Callie and Mary joined them too, and Non enjoyed being in the middle of a group of people—even if she still didn't really have anything to say. It was just nice to feel like she belonged there.

"The thing is, Non," started Ellie. "When we were at home, you always acted like you hated going outside the walls, but now we're here, you're really brave when you're outside. Killing demons, running from demons, taking charge! Are you sure you don't want to be military?"

Non was sure of nothing anymore. Nothing. She took another swig from the bottle. Some of the time she was only tilting it up to her lips and pretending to swallow—but this time she took a big swig.

"Did any of you kill any demons?" asked Mary.

"Yes." Everybody nodded.

"Do you know who killed the pacer?" she whispered.

Non shook her head.

"Was it you?" Callie whispered to Mary.

"I don't know! It might have been! I think I killed about six of the monsters."

Callie looked at her, open-mouthed.

"Honestly, I quite liked it. It was really satisfying. Their heads make this amazing crunch, don't they?"

All the girls started to laugh.

"If it was you, you can never admit it," said Meg. "You've got to never speak of that one again."

"I know, right?" said Mary.

Later, somebody started to sing, and the Kintaborel Castle girls danced. And then everybody danced. Crazy, and fun, and pretend drunkenly even if they weren't drunk.

As the sun went down, they left the dormitory, and as the stars came up, they sat around in groups on the hillside chatting, laughing, drinking, and watching the beauty of the sky.

"You're one of my best friends, you know, Non," said Ellie. "You're so lovely. We should hang out loads when we get back to the citadel."

Non gave her a hug. That would be fun. She hadn't realized how much she liked Ellie until they came here either.

"I wonder what they're doing in the citadel tonight," said Ellie. "I hope they're OK. Do you think they're OK?"

"I have zero clue, Ellie."

"We'd have heard if they weren't OK, though, wouldn't we? I imagine it means absolutely nothing that we haven't had a supply cart from them in ages, and you're not allowed to tell me differently."

"OK. I won't."

They hugged again and sat there for a few minutes just watching the dancing and the stars.

<hr />

At some point, the Castle Goch boys started a crazy game that seemed to be part obstacle course, part excuse for more drinking. They had to run up and down the hill, climb the dormitory walls, and then walk the whole way around them before downing a shot. Although each of the participants was taking it seriously, nobody else was, and it just led to more laughing. Very few of the boys made it the whole way round the walls without falling off, and it got to the stage where everyone was just chanting, "Fall, fall, fall, fall," until Non thought some of the boys fell on purpose. But it was hilarious, and Non laughed until her stomach hurt and she couldn't breathe. When it was Sam's turn, he got down on his hands and knees to try to crawl along the top, but eventually he gave up and slid to the floor. There was a chorus of boos, and as he walked past Non, she called, "Pathetic attempt!"

He stopped and grinned. "It was hurting my knees," he said.

"Well, can you do it walking, like normal people?" she said. "That wouldn't hurt your knees."

"It might hurt my body if I fall."

"Excuses, excuses. We fought demons today and you can't even walk along a wall, for no valid reason, in the dark."

"Right." He clambered back up again.

"Hey!" she called. "Come on, Sam!"

He started walking slowly, his arms out for balance.

"Come on, Sam," a few other people called, echoing her.

"Come on, Sam!"

"So," said Ellie. "Sam, eh?" Non couldn't see her winking in the dark, but it felt like she probably did, or at least as though she gave a significant look. It silenced Non anyway, making her feel self-conscious again, even with the darkness hiding her. But then Meg walked past, heading toward the far end of the hillside with her arms round two Kintaborel Castle boys. Ellie and Non laughed again.

⸺ o ⸺

When things were starting to quiet down a bit, and when people were starting to go to bed or were disappearing off to secret corners of the hillside, Non climbed up onto the wall again. The moon was high, and she knew she should be careful—she could feel the fuzz of the alcohol in her head, but she also felt focused and brave. She walked along the wall to the broken section over the cliff and dangled her legs over as she always did. She was hoping Sam would come, as he had earlier that day, but she also knew she didn't mind if he didn't.

The night was very still, and from up here the voices of the other students seemed dulled, deadened, like they were shouting and singing into a saucepan, the sound trapped inside the castle walls. Non turned her head toward the valley to see if she could hear anything from the outside, but there was nothing apart from the breeze brushing against her face. Nothing seemed to be moving down there either. Even the river seemed motionless, the water, at this distance, just a solid strand of darkness cutting along the valley floor. There were watchers on the walls too, their backs to the students and their eyes still on the plain below—but tonight their stance was relaxed, their movements routine. It was a normal night out in the valley.

Non saw him out of the corner of her eye. He'd climbed up onto the wall at the bottom of the hill, and now he ambled along the ramparts slowly, stopping occasionally to laugh with one of the guards, or to just look out into the night. She checked behind her to see if anybody else had seen, but there was nobody about. The hillside was empty.

"I thought you might want another drink," said Sam, holding out a bottle to her and sitting down. She took a swig. Then she took another swig.

"I guessed you'd be up here. Is this your favorite place in the castle?" he said.

"Yeah. I like that I can see out so far but still be protected. What's your favorite place?"

"My favorite place is anywhere outside the castle. I don't like being stuck in here."

His hand was still tonight as he rested it on the wall, and his body didn't have the tension or energy it normally seemed to fight against.

"It's a bit dangerous here, Non," he said. "And it's a long fall down that cliff. I don't know how protected you are."

"I think I like the danger a bit too," she said. And they smiled at each other. "I like looking at all these miles of trees. They look quiet and peaceful, but they could be hiding anything."

"They are hiding anything. They're hiding loads of things. You know that from today."

"Yeah." Non struggled to explain it, to put the feeling into words. "I guess I just like that you don't know where in these trees they're hiding. And there're probably some out there right now and we don't know where. It's just mysterious. Not quite exciting . . . but it is almost."

He nodded. "I sort of know what you mean. You're mad. But I know what you mean."

"It wouldn't be exciting or mysterious if I was down there wandering around the woods in the dark. It would be terrifying."

"Yeah." He laughed and took another drink.

"But I think it's that possibility and all of the unknowns up here, where I'm safe, that I find exciting."

"I know what you mean. But I'd still rather be down there, dealing with the unknowns. It feels like we're hiding from them in here."

"We are!" She turned to smile at him. In the night, he looked different, the shadows and the whiteness of the moonlight outlining different sections of his face, highlighting different parts of his body, and she watched him for a moment, for as long as she could without it being weird, seeing how the light made him look new.

"But when you're playing hide-and-seek as a child, the winner is always the one who knows where the others are," he said softly. "The winner is always the one who can find the others. If we're all in here, locked deep inside our walls, then they know exactly where we are, and we have no way of finding out where they are. I know it's a good idea and the walls keep us safe. It just feels a bit like we're the losers."

"It's not a game, though. In the children's game, nobody's life is on the line. Well, they weren't in the citadel anyway—don't know about your castle." She grinned at him.

He laughed. "You know what it's like in Castle Goch—always danger!"

"I don't, actually. What is it like?"

"It's colder, because it's higher up and there's more wind."

"More wind than here?"

He nodded. "But it's bigger. The walls are much longer, and the top of the hillside is much flatter. We have a football pitch in the middle, which is still grass, so it's much more spread out than here."

"You play football in the middle of your castle?"

"Not very often," he admitted. "And it's mainly the little kids. We use it mostly for grazing animals, because there isn't much grazing land outside. Our houses are round and have space between them. I heard it's not like that in the citadel. Your houses are all right next to each other."

She nodded.

"Our houses are sunken a bit into the ground, not like here, so that they are protected from the wind and the cold. Only the roofs are exposed, and they are mainly thatch. It's not dangerous at all, just in case you didn't realize I was joking."

"Do you miss it?" she said.

"Yes. Though I think these buildings here are going to be posher than our houses, maybe. I miss the space at home. And there's not much woodland around there either, up there at the top of the valley. The hills are open, and you can see for miles. If anything attacks us, we get lots of warning."

"What about your pacers?"

"They live outside the castle. We feed them with leftover meats if we have any, and we declaw them once a month. They're harmless."

"Would you show me one, so that I can have a proper look at it tomorrow?"

He nodded. "Yeah. Sure."

Chapter 23

The party had completely broken up by the time they went down, and clouds had shifted across the stars so that it was darker. The night felt cooler, and some of the magic had gone. Non held on to the dormitory wall as she walked along it to the doorway, feeling her way with her hands. The ground was uneven and, although she knew the pathway, she also knew there were holes in it that she didn't want to trip in. She could hear the soft snoring of at least a couple of people, but otherwise the night was silent.

"Non," whispered Sam. She turned to face him. She could barely make out the outline of his body in the shadow of the wall and couldn't see the detail of his face at all. He reached out for her hand, and their fingers entwined, his thumb stroking hers. She took a step closer to him.

"It's always good being with you," he whispered, so softly she could barely hear it. He paused a moment, then reached out so that his hand was cupping her cheek. Then he leaned forward and kissed her, their lips barely touching. But she could feel the warmth of his body, and she reached up for his waist. He slid both his arms around her and kissed her again, this time for longer, so that silvery shivers ran down her spine.

When he moved his lips away, or maybe it was her, he kept his arms around her body, and they leaned in close together, their foreheads touching. She could feel his breath hot against her cheeks, his arms enclosing, protecting.

There was a rustle from inside, somebody muttering something in their sleep, and Non put her head on his shoulder, half on his chest, instead. She nestled into him, smelling the soap, and the alcohol, and the fire, but underneath it all, just him. He kissed her hair and, his voice muffled, whispered, "I should go."

"Yeah." Non pulled away, but then she leaned in again and kissed him again. "See you tomorrow."

"Mm," he said.

———o———

When Non woke the next morning, it was the first thing she thought about. It felt so special she didn't want to share it with the others—though after a few moments, she wondered whether she'd just dreamed the whole thing.

But she could still feel where his arms had been around her; her skin still tingled with the memory of his touch. She put her blanket over her face so she could smile without anybody seeing.

"We've got to hide the bottles," said Meg. "Come on. Quickly!"

Around her there was the *chink* of glass, and giggling.

"There's loads of them!" whispered Meg. "Where are we going to hide them all?"

"Just get them out of the courtyard," said Mary.

"I'll check the hillside and pathway," said Callie. "Nobody'll come into the dormitories. We can just put them under our blankets here and then chuck them off the side of the castle later."

"Quick!"

There was a mad scrambling of people getting dressed and running around, half-naked. The Kintaborel Castle girls rushed their prayers this morning, mouthing the words individually as they pulled on their clothes, and people ran in and out with bottles. Jane sat up and then lay down and then sat up again—as though she was thinking about doing her morning sit-ups. But then she lay back down again and pulled a pile of clothes over her head.

They were ready, and in the courtyard, as Commander Daffy came up the hill with breakfast. It was only him carrying it this morning—there was only one plate and, though it was heaped high, it wasn't much for all the people it was feeding. A few people, Non noticed, were looking pale or were resting their heads in the hands, but there was still a feeling of happiness, of shared rule-breaking togetherness, and it was great.

"A busy day today," he said, passing round the bread. Non took a chunky heel and started picking off the mold. "Lots to do. We could start doing some cooking with the food collected yesterday."

"Yeah."

"Oh, yeah."

A lot of people nodded at this, enthusiastically.

"Then we're going to look at some military strategy, because there are lessons to be learned from yesterday's experience. Plus, obviously, light building work and weapons training."

There were more nods, and people looked like they might actually pay attention this time.

"I'll be back in half an hour to start work, then!" He beamed at the students.

Non searched for Sam as everybody was sitting round chatting, reliving and exaggerating the comedy moments from last night—comparing notes and remembering what had happened. He was, predictably, sitting in among a big group of Castle Goch boys. They were laughing loudly, teasing each other. His hair was wet again, and she tried not to let herself imagine him swimming in the moat or, perhaps with his top off, washing at the well. He caught her eye, though, as she was staring at him, and smiled.

"You OK?" he mouthed.

She nodded and smiled back.

Meg coughed, spluttering on her hard bread. "Did anything happen with Sam last night?" she said.

"Non didn't come to bed until late," said Ellie.

"What were you doing?" asked Meg, her eyes narrowed.

"What were *you* doing?"

"I tell you everything."

"No, you don't."

"Well, I would if you asked."

"I don't want to know, though."

"I was with two boys last night, and they were both lovely. First . . ."

"Aggggh, no!" said Non. "I really don't want to know!"

"Then did anything happen with you and Sam?"

"We talked for a bit on the walls. Just about stuff."

"Anything else?"

"He's going to let me see their pacers today."

"Oh, what?" said Ellie.

"Ugh!" Meg screwed up her face. "Is it a date?"

"That is the least romantic thing I can imagine."

"It's not a date. He's just helping me look at demons."

"Why? I want to stay as far away as possible from them forever," said Ellie.

"Oh my God, have you found somebody just as weird as you?" asked Meg.

"It's really not a date. We're looking at monsters."

"You like him, though, don't you?"

"He's a nice person, yes. Lots of the new people we've met are."

"Non, you are so annoying," said Meg, and all three of them laughed.

It was late afternoon before Non talked to Sam again. Commander Daffy's lesson on military strategy felt even more difficult to follow than before, even though it also felt more important. Maybe because they were tired, or because it was warm, but Non found the diagrams he drew particularly abstract and the points he made almost meaningless—even though they'd experienced the attack yesterday, so everything about demons should have felt personal. Somehow he made it all feel impersonal again, and she would have liked to ask him some questions, but they never seemed relevant, and also she couldn't quite express exactly what it was she wanted to know anyway. Plus, she didn't want to speak in front of everybody. He did answer other people's questions, though—but in ways that just made Non wonder even more.

Mostly, though, she was distracted. She kept searching for Sam out of the corner of her eye but without turning round too frequently, because she didn't want Ellie and Meg to know she was looking for him. A few times she thought she felt his eyes on her, but when she looked round for him, he was always busy with something and not looking in her direction at all.

Later, when they were up near the dormitories chatting, he came over again. Most of Kintaborel Castle had disappeared off for a run, so Non had relaxed, lying out on the hillside in the sun.

"Hey," he called as he ran up the hill. His hair flopped over his forehead, and his face was bright with exercise. "I brought you a present."

Non stood up, flustered. She could feel herself flushing, just as she could feel the grins of Meg and Ellie as they stood up next to her to watch. There was nothing in his hands, and she couldn't see anything behind him.

"I'm kidding. I've just got the pacers outside, if you still want to see them? They followed us back."

Ellie fell back on the grass, laughing.

"Oh. Yes. Yes, I would like to see them." Non stood up, grabbing her notebook.

"Be careful, Non," said Meg. "You know . . ."

"They're fine. Honestly," said Sam. "Completely safe. You'll be safe with me, Non."

———o———

There were three today. The guards hadn't bothered shutting the castle gate against them; the pacers just stood on the drawbridge while Becky and Jane held their spears out, waving the weapons around occasionally when one of the pacers made to step forward.

Looking at them properly now, they were very different from other demons. They were fiercer, if anything, low growls and soft howls coming from them as they bared their filed, toothless mouths and clawless fingers. But their bodies were plumper, a layer of yellowish fat surrounding their stomachs, and their muscles weren't as taut.

"Hi, Non," said Jane. "These are our pacers." She smiled proudly and looked at Non directly.

"They're lovely," said Non. It wasn't entirely a lie—though it was mostly.

Jane's smile broadened. "Oh, they're cheeky old things," she said. "Cause us loads of trouble."

"What are their names?"

"This is Stubs." She pointed to one, which seemed to have had its fingers filed off as well as its claws. "And this is Elizabeth."

"Right," said Non.

"Named after my mother."

"Oh." Non wondered whether this was an honor or not. Judging by Jane's happy smile, she decided it probably was.

"And this is Poppet." Both Jane and Becky looked fondly at the larger of the three, and Jane gave him a pat on his arm. This seemed to enrage him further, and he waved his arms wildly, leaning forward to try and get at her. She winced away, and Becky prodded at the monster with her spear. "Oh, Poppet," Jane laughed. "Get down, boy!"

"We've had these ones for . . . about four years?" said Sam.

"We've had Stubs for four years. But we've had Elizabeth for four and a half years," Jane corrected. "Poppet we've had for almost eight years."

"Eight years!"

"Yes."

Paul came through the gate, clutching his spear. He walked straight toward the pacers and started tapping the spear lightly against Elizabeth's chest, as though he was pretending to stab him. Elizabeth grabbed at the spear, growling. But it was pretend growling, Non could see. Like a kitten play-attacking a shoelace.

"Stop it, Paul. You're winding him up. Non wants to see them."

"What do you want to know?" asked Sam.

"How did you get them?" She hoped this might lead to them explaining *why* they'd gotten them, which was something she didn't really think she could ask outright.

"I got Elizabeth for my birthday," said Jane. "And I think the others were for special events, weren't they? Christmas? Harvest festival."

"Yeah." The others nodded. Non could see Sam was watching her carefully to see her reactions. She smiled to reassure him that it was fine.

"How did you catch them?"

"The soldiers catch them," said Jane. "Some of them were caught on purpose, as presents for us. But Elizabeth was a stray and was found, injured, in the hills."

"They're normally injured," said Sam.

"That's because the soldiers injure them," said Paul. He was still playing with Elizabeth, but more gently now. "They injure them because that's how we tame them."

"How do you tame them?" asked Non.

"Like you tame any wild animal. With food. Or with *not* letting them have food," said Jane.

"We haven't toilet trained them, though," said Becky. "Nobody's managed to do that."

"That's because nobody wants them in their house!" said Sam. "So there's no need."

They all laughed—Non a split second behind the others, because she wasn't sure why that bit was any funnier than the rest.

"Elizabeth was injured in the leg, here." Jane pointed to a darker line along the thigh. There was an indentation in the muscle there, and now that she'd seen it, the mark was obvious. Similarly, Stubs and Poppet both had irregular lines or worn patches on their bodies. "He couldn't walk properly when we got him, so we had to let him rest for a couple of months until he could run away into the hills. The others were similar. But they were hurt in different places."

"So they stayed with you because you looked after them when they were injured?"

"Yes," said Sam.

"Even though some of you might have injured them in the first place?"

"Erm. Yes. But we give them nice rats as a treat and they forget about it?" Sam grinned.

Non grimaced and laughed. "Can I see the claws?"

Sam stepped forward and grabbed Stubs's hands, pulling them toward Non, though the monster kept writhing behind.

"Look," said Sam, holding down the fingers. "When we first get them, there is fluid all down here." He pointed to a long strip of red, running the whole way down the demon's arm. It was almost the same color as the rest of the arm, so Non would have taken it as being part of the ordinary muscle. But, in fact, it was ridged and hard to the touch—like the skin on the back of your foot. It was also very slightly a darker color. It didn't feel loose, like it could be inflated with liquid.

"The skin is hard here so that it would be difficult to puncture in battle or, I guess, so that the demon wouldn't scratch it open just on a tree branch or something. We declaw the demons once a month, and the fluid never comes back if we do that."

"If you leave the declawing longer than that, it does," said Paul. "Remember Pox?"

They all smiled, fondly.

"Well, do you remember that time he went missing for a few months? When he came back, his claws were properly long again and we weren't allowed near him until they'd been cut and the liquid had been squeezed out."

"Somebody squeezed it out?" asked Non.

"Yeah. It's like milking a cow, a bit. Or a snake. I've seen them. You just hold the fingers up and press them firmly against the side of a cup, then the stuff comes out. It looks a bit like milk too. Probably best not to get them mixed up!"

Non looked at Sam.

"You'd like some of that liquid, wouldn't you? I can try and get you some, if you want?"

"*How* would you try and get it for me?" asked Non, wide-eyed.

He shrugged, casually, but looking at her intently. "I'd just have to catch you a demon."

She grinned at him slowly, and he was just about to say something else when there was a call from the castle above. "Sight!" shouted one of the watchers.

"Sight!" Another voice echoed the first, followed by the sounding of the horn.

All the soldiers suddenly ran along the wall, and the watchers left their posts, leaping over the gaps in the ramparts. They were still armed, Non noticed, even though they were just watchers, not archers, and their bows clunked noisily against their shoulders as they ran. Had they always been armed?

"Get inside," shouted one of the guards. "Get out of our way!"

Jane ushered the pacers across the drawbridge, and they scattered onto the plain. Running, but looking back over their shoulders at the people, they headed toward the trees.

Non ran inside the castle with the others. There were already more soldiers down here—Commander Edwards and Dog too, their crossbows pointed right at the gate even as Non was running through it.

"Up here, Non!" called Meg from the walls.

"What's going on?" she said, clambering up. It felt odd, even then. There wasn't any feeling of panic from the soldiers. They hadn't pulled up the drawbridge, or released the portcullis, or any of the things that would happen in an emergency. They were grim-faced, though.

"The supply cart!" came a shout.

Non edged along the wall to reach Meg, and there was a line of other students there too, and at that call they looked at each other expectantly. Food! Mail!

As it came round the corner, Non could see that the cart was fully laden, piled high with colorful bags and sacks and boxes, all jammed in together and tied on firmly with a bright-blue rope. But the dusty white tarpaulin that had once covered the load now flapped gently in the breeze, lifting up and then down again in time with the horse's lumbering steps. Even from up here, Non could see the bloodstains, spattered wide across the length of the cart and now dried to a deep, rusty brown.

The driver was slumped, still seated, but with his head tipped back and his arms wide-open as though in invitation, exposing the jumble of flesh and guts that remained of his stomach. His intestines still glistened with the wetness of fresh blood, and little crimson rivulets seeped down the creases in his trousers to the bloody pool beneath him.

His head was held rigid, but beneath that his arms and body swayed from side to side as though disconnected in a dance of death, like the puppets in the shows Non remembered from Christmastime.

Meg grabbed her hand.

"Do you think the demons got to him?" asked Ellie, her voice jarring in the stillness.

Nobody replied, because the answer was obvious.

"When should it have been here?" asked Non. "How long has it been since the last supply cart?"

"There was that one on Sunday," said Sam, "but I don't know if there's been another one since."

"The food's been really bad this week," said Ellie. "There can't have been another one. And I bet this one's late."

"Where . . ." said Meg. "Where . . . are his guards now?"

"Some of them might have made it," said Non. "They might have made it back to the citadel." Meg squeezed her hand, though they all knew she was wrong.

There would be at least three more demons growing somewhere. And they'd be growing inside bodies wearing the uniforms of citadel soldiers.

Chapter 24

Non had never seen a dead human body before—not a new one anyway. People did die, and she'd attended funerals. But in those, the body was always covered, a shroud politely wrapped round it so that only the outline of the body was visible. She'd seen pictures, of course, and they had the skeletons in the surgery for her to study anatomy. But hypothetical death, neatly arranged and documented in a book, was very different from the recently spilled guts of a man doing his normal job.

Those people in the church and those people on the farm were ancient. Almost unreal. Non had to struggle to imagine them doing anything. There was sadness with them when she thought about their deaths and lives. But the point was, she had to think about it with them. With the dead man in the cart, the death and the struggle and the pain and the mess were right in front of her.

Meg started to sob. Loudly and without self-consciousness.

"His poor family," she sobbed. "Oh, those poor people."

Non felt shock more than tears. The soldiers were shouting to each other, a line of them standing above the gate, crossbows armed and pointed at the empty plain. Sam and a couple of others didn't wait for the cart to cross the drawbridge but jumped off the wall to tend to the exhausted horse. Non looked around the plain in case there was something threatening there. But it was empty, the morning lovely, the dew fresh and glistening on the grass, the sky bright blue with only a few wisps of white cloud left behind, as though they'd lost their way. The red kites were still sitting in the far trees or were idly pacing back and forth on the other side of the moat, their feathers twitching in the breeze. But their eyes saw everything. Even when they faced the other way, nonchalantly, they would normally be upon a mouse-monkey that dared to flit across the grass within seconds. So why weren't they hovering over the cart? Had they already feasted this morning? And, if so, what had they feasted on?

Somebody placed a sheet over the driver, his insides too intimate for display, and the cart was guided under the gate. The soldiers were still shouting. Too many people were helping; it felt urgent and desperate. As the horse made it onto the cobbles beyond the gate, a rush of people ran forward to start unloading the goods, untie the horse, gently lift down the corpse. The portcullis dropped, with its smooth, rattling shriek of metal; the watchers started making their way back to their positions.

But even through the panic and chaos, Non noticed how similar the insides of the victim were to those of the demons. How the guts and muscles of one were almost indistinguishable from the other.

Her notebook was still in her hand, and she opened it to check the anatomy. To write down something, to organize what wasn't organized. She wrote intently, nothing in particular, just thoughts and questions and ideas. But she drew a diagram of the cart they had been on when they were attacked, and now this cart. She tried to go through her memory and think about possible places on the track between the citadel and Cirtop where an ambush could have taken place, but there was nowhere she'd felt as threatened as she had on the way back from the farmstead. The tracks around the citadel were kept fairly clear, probably to keep away threats.

She thought about the position of the cart driver in comparison to the horse. She thought about his body; she thought about attackers; she thought about the parasites and those people in the church. She flicked back and forth through her book, just writing down different questions, adding to notes here and there.

She thought about the pacers, about their hands, about the way they ran in comparison to the way the wild demons ran. She was thinking so much she didn't notice Dog standing behind her.

"What exactly do you think you're doing?" Non jumped. She felt suddenly flushed with guilt, as though she'd been caught doing something very wrong, something indecent.

"I'm just writing things about the demons again." Was it indecent? Non wasn't sure. She'd have definitely hidden it if she'd been in the citadel.

Dog gave her a long look. "Have you thought of anything useful?"

Non paused. Was this a trick question? She felt herself flushing just talking to Dog. "I guess I'm wondering when this attack happened. Whether it was before or after the attack on our cart?"

"Why are you wondering that?" Dog spoke abruptly but not angrily, her eyes on the scurrying people by the gate.

Non took a deep breath. "Because I'm looking for patterns. I've never read anything about demons attacking carts in big groups, so I'm wondering if this is a new thing or if it's a pattern of behavior that has always been there but we haven't realized before."

Dog looked up the hill behind her and gave a nod to Commander Edwards. She turned back to Non. "Continue," she said.

"And, I guess, there's lots of things. Did they learn how to attack carts better by the failed attack on ours?" She coughed and looked down at her book, as though the answers to the questions she hadn't even figured out yet were there.

Commander Edwards sauntered over, his hands in his pockets. "Looking at the state of the corpse," said Dog, "I would estimate the attack to this cart came after the attack yesterday. But that's not definite, because we would have expected a delivery of food before then."

Non nodded.

"So what does that make you think about your patterns?" Dog asked.

"Just—I'm really not sure," she said. Non glanced up. Both commanders were staring at her, and she knew she needed to say something. Was this a test where there was a right answer? Or were they genuinely asking for her thoughts? "The one thing that would have slowed us down, and that would have prevented us getting away when we were attacked, would have been if the drivers of our carts had been killed. The demons haven't infected this driver, or, if they have, he's useless to them now because he's dead. They haven't eaten him either. So I'm just wondering how the death of this driver benefits the demons."

"Yeah. It doesn't appear to, does it?" said Dog, with her eyes narrowed. "Though they're animals. Might they not just kill for fun?"

"They do sometimes," said Commander Edwards. "We know they like to play with their food too, sometimes."

Demons played with their food? Non quickly wrote down that idea too.

"But were you suggesting the demons had learned from one failed attack?" asked Dog.

"No. I don't know. Maybe?" said Non, which was the most coherent explanation she could give for anything right then. "I guess, by killing this man instead of just infecting him, it would have slowed down his guards—so made them easier to attack. Also . . ." She paused. "The food has gotten to us more slowly too, which could make us vulnerable." Non felt herself flushing again at the awkwardness of talking to these two.

"You don't have to work today," said Dog. "There are lots of books up in the guard tower that haven't been read for decades. Keep on with your research. You can summarize your findings to us."

Commander Edwards nodded. "Yes, there do seem to be rather a lot of the beasts around at the moment. Bit of a pain. Getting in the way a lot."

———o———

So Non spent the rest of the day reading. She spiced up the long books of paragraphless military history with the occasional flick through her mum's notes. When she read enough to realize a book wouldn't be useful, she put it aside. But she was overwhelmed with how much they didn't know. The many, many details that seemed crucial and useful that, for some reason, nobody had bothered to write down before. Was it that nobody considered them a military issue? There were no books there on dragonites, gormads, or even wood-lions either. Were the animals not considered as big a threat as humans? It did look like it, which Non thought was a mistake. She could have had a conversation with a bandit, or an island pirate, and explained to them why they shouldn't kill her. You couldn't exactly negotiate with a gormad.

A couple of guards passed through the room while she was in there, either nodding to her or ignoring her completely, but nobody stopped to talk to her. It felt isolating, but she didn't dare leave until supper time, since she had orders to be there—even though those orders hadn't been specific about what she was looking for.

Chapter 25

Porridge the next morning was lovely: perfect, soft oats that melted in the mouth, with layers of opalescent cream slowly oozing and pooling into the gaps left by Non's spoon. She'd paused momentarily when Meg had scooped a generous helping of banberry jam into the center of her bowl, but more because she felt some sort of politeness demanded it than because of any feeling of sadness or disgust. The bright, intrusive red swirls against the whiteness of the porridge were an obvious reminder of yesterday's deaths . . . but they also tasted really good. Non tried to savor each mouthful in memory of the guard who'd died keeping them fed, but she ate it so fast there wasn't time to think about him too much.

And then, suddenly, there was too much time to think.

"You're all staying inside today," said Dog, appearing in the courtyard after breakfast. "You know why. Keep out of everybody's way. Cause no trouble. Do as little as possible to bother anybody."

She looked exhausted. Her face, against the red blotches on her skin, was pale with almost a yellowish tint, and the bags under her eyes were deep.

"Can't we help?" called a few people.

"Yes," she said. "By staying inside this castle. Do not disrupt the work of the soldiers. We don't have the resources to be going out looking for you or to defend you if you get into trouble.

"Build something, or do weapons training if you're bored. And . . ." She looked around for Non. "You. Keep studying."

A few people looked over at Non curiously. Dog made to step away, and Callie stood up. She coughed.

"Commander." A lot of people frowned in surprise. "Commander, can we do the cooking? Would that make it easier?"

Dog looked confused.

"It's just . . . we were always told that was just as important as the fighting. Food, and keeping the castle clean and tidy, are all part of the battle."

"Yes," said Dog, her eyes brightening for a moment. "Yes, you definitely can. The food needs to be rationed, though. Can you sort that out?"

Mary stood up next to Callie. "Do we know when we will be getting more deliveries?" she said.

"No," said Dog. "I think you can see that. We might not be getting any . . . for a while."

"Do we know about the situation in the other castles?" asked Sam.

"No. I think you can see that too."

"We'll ration the food," Mary. "And we'll plant some more. Leave it with us." The Kintaborel Castle girls moved closer to each other and bowed their heads as they conferred.

Dog wavered a moment. "Just stay inside the castle," she said again, but she said it with less certainty this time. And then she walked out.

Immediately there was a hubbub. People guessing what was going on at home, trying to work out what Dog was doing, wondering where Commander Edwards was. But then Callie stood. She held her arm up for silence, and the room quietened.

"This castle is a mess," she said. "There is a lot that needs to be done to improve it. More than we can do ourselves in a day. We're going to take charge, but we need help."

"What needs doing?" asked Meg. "We'll help."

"We need to sort out the food. We need to clean the communal areas, and it's a nice day, so we'd like to get a load of washing done."

"I think we should sort out the spears and prepare for war," said one of the Castle Goch boys.

"Yes, absolutely. Your little boy jobs. Do those."

There were gasps from Castle Goch. She shrugged.

"And while you're busy, we will focus on making the castle work more efficiently and on making sure that the soldiers are fed and have somewhere to sleep. Because that will make them better fighters. You'd probably like something to eat, I imagine?"

There were nods from a lot of people.

"I don't know whether the archers, watchers, and guards have had much sleep recently. Perhaps you could check that, and some of you could take over from them so they can rest?" She grinned. "Before you prepare for war, that is?"

Non went up to the guard tower again and continued working her way through the books. She felt like she was learning very little, except how much fighting had gone on in this valley over the past thousand years. Also how many of the commanders had had similar names. The reasons for some of the battles weren't even mentioned, and she thought it was sad but interesting how the historians of the battles had just assumed the reasons for them would be obvious. It really didn't seem obvious now.

By midmorning, she had managed to find several mentions of demons, alongside dragonites. Somebody had suggested in the past that the two might be linked, but Non had never even seen a dragonite, so that clearly wasn't the case right now. Still, it felt useful to know that somebody had once had a thought for demons—even if it now only merited a few sentences in the history books.

Non went down to help the others in the castle after lunch. The castle was full of noise, and none of the things she was reading seemed linked to reality. Somehow, all those old battles and leadership struggles seemed like pointless stories or lists of deaths. She kept just thinking about all the things that weren't mentioned—like who was keeping the castles supplied with food while they were fighting the big battles? Like where did the enemy go to the toilet? Like what were the weather conditions? Like what were the people who weren't in the army doing? And what were the demons up to when there was a war?

Callie and Mary were firmly in control of the castle, and Non arrived down just in time to see them issuing a new set of instructions for that afternoon—including a command to leave the castle. A few students hesitated, as though they were going to disagree, but right now the Kintaborel Castle girls were scarier than Dog, and it was clear that sweeping the drawbridge had not been the sort of thing she'd been forbidding.

"It's just covered in dirt," said Callie. "Which would make it slippery if it rains, or the soldiers could skid on it if they're coming back in a rush. Those cobbles too. Make sure there is absolutely no dirt on the cobbles."

The Kintaborel Castle boys were the first to do what they were told, obeying all the commands given by the girls. "I told you they were nice," said Meg. "Very considerate to women. They'll do anything you ask." She smiled to herself then, and Ellie pulled a face.

Within a couple of hours, washing lines had been set up underneath the castle ramparts on the sunny side, and lines of sheets and bedding from the guard towers were drying in the breeze. Other students were washing several loads of soldiers' uniforms and sheets in the moat. The shutters were open in all the windows, and inside floors were being swept, surfaces were being dusted, latrines were being cleaned.

Outside the kitchen, pots of newly planted herbs had appeared, and on either side of the castle gate there were now blue roses. The grazing sheep were being organized and counted, and across the moat a square area of land was being dug up for planting.

There were also now only two adult watchers on the ramparts. The rest had gone to bed, and their places had been taken by serious boys, swaggering with the importance of their role.

"It's silly not having floors in our dormitories," said Mary.

"Especially when the floorboards are just here." She pointed to a shed nobody else had noticed.

In the late afternoon, people had ventured farther out from the castle.

"We need to be realistic," said Callie. "And we are very badly prepared for a siege. We have enough food for a few weeks, but we need to become self-sufficient. We need to chop wood for the fires, and we need to plant vegetables."

"There's not going to be a siege," said Paul. "The demons are a problem, yeah. But they're not exactly an entire Southern army."

"It doesn't matter. Any castle should be ready, at any time, to close its gates and keep its people inside the walls," said Callie. "If we had to do that right now, we'd starve."

"No, we wouldn't," said Paul. "Because we could just climb over the walls and go off to hunt in the woods or something. And if we couldn't climb over the walls, there's bound to be a siege tunnel some-where for smuggling food in and out—like there always is in castles."

"Know where the siege tunnel is, do you?"

"Sure I can find it," muttered Paul.

"Well, it's usually hidden very well—because hiding them from the enemy is the whole point. I'm not convinced that it would be in any better condition than anything in the rest of this castle. If there is one. But after you've found it, do you want to go out and quickly hunt something for us? Get some meat in for us to cure?"

"I'm just saying that I don't think there's a need to do any of this stuff." Paul looked up into the hills, and then at the moat, and anywhere instead of meeting Callie's eyes.

"I don't think we should be relying on the other castles, though, should we? At the moment we're a drain on their resources. And I'd rather not require them to send deliveries here. What do you think?"

A few people glanced at each other then, or deliberately didn't. Because why hadn't they heard from the castles for a while? Was the plague worse than they'd thought? Were people dying at home? Callie's words were very uncomfortable, a reminder of something that nobody wanted to talk about but that everybody was thinking about constantly.

Paul nodded. "Fine. I'll chop wood," he muttered.

———o———

By early evening, the smells of baking bread and stew and, Non thought, maybe even biscuits filled the air. Kintaborel Castle girls patrolled back and forth, ambushing with ruthless efficiency. They drafted everybody into jobs so that things people had never even noticed before were suddenly finished. Doors had been hung on the dormitories, floors laid, bunk beds put together. They marched students up and down the hill to plant potatoes and carrots. Everywhere they battled with mess, fought against poor organization, and attacked the basic living conditions. The transformation they managed in just one day was incredible. Commander Daffy wandered around, occasionally shaking his head and muttering, "Lovely. Lovely."

Then, in the evening, the Kintaborel Castle girls let them rest—after they'd eaten supper, washed up after supper, put the plates away, tidied up the dormitories, and washed in the moat, that is.

Sam and most of Castle Goch went for a run—but only around the castle. Non did a bit of target practice at the same time, but not for long because she felt like Meg and Ellie were laughing at her, or watching her, that they were suspicious of her motives for wanting to practice right at the exact time that Sam was running with his top off. They were right, actually, because Non did like the way his muscles rippled as he ran.

So she went up to sit on the wall above the cliff again. There had been talk from the Kintaborel Castle girls of putting a barrier up to make it safer, but nothing had happened yet, so Non dangled her legs off the edge and watched Castle Goch completing their circuits below. A flock of birds flew up the valley, twisting and curving above the trees, turning in unison at some invisible signal. The red kites were hidden, though—either perching somewhere, nesting somewhere, getting ready to sleep, or away feasting on something dead. There were none of them out in the open. And on the plain below, a lone pacer stood, tethered to a stake in the center of the newly plowed earth. Seeds had just been planted there, and the waving of the demon kept the birds away.

She looked up the valley toward the citadel. It was hard to imagine from this distance what was going on there. The lack of contact couldn't mean anything good, though. She hoped her father was OK, that it was just quarantine within the citadel walls that was preventing contact with them—just precautions, and not that the plague was too bad.

Non opened her mum's notebook and turned to the middle, where the pages were blank. She looked again at her mum's last entry—a set of drawings on the development of the parasite. And then she wrote a title on the next page: *Practical Demonology, by Non.* She underlined it and began.

Chapter 26

Non wrote until she couldn't see the words anymore, and she wrote after that too, forming the letters by feel, desperate to organize the ideas in her head, to try to sort out the contradictory, interesting, new, and old layers of information. And the more she wrote, the more questions she had. There seemed to be so much they had just accepted about demons, taking them for granted as things that were always there, like the grass or the trees or the castles.

But the more she thought about it, the more she was certain that the attack on the way back from the farmstead was an ambush. The position of the attack, but also the numbers of the demons showed that, and maybe the supply cart too? It showed more than just animal intelligence, surely—something the demons weren't supposed to have. Were there demon military commanders, then, who had told them to be there? But also, where were the young demons? If they hatched from eggs, why had she never heard of demon babies? Anything hatching out of those eggs would be a similar size to a human baby—so where were they? And how long did they take to grow?

It was properly dark when Sam came to sit next to her, and for a few minutes she pretended she was still working, suddenly awkward and not sure how to be around him.

"Have you discovered anything interesting?" he said.

"No. Yes." She sighed. "I guess—there's just so much we don't know. Or maybe it's just me. Maybe it's stuff I don't know and can't figure out."

"No, I think it's all of us. I've never thought about demons much before talking to you. The pacers were just always around, you know?"

"I mean, do you know where all the demon babies are?"

"No!" He laughed. "That's a really good question. Mind you, I've never seen a squirrel baby either. Or a snail baby. Don't even know if they come from eggs or whatever."

"Snails do come from eggs. But I think snails are a bit like demons, because they're not definitely male or female. They can be both."

"I always think of demons as being male. Because, you know . . . their bits."

"It's not a proper penis. It's just for urine. They don't reproduce sexually."

"Good to know," said Sam. "Though I definitely didn't think we'd be talking about demon sex when I came up here to see you." For a split second it was awkward again, but then Sam laughed. "I didn't think I'd be lucky enough that we'd be talking about sex at all."

Non grinned. "Not even in snails?"

Without her noticing it happening, somehow her hand was in

his hand, his fingers between hers. His skin was callused from gripping his spear, and she stroked that part with her thumb, the hard ridges catching gently against her nail.

They were quiet. The first stars were up in the sky, though the horizon on the other side of the castle was still bright. There were the soft murmurings of the other students, their voices enclosed by the castle courtyard, the glow of the fire a soft square of yellow in the shadow of the hillside.

He leaned in to kiss her again, his fingers cool against her cheek. His touch was gentle, his lips soft against hers, but then she pulled him closer in answer, and they kissed like that until the Milky Way filled the sky.

She shuddered suddenly with the cold, and he put his arms tightly around her, holding her close. "I don't know how to act when I'm around you in the daytime," she said. The words came out of nowhere and were the sort of thing she'd normally only have confessed to Meg. "I just think I'm a bit of an idiot around you in public."

"You're not an idiot. There's lots of people who are bigger idiots all the time. Do you mean that you're a bit quiet?"

"Maybe." No. She meant that she didn't know where to look, or where to put her hands, or what to say.

"Are you embarrassed to be seen with me?" He pulled away from her, and she felt the cold filling the place where his arms had been.

"No! I think I'm just embarrassed. Definitely not about you. I'm just permanently a bit embarrassed in public."

"Embarrassed about what?"

"Everything."

"Even though nobody cares?"

She reached out for him, and he wrapped his arms round her again, warm, protecting, and comforting. "Oh, look, I'm just apologizing for how I'll be tomorrow. I already know I won't know how to behave when I'm around you. It would be fine if I was alone with you. It's just in front of others. I'm just worried they're watching me."

"They're not watching you. They're just staring into space because they're bored and you happen to be in the way." He added, more quietly, "Does it make it worse if I say nobody cares about you at all? And they're not watching and they're not bothered?"

She laughed. "No. That's harsh, but it makes everything loads better."

"Anyway, I'm going to kiss you and grope you in front of everybody first thing before breakfast tomorrow morning."

"Please don't."

"But that'd give you something to properly worry about, wouldn't it?"

Her teeth were chattering now, but she didn't want to leave the warmth and magic of his arms. They kissed for a few minutes more, but her shivering became too obvious and turned the kissing into laughing.

"Shall I get a blanket?" he said.

"We should probably go down."

"That's not a no. You're worrying about what people will think if they see me going to get a blanket to share with you, aren't you?"

"Yes." She laughed. It was so true. Somehow kissing on the wall was much more respectable than kissing under a blanket on the wall.

She was just about to tell him that and turn it into a joke when she saw movement from across the valley.

"Wait," she said, pointing.

Up on the hillside, a line of lights had appeared. Sam glanced up to alert the watchers, but they'd already seen, and several were now standing on the guard tower facing the church. As before, the lights were evenly spaced and moving slowly as they crept along in the same direction, shimmering and flickering as they went behind bushes or leaves. But this time, there were around twenty of them.

Non thought they were heading toward the church, higher up along the brow of the hill, above the abandoned village. When they'd gone scouting around there, there hadn't been anything of interest up in that part of the hillside—though they hadn't looked closely, because they'd been too busy running away. Non tried to remember what she'd seen from the top of the church tower, but she'd been looking for escape routes, for danger. Maybe there had been something there—something that might not be of interest from a military perspective but might be of interest to demons. Or others.

There was a distant shriek, and Non flinched. But it was just a night bird, hidden somewhere in the darkness.

"What are they?" asked Sam.

Non took a deep breath before she answered. "It's from the children's story. You know. They light the way for a funeral. Seeing them shows that a death is going to happen."

He was silent for a moment. "Have you seen them here before?"

"Yes. I think . . ." The watchers muttered something to each other and pointed down to the plain. "I think they come every night."

Chapter 27

"Did you get all your studying done last night?" asked Meg.

"I did some," said Non. "What did you get up to?"

"Oh, we just sat around chatting. It was quite relaxing really, wasn't it, Ellie?"

"No. Non, most of the male population of the castle sat around staring at Meg and sighing. It was really stressful. It was like sitting in a circle of sad wood-lions."

"No, they didn't. It was fine!" Meg tossed back her hair, and a couple of the Kintaborel Castle boys slumped farther against the walls.

"Ugh. When do you think we can go home?" asked Ellie. "I am so sick of it here."

"You're not actually sick, though, are you?" Meg asked pointedly.

"No. No." Ellie pouted and leaned back against the wall. "I know I should be grateful, and I am. I just worry about everybody back home, and I'd rather be there. I know we're still better off here, though. I just really, really hope everybody's OK in the citadel, that's all."

"Yeah. Me too," said Meg.

Ellie sighed. "Why do you think loads of demons have appeared at the same time as the plague? You don't think it's connected, do you?"

"Ugh, no! Demons can't grow that quickly. And please don't look for other things to worry about! We don't need more!" said Meg, and Ellie smiled. "They're probably just taking advantage of the fact that there are fewer people around to come out from the hills."

Non looked up for Sam. As usual, he was sitting in among the Castle Goch boys, but he caught her eye as she looked at him and winked. She smiled back and looked away.

"Right. Good morning," said Commander Edwards, sauntering into the courtyard. A number of people frowned or raised their eyebrows, but he didn't acknowledge their surprise at seeing him. "It's lovely weather today for a bit of target practice. And also a run. Bit of exercise." He yawned. "We've got one or two demons I'd like you to get rid of, maybe after breakfast. I'll be back for you in five minutes. Be ready."

"Commander, breakfast isn't here yet," called somebody.

"Oh. Then let's go now. We can get it out of the way before we start the day." He gave a casual wave of his hand, as though he was suggesting merely nipping out to buy a loaf of bread.

"Archery first. All of you fetch your bows and get on the wall."

There was a scurry as people ran off to find their things. Nobody thought this would be quick. Everybody remembered that time a few of them had been asked to just go and gather a few things from the farmstead, or the time before that when the students were told to go out and have a little look for "things of interest" in the valley. They assumed this would be the same sort of highly dangerous, lengthy mission.

When the Kintaborel Castle girls arrived with a steaming cauldron of porridge, Commander Edwards turned to them and said, "Ah. Callie, Mary, no need for you to join us, unless you'd like to, that is? An excellent stew last night. Love what you've done with the place. Keep doing it. Can you keep the porridge warm for a few minutes? We're just going to kill some demons."

Callie and Mary nodded. And then they turned to stagger down the hill with the heavy cauldron again.

"I think we'll go to the section over the gate, where the wall is lower," he said. "Might make it a little easier."

The portcullis was down, the gate still shut, and as each person climbed up onto the wall, they gasped or paused at what they saw on the plain. Non was toward the back of the group, so she had time to imagine what it was they could see. She didn't have to think very hard.

The early-morning mist clung to the valley bottom, layering the world with a glistening white softness and concealing everything but the telltale invading smell of mushrooms and decay. Fog patches drifted slowly across from the river to weave in and out of the bushes surrounding the castle, and Non could just see the outlines of the motionless shapes coming in and out of focus—a deeper darkness within the hazy, shifting world.

There were ten, maybe twenty, or perhaps even thirty deathly statues standing sentry outside the walls. They were facing the walls with their terrible eyes.

The otherworldly call of the red kites was the only noise, harsh and cutting in the stillness of the valley. The birds already filled the branches overhanging the demons, and Non wondered how it was that they could sense impending death. How did they know that the demons would bring them a feast?

"It's these I'd like you to get rid of," said Commander Edwards. "It's the ideal opportunity to test your shooting skills and, while it's a bit tricky with the mist, they're also not moving at the moment.

"Use as many arrows as you need. Somebody can go down and fetch them later."

Meg raised her eyebrows at Non. "That's the sort of thing that crazy Castle Goch boy would do. Sam, the one you like."

"What?" said Non, looking over at Sam.

Meg grinned. "I knew it! You've basically admitted it now! Well anyway, you can ask him to fetch the arrows for us."

The eyes of the demons were moving, Non could see—without eyelids, they couldn't conceal the direction of their glance. They were looking back and forth at the line of students, just as the students were looking at them. Seeing so many of them in one go, Non could see how they were different from one another—not just in height, but in face shape and even color. Some of them did seem to be slightly darker than others, or they had broader chests or more muscular arms. The pacer, tied to his stake as a scarecrow, was facing the castle in the same pseudothreatening way, even though there was little he could do to harm anybody.

"Our pacers are there," shouted Jane. "Don't hurt our pacers."

Commander Edwards gave her a long look. "Would somebody from Castle Goch care to point out the pacers, just in case it's not obvious to everybody else?"

"Stubs is the scarecrow," said Jane. "Then Elizabeth is over there, and Poppet over there." She pointed at the two opposite ends of the plain. In comparison to the other demons, Non could see that Elizabeth and Poppet looked a bit raggedy. Their muscles were less defined; they also seemed to slouch and, she may have been imagining it, but their eyes seemed to watch the castle and the students without the intelligence she could see from the others.

The demons were in range, that's true. But they were also slightly too far away for a kill to be a guarantee—if anybody managed to hit them. Non thought it more likely that they'd injure the demons and enrage them.

"Raise your crossbows," called Commander Edwards. "And . . . fire at will."

There was something genuinely disturbing about the silence and lack of movement from the demons. Partially concealed by the mist, they seemed almost unreal, lacking in substance, part of a mystical dream world. But then they would emerge from a patch of the spiderweb cloud, and you could see that they were all too unpleasantly real, with their stretched, grinning mouths and long, powerful claws.

There was a soft *woomph* as the first arrows were released, but from where Non was standing, she couldn't see that anything had been hit. She positioned her bow carefully, lining the arrow up and squinting with each eye in turn to check her aim.

There was the metallic twang of more arrows being released from around her, but Non focused on a thinner demon several feet beyond the moat and slightly to her right. As she delayed, another student's arrow hit the demon's shoulder, and his body seemed to flinch backward as though with pain—though she knew it could also just be the force of the arrow strike. She took one last squinting look and, aiming straight for the head, she pressed her trigger.

He crumpled gently, slowly falling to the ground. The red kites immediately leaped down onto the carcass, hopping onto the exposed flesh and pecking cautiously. *How could they tell he was properly dead?* Non wondered. *What was so different about him now?*

"Did you get that one?" asked Meg, pointing at her dead demon.

"Yeah." Non nodded.

"Well done."

Meg raised her crossbow again, but she did so slowly and with a glance at Commander Edwards.

"I don't like this. Do you?" whispered Non.

"No. The whole thing's really weird," whispered Meg. "It feels really strange. Like they're inviting us to kill them."

"I don't think they'd do that, though, would they?"

There were lots of arrows down on the plain now. Quite a few of them feet away from the nearest demon. The students weren't shooting their best, and there were only six or so bodies on the ground. The whole situation felt very uncomfortable.

"Right," called Commander Edwards. "Time for breakfast, I think. Though that was pretty rubbish. Well done, those of you who've hit a target, but it did take you a while, didn't it? Those of you who've managed to kill one, I expect you to be working on improving your speed this week. Those of you who didn't hit the target, and I know who you are, you need to come and see me after the lesson, because you've got some serious work to do or, you know, you'll probably die.

"The enemy are not behaving in a . . . normal . . . way today. They don't usually stand around and let you shoot them." He laughed joylessly. "Normally, they're going to be moving toward you, fast, trying to kill you, so, yes, it's nice of them to stand still . . . but I don't think we should relax. Do you?"

Chapter 28

Non didn't feel like she wanted to eat her breakfast. But she also felt like she should eat whenever she had the opportunity to do so, because food was precious right now. The porridge was claggy in her throat, and it didn't sit right in her stomach when she swallowed. There was a hush in the castle courtyard as people ate, and nobody quite knew what to say or do. Meg leaned her head against Non's shoulder, but she wasn't really doing anything or saying anything, just methodically eating her breakfast too.

Even Callie and Mary seemed to move more quietly, and Non noticed that they'd managed to find time to arrange their hair beautifully again—though their skirts remained shorter, and their shoes stained.

She looked over for Sam, and he was sitting in the same place he'd been earlier—a few minutes ago. Was it really only a few minutes? He'd finished his breakfast already and was listening to something one of his friends was saying, but his leg was restless, and he was tapping his foot lightly against the flagstone floor. For a moment Non worried about people watching her, but then she also remembered the demons watching outside. And that worried her more. She gave

Meg's hair a stroke. "I'm just off for a minute," she said. Then she stood up and walked over to Sam.

"Sam, will you come with me?"

"Where?"

"Back up to the wall. I want to look at the demons again."

He sighed dramatically, but he was smiling underneath. "Of *course* you want to see them again!"

"I've got an idea and I want to do something."

"Yeah. OK." He stood up.

"It's a bit silly . . ."

"Is it?" He raised his eyebrows at her.

"Maybe not," she whispered.

———o———

When they climbed up again, the mist had cleared, and several watchers were lining the ramparts, their binoculars raised to scan the valley—Commander Edwards among them. He saw both Sam and Non arrive but said nothing, returning to frown at the forest. The demons had mostly moved back to the protection of the trees, standing beneath branches that would shield them from arrows, but many remained in sight. Non wondered how many more were hidden there or up in the hills.

The pacer was still tethered to its post, and it waved its arms feebly again, growling half-heartedly at nothing in particular. The ground around it was trampled now by many feet—though the seeds planted yesterday were probably safe, as the only birds nearby seemed to be the many red kites perching in the trees. They were still there, waiting, their eyes watching the plain; they hadn't had their feast yet.

"Where have the bodies gone?" asked Non. Commander Edwards looked over, and she lowered her voice. "There were six kills, I think? Weren't there?"

"I didn't see exactly," said Sam. "Was it the dead bodies you wanted to look at?"

"No. But dead demon bodies aren't that easy to get rid of. I speak from experience."

Sam started shaking with laughter, so that this time all the watchers looked over too.

"Commander," he said, in between laughs, "where are the dead demon bodies? They're hard to move, apparently."

The corners of Commander Edwards's mouth twitched. "They are hard to move, aren't they? Interestingly, we're not quite sure. They seem to have been removed by the other demons, which is something they do occasionally. The other demons eat them, apparently."

This information was definitely not mentioned in any of the books Non had read.

"What do you two want?" asked Commander Edwards.

"Non?" Sam gestured to her.

"Um." It definitely sounded crazy right now. But then, so did the world. "I want to mark some of the demons with ink so I can track their movements."

Commander Edwards narrowed his eyes at her, but it wasn't an angry look. "Ah, Non the demon studier. How are you going to do that?"

"Shoot them with arrows that have ink pellets attached?"

"All right. Have you got the ink?"

"Yes." She held out a couple of cartridges.

"Give them here. I'll do it. Which demons do you want?"

"Whichever ones you can get. But I need a distinctive ink pattern."

He smiled and stuck the first ink cartridge onto an arrow. He loaded it into his crossbow, aimed, and fired. The arrow looped into the air, spinning, its course uneven with the extra weight of the ink. The demon he was aiming for had time to see the arrow and flinched out of the way. The arrow caught on a branch and fell to the ground uselessly, its ink leaking out onto the grass.

Why were the demons moving away from the arrows now? What had changed?

Commander Edwards stuck another ink cartridge onto an arrow and passed a second cartridge to the watcher next to him. Both men loaded their crossbows at the same time, pointed at the demon, and fired. This time, both arrows hit, the cartridges on their tips exploding, covering the chest of the demon in black. The monster looked down in confusion as both arrows fell to the floor, having barely broken the skin, and he rubbed at his chest, smearing the ink in and spreading it to his hands.

"Distinctive enough for you?" asked Commander Edwards.

"Yes, thanks," said Non, though she could see that his lips were twitching with laughter.

They got another two demons—one all over its head, and one on its left thigh.

"Is three enough?"

"Yes," said Non. "I think so."

"Is there anything else you two want?"

"No," said Non. "It's just . . . do you know how many demons there are?"

"Quite a few more than we thought," Commander Edwards said.

"It's just . . ." Non said, and several of the watchers turned to her and the commander. "It's just, shouldn't we know exactly how many there are?"

Commander Edwards narrowed his eyes.

"I mean, if demons can't reproduce without killing a human, doesn't it mean that we should be able to tell exactly how many there are because of how many humans are dead? And we'll know that if we add up the totals from the castles, won't we?"

He nodded slowly.

"And then, don't the military manuals all say that soldiers have to report how many demons have been killed? So if we just do the math for the past seventy years, we should be able to work it out exactly."

"You're right, of course. We should be able to do that. Except you're forgetting one crucial thing. We have no idea how many of our enemies were taken: the Southerners, the Northerners. When we were at war with them, we didn't know if the demons took any of them, and I guess our enemies couldn't tell either. Looking at the numbers of demons now—well, there are more than the people who've been taken from just our castles. Whole armies of people marched through here to attack us, but while we were safe inside the walls, they were out here in their flimsy little tents holding us under siege."

"So there could be hundreds of demons?" asked Non.

"There could be," said Commander Edwards. "Any further questions?"

Non paused. Several of the soldiers had moved closer too. "Well . . . shouldn't we still be able to tell, roughly, based on how much food they're eating? Because they hunt, don't they? So why can't we tell based on the animal population and how that's changed over the past few decades?"

"What do you feed the pacers?" Commander Edwards turned to Sam.

"They eat anything we eat. Though they prefer uncooked meat. They do hunt, but they also eat slops like you'd feed pigs, so, like, oats and vegetables and stuff. I don't think they'd eat each other. And when one of them has died, the others haven't eaten the body. They've sniffed at it and had a look, but they haven't done anything with it."

"So they could eat vegetation too."

"Yeah. And oh," said Sam, "they sometimes stand in the rivers and catch fish. They're quite good at that, actually."

"Does that tell you anything?" asked Commander Edwards.

"No," said Non. "I don't think so. I think . . . it makes me wonder where they all go, though?"

Nobody said anything, but they kept looking at her. So she continued.

"Where are they? The other day on the cart it was an attack, like a troop of them. But we won that, even though we almost didn't. And today they've deliberately let themselves be killed—five or six of them. In the past few days, that means I've seen more demons than I thought existed in total, but there must be even more, because they'd only risk attacking us if they have a whole army to spare."

"Unless they're getting desperate," said Sam.

"What?" Non frowned.

"Well, unless they're getting desperate? We haven't been at war with a human enemy for decades, which means that most of the demons must be old—they don't have battle casualties to make into new demons."

"You two," said Commander Edwards, "go to the guard tower and write me some more questions. Answer some of those questions. Read some books. Look at maps. Find out where they could be." Then he pointed to one of the soldiers. "You."

"Sir."

"Let's track those dead bodies."

Chapter 29

Non took all the books off the shelves. She was sure that there must be some useful information in them somewhere—or what was the point of them? They seemed to take up more space on the table than when they were on the shelves, and she started by arranging them around her, like a little fort of words with knowledge trapped inside.

She sorted them out so the ones she'd already read were on one side and the ones she hadn't yet looked at were on the other, then she placed her notebook open neatly in front of her and her pens and cartridges next to that. She had no idea where to begin or what to begin with.

"You're really pretty when you're reading," said Sam. "It's really . . . exotic?" He frowned. "Yeah. Exotic. I've never seen anybody read so much before."

She grinned and shook her head. "I haven't started yet. It feels like there's so much to do and not enough that we know."

"Well, just treat it like you're going for a long run."

She raised her eyebrows at him.

"It feels impossible at the beginning, but you just put one foot in front of the other at a steady, slow pace, without thinking about how far you've got to go. And then, about halfway through, you can see how far you've come, which spurs you on to run more. The last bit is hard because you're tired, but you keep going because the finish is in sight. And then you've done it, and you feel amazing."

"So the main reason you go for a run is because it feels amazing when you stop?"

"Yeah." He wrinkled his nose as he smiled. "Yeah, I suppose so."

He unwrapped the maps of the valley. There were several older ones, their edges uneven and crumbling away, and he laid them out delicately on the table; the newer maps were neater, more professional and detailed, but they covered only the areas around the three main castles. He laid them out on the table too and stood, staring at all of them, looking up occasionally at the valley drawings on the walls. Sometimes he went to add something to the images in chalk.

They read like that for a while—maybe an hour—before Commander Daffy came in. He opened the door so quietly, Non didn't notice him at first, so afterward she didn't know how long he'd been there. There wasn't a smile on his face this time, and without it she almost didn't recognize him, his cheeks wrinkled and sagging with surplus skin. She wouldn't have noticed him if she'd passed him on the street—he was just one of those generic older white men, the sort who all looked the same. But he beamed when he noticed her looking, and his face seemed to shape itself again into what looked like a more natural position, the wrinkles and sagging gone.

Sam spoke first. "Commander Daffy, we've been sent up here to look for more information about the demons and any sieges in this castle. Do you know where we should look?"

"Oh, how interesting!" said the commander, and he widened his eyes so that the skin on his face stretched even farther, now perfectly smooth. "That sounds like super fun. I don't think I can help you, though." He put his head to one side sympathetically. "You're Castle Goch anyway, aren't you? So I should have thought it would be a bit tricky for you to manage lots of words."

"Yes, it is." Sam and Commander Daffy both smiled. "Which is why I'm looking at the maps and Non's reading the books."

The tiniest wrinkle appeared between Commander Daffy's eyebrows, but then it was gone again, and his smile seemed even wider. "Maps, eh? Well, I'm in charge of those—for my sins." He laughed—jolly and infectious, so that Non found herself smiling too, though she wasn't sure why. "There's not much useful there, I'm afraid. And the scale is very strange on some of them. Very strange indeed."

"Yes, I am finding that. They don't really match, do they?"

"Not at all. Not at all!" Commander Daffy walked round the table and idly picked up one of the books from Non's pile, opening it to a random page.

"I'm wondering, sir, if this is all of the maps, or if maybe there are some other bits somewhere?" Sam asked. "Some of these older maps seem to be in fragments. And did nobody make any maps last century, or the century before?"

"It's a bit of a mystery, yes." Commander Daffy pulled a face and closed his book, tucking it under his arm. "There are sections missing—but where they are, I'm afraid I don't know. My guess is rats have nibbled at the edges. Squeak, squeak, squeak!" He raised his hands and twitched his nose as though pretending to be a rodent.

Sam smiled politely but continued. "I can't see that farmstead marked anywhere. And I also can't see the church—which is strange."

"I know!" said the commander. "We're trying to repair what we can and find out as much as we can. But it's a good thing people like you are here to help us, isn't it? If you do find anything useful, make sure to note it down for us. How lovely!" His smile returned to normal, and he looked at Non too this time. "What about you, sweetheart? Have you found anything interesting?"

Non shook her head.

"Oh, that is a shame. Well, let me know if you do or if I can help you in any way."

With one last smile, he walked out the door, still clutching the book from Non's pile. She hadn't read it yet—but then there were a lot of others she hadn't made it to either. It had a red leather cover, which was worn either with age or use—probably age—and she reminded herself to have a look at it later.

Suddenly there was noise outside.

The window shutters were open wide. Through them came the anxious shouts of the other students and, occasionally, Commander Edwards's lazy drawl. His voice was louder than it felt when you were near him, but even from the distance of the guard tower he was managing to give the impression that nothing more than a relaxing picnic or tennis match was happening outside.

"I think he's sending out the ones who didn't manage to hit a demon," said Sam, moving over to the window. "Yeah. He is. He's actually a complete psychopath, isn't he?"

"What!"

"Yeah, they're running back and forth fetching the arrows. They're on this side of the moat, but they're completely terrified."

Non stood up and went to the window. There was no danger to the students, she could see that. A couple of demons had moved from beneath the trees and were watching, but they'd moved only a few inches, still staying well out of the range of the arrows. The other students were on the wall, their bows trained on the demons, ready to fire if they should get closer. But even from here, Non could see that several of the bows were shaking as the students, white-faced, tried to focus on defending their friends.

Meg and Chris were among the ones running on the plain, but the other students from the citadel were up on the wall above. Commander Edwards was standing on the drawbridge, casually leaning on his spear, though Non could see that his grip was secure, and she was sure he knew the location of every single demon under every single tree. Meg's face was crumpled in terror, her movements erratic and panicky. She was running back and forth picking up any arrow she happened to stumble across rather than standing still and searching for them one by one. She bent down to pick one up, but her fingers were clumsy and she dropped the others she was holding so that she had to bend and pick them all up again, fumbling and desperate. Non saw that her mouth was open in a sob.

"What is wrong with him?" she said. "Oh, Meg!" She covered her face with her hands so she didn't have to look, but then she looked anyway because she couldn't not.

The students on the wall above were just as panicky. Paul's face was frozen in a frown of concentration, his bow scanning back and forth along the tree line. Becky was crouching down, steadying her arm on her knee, her bow trained on one of the closest demons.

"Great," Commander Edwards called as a soldier collected the arrows from the students. There was a pause as everybody waited for what he was going to say next, though all of them must have known. "Now get the ones on the other side of the moat."

Non covered her face with her hands again, and Sam put his arm around her waist. She leaned into him, and the strength of his body made her feel weak.

"I can't watch," she said. "Oh, Meg! He's a terrible person."

"Yes, he is. But we also can't waste arrows. Where are we going to get new ones from? There's nowhere to make the arrowheads in this castle."

She shook him away.

"I'm sorry. That wasn't the right thing to say, was it? Do you want me to go down and get the arrows instead of her? I don't mind. I'll do that if you want?" He was biting his thumbnail, his other hand tapping on the windowsill even as he gripped it. He was wired with energy again, his body taut and ready for running.

Non shook her head and sighed. "Meg said you should be the one to do it. That you'd be crazy enough."

"It's not crazy. Not if you've got everything set up so you can't fail."

"Edwards *is* crazy, though, isn't he?"

"Absolutely. And I'm sorry," he said again.

"It's not you who should be sorry," muttered Non. Meg and the other students were sticking close to the moat, but they were working more sensibly now. Meg was no longer running erratically but looking from arrow to arrow. She had a bunch already in one hand—almost too many to carry. Several of the demons had moved, inching closer to the running students, but none of them had yet moved enough so that they were within range of the arrows. Non could see that the students on the wall were more organized too, and between them they now had each of the demons targeted. She reached out for Sam's hand, and they watched for another few moments until Commander Edwards sent the students back over the draw-bridge again.

Non turned to Sam. "I don't think I've learned anything all morning. What's he going to do to us if he thinks we're wasting time?"

Sam leaned forward quickly and kissed her. "Now no time has been wasted."

"Oh, help!" Non smiled despite herself. "I think this is the most stressed I've ever been."

"No regrets," said Sam. "And one foot in front of the other."

They worked steadily until midafternoon. If there was lunch, then nobody came to call for them, and Non didn't want to remind Commander Edwards they were still there until she had something to report. Sam had filled in the gaps on the walls with chalk drawings—though many of them had question marks or arrows over them. Most of Non's books were now back on the shelves.

He sighed and stretched. "What are you doing?"

"I'm making a time line of the main times we've been at war. Roughly. And then I'm trying to see if that corresponds with a rise in demon numbers a couple of decades later."

"And does it?"

Non paused, because it was a big thing to say. But there did seem to be a pattern, even if a couple of books were missing—more than just that red one Commander Daffy had taken. It wasn't a very clear pattern, because the demons rarely seemed to attack all at once, more just here and there. And the official military records didn't seem to bother mentioning them in a formal way, so she was looking only for occasional references. Yet those references did seem to increase a few decades after one of the castles had been held under siege or there'd been a big battle. One of the books suggested that regular "demon culls" were necessary, because the herd was getting "out of hand."

She nodded. "I think so. What about you?"

"Well, there's a lot of problems with the maps. The commander's right. The scales don't match, and I don't think any of them are accurate. I'm having to guess a lot. There are quite a few places the demons could hide. We've got seven more abandoned villages in the valley, and we know they do use human houses sometimes because they used this castle for a bit, didn't they? But I think we're looking for somewhere bigger and more permanent. I think they must live underground, because otherwise somebody would have noticed them at some point."

"Maybe somebody did. Maybe they just got killed and couldn't tell us."

"Yeah. Probably. Can you tell where the most demon attacks have happened?"

"No. I looked for that. But all the castles have lost people. I think . . . it might be this castle, though, if it's anywhere."

"That's what I was thinking. Most of the battles have been around here, as the armies make their way up the valley."

"And this is the only castle that's been abandoned because of demon attacks."

"It wasn't abandoned because of demon attacks. It was abandoned because there were too many enemies to fight at once."

"One of which was the demons. I can't find that book, though, the one that would give us that information. It must be somewhere, because Commander Daffy knew about the history of this castle, but there's nothing here."

But it wasn't until she'd almost finished looking through all the books that the real breakthrough came. She'd left the book until the end, because it was one they had at home, in her dad's study. It wasn't particularly special—just a slim volume outlining the main health problems in the valley. There was canker, obviously, and details of the sporadic cholera outbreaks faced by the castles—the leper colonies, some of the ailments of childbirth, fever, stomach complaints. And both types of plague: the rash and fever, and the milder stomach cramps and diarrhea—as well as the years in which they'd struck. Though she'd seen the book many times and had even glanced through it on a couple of occasions, she'd never thought of its significance. Even as a guide for the plague and how to treat it, it was of little use.

But when compared against the military data, the information about the battles, the trends in demon numbers, the plague years also fit into the pattern. It wasn't an exact pattern, and the numbers didn't quite work—but there was no doubt there was a pattern, and it was a repeating cycle that had occurred time and time again. For a few years, demon numbers would be low, and no attacks would be mentioned in the chronicles—or very few. Then there would be a battle, a war against somebody, and demon numbers would spike a couple of decades later. The chronicles would report demons as being a problem and a worry, and the humans would start working together to defeat them. At around about this time, plague would also normally strike the castles—all three of them—making a coordinated military response to the demons more difficult. It wasn't quite how she'd meant it, but Ellie had been right.

"Sam. Sam!" she said. "I think you should get Commander Edwards now."

Chapter 30

But Commander Edwards wasn't there. Dog wasn't there. Commander Daffy *was* there, but there didn't seem much point in talking to him. So Sam and Non went to the castle wall to stare down at the demons staring up at them, because it's what most of the other students were doing.

Meg was surrounded by a number of young men. She had a blanket over her legs and a range of treats—apples, biscuits, barley sugar—and she was chatting away prettily. As soon as she saw Non, though, she pushed the blanket up and stood, going straight over for a hug.

"We saw what happened," said Non. "Are you OK?"

"Yeah," said Meg, though she held her hug for longer than normal. "I think I might go and do a bit of target practice in a bit, though. It's inspiring me to think about improving my technique. Or getting a technique, actually." She grinned.

"I can't believe Commander Edwards made you do that," said Non.

"I think I fancy him a bit, you know," whispered Meg. "He's just so mean and manly." Her eyes were wide and excited.

"Meg, No!" said Non. "Just, NO!"

"He's not conventionally handsome, I admit. And he's not the type I normally go for . . ."

"Oh my God."

"But one of the Kintaborel Castle boys has started writing me poetry, Non. Poetry! Commander Edwards would never do that." She sighed.

Sam was already holding a spear, idly running his finger over the sharp tip while he chatted with some of the Castle Goch boys. They were gesturing to the demons and, Non guessed, discussing their locations.

"Where have you been? Ellie said you were studying again. Studying with that Castle Goch boy who can't read anything. I can't imagine what the two of you must've been doing."

Non didn't blush this time. She just shrugged. "He was looking at maps to try and figure out where all the demons go. I was trying to see if there's any patterns in the numbers of demons in the valley."

Meg hugged her again. "I absolutely love you. You're awesome. I bet there are patterns, aren't there?"

"I think so."

"That means yes."

But saying it out loud to Meg made Non feel less confident in what she'd seen. It was only in the books. It was only numbers. It was only guesses. *Was* it even real? Non was too twitchy to watch out for Commander Edwards and Dog, so they went back up to the dormitory so Meg could brush her hair. Non thought she might like to brush her own hair too, maybe just check she looked OK. There were a few others already up there—one or two trying to catch up on sleep—but Cath, Callie, and Becky were also there chatting.

As they walked in, a hush fell.

"Shall we walk back out again?" offered Meg. "If we were interrupting?"

"No!" said Mary. "We weren't talking about you—but about what happened. To you. It was horrible."

"I'm fine." Meg waved her hand casually, but the dimples were back in her smile, and Non could see the other girls were already making her feel better. "They're just all a bit crazy, the commanders, aren't they?"

"So crazy!" agreed Callie, and the others nodded. "We were wondering if that's why they've been posted to this castle—to get them away from the normal castles?"

They all smiled.

"I should think so," said Meg. "That makes loads of sense. Except Commander Daffy. He's normal, isn't he? At least—he doesn't strike me as being completely insane, which is what I'm measuring him against with the other two."

"He's rubbish as a military leader, though, isn't he?" said Becky.

"Yes, I can't imagine him either leading or doing anything military," said Meg. "Napping seems to be his main skill."

Non wasn't entirely sure he was sane either, but at least his weirdness wasn't as obvious as in the others.

"How do you think he passed all of the military tests?" asked Becky. "I'm not being rude, but are the tests easier if you're from Kintaborel?"

"We'll not take that as being rude," said Callie. "But our other leaders are very good—the ones back in our own castle—so I don't think so. He does come back there and always corrects people if they don't give him his full title of commander, so I always thought that was an important thing, but Dog doesn't seem to care about rank."

"No," said Becky. "But maybe that's because she's just so good at what she does that the job title is obvious?"

"I wouldn't want to hang out with her in the mess room, though. Or Commander Edwards," said Meg. "They're both a little bit too good at being military—like killing is a lifestyle choice for them rather than just being part of the job. I reckon you're right, Callie, that's why they're all here. This castle, far away from the others and broken, is somewhere where the military can be a bit unusual, or rubbish, and nobody would notice what they were up to."

"Or care," agreed Callie.

"Except now," muttered Non, and everybody looked at her. She shrugged and spoke a bit more loudly. "Now they do notice, because we're all here."

Non also felt too twitchy *not* to watch out for Commander Edwards and Dog, so after a bit she found herself back at the front of the castle again, on the wall and watching over the plain. For an hour or so, there was nothing, but then the red kites flew into the air suddenly, startled, their wings momentarily clumsy, the angle of their flight forced and awkward, though they quickly righted themselves and swooped higher, swift and buoyant again.

A unit of soldiers emerged from the trees. They were running along the track that came from the citadel, but their boots and legs were spattered with dark mud, and several seemed to be wet up to their waists. It was possible that some of the stains on their trousers were not from mud, were deeper and richer, but Non couldn't be sure. Commander Edwards led the group, his running pace steady and practiced. Non realized this was the first time she'd seen him properly moving, and it looked like he was barely out of breath. He stopped as they got to the drawbridge, and he waved the other soldiers on.

"You and you." He pointed to Non and Sam. "Report to the guard tower, now."

———o———

The room was already packed when Non and Sam arrived, many of the soldiers examining the walls where Sam had filled the spaces with drawings.

Dog stepped forward. "We are well supplied in terms of food and can remain on full rations this week, but I expect to be halving rations next week if we don't receive any more reinforcements. All supply routes remain under attack, and, combined with the medical situations in each of the other castles, we have to expect no contact in the near future. We are working on the basis that we are isolated and must assume we may need to be self-sufficient for a time."

There was no reaction from anybody in the room. It was clear this message was not a surprise to them. It wasn't truly a surprise to even Non or Sam—though hearing Dog say it out loud felt very uncomfortable.

"We are outnumbered many times over by the demon forces," she continued. "Best estimates are five demons to every soldier."

"They're not considering the students, then?" Sam whispered.

"That would still mean we're outnumbered," said Non. She didn't add that the students weren't very good at fighting.

"But we have weapons and they don't."

"You two. The students. What did you find out?" said Commander Edwards, nodding at the walls.

Sam stepped forward. Knowing him better now, Non could see that he was nervous—but she could only tell because he was almost overcompensating for it. His back was too straight, his walk too confident, his voice too loud.

"I don't have anything definite," he said. "Except that we think most of the demon attacks over the centuries have probably been around this castle, or lower down the valley instead of around the three big castles. That's the only way they could have hidden their numbers. There are lots of places the demons could hide or be living in the valley, but nowhere permanent that we've been able to find. And I think there probably *is* somewhere permanent, and big, because there must be somewhere secure they take the humans who go to them, and also somewhere they raise their babies.

"So I think we're looking for somewhere underground—probably caves. We're looking for somewhere around this castle, or maybe lower down the valley, because these are the areas that aren't mapped so well."

The room was completely silent, then Dog spoke. "Interesting. We should be able to identify it because there would be a high concentration of demon movement. Can anyone think of anywhere that fits that description?"

A few people spoke to each other, but Non already knew there were quite a few areas round the castle that had a lot of demon movement. Nobody offered a suggestion publicly.

Commander Daffy unfurled a couple of the maps and, balancing them both awkwardly, checked them against Sam's drawings. He wasn't smiling now, and his mouth was partly open in concentration.

"You," said Commander Edwards, pointing at Non. She felt her throat tightening immediately, the room now a blur of heads—too warm, her legs and arms heavy and awkward. She opened her mouth, but nothing came out.

"There's no time for shyness," said Dog with a tut. "Hurry up and speak."

Non opened her mouth again. The blur of heads was still staring at her.

"Come on, girl!" said Dog, tutting again impatiently. Sam smiled encouragingly.

Non took a deep breath and started explaining what she'd noticed. It was a gabble of words to start off with, and she spoke very quickly—she knew she did. But people nodded, and they did listen. Nobody looked at her as though what she was saying was stupid—and she knew it wasn't. She knew she'd discovered something important, but at the same time there was still that self-doubt—that feeling that maybe she was just making a fuss or being a silly little girl.

There was silence for a few moments after she spoke, aside from the slide of paper on wood as Commander Daffy removed books from the shelves to check her information. Then Dog stepped forward again.

"Plague and demon attacks are linked, eh?" She raised her eyebrows. "Well, based on what we're living through, that doesn't seem like an implausible idea." There was scattered laughter in the room, but it felt respectful, positive. She looked directly at Non. "We'll send a message to the other castles as soon as the next supply cart comes and get that link investigated."

The people in the room nodded, and Non felt herself relaxing. She'd shared something important, but it was somebody else's problem now.

"Right. Next. Six carcasses were removed from the plain this morning," said Dog. "We were able to track the demons removing the bodies over some distance, and they seem to have been heading toward the citadel, perhaps up to a location on the valley side. They became aware that we were following them and must have become scared, because they dropped all the bodies and separated into the woods. We gave up following at that point and returned."

"Was there anything unusual about their behavior? Anything else to report?" asked Commander Edwards.

"Other than that they were carrying the bodies? No. They had a definite direction in mind and were more focused on heading there than avoiding detection. I suggest we prioritize scouting round the area tomorrow—in particular to see if there are any caves."

Commander Edwards nodded. There was silence in the room for a moment while everybody reflected on what had been said. Then he turned to Non and Sam. "What do you think?"

All eyes were on Non again, and for a moment she thought about being anxious. But there was also an idea stirring within her, an exciting but horrible idea. And for a moment that emotion took over. "Where . . . did they drop the bodies?"

"In the woods, right about where the terrain was about to become more steep. In a ditch."

"A ditch?"

"A small stream, perhaps." Dog looked at a couple of the soldiers, and they nodded. "A stream," she confirmed.

"Did . . . the water from the stream run into the river? For our moat?"

Dog frowned. "Yes, it did, didn't it? We had to wade through it."

Non took a deep breath. "I don't know this. I haven't tested, we haven't looked at the water, and I'm only guessing."

The room was silent.

"But . . . it's the rest of the information, isn't it? The type of plague we have now seems to match exactly with the times when demon numbers are highest and so the castles were starting to fight against them. I think they're poisoning the water to the castles."

The room was deathly silent. Her voice sounded strange and croaky. When she had been speaking, she realized, she had been forgetting to breathe regularly. So now she needed to pant to catch her breath, like she had been running in a race. She put her hand over her mouth to try and cover that up.

"Go on," said Dog. Commander Daffy took another few books down off the shelves and started leafing through them.

"Well . . . we don't know how the plague is spread. We know the symptoms, and that's what we check for when people come to this castle. But why *has* nobody here gotten it yet? None of us brought it with us; it hasn't spread with any of the supply carts. I know everybody is being careful—but they were careful when traveling between the three other castles, yet the three main castles still got it at the same time. And that's strange. We knew exactly how the other illnesses are spread, but not this one. I think we've always been confused about this plague, because the three castles always seem to get it at the same time—and that doesn't happen with cholera, so it looks like it's spread by human contact. Unless the water is being deliberately poisoned, that is—and you can do that with rotting bodies.

"I think . . ." She took another deep breath. "I think, if you went to look at some of the other streams upriver of our moat, you will probably find some dead demon bodies in them. But in this castle, we're not using the water from the moat except for washing, because there's not very many of us, so the well is still usable. I think that's why we're not affected."

This time there wasn't silence. The room erupted into loud discussions—people calling back and forth, checking information, making suggestions. Commander Edwards and Dog both conferred.

Finally, Commander Daffy stepped forward. "Some very important ideas. Absolutely worth looking at and considering further. I'm going to suggest we go away and think about it more. We can return to this tomorrow."

"Stop!" interrupted Commander Edwards, holding up his arm. "Send the soldiers out again. We need to check other ditches and streams for dead bodies. If she's right, it's important enough that we have to send word to the other castles. We need to do that tonight, because there are lives at stake. Probably our own."

"That's very hasty," pointed out Commander Daffy. "If there is a pattern, like this child has suggested, I would find it surprising that it hadn't been noted before. And as for a link with the demons? I am very wary of wasting the other castles' time and endangering the lives of our soldiers to get that message across to them. Because yes, lives would be at stake—the lives of *our* soldiers, that *we* have responsibility for."

Dog ignored Commander Daffy. She looked at Non, then at Commander Edwards. "Be down at the drawbridge in five minutes," she said.

Chapter 31

"I don't know if I'm right," said Non. "What if I'm wrong, and everybody in the whole valley makes a big fuss about water and stuff just because of me?"

"But what if you're right?" asked Ellie. "What if you get the chance to save lives because of what you've found?"

"I agree with Ellie," said Meg. "If you're right, and we wait to check that you're definitely right, people will die while we're making sure. I get why you're scared, and I'd offer to take the blame in case you're wrong. But that would also mean taking the glory if you're right."

"I don't want any glory. I just don't want to be really embarrassed." In the guard tower, her self-doubt had felt annoying, indulgent, something that was wasting the time of people who had more important things to be doing. The thing was, if she was right, then, yes, her lack of confidence was selfish and would have been costing lives. But now that she was out and had had time to think, it felt unlikely that she was right. She couldn't possibly be right. She wasn't good enough to have spotted something loads of important people had missed. No way. But if she had made a mistake, then she'd have to hide away forever—which was difficult in this place with nowhere to hide. Non put her head in her hands and stared out at the plain.

Meg reached out and grabbed her hand. "You're being very brave," she said. "I get it. But some things are worth the shame."

Ellie glanced at them both. "I think you have different things in mind."

Meg giggled. "I wouldn't know. I don't ever really feel shame."

"Don't you?" asked Non.

"Oh, I suppose so. Of course I do." Meg gave her a sideways look. "I've just had more practice at getting over it than you. The feeling goes away quite quickly if you ignore it. But if you spend too much time focusing on it, then other people get involved too. They start thinking you *should* feel shame, so you start thinking maybe you should too, then people start thinking you should feel even more, so you feel even more. It goes on forever if you let it, so it's better just to ignore it. Or to confuse people by doing something even more shameful so they don't know what to focus on."

Despite herself, Non grinned. "Something even more shameful. I'll bear that in mind."

A squad of soldiers had gone straight out with Dog after the meeting, before Non had made it back down to the wall. Most of the students were still sitting there, and though there was a sense of unease, it was a feeling that was starting to become normal—the swimming and swirling in the stomach, the tightening of the throat, the stiffness in the shoulders. They stared at the demons for a few minutes. There were at least four that Non could see easily, half-concealed by the branches above them but with their legs showing beneath.

Every so often, as the branches gently moved and shifted, the leaves flickering in the breeze, a new part of their body would be thrown into the light so that they'd see a muscular arm or the bulging ball eyes.

"There's more over there," said Ellie. "A whole group of them."

She pointed at a strange darkness. Something the light couldn't filter through, that absorbed it rather than shifting it into the shadows. Non watched for a while, but it was the stillness that was so strange. They didn't move like the valley did. They didn't blow or bend with the breeze or lift and shift as the clouds moved across the sun.

When the red kites flew up this time as Dog and her soldiers emerged from the woods, Non could already tell what Dog was going to say. And it almost would have been better and easier if Non was wrong, if all her studying of the books had been a mistake. But Dog nodded her confirmation to Non even as she stood on the drawbridge ushering the exhausted soldiers in. The painful sliding of the portcullis and the answering groan of the rising drawbridge were chilling that evening, both sending a shiver down Non's spine. The relief she felt at being right was only for a split second, because it was just such an awful thing to be right about. It was a horrible feeling, knowing they were sitting on this knowledge that could change people's lives, prevent them from dying—but having no way to share that knowledge without also, possibly, people dying.

Dog called them all to a meeting an hour later—everybody in the castle. The courtyard was filled with students, but soldiers also leaned against the walls or sat perched on the stonework above. She didn't start with sharing the information Non and Sam had found out. She, rightly, assumed this would be common knowledge by now. Instead, she got straight to the point.

"Good evening," she said. "We need to inform the other castles about the origins of the plague. It is our duty to do that, because not knowing leaves them vulnerable to illness and attack, which in turn leaves us all vulnerable. Tomorrow morning, at first light, we will send two units to the citadel, as the closest castle. We will take the most direct route, and we will expect attack. Thirty minutes later, a third unit will leave. They will take the route through the woods on the other side of the river. Their role will be supplementary, in the event of the first two units not making it. We will assume that the first two units, as the bigger force, will attract most of the demon army, but the third unit should also expect attack."

A few of the soldiers whispered to each other, but there was no arguing or disagreement with what she'd said.

"The numbers required will mean that we'll be leaving only Commander Daffy behind. This is unprecedented, but it is important that we pass the message on. Therefore, students, from tomorrow morning, the castle will be yours. You are to close the drawbridge and portcullis behind us, and you should not open them again until early evening, when we will return. You are not to engage with the enemy, you are not to antagonize them, you are just to keep the castle functioning. I don't foresee any problems . . ."

She gave a wry grin, as did a few other people.

". . . apart from all of the obvious ones. But I don't expect to get back and find this castle trashed. OK?"

Everybody nodded.

"Right. Thanks very much." She dismissed them and walked away, most of the soldiers following. A few climbed up onto the ramparts, returning to their posts watching the plain below.

———o———

Non, Meg, and Ellie sat there for a moment not speaking.

"So," said Non, "shall we talk about sexy boys or something?"

"Yeah, I suppose so," said Meg with a sigh. "That is always a bit interesting."

"But only when there's nothing more interesting to talk about," said Ellie.

"Yeah. I think I'd rather talk plague than sexy boys."

"Poisoning," corrected Non. "It's not really a plague, is it? It's poisoned water."

"What exactly do you think is causing the . . . poisoning?" asked Meg.

"I don't know. Are you asking about whether it's the parasite leaking into the water?"

"Yes, I suppose so. The idea that they're deliberately letting themselves get killed because it'll weaken us is just really scary."

"That's the bit that we can't check without looking at water samples. But the symptoms don't seem to be in any way linked to the parasite. I think it's more like just a nasty stomach bug, but for a long time—and you would get that just from having something bad in the water."

"Like any dead body," said Meg.

"I guess. Normally dead bodies don't get left lying around much, though."

"Oh, actually, can we talk about sexy boys?" said Ellie. "Thinking about rotting dead bodies is making me feel a bit sick."

"Imagine kissing Commander Edwards," said Non. "How does that make you feel?"

"More sick. Bleurgh."

Meg was frowning in thought. "Do you think that's why the plagues ended before then? The bodies had just finished rotting away so that it was only the skeletons left?"

"Maybe. I don't think we can work that out, because the books aren't that clear about how long each plague lasted."

"I think . . ." said Meg. "Do you want us to go back up to the guard tower and double-check what you've found? Would that make you feel better? We can see if either of us spot anything extra?"

"Yes!" said Ellie, her eyes lighting up.

"That really would make me feel better," said Non, reaching out for both their hands. "Thanks!"

Chapter 32

The fire in the demon pit was still smoldering with the burned bodies of yesterday's kills. Non could make out at least two ashy, humanoid shapes in among the pile of dust and smoke, and the sharp tang of burned flesh lingered in the air like an omen. But the students sat on the wall overlooking the plain anyway, and the demons stood under the trees too, silently staring back at them.

The first two units of soldiers had already gone, and with them, some of the demons. But Non thought they had followed behind half-heartedly, without the passion of killers, more just because running after humans was what they did. It wasn't any of the demons she'd marked who'd gone, and Non wondered, after all, if it had perhaps been the pacers who had just fancied a bit of morning exercise.

And now the third unit left. The students raised their crossbows, pointing them at the staring demons. As the soldiers went under the gate, the demons turned, as one, toward the unit. There was a pause, a moment when even the wind seemed to stop, the noise of the world dulled in Non's ears. She could hear, or maybe feel, the *thud* of the soldiers' feet as they crossed the drawbridge, and then the change as they moved onto the grass beyond. The students waited and the soldiers ran. Closer, closer. Non's crossbow was taut in her hand, ready to spring and fire. The soldiers ran farther across the plain. They were almost at the tree line, the point where the moat joined the river, when the demons suddenly charged. Eight of the monsters ran, with a ferocity and violence that was startling and gut-curling, their clawed fingers out to grab and scratch.

Non felt herself recoil, and even as she released her arrow, she took an involuntary step backward. Some of the arrows hit, and the soldiers quickly killed the other demons who had run, their bodies falling to the grass as the red kites circled overhead in their repeating spirals. But it was the ones who hadn't run that Non looked at. A sudden gust of wind blew the branches away, exposing a stationary demon army standing beneath ripples of curling green leaves, and Non imagined one behind every tree as the forest moved up the valley sides. They didn't move. Nothing. Not even a twitch. They remained, staring, heads angled to face a point slightly above the wall, toward the castle itself on top of the hill.

As the soldiers ran on without being followed, one demon, or maybe more, let out that droning, haunting wail. Some trick of the sound meant that Non couldn't make out which of the creatures was making the noise. It seemed to echo round the valley, distorted by the slope, deadened by the river. It went on for a minute or more, as though the creature didn't need to draw breath.

Non turned and looked up to the castle, trying to see things with the enemy's eyes. She felt not so much panic as cold dread, like a solid, heavy, heaving mass in her stomach. There still wasn't really anything here. Cirtop looked nothing like the impenetrable stronghold of her childhood in the citadel. The outer walls were higher than a person, yes, but they weren't feet thick. You could barely walk along them in some places. And the castle itself was still clearly ruined. It was much better than when they'd arrived, and much stronger too, but it wouldn't hold out against an army of demons forever. It was impossible to escape the feeling that they'd just fallen into a demon trap.

All around her, the other students were coming to the same conclusion, their eyes wide, their mouths slack. Some of them were whispering to each other; some gripped their weapons, rearming them. What should they do? What *could* they do?

Then Non caught movement out of the corner of her eye. It might have been a tree branch waving, or an animal flitting through the trees. But others had turned too. There was a wave of shifting darkness in the woods. Concealed in the undergrowth, hidden behind the branches, something was moving. Lots of things were moving, like a shadow spreading across the valley.

"Close the portcullis! Pull up the drawbridge!" yelled Paul. "Do it NOW!"

Others shouted too—and wordless echoes, screams.

They sped to the gate and the drawbridge pulleys, three, four people turning each one. It juddered up, painfully slowly to start, so that Non felt her body frozen, filled with fear, but then it rose quickly, smoothly, the chains barely clanging, such was the speed. Darkness filled the gateway, and for a split second Non was blinded, the gateway just a room filled with shadow. But then the portcullis was released with the sound of sharpening knives.

There were shouts from up on the wall, and Non heard the metallic twang of the arrows. She took a deep breath and calmed herself. She realized her legs were feeling shaky. She stood taller to hide it.

Others were calming down too. Apart from the few who had remained on the wall, most people were now down by the gate, standing on the cobbles.

"What shall we do?" asked somebody.

"Well, nothing," said Commander Daffy. "If we do nothing, they can't get us. We've got food, we've got water—uninfected water. We just sit tight. They don't have weapons, so there's not much they can do, is there?" He beamed at the students in what he obviously hoped was a reassuring way, though Non thought his cheeks were a little stiffer than before.

"Commander, sir," said Paul. "It really looks like they're going to try and attack."

"Well, what are they going to do? Throw themselves against the walls? Leap over the moat? I don't think that's going to be possible, my lovely."

Paul winced, and a few others frowned too.

"Now, it would be helpful if a few of you would take shifts on the wall, just as watchers, so that we know when the others come back and we're ready to lower the drawbridge. And all the girls can go and help in the kitchens or with the cleaning—so nice to have a feminine touch around." Callie raised her eyebrows, and Mary's mouth gaped. "But otherwise, you've got a free day just to relax and enjoy yourselves. Have fun!"

"I think we should throw *him* to the demons," whispered Meg. And she said it in a deliberately loud whisper.

"Have fun?" said Ellie. "Really? With a horde of slavering demons outside?"

A low wail started again from the woods. It was quieter this time, but again, Non couldn't place it, couldn't even work out if it *was* actually quieter or just if it was farther away. A few moments later, its call was taken up by another voice, a different tone, and then in turn by a different voice.

And though they waited beyond dusk, they didn't need to lower the drawbridge, because the soldiers didn't return.

Chapter 33

The wails had continued all day, so that it became an undertone to everything they did. Non almost got used to it. They talked louder, or they stayed indoors working, and after supper they played a game of football, laughing loudly, calling to each other and cheering with false and exaggerated happiness. Except for those doing their shift on the walls. Those students stood silently, watching the plain.

It wasn't until it got dark that people admitted to each other, and to themselves, that things were definitely very wrong. A few voices suggested that the soldiers must just have decided to stay at the citadel, that maybe they were tired after the journey there and didn't want to return today. But their cheerfulness sounded fake, like they couldn't quite get the tone of their voice right. A few even suggested that the soldiers might have decided to go on to Castle Goch and Kintaborel today too, rather than sending messengers from the citadel onward. They managed to make that theory sound convincing, nodding to each other and agreeing in earnest voices, adding in extra details each time they repeated it, as though they were constructing a story in their heads.

Eventually people started going to bed. Some lay in the

dormitory with clothes or blankets over their heads to try to drown out the sound. Others were crying to themselves. Everybody pretended to ignore everybody else's misery so that they could deal with their own. Meg wasn't in the dormitory; she had disappeared off with some boy when Non hadn't been looking, to one of those nice, snug dips in the hillside.

Non didn't try to sleep, because she would have failed. She went and sat on the wall, the higher section overlooking the cliff. Up here the air was cool, but it was also fresh and from somewhere else—anywhere else. She felt as though she could stay awake for days. She felt like she was more aware of everything: her own body, the feel of the stone beneath her, the wail of the demons, but also the silence and mystery of the dark forest.

There had been no demons visible on this side of the castle earlier in the day, though surely there must be some, hiding somewhere along the track to the citadel, waiting to ambush. But it wasn't the ones she could see that worried her—or was it a worry? Was it instead a thrill that there were so many? A bit of excitement that they'd managed to hide for so long without the humans in the valley noticing? Did she feel awe at their cleverness, at the repeating pattern of their threat over time? Was she even, maybe, interested in what they were going to do next? She could imagine reading about this moment later, seeing "The Demon Siege of Cirtop" as the heading in a worn-out book, and then a couple of paragraphs outlining the facts of the case. The language would be boring, the words unemotional, the sentences short, and there would be lots of statistics. She just couldn't imagine what, exactly, the content of those paragraphs would be.

After a few moments, Sam came to sit next to her, as she'd hoped he would. She turned to kiss him straight away, and they stayed like that for a while, at least partly because it meant they didn't have to speak. But it was good being with him, feeling the warmth of him next to her. His arms were protection when they wrapped around her, and she felt safe inside them. His strength, his muscles, his chest. Everything felt better and became better with him there, and kissing him made her feel like everything was going to be OK or like if it wasn't, it didn't matter so much. The terrible wails from the valley became quieter, just a soft buzz in the background, when his breath was on her cheek and his hands were intertwined with hers.

But he pulled away after a time, and they sat there, his arm around her, looking up at the hillside opposite and waiting.

"I think you should take charge of the castle tomorrow," said Non.

"Commander Daffy's in charge," he said quickly. "And we were told to do nothing."

"Commander Daffy's a wet biscuit. And we were told to do nothing based on military assumptions that were wrong. And we can see they were wrong, can't we?"

He paused before saying softly, "How wrong do you think they were?"

"No clue. I don't know how many demons there are— hundreds, maybe?"

"What's worrying me . . ." he whispered, and held her more tightly, "is what's happened to the soldiers. And Dog, and Commander Edwards. What . . . do you think?"

"I don't know. We didn't see many demons go after them, so

unless they were ambushed later on, near the citadel, I don't know. But it must be something bad, mustn't it?"

"Yeah," he whispered.

"I think it would be literally impossible to kill Commander Edwards or Dog, though. I feel like quite a few people have tried before and failed."

He laughed and put his head on hers. "They do look like they've had mysterious stuff happen to them that you wouldn't want to know about, don't they?"

The lights came then. To start with, they were faint, and Non had to squint to make sure, but they became stronger, different, a blue tonight that was like the night sky and the stars combined, all mixed together and swirling, changing, flickering.

"Why do the lights start out dim?" she asked.

"More tree branches blocking them? Or maybe they have to turn them on?"

The lights moved slowly, slowly, one by one, just below the brow of the hill toward the church. Non and Sam watched them for what felt like a long time until the lights reached it—they could see its silhouette—and disappeared.

"Are they going inside?" asked Non.

"No way." But Sam was tense now, sitting up straighter, and Non could feel the energy in him again. "There's no way they can get in that door."

"Why? Weren't the barricades off? Can they open doors?"

"No. They have hands, but their claws would get in the way. Our pacers can't even pick up sticks to use as weapons or tools."

"How are they holding those lights, then?"

"I don't know. I don't know what the lights are."

The lights emerged again, one by one, as though in a procession. It *was* like a slow, respectful funeral procession, and she wondered now if that's exactly what it was—but for the demons themselves, not as a warning to humans. She wondered if that's another one of the many things they'd gotten wrong.

The lights continued and continued—but this time they were faster, and they processed past the point where Non thought she'd first seen them. Others were watching now too—the students on duty as watchers were standing on the ramparts nearby whispering to each other. The lights continued heading farther along the hillside, lower down. They seemed to slow again and pause, but then they were definitely going downhill, the line of lights now at an angle as they walked along the old road. Non was really cold now, her teeth chattering, and she leaned into Sam for warmth while they waited. But as the lights went into the thick, tree-covered section of the road, they disappeared and, though Sam and Non waited longer than it would take to walk that section, the lights didn't emerge.

"We have to get up to those buildings again," said Sam.

Non laughed through her chattering teeth. "A lot of people would think the complete opposite."

"But you secretly like danger, don't you?" he said, then added, "And if nothing happens tomorrow, I *will* take charge."

Chapter 34

The next morning, they ate breakfast on the wall above the gate, overlooking the moat, the plain—and the watching demons. There was no point in pretending that anything else was going to happen, and nobody suggested or offered to do any other work. Some students stood up on the tower overlooking the cliff where the track emerged from the forest, the horns clasped in their hands, ready to announce the return of the soldiers. Others stood behind the gate, ready to let the drawbridge down urgently if the soldiers should arrive. But midmorning came, and then lunch came, and the soldiers didn't arrive.

Non sat with Meg and Ellie, but though they started the day chatting away happily enough, it didn't take long for them to drift into silence. It didn't take long for everybody to drift into silence. The howls of the demons were almost continuous now, barely a pause between them, but every time a new voice started up, it was in a different tone, and that tone seemed to jar, to penetrate Non's insides so that the sound vibrated unpleasantly in her stomach and through her body. Everybody's faces were pale, and a few sat with their heads in their hands, as though that would block out the sound.

But it didn't. Instead it seemed to trap it inside their heads. What had seemed like an unhappy noise, a mourning cry, now felt like a threat, a promise of pain.

The red kites circled overhead, twenty, thirty of them maybe. More perched beyond, in the trees around the plain, their eyes focused black spots of brightness glinting in the shadows. Non felt tense, wired, ready for action, the adrenaline pumping through her again and again, but they'd been like this for hours, and her limbs were starting to ache as though she'd been exercising for all that time instead of sitting on the wall.

Everybody ate the lunch Callie and Mary passed around—of course they did. But Non couldn't have said what was in the sandwich they gave her. Or even if it was a sandwich. The noise of the demons seemed to remove all feeling apart from fear, and she ate hunched up, each swallow just something else that could churn around in her stomach.

Then, midafternoon, Jane jumped down off the wall without warning. She took with her two spears, one for each hand. Everybody scrambled up to get their weapons, to point them at the enemy and protect her. There were shouts, but Jane ignored them. She walked straight toward the moat, jumped as far as she could across it, then pulled herself up on the other side.

Two others jumped down behind her—Becky and Paul—each clutching two spears. More people shouted and called to them to come back, but all three remained focused on the enemy.

Jane strode forward. Becky and Paul both ran toward her until the three were walking side by side. They slowed as they got within range of the demons. Then they crept closer and closer, inches at a time, until they were within feet of them.

"I reckon she's got about two seconds," said Meg.

Jane stopped, the two other students slightly behind her.

"Oh, I can't watch," squealed Meg, covering her eyes. "Tell me when it's over."

Jane took another footstep. And she raised both her spears, angling one directly at the closest demon. But there was nothing from the monster. Still no movement.

Jane tightened her grip, her muscles tensed and ready to throw; she pulled her arm back to get more force behind the throw. Nothing.

Then suddenly the howls stopped. The lack of sound was shocking, and for a split second Jane wavered too, a flicker; she turned her head slightly toward Becky.

And the demons leaped suddenly, six of them charging toward the wall. And equally suddenly, Jane and the two others turned and ran.

Meg gave a screech from behind her fingers. The gasps from all around were startling and strange without the howls beneath them—echoing and loud.

"They're going to make it," said Non. "It's fine."

Jane, Becky, and Paul were ahead of the demons, and Non could see the monsters following them were thinner, spindlier—maybe elderly—than most of the others. They were well ahead of these decrepit demons, and the gap was widening as they ran faster and faster. They were easily going to make it over the wall.

"Raise your bows!" shouted Sam. "And hold your fire. Hold!"

Non could hear the shouts of the Castle Goch students, but sound still seemed distorted, her ears still adjusting to normality. Jane seemed to run faster. The demons were now coming within arrow range, but the archers waited. And waited.

The students ran on, and Paul cleared the moat completely, Becky and Jane making it almost to the bank but scrambling up quickly. Swiftly they ran to the wall and were lifted up and over. The demons kept running, their arms outreached and awkwardly twisted to claw and grab.

Sam gave a shout, and the first arrows were fired. One of them hit a demon in the eye. It was a spectacular shot, and the monster fell forward immediately with its hands still raised.

But then, like a switch had been flicked, the demons stopped. The five remaining demons reached down, as one, and grabbed their dead comrade, pulling him back toward the army hiding in the trees.

Back at the wall, Non could make out Jane, crouched, her head in her hands and hunched with despair.

"More!" shouted Sam. "Fire again!"

Another round of arrows was released, and two more hit demons in the back so that they flinched, but those demons continued toward the forest with the arrows hanging from their flesh.

"Put your bows down!" yelled Sam. "Down!" He picked up a spear and, lining it up, squinting with one eye, he pulled his arm back and threw—so hard his whole body twisted. It flew through the air faster than most of the arrows and hit the closest demon so hard that it went right through its torso. The monster stumbled and then fell. The remaining four demons ran for the forest, leaving the two corpses behind.

"Right," said Sam. "We need a meeting."

The meeting was held up on the wall, so they could shoot any demons who might come back for the bodies. And the bodies were covered in twitching, fighting red kites, jostling to get at the best meat, occasionally screeching at each other with piercing calls that echoed across the valley.

"Let's figure some stuff out," said Sam, "just in case Commander Daffy's busy."

"Commander Daffy's gone to bed," said somebody, and there was a ripple of laughter.

"Well done to Jane, Becky, and Paul for turning off the noise," he said, and everybody gave them a round of applause. "But running out onto the plain wasn't a great idea. I'm not saying we're not up for doing it again, but some warning next time would be good. And if we do it too many times, somebody's going to have to go and collect the arrows."

Meg shuddered next to her, and Non realized Meg's hands were shaking. Had she been shaking the whole morning? Or was it just the mention of fetching the arrows? When Meg saw Non watching her, she smiled and tossed back her hair as normal, but it seemed limp, somehow, her movements unsure.

"How much food have we got?" asked Sam.

"With just us, easily enough for two weeks," said Callie. "If we halve it, we can survive for a month, and by then the potatoes will almost be ready."

"So we could stay here securely," said Sam.

"Yes." Mary nodded. "The food might not be great, though."

"It's only since you took over that anybody's cared about that," he said. "I suspect you'll still work magic."

"Are you interested in him?" whispered Meg. "Tell me now. Because I am loving that he realizes Callie and Mary are our most important military asset."

"I like him, Meg," whispered Non. "Please leave him alone."

Non could feel Meg looking at her, but she kept facing forward so that she didn't have to make eye contact. Meg stroked her arm and turned back to the meeting.

"I think our big problem is that we have no idea what numbers we're dealing with," Sam said.

A lot of people nodded.

"Mary and Callie, in your opinion, how much food do the demons have? How many demons do you think they can feed?"

"A hundred and fifty or so," Callie said without even pausing to think. "There can't possibly be more than that without a regular food supply—like a farm or something. And there isn't. I don't think they could support more than about two hundred in this valley just scavenging. Demons do take farm animals, but rarely, so they've been existing mainly on wildlife and wild plants and nuts."

"That's really interesting," said Sam. "How confident are you about that?"

"As confident as I am about how much longer our food will last here, and as confident as I am about how many potatoes I'll need to put in tonight's stew," said Callie. "So, very." Mary nodded in agreement beside her.

"Excellent," he said. "That changes things a bit. Because with that number, we could fight them."

"Dog said not to do anything," Paul pointed out.

"Yes. But Dog's not here, is she?"

Paul didn't argue further, and nobody pointed out that Paul had already been one of the first to break Dog's command.

"I think we need to plan. It really feels like this situation has been set up and we've played into the demons' hands. Claws. I suggest we spend the day checking weapons just in case.

"I think we should also watch the demons even more closely. I'd like to know exactly where each of them is, and if they move, I'd like to see if we can tell where they're going and if there's any pattern to those movements."

Chapter 35

The mood was uneasy for the rest of the day. The whole thing had a feeling of unreality to it and, even though she knew by now that it wasn't going to happen, Non kept half checking the plain, walking along the walls or peering over just in case they'd made a mistake and there was a whole army of soldiers outside that they'd forgotten to let in. But the students watching above the cliff didn't raise their horns. And nobody lowered the drawbridge.

Sam called another meeting as the sun was going down, the sky red and orange and yellow behind him with those disappearing streaks of light. He leaned on a spear as he spoke, twiddling it round and round between his fingers—the only clue that he was nervous.

There were twenty or so chalk arrows drawn along the wall—in between the students still watching the demons across the plain—and he pointed to them now.

"The arrows show where a demon has been spotted. Tomorrow morning whoever is up here needs to check again to see if the enemy are still in the same positions or if they've moved in the night.

"It should give us a lot of information—even if they stay in exactly those positions, that'll tell us something. We will add an extra couple of watchers to our night shifts, and I'd like you to look for any change at all."

Non put her hand up. He caught her eye, looked away, and then said, "Any questions? Oh, yes, Non."

Beside her, Meg sniggered, shaking her head.

"Thanks. I'm wondering if anybody has seen any of the demons that we marked with ink? We marked three. They should have large black splodges on their bodies."

"Yes!" called one of the students at the far end of the wall. "One over there!" He pointed to a spot in the middle of the forest where there didn't appear to be anything visible apart from the darkening greenery of the trees. "It's this one." He moved over to a chalk arrow and put a star next to it.

"Which one? Where's the mark?" asked Non. "On the demon, I mean."

"All over its chest—which is why we almost didn't see it for a while, because it was camouflaged in the shadows."

Non looked in the direction he was pointing, as did most of the other students, but in the dim light, it was impossible to make out anything.

"Also—" Sam coughed. "A few people have noticed lines of lights moving along the hillside up there at night. We think they were going to the church and then back. Maybe along the track too . . ."

There was a lot of muttering, and Non could hear the regular syllables of people reciting the children's rhyme. Sam spoke louder.

"Can you look out for that again tonight and see if there's a pattern to where the lights go? It does seem to have been happening just after the stars come out. If you're not doing a shift on the wall, can you make sure you're sleeping? We need to be ready for . . . whatever tomorrow brings."

"Yeah," said Meg. "Sleep like Commander Daffy." There was laughter from all along the wall, and the meeting broke up—people going to their positions, or going to bed, or just standing round discussing the day's events with their friends for a bit.

Sam went along the wall, speaking to each of the students on duty in turn and still clutching his spear. On the plain, the light was dimming rapidly, but the corpses of the two demons were still there—a darker mark in the grass, the shape of their bodies no longer discernible. Non wondered if they'd still be there tomorrow.

"Are you coming, Non?" asked Meg.

"I think I might just stay here for a bit," she said.

"Oh. OK," said Meg. "See you later, then." It was difficult to see Meg's facial expression in the darkness, but Non could hear the smile in her voice. Somehow, the fact that she couldn't see her look took away some of the awkwardness—or maybe it was just that there wasn't much awkwardness after all.

Non waited there for a few minutes, until most of the people had gone, and she looked at each of the chalk arrows in turn, their whiteness still standing out against the dark of the stone. They were evenly spread along the wall. Very evenly spread. She crouched down by one and followed its line of direction to look into the woods. She couldn't see the demon it pointed to in this darkness, but she thought maybe that she could make out a softer shape, maybe a part of the tree that wasn't quite as straight or solid.

When Sam came up alongside her, she had almost forgotten why she'd waited, she was so engrossed in looking into the darkness, where the arrows pointed.

"Are you going to bed?" asked Sam.

"Yeah. In a minute."

"Or do you want to go and just chat for a bit? It would be good to have someone look over the plain and watch for the lights with me. To see what the demons do tonight."

"I'd like to go and sit on the wall with you," said Non. "But let me just get a blanket first."

In the end they didn't make it as far as the wall. Instead, they found one of those dips in the hillside, and they stayed there for a time in the warmth. Later, though, in the silence of the night, Sam spoke.

"What if I mess up, Non?" he whispered, so quietly that for a moment she wasn't sure it was his voice.

"What do you mean?"

"What if they attack and I get it wrong? I mean, if I can't get people to defend themselves properly or I don't know what to do? What if I'm just not good enough?"

"But you are good enough." She didn't know what to say in reply. She leaned up so that she was resting on one arm and looking down at him. "Who's better than you?"

"Thanks for your faith in me."

"No, I mean it. Honestly, who's better than you?"

He covered his face with his hands and groaned.

"I'm just really surprised you're even doubting yourself."

"Everybody doubts themselves, don't they?" he said, his voice muffled from beneath his hands. "You'd be insane not to."

"Really?" Non slid back to the ground and lay down next to him again, staring up at the stars. "So is everybody just really good at faking their certainty about everything, then?"

"They're either faking it, they're insane, or they're genuinely brilliant at life, I guess." He took his hands away from his face and kissed her lightly on the top of her head.

She was silent for a moment. Everything about Sam made her see the world a little differently.

"Well, I think you're genuinely brilliant," she said. "But I suppose if you don't agree, then you're just going to have to fake it. Because if anything happens, then we really need you, and everybody else needs to believe you know what you're doing. And I think you do, Sam. I think you do know what you're doing—or, at least, you're better at it than anybody else."

"Thanks," he said quietly. "I'm still really nervous, though."

"Me too." She turned over and kissed him. And they kissed until they fell asleep on the hillside, under the stars and the blanket. She knew she should have been nervous about what was lying outside their walls, but inside Sam's arms the night felt full of magic—excitement, joy, anticipation, beauty, safety, warmth, perfection. She felt like they could work anything out, figure out a solution for whatever the problem actually was.

So when they were woken up, first by shouts, and then by the sounding of the alarm, it took a few seconds to work out where she was.

Chapter 36

"To your battle stations!" shouted Sam. "Battle stations!"

The bell by the gate was being rung again and again, the sound shrill and uncomfortable.

"Are you OK?" He turned to Non.

"Yeah."

He kissed her. "We can do this," he said.

"We can," she said. "You can!"

And he ran toward the wall. All around the hillside, people were running down to the shouts. But they weren't screams. And there was no sound of weapons being used. Even as they all ran down, Non noted that. The shouts were ordered—people calling instructions—and they were surprised, not panicked.

Somebody ran to the tower and grabbed the extra weapons, and these were being put in their places as Non arrived, but she could see they weren't going to need them.

There was a group of students standing on only one section of the wall—the lowest point, just near the gate. They weren't spread out, and they weren't fighting off a desperate enemy. Non climbed up slowly, alert and thinking. The night was quiet, cool, and there was that early-morning feel of moisture in the air—the settling water damp against the skin as the world was getting ready for dawn. There was movement at the far end of the plain, sudden scurrying shadows, too fast to just be the trees, but they were distant, too far away to be the problem.

Non looked on the other side of the moat, searching for the black patch of irregular shadow that was the corpses, but there was no shadow big enough.

There were several large logs standing upright below the wall. The students were pushing them away with spears, tipping and rolling them back toward the moat. But they were heavy and the angle difficult. People were having to lie down on the wall to get a long enough reach.

"They just appeared," said Becky, her voice high and tearful. "We didn't see them. They're the same color as the moat in the darkness. But they came from the water. They must have floated down, and then suddenly the demons were pushing them up here, loads of them, and then we realized they'd be able to use them to climb up."

"We need to get down to push them farther away," said Paul.

"Stay where you are!" said Sam. "*Don't* get off the wall."

Paul wavered, looking at the logs.

"Where did the demons go?"

"I don't know," said Becky. "They just ran away into the darkness."

"We didn't see," said Paul. "We were pushing the logs away."

"And that's why you're not going down. You didn't see, and they could still be hiding in the water. I'm relieving you. Everybody who was doing this shift, go and get some rest. Get your heads sorted out.

Paul, you can help move the logs away in the morning when we can see to do so. We need to double numbers here in case they attack again. I want volunteers."

Most people put their hands up—because who was going to be able to go back to sleep again? Sam pointed to the twenty people nearest him. He didn't choose Non, but she sat on the wall anyway, her head still buzzing with thoughts—too many, spinning round, messy, incoherent. She would have liked to get her books out and write some ideas down to try and put them in some sort of order—but the night was still too dark to see.

It took only a few minutes for something to happen—quicker even than Non had thought. She was staring so hard at the hillside that at first she wasn't sure whether she was imagining it or not, but gradually, slowly, the darkness of the brow became dotted with spots of brightness. First one, then a second, and so on until there were twenty or more. The lights processed toward the church again, as they always seemed to. From somewhere on the hillside, there was a wail.

There were gasps and whispers all around her, but everyone on the wall was watching, pointing, discussing.

"Everybody note that spot," said Sam. "I want to know exactly where the place is that they come from. We need to be able to look for that tomorrow."

"And are they going into the church," asked Non, "or around it?"

There was silence now as everyone watched. The first lights of dawn were starting to appear, the black of the sky starting to change to streaks of softer blue. The shadows on the plain were fading, and Non could see with certainty now that the two corpses had gone.

The moat was also more visible, and although you couldn't see what was beneath the surface, you could see that there was nothing *on* the surface.

This time the lights were moving more quickly, but so evenly and steadily that they seemed almost to be joined together—a ribbon stringed with swirling blue lanterns. The church was still a black silhouette against the sky, but this time the individual buildings and trees around it were almost visible in the coming dawn. Non stood up as the first of the lights reached the church, as though the extra height would make her able to see more clearly. The light wobbled a little in front of the building—the demon going in through the gate—but then it turned slightly to the right and disappeared.

"They're going round the building," said Sam. "Not inside."

The other lights followed steadily and disappeared momentarily before reappearing on the other side of the church and, one by one, returning the way they had come.

"What do you think is going on, Non?" Sam called.

"I don't know." Right now she felt like she never knew the answers to any of the questions people asked. "But they must have held the people inside that church under siege for ages, while those eggs developed. So maybe it's an important place for them. The grass was really trampled in the churchyard. I thought it was animals at the time, but I guess it's just the demons. Maybe the church is special because demon babies died there and so they're remembering that. Do they remember things, Jane?"

"Yes," said Jane. "Sort of. They remember who feeds them, and they remember where the hunting is good. They remember where they live. They are really intelligent."

"Anything more than that?"

"Not really. But I think it's because they don't want to; they're just not interested in the same sorts of things as us. Some people say that's a sign they're stupid, but I think it means they're pretty clever, because when people try to talk to me about things I'm not interested in, I'd like to walk away too, but I can't because it's not polite. Demons don't have to worry about being polite, which must be nice."

The lights were returning along the brow of the hill now, dimming in the glow of the rising sun. They began to disappear altogether at a point just below the highest trees, in an area of the forest that looked no different from all the rest. It looked to be above a couple of the abandoned houses, slightly after the clearing with the rabbits—but Non couldn't be sure about that.

"Try and remember where that point is," said Sam. "Because someday we're going to need to go and have a look at what's there. And that day might be quite soon."

The students were silent for a few moments, mostly still as they watched the remaining lights disappear and the trees around the plain coming into focus. The dew glistened as the sun reached it, and the morning was golden, pink and rosy shades. Nothing moved in the valley now, the world like a stage set, a backdrop for what must surely happen today.

Chapter 37

And then . . . nothing happened.

By midmorning, there had still been no movement from the enemy. The red kites were back, which was the only clue a battle might be about to start, but the demons were just standing around again, in exactly the places where they'd been the night before.

The students had had breakfast on the wall, and every time a slight breeze flickered through the woods, Non and the watchers desperately peered at the trees to see if any branches lifted to reveal the unmoving demons beneath. It had been slow work, but they'd ticked them all off now. All the places where the white arrows pointed still had a demon there.

But they'd all been up for hours, so the feeling of waiting was insufferable, the feeling of inaction, as the minutes ticked painfully by, agonizing. Non used the time to make notes in her books—they were both almost full now, her writing overlapping with her mother's, her ideas and information adding to what had already been there so that the pages were covered in black lines of thoughts and facts.

As she was squeezing notes onto another one of the pages, a particularly strong gust of wind blew across the plain, and she looked up, as she always did, to glance into the woods for the demon enemy, and it was then she noticed it. A wave of rippling branches ran across the woods, momentarily exposing demon after demon in turn as the leaves swayed in the breeze. Each one was exactly where they should be—but where the one with the black splodge on its chest had been, there was now one without ink. And on the edge of the woods, where yesterday there had been one without ink, there was now one with a stain of black on its thigh.

Non stood up and stared at them both, checking to make sure. But she was already sure.

"They've moved," she said. Most of those on the wall turned to her, frowning. "They've moved," she repeated. "There are demons in all of the spots where they stood yesterday, but they're different ones. I think they're doing shifts."

Sam wasn't on the wall, but somebody ran to get him, and within a few minutes everyone had gathered once again on the ramparts. Sam was one of the last to climb up, and as he walked past Non, she let her hand brush against his chest and he smiled. He went to the middle of the students and, with his back against the plain, turned to face them.

"So they are moving in the night then," he said. "That seems to be when everything happens. Non, have you got any more thoughts?"

"They're not completely nocturnal," said Non. "We can tell that. But they can obviously see better than us. They're moving around at night without us noticing, which means they're able to walk through the woods and see where they're going."

"It also confirms their base is nearby then, doesn't it?" said Sam.

He paused before continuing. "We are going to need to go down onto the plain," he said. "The logs were a deliberate attack, so we should expect the same tonight. With logs of that size, they can easily reach the top of this wall, so we need to prevent them getting up here. We're going to need light. If they're going to attack us at night, which it looks like they will, then we need a way of seeing them. Any suggestions?"

"Bonfires," said Paul.

"OK. How are we keeping them lit all night? Who's going down to replace the wood?"

"Well, I don't mind doing that," said Paul, and Sam shook his head, "but we could set them up, pack loads of kindling in, and then light them with flaming arrows when we need to."

"Are you happy to go down on the plain now to set up the bonfires?"

"Yes."

"And me!" said Jane.

"Couldn't we just set up a string of lanterns?" said Non. "I know it would mean somebody having to go to the nearest trees, but couldn't we tie a rope from the castle wall to a tree? And then there'd be light all night."

"Anybody happy to do that?" asked Sam.

"Yes!" said Jane.

Paul and Becky nodded too, as did a number of other Castle Goch students.

"Also—" Callie coughed. "These planks of wood might be useful, so we brought them." She pointed to a stack of thick, sturdy planks leaning against the wall. "They're for floorboards on the second story of the dormitories, but we haven't made a second story yet. Just thought they might work well as levers if the demons attack with any more logs."

"Excellent," said Sam.

They spent the next few hours working steadily, and at around noon, when Non was sitting with Meg and Ellie, Sam came to find her. His face was flushed, and she could see that he was full of energy—even as he spoke to her, he moved several paces back and forth on the spot.

"Come for a walk with me," he said.

She tipped the arrowheads she was sharpening into Meg's lap. "Can you do these?" she said and, though Meg's eyes were wide and her face more neutral than was natural, she nodded silently in reply.

Sam walked straight up the hillside, so fast that Non was panting by the time they got to the top. He went straight for the part of the castle wall above the cliff, and they walked along it to the guard tower before he slowed.

"Are you OK?" she said.

"Yeah, yeah, fine!" he said. "I'm fine. You?"

She nodded.

They both leaned on the battlements and looked up the valley. There was nobody stationed on this section of the wall because there were more important places for them to be. No demons were in sight on this side, and a few wisps of cloud drifted slowly up at the top of the valley, casting shadows on the hills below as they moved across the sky. The shadows from them seemed to move faster over the ground than the clouds did through the sky, undulating and wiggling as they ran over the dips and cliffs and outcrops.

"What if it doesn't work?" he said. "Everything I've told them to do."

"It has to work."

"What if I'm a bad leader?"

She shrugged. "I guess we could put Commander Daffy in charge instead?"

He laughed. "I knew you'd make me feel better."

She reached out for his hand, and they stood quietly for a few moments.

"What have we missed?" he said.

She sighed. "Probably lots of things."

"That's what worries me. I feel like there's more information missing from those military books than there are stones on this hillside."

"Well . . . how about, could there be fewer than a hundred and fifty demons?" she said.

"Yeah. Why? What are you thinking?"

"I'm probably wrong."

He laughed. "Stop apologizing before you say anything!"

"I just don't know much about military things, and to be honest, I find those books quite boring. But I wonder if the attack on the carts was the demons' main attack? It makes much more sense if you want to injure lots of people but don't want to kill them because you need them to make more demon babies. Attacking us while we're inside a castle is much more difficult from their perspective. I mean, they don't really want us to stay in here, do they? They want us to leave so they can more easily infect us."

He nodded.

"So I thought about the math. Callie reckons this valley could only support two hundred demons, maximum, and we've killed maybe sixty—some of those because they were deliberately poisoning the water. Well, there are three other castles where the water was also being deliberately poisoned. That means more demons will have needed to die to lie in their rivers—so that's maybe, what, another fifteen?"

"Yes. You're right," said Sam. "And there are probably some demons, at least, left around those castles too. Say even if there's ten outside each castle, then that's another thirty who aren't here." He laughed again. "Remind me to never get in the way of your 'I'm probably wrong but' thoughts."

Non grinned despite herself. "I don't always think I'm wrong. I'm just not definitely sure I'm right."

"I'm sure you're right." He leaned in and kissed her. For a moment, she thought about glancing down at the hillside to see if anybody was watching, but then she thought she'd rather just kiss him again. He held her very tightly, and she could feel the tension in him.

"You'll be OK," she said. "You can do this. Because with that math, we're only outnumbered two to one."

Chapter 38

When Non woke the next morning, it was later than normal. Around her most of the girls were still asleep, but the angle of the light and shadows in the room felt wrong. The feel of the world outside—the sounds of the animals, something in the air—hinted that the castle should have been up for hours, yet all was quiet. Non eased the covers off herself and pulled fresh clothes on. She brushed her hair, plaiting it so that it would still look good even in a battle.

Walking down the hillside, it felt like the castle was under a spell. There were no sounds from anywhere, although the sun was high. She was glad to see the students sitting guard on the wall—but even their positions were relaxed, and a couple of them waved at her as she walked past. Clearly, nothing was happening outside the walls. She hoped the demons were getting tired standing watch and were not rebuilding their strength like everybody inside the castle.

After Non got some food from the kitchens, there was nothing much else to do. She had a quick look in the armory, but the weapons there were gleaming and battle ready.

The tower room was clean and neat—Callie and Mary had clearly been there. The books were stacked up again on the shelves, and the maps were rolled back up, as they'd been when she'd first seen them. Non looked along the shelves, but the book with the red cover—the one that Commander Daffy had taken—still wasn't back, and she thought there were a few more missing too. It wasn't as if one book was going to answer all her questions or fill in all the gaps in the history of the valley—but the red book was now the only one she knew she hadn't read. Had Commander Daffy taken other ones too? Might those books be useful? Supposedly his job had been to organize maps of the valley, but he was clearly rubbish at it, when he didn't seem to have noticed large buildings that were clearly visible from the castle. She could see how he might have forgotten about a couple of useful books.

And where had he been the past few days?

She opened the door he always entered through, but it led to a dark corridor and then narrow stairs twisting down. There were two doors off the corridor, and maybe more lower down. There was a smell of damp, and the air trapped in here was cold. She listened, but there was no sound at all. Did she dare open the doors or knock on them? She could easily pretend she was looking for somebody—or even tell Commander Daffy the truth. He'd offered to help her find information about the demons, hadn't he? So why did she feel like she didn't want his help?

"Commander Daffy," she called softly. "Commander Daffy? Are you awake? Would you like a cup of tea?" There was no reply—and she couldn't hear even the rustle of somebody who'd heard but was ignoring her. She knocked lightly on the closest door and then opened it. Light spilled into the corridor immediately. The room was empty but very neat—the bed covers pulled so tight and smooth, they were flatter than the floor. She recognized a couple of Dog's tops hanging up on a rail at the side, but there were no other personal possessions in here.

She shut the door again and knocked on the next one. Again, there was no answer and Non softly called, "Commander?" before entering.

This was clearly Commander Edwards's room. There was nothing in there of his that she recognized, but there was a series of knives and machetes hanging on the wall—perhaps as decoration, perhaps for some weird hobby. She couldn't picture this being Commander Daffy's room anyway. She was just about to close the door when she also noticed one of Dog's tops in here too, and then a pair of boots that were too small to be Commander Edwards's. The bed here had clearly been slept in. It was made, but the covers weren't as tidy as the ones in the room opposite. Non wondered what the sleeping arrangements were, exactly. And then she wished she hadn't had that thought at all, because she really didn't want to know.

Non crept down the stairs, knowing that Commander Daffy must be in the room below—even though the twisting stairs were leading down to what would have been the dungeons. She supposed in a castle where so little was built, any accommodation was better than none. It did still seem a little rude, though, that when Commander Edwards and Dog were clearly only sleeping in one room upstairs, they still made Commander Daffy sleep in a cell.

She called again, "Commander?" and again there was no answer. She knocked and then pushed the door gently. There were curtains on this window, but also bars. The door was wooden, but it was the original sturdy one, and there was a barred hatch at the top for giving prisoners their food back in the old days when this had been used as a cell. All was still, and there was no sound of breathing. The room was very messy—clothes strewn everywhere, along with papers, notebooks, and a stack of books. The bed had been slept in—the covers were pulled back. But there was nobody there. Commander Daffy was definitely not in the room. For a second Non considered closing the door again and pretending she'd never been there. But she also wanted to see the books.

There were at least ten in the stack—some of which she recognized, but others she'd never seen. Could she just take them, sneak them out now and then sneak them back in later? Would he even notice?

The one with the red cover was near the bottom, and she lifted it out. Even as she was easing it from beneath the others, she saw that same circular symbol on it, the one from the church—the elaborately decorated, knotted, interlocking lines and loops, with a gap in the middle for the shape of a cross. And it was something about the shadows in the room, or maybe just seeing it more clearly, but that missing cross suddenly seemed sinister—an inside-out idea of religion.

Non opened the front cover carefully, trying to make as little noise as possible—though surely she'd hear him coming as he walked along the corridor up above. The frontispiece to the book was an elaborate woodcutting containing three dancing figures. They were grinning, grotesque caricatures. One was small and hairy, clearly a monkey, its arms as long as its legs. It didn't look funny, as monkeys normally did in pictures—perhaps it was the fact that its eyes were staring out at her threateningly. The second figure was clearly a human—a man—and he had the same stance as the monkey. His grin didn't look happy, despite his human features. Perhaps the artist wasn't very good at faces, because despite the fact that he was dancing, he looked angry, as though his teeth were bared in rage rather than jollity. The third figure, as she knew it would be before she looked, was a demon. It was slightly taller than the man—but like both figures, it was also dancing, and its arms were in exactly the same position as the others. Alongside each other, the three looked very similar—though perhaps that was the intention. And it was the dance of death, Non realized, the danse macabre. Behind the three characters, in among the decorations in the border, a hooded figure stood, holding a long scythe.

She'd seen the image before on churches, or in pictures at home, but in those the three dancing figures were always human, and the image was supposed to be a lesson in humility. The idea was, she supposed, that life is just a pointless exercise—like a dance. You fill your time on earth, have fun, but it's all meaningless because soon you will die when the music of your life stops. The images she'd seen before were quite fun, colorful—a not-very-subtle warning to behave on earth or you wouldn't get to heaven. But this image was far more disturbing than that. The dance horrible, the three humanoid figures linked together by the artist in the pointlessness of all earthly life. The hiding figure of death was somehow the most unpleasant. In the danse macabre pictures she'd seen in the citadel, death was at the front of the picture—because death was the whole point of the warning. Somehow having him hiding, watching the dancing, grinning, naked creatures without being seen, made her skin crawl.

She was just about to turn the next page when the lunch bell started to ring from the kitchen. She slid the book under her top, looked once more round the room, and shut the door behind her.

She knew the book had to be about demons—but it also had to be linked to that church, because the symbols on it were the same. Why had Commander Daffy lied to her?

She ran back out of the guard tower, half expecting to see Commander Daffy in one of the shadows or sitting in a corner somewhere. But he wasn't anywhere. Where else could he be hiding?

In the kitchens, Callie and Mary were dishing up bowls of stew. Most people were awake now, and another shift of students was standing watch on the wall.

"Have you cleaned in Commander Daffy's room?" asked Non.

"No," said Callie. "He's always in there and says he's busy so can we come back later." She looked up at Non across the steaming pot. "You OK?"

"Yeah. I'm just wondering about a few things, and I'd like to know if there's anything weird in his room."

"Like what?" replied Callie.

"I don't know. He just . . ." Non screwed up her face and dropped her voice to a whisper. "He lied to me about something, which doesn't make sense. And it was about demons. He's hiding information about them—and I'd really like to know why. It might be nothing, though."

Callie raised her eyebrows. "That sounds really strange." She looked at Mary. "How about we insist on cleaning his room and get him out?" Mary nodded.

"He's already left his room," said Non. "He's not there now."

"He can't have done," said Mary. "I brought him breakfast a couple of hours ago, and he was in there then. We'd have seen him if he left. He'd have had to walk right past us—and it's not like there's anywhere else to go, is there?" She gestured round the castle.

For a moment, Non doubted herself. Had there been a cupboard he could have been hiding in? But no, the wardrobe was open and the clothes were spilling out. Behind the curtain, maybe? But why would he hide?

And where was he now?

Chapter 39

Mary and Callie grabbed their cleaning things, and the three of them walked quickly through the guard tower again.

"Lunch is ready, Commander," Callie called as she walked down the stairs—her voice too falsely bright and cheerful for lunch during a siege.

Immediately, there was an answering *thud* of things being shut and somebody moving around. "It's all right," called Commander Daffy. "Thanks for bringing it to me, girls, you are so lovely. Leave it outside, please."

"Oh, we haven't brought it to you," said Callie. "We thought you might like to go and get it yourself this time. Perhaps sit down at a table and relax? I think some of the boys might have a few questions for you—about military strategy, and that sort of thing."

"Men's things. That we don't understand," added Mary.

The door opened slowly, and Commander Daffy peered round—his eyes blinking in the light from the corridor.

"We'll clean your room while you're out," said Mary. "Change your sheets and make it more comfortable."

"Oh, no, no need to do that," said the commander.

"It's no trouble. And there are a few cobwebs we could sort out too."

"No, no, it's fine."

"It's the only room in the castle we haven't cleaned," said Mary. "We won't be long. And we won't touch any of your things. Just pile them up on the bed?"

The commander opened his mouth and shut it a few times, clearly not quite knowing how to refuse—or what possible reasons he could give. He had his normal smile on his face again, and this time, somehow, it reminded Non of the creatures on the frontispiece from the danse macabre—unconvincing, as though drawn on by a bad artist.

"Lovely, lovely," he said. "Well, perhaps I could take a little break from my work. So important, you know." And then he saw Non. His forehead wrinkled momentarily before his smile became wider. "Perhaps you, Non, could take me there. Dish up for me and whatnot."

"Ah . . . yes," said Non, turning to follow him. Callie winked at her as she went into the commander's room, clutching her cleaning cloth and broom.

⸺ ∘ ⸺

Non had an awkward fifteen minutes or so making polite conversation with Commander Daffy. She was suddenly very conscious of the stolen book under her top, so she hunched while she ate, keeping one hand in front of her stomach. Commander Daffy talked mainly about famous military operations of the past—big battles where the Northerners had been defeated. The battles he favored usually involved machines too—trebuchets and battering rams. He liked talking about those and was able to keep talking even while eating his stew, loudly slurping up any of the liquid that dribbled out of his mouth in his enthusiasm. Non tried desperately to think of an excuse so she could leave, but every time there was a gap in the conversation, he filled it with some more anecdotes about military transport, laughing heartily to himself so that she had to smile politely in reply.

Callie and Mary returned shortly after he went back to his room, their eyes wide.

"We need to call a meeting," whispered Callie. "Now!"

Again the meeting was held on the wall so that everybody could attend—though this time, Mary sat on the ground inside the castle walls, watching the guard tower for Commander Daffy.

"There's a siege tunnel in his room," said Callie. "And he's been using it."

"We saw mud that shouldn't have been there, given that he never leaves," Mary said. "It was on his shoes and clothes too—particularly the knees of his trousers, so he's obviously been crawling through something."

Sam nodded, serious and calm, but he was tapping his fingers against his leg, and Non could see he was already working out what to do next.

"And we saw the outline of the entrance to the tunnel," said Callie. "It's just a loose flagstone on his floor—near the wall. There must be a way of getting the flagstone out, but we didn't have long to look."

A few people whispered to each other, but it was difficult to work out the implications of this news, aside from a general feeling that it wasn't OK.

"Did the flagstone look secure?" asked Sam. "So any person—or demon—coming in would have to push up a large stone block to get access to the castle?"

"Yes. Definitely."

"So—there might not be a problem then," said Sam. "I'll go and talk to him and find out. Any demon trying to get in that way would be very vulnerable to attack from above, so it's probably not much of a threat. But it's . . . odd nobody's mentioned it."

"If Dog knew about it, she would've told us," said Jane. "Especially with what we're facing."

"Well, maybe. We've got to ask Daffy," said Sam. "Trying to solve a problem before we know whether there's a problem or not is pointless."

He turned to go toward the guard tower.

"Sam," called Non, biting her nails. For a second, she worried about being wrong or the fact that everybody was looking at her. But she knew she wasn't wrong, and she knew she didn't like Commander Daffy. "Sam, what do you think he's been doing, going through the tunnel?"

Sam paused, and a few of the students started whispering to each other.

"I mean, because I *do* think we've got a problem here," she said. "And it might not be solved by asking him about it nicely." Sam nodded slowly, as did a few others. "What can he possibly be doing, in the middle of a siege, sneaking out of the castle? We've got enough food in here for a couple of weeks—and he knows that. I don't think he'd be good in battle, so I don't think he's secretly off killing demons to help us."

"Any theories?" asked Sam, turning back toward everybody again.

"Whatever he's doing, it's not good. He's lied to me about the demons. He knows more than he's letting on." Non felt more confident the more she spoke. And then, before she'd even been able to form the ideas in her head, she was saying what she realized she somehow knew. "I think he already knew about the bodies in the church. We weren't the only people to visit that church in the last century. Somebody had painted over the symbols on the door, refreshed the DO NOT ENTER sign, stopped the gate from falling off. I think that person was him."

"How sure are you?"

"Well—let's go and ask him. But let's take backup."

This time Non entered the guard tower behind Sam, Paul, Jane, and Becky, all armed, all walking quietly. Commander Daffy's door was open when they climbed down the stairs, his curtains pulled back so that the light shone into the corridor. His room was still messy, but there was a rug covering the floor. He had his glasses on and was sitting reading at his desk.

"Oh, hello," he said. "How lovely! A deputation! What can I do to help you all?" He put his book down and swung round toward them.

"Commander," said Sam, "we'd like to have a look at the siege tunnel in here, and we're wondering why you've been going through it."

"Goodness me," said Commander Daffy. "Is there a siege tunnel? I suppose there probably was somewhere in the castle, many years ago. But there isn't one in here."

"It's against the wall," said Sam. "Probably under your rug."

Sam strode toward the wall while Paul and Becky stood in the doorway, their spears grasped firmly in their hands. Commander Daffy beamed at them both.

As Sam lifted the rug, Commander Daffy turned, still smiling that smile that now made Non uncomfortable. "Oh, dear. Do put that old thing back carefully later, will you? There's a loose flagstone there, which I keep meaning to have fixed."

Sam prodded at the flagstone, which wobbled but didn't seem to do more than that. He took his spear and tried to lever up one of the corners, but though he managed to raise it by an inch, it was hard work, and he dropped it again.

"Goodness me, is it that flagstone that you think is a siege tunnel entrance? Because that would be a bit silly in a dungeon, don't you think? It would make it pretty easy for any prisoners trapped here to escape." He laughed, and Sam pulled the rug back. Becky and Paul had relaxed their hold on their spears, and for a minute Non felt her cheeks flushing with the embarrassment of having made a mistake, but then she decided this was just another one of those things that was worth the shame.

Sam stood uncertainly. "Well, sorry to bother you, sir. Let us know if you do find out where there is a siege tunnel."

"I will, Sam. I will."

Commander Daffy glanced at Non then, and she saw his smile waver again when he saw her. It was all the reassurance she needed. "Commander," she said. "Can I borrow some of your books?"

"Of course! I think you've read them all, though, haven't you? And made notes for your little demon project. This is a lovely one." He held up one of the ones she'd already read. "And perhaps this one."

He slid a slim brown book slowly across the desk. "It's got a bit about the history of this castle. Don't know if you'd be interested in that?"

She didn't let herself be fooled. "What I'm really interested in, Commander, is that one with a red cover. The one with the inverted crucifix on it?"

"Oh, dear, I don't know which one you're talking about, I'm afraid." He patted down all the books on his desk, as though he was humoring a child by looking for a fairy inside a tree.

"I already took it, Commander," she said, pulling it out from under her top. Immediately he lunged for her, but Becky and Paul stepped forward with their spears. He sat back in his chair, eyes narrowed, no longer the pretend fumbling old man of a second ago.

"You should have just asked for it," he said. "I would have been more than happy to show it to you." There was laughter in his voice, though, mockery. He raised his eyebrows. "Have you looked inside it yet?"

Non opened it and flicked through. Several different people had written neatly in it, and it contained columns and columns of names. Sometimes numbers had been written next to them, and sometimes arrows were drawn between names. There were other words too, written in capital letters—words that looked pseudo-Latin. Around half the pages were blank, but they were numbered, as though ready to be filled.

"Reading it will give you something to occupy you, at least. Sieges can be terribly boring. All that waiting for something to happen. I do hope you enjoy it."

"What is it?" she said.

He smiled, and Jane started tying up his arms.

"Are you going to tell us what you've been up to?" asked Sam.

"Don't be ridiculous. Of course I'm not."

"What were you doing up at the church?" pushed Non.

He laughed and shook his head. "Oh, you're lovely. Just lovely."

"Ugh. What shall we do with him?" asked Paul.

"Lock him in here," said Jane. "This is a dungeon, after all. It's set up for keeping prisoners."

"Apart from the probability that there's a siege tunnel here," pointed out Sam.

"Tie him up, then, *and* lock him in. There are manacles still on the walls."

Sam pulled at one of the manacles, testing it—still strong. Commander Daffy had had a scarf hanging from it. "What do you think, Non?" asked Sam.

"I like the idea of locking him in here. Just like those people in the church." Commander Daffy started to laugh again. "Plus, if he's locked in as well as being tied up, then even if there is a siege tunnel and it opens, nothing can get past the door."

Chapter 40

They were too well rested now. Non felt herself alternating between feeling lethargic and feeling so twitchy she couldn't stay still. Most people sat on the wall when they weren't sleeping or walked along the wall up to the top of the castle to stare along the track to the citadel—just in case help was coming. Even though, by this point, everybody was fairly sure it wasn't.

And the demons stared back at them, just out of range, or in their dark hiding places in the woods.

Meg sighed. She picked at some of the mortar between the stones.

"Don't do that!" said Ellie.

"What?" Meg turned to her.

"You'll break the wall."

"I'll break the wall! I'm just touching a bit of loose stuff. That's not going to break the wall in a crappy castle where everything is already broken."

"Well, it's not exactly helping, is it?"

"Oh. OK. Well, what are you doing that's helping anything ever?" Meg scowled at her and then relaxed before sighing again. "Sorry, Ellie. I just said that for drama. You are brilliant and always helpful."

"No, I'm not. I'm useless." Ellie hung her head.

"You're not useless," said Meg. "And at least you're not breaking the castle."

"Please, no," muttered Non.

Ellie and Meg both grinned at each other. "Sorry, Non," said Meg. "Are we annoying you?"

Behind them there was a sudden burst of shouting and laughter. Some of the Castle Goch boys were leaping over the jagged rocks that cropped out of the hillside. They had set up a course that required them to jump three, with a zigzag run between. Each one was a long distance to jump, and it wouldn't take much to miss. Missing would certainly involve cuts and bruises—and maybe more.

Sam was watching the game with a frown. He was drumming his fingers on the wall, and he crouched there rather than sitting. Every so often he would also look back at the plain in case the demons had moved, and then up at the towers in case one of the watchers had spotted help coming from the citadel track.

Non caught his eye and smiled. He smiled back, but she could see the stress in his face. "It's not going to happen today," she said.

"No," he said. "I don't think they'll attack in the daytime."

"Do you think they will attack, then?"

He grimaced. "Looks like they're going to do something, doesn't it?"

She nodded.

"What do you think?" he whispered.

"I don't know. Do you think they wanted to get in the other night, with the logs?"

"Definitely. And they almost did." He drummed his fingers on the wall again. "I feel like we're not as safe in here as we think we are. Even with Commander Daffy tied up."

"But we're not safe if we leave."

He looked back out at the plain once more. "We need to do something," he said. There was a particularly loud cheer from the Castle Goch boys, and he glanced back. "Yeah. Anything."

"You do it, then," said Non. "You."

He looked at her, and she nodded.

Slowly he stood up, with his back to the plain. "All right. Listen up!" he shouted. From all over the hillside, people turned to him. "Listen up!" he shouted again. People started to walk down and gather around him. "Nobody's coming," he said. "And we're probably going to be attacked again." People were grim-faced, but nobody looked shocked. "So let's spend the day getting ready. Let's spend our time, now, making sure we're the best we possibly can be, and that we know how to defend ourselves." There were nods from all over the hillside. "And win!" he added. There were cheers. "Because we can do this!" There were more cheers. He raised his arms above the crowd. "Let's get ready for war!"

———o———

Sam seemed to be everywhere at once. Never rushing, always seeming to be spending time with everybody, but all over the castle, people were suddenly doing useful things. Targets were set up by the gate, and Meg stood there with a stack of arrows lined up next to her. She shot them one after another, and some of the Kintaborel boys fetched them for her. Then, later, some citadel boys. Later still, when they'd gotten bored too, she fetched them herself.

Teams of Castle Goch boys ran up and down the hillside, practicing charging and defending the castle. They pointed out the rabbit holes to each other and removed the loose stones that might trip someone. They ran until they collapsed on the ground, panting.

Ellie and some of the other girls took a large bucket of mortar, removed any of the loose mortar from between the stones on the wall, and replaced it with new. Then, later, they threw spears. Close range, and just at the hillside behind them, but with determination and with increasing skill.

Water was pulled from the well and set up below the wall. Food was cooked, the sheep were penned up, the scarecrow pacers were released, the portcullis chains were oiled. Wood was chopped, fires were lit, arrows were checked, weapons were sharpened.

Becky, Chantelle, and Jane practiced using their swords—but just the lunging and stabbing and blocking and cutting. Later, others joined them—Ellie, but also Cath and some of the Kintaborel girls. With narrowed eyes and focus, Becky corrected their grip and showed them again, and again, and again, until they moved like her and were holding their swords like they could hurt.

But again, it was Mary and Callie who worked the hardest and had the most effect. They walked from person to person checking their clothing. They sewed thick army gloves onto sleeves so that there would be no exposed skin. As the night wore on, they tied scarves around students' necks so they were protected there too and, at some point, the Castle Goch girls were suddenly wearing tops that covered their stomachs. They checked for holes in clothing and material that might be too thin. Some students were given extra army tunics, and those on the wall the thicker helmets.

Before supper, Sam called everybody over again and divided them into teams so that there would be rows of archers, rows of those throwing spears, and rows of those deflecting attackers. He made them practice moving on his command, and then practice moving when there was nobody giving commands. At first they tripped over each other's weapons or had to duck out of the way to avoid spears or bows, but he kept them going, again, and again, and again, until eventually it felt like they were helping each other. Supporting each other rather than getting in each other's way. He sent people to run back and forth under the wall with water, extra weapons, and supplies, and he even made them practice swapping those weapons.

But eventually, Sam released them for the day. A few people stayed on the wall—those whose shift it was—and he turned to Non and smiled. The anxiety was still there behind his smile. "You faked it really well," she whispered, and he started to laugh.

"You think so?" he said.

"Yeah. It's almost like you were actually really good at it and weren't faking."

He groaned and covered his face again. "Let's wait and see what happens when it gets dark."

Chapter 41

Thick clouds covered the sky, gray and low, so that it felt like dusk for an hour before it was. The plain, the castle, the woods all seemed covered in shadow, and the air was cooler, sharper, harsher, every gust of wind sending a chill through them. The red kites hovered high above the plain, the wind blowing them upward and backward, but they always returned, their bodies moving effortlessly against the invisible force of the air.

The lanterns had already been lit, and their jollity as they swung on their line in the wind was like a promise of the worst party ever. But the light they cast did stretch down to the moat and illuminated the lowest, most vulnerable part of the wall. There were piles of dry wood on both sides of the moat, ready to light if needed, and the braziers on the wall were already burning. Non sat beside one for warmth.

A few students had gone for a sleep after supper, to rest up for battle. But Non didn't know how they could. Her head was still pumping with thoughts, things she'd half forgotten, worries about people at home, about themselves, about the missing soldiers, Commander Daffy. Images of the demons kept coming into her head, intruding on her ideas, sneaking into anything she tried to focus on, with their clawed hands and their snarling mouths.

And Sam was in her head too. She felt like she was aware of him always, could feel his body wherever he was in the castle, and she was constantly looking for him out of the corner of her eyes as he moved around checking everything was battle ready. She could feel his eyes on her, knew he was checking for her too, and his smiles made her feel beautiful.

The minutes ticked away; the shadows of the valley gradually grew into darkness; the wind became stronger, so that it was pushing against the students on the wall—battering them as they hunched smaller, bending down away from it. And the flames in the braziers threw dark, creeping shapes into the castle, twisting and dancing on the hillside.

It was almost time for a shift change when the attack came. The wind was high and was taking up so much space as it brushed past the students' ears that there was no room for any other noise. They had long ago given up trying to chat with each other, the shouted conversations just too much effort—not that there was much that seemed worth saying. A watcher at the far end of the wall—the point where the castle ramparts joined to the cliff—stepped forward suddenly. She peered into the darkness, looking for something nobody else could see. The others readied themselves, grasping their weapons tighter, but the narrow brightness around the lanterns blinded them to the rest of the plain, and anything beyond the moat was screened by the night. She stared at the nothingness, her eyes narrowed and searching, her ears turned toward whatever it was she had heard, but after a moment she leaned back again. Just the wind. Just that.

The others relaxed, hunching back against the wind, heads bowed and staring again at the moat. The wind howled against the stone of the cliffs, unearthly and strange, eerily similar to the wails of the demons, but the sound was not alive as theirs was—there was no horror there, just two forces meeting each other at speed.

And then the watcher stepped forward again, this time pointing her spear into the darkness. She listened, crouched, and half turned. But then something made her certain and she whipped round to the others, her face screwed up with fear.

"Attack!" she screamed. "They're here!"

"Light the fires!" shouted somebody. "Light the fires!"

Non thrust an arrow, heavy with oil and fat, into the brazier. It went up with an *oomph*, and the heat stung her fingers as she aimed it at a woodpile and fired. In the strength of the wind, the arrow hit only the edge of the wood, but it caught with a splutter and then a spreading burst of orange anyway. Along the other side of the moat, each of the bonfires went up in turn, the flames fighting against the wind.

But with the wind now came spots of rain, pinpricks of cold against Non's face, and the fires fizzed and spat against it. Floating down the moat, smoothly and effortlessly, came dark, thick logs; behind each of them, two white eyes glinted, glowing in the night.

From the gate somebody started to sound the alarm, the noise coming in waves as the wind carried it swirling around the hillside.

"Don't waste your arrows," came Sam's voice. "Wait until they get out. Get ready. Aim . . ."

Non felt for the arrows at her waist, checking them for the hundredth time. She loaded her crossbow and aimed it at the pair of eyes sliding closer. They were looking directly at her, the pupils wide and flickering with reflected flames.

For a moment, time slowed again, even the wind delaying as it grazed across Non's face. The logs moving steadily, closer and closer, those eyes fixed on Non, the pupils staying on her even as the log slid past.

Then suddenly the light changed, large shadows falling across the water and the wall: something moving in front of the fires. With a growl, the demons pushed their logs out of the moat to just beneath the wall, the water on them reflecting the firelight so that they seemed momentarily to glow—a moving shield of fire and death.

Out of the corner of her eye, Non could see that the string of lanterns had been cut, their light now falling only on the wall, exposing the students and keeping the demons in darkness. The bonfires were still lit, but their light was only on the moat, and it was dimming, a glow that hid any enemy beyond.

There was one demon in front of her, shielded by the log it was inching toward the wall. To either side, there was an advancing line of other shapes moving forward, but the light, and her panic, made the rest of the world a blur.

She became aware of the voices behind her, the calls and shouts as others gathered, running along the ramparts, running behind and handing up weapons. Everyone was in their positions, and the wall was bristling with weapons and adrenaline.

Beyond the moat Non could see other movements, a darkening of the night there, a shifting in the shadows. The demons and their logs took another step forward.

"First line of arrows," called Sam. "Stand tall! Aim for behind the logs. And . . . fire!"

The arrows flew, and though the demons slowed, crouching behind their logs, Non couldn't see that any had hit.

"Second line of arrows. Aim across the moat. Ready . . . fire!"

The arrows flew across the moat and into the darkness where nobody could see. And this time there was more success—yelps of pain, and shadows that seemed to pause.

But still the logs slid forward across the grass, the demons barely visible behind them.

"Get the levers ready," shouted Sam, and students lay down on the wall, the floorboards in their hands—Meg just next to Non. "First line, spears!"

Non unclipped her spear and readied it, aiming it at the closest log.

"Second line, reload arrows . . . and fire!"

Another set of arrows flew across the moat, whistling as they cut through the wind, and as they hit there were more yelps. In the distance a wail began. Then another from closer by. Non took a deep breath and shuddered as the sound hit her, but the wind took it away, each gust bringing new, fresh air that distorted or moved the sound beyond so that it didn't bring its usual paralyzing fear.

"Get ready," called Sam. "Hold . . . hold . . ."

The logs were a few feet away, now just a foot, the demons' legs visible behind. But the angle was awkward—tricky for an arrow to hit. Non gripped her spear more tightly.

"When they stand on the logs," called Sam. "Wait for that moment . . ."

Next to Non, half lying, half kneeling, Meg crouched awkwardly, her floorboard ready and protruding off the back of the wall, but Non could hear her panting—her breath too heavy and panicky.

"Calm down," Non whispered. "We can do this."

On an unseen signal, the logs moved forward at the same time, and suddenly the demons were leaping on top of them, their heads level with the top of the wall. Teeth bared and eyes focused, their clawed hands were reaching out not to climb the wall but to scratch at legs or arms. Meg flinched backward, and all around there were screams or shouts or snarls. Non stabbed at the closest demon with her spear, but it arched its back and the tip of the spear grazed its chest, leaving its arms free to scratch and grab. It lunged forward, and Non stabbed her spear at its face. It grabbed the tip and held on, its claws scraping against each other with a harsh screech that sent chills down Non's spine. She tried to shake it off, but its claws were intertwined now, locked together, and the more Non shook, the closer it seemed to get, and the tighter it seemed to grip.

"Meg, push the log away. Meg. Now!"

Non could hear her still panting, but Meg crawled back across the wall again and let the plank slide through her fingers. Then she grabbed it once more and pushed. Then she pushed more.

Non couldn't see what was happening, but the demon wobbled and righted itself, its spare arm arcing toward Meg's face. Non kicked the hand away and pushed her spear again.

"On three, together," she said to Meg. "One, two, three, push!"

Both girls pushed, and the demon fell backward, the log rolling away beneath it. Non had to let go of the spear, and the demon still clutched it as he stood back up again, but the log was now on its side and Meg pushed at it with her plank, rolling it away from the wall. Non grabbed her crossbow, and without even noticing herself loading it, she fired first one, then another arrow at the demon. The arrows hit—somewhere, anywhere—the demon fell backward, head lolling into the moat, and Non looked around. She realized she was breathing fast too—and wondered whether the panting had been hers, not Meg's. She could feel sweat on her forehead, now cooling rapidly in the wind, but her heart was still beating too fast in her chest. She breathed in and then exhaled slowly.

There was a mess of demon bodies lining the thin area of ground between the moat and the wall, and a set of logs still lay among them—all close by. None had been pushed back in the water, though people were trying now, poking at them with the planks. The bonfires on the other side of the moat were still lit, flaming and spluttering in the drizzle—they had hardly burned down at all.

Students were crouching down, hands on their knees, or wiping their faces with their arms, or hugging each other, or reloading their weapons. They were quiet now. The noise of a few moments ago was gone, the wind the only sound. There was a feeling of waiting. Non caught Sam's eye. He smiled at her, but the tension was clear in his face, and he turned back quickly to look at the battlefield.

And across the moat, another line of shadows appeared behind the bonfires. More than had attacked before—double the number, maybe triple.

"Second-line archers, get ready!" shouted Sam. "And fire!"

The arrows flew across the moat, but the wind blew most of them off course, and many of the shadows shifted quickly—ducking or dodging. There were no yelps this time, and Non saw most of the arrows falling uselessly on the ground beyond.

"First line, spears, get ready!" shouted Sam.

"Oh, no," hissed Non.

"Take the plank," said Meg. "Quickly!" Meg slid off the wall into the castle and ran for more weapons. Non crouched down. The plank was rough, and she could feel where it would give her splinters.

"Second-line archers get ready," shouted Sam. "Hold . . ."

The wind against the cliff rose in tone, two howls at once, as though the valley was playing a ghostly chord. The flames of the bonfires stretched out almost vertically, the wind trying to pull them with it as it flew through the night, and the rain started properly.

"Hold your fire," called Sam.

The rain flew in thick curtains of water at the head of each gust, flinging itself at the students so that they were soaked within seconds. The fires fought against it bravely for a few moments, but they quickly fizzled and smoked. Only the lanterns remained, lighting the corners of their eyes, outlining the area that needed protecting.

And then the demons leaped. Straight over the moat, they were suddenly there, pushing the logs forward again or jumping up at the wall snarling, so that students ducked back. They were a writhing, scratching, almost-invisible mass of fear.

Non just leaned on the plank and pivoted it from side to side, keeping them back. Every so often the plank hit and she felt a creature wincing away. There were shouts and calls and orders from all around her, but it was too much to hear; she focused just on keeping them away from her—those sharp claws and the bared teeth. Suddenly Meg was behind her, and a spear was back in Non's hand. She thrust it forward blindly, and it found soft flesh. She thrust it in farther, pulling away when the flesh went still.

"Get out of the way," shouted Callie. "Duck!"

Non and Meg ducked, and Callie threw a cauldron of boiling water into the crowd of demons. There were yelps and whimpers—like those from an injured dog—and then splashes as some jumped in the moat.

"More arrows," shouted Mary from behind. "More arrows!" She walked along the wall on the castle side, passing arrows to every student.

"Fire at will!" shouted Sam. "Fire at will!"

Non loaded her crossbow and peered into the night. The rain was easing and the moon rising as the cloud withdrew, so that the wet bodies of the moving demons gleamed on the grass below. She aimed carefully and fired. The arrow hit, and around her she could hear other arrows hitting, so that the moving bodies slowly became still or withdrew to the darkness across the moat.

"Are there any alive down there?" called Sam. "Anybody got any alive?"

The last of the demons slid backward into the moat. Non thought it might have been injured, but it disappeared into the water with a ripple as it swam away.

"Position your planks outward," he said. "As a barrier. They'll protect us for a minute as you rest."

Non could already see more demons gathering, their forms indistinct and larger than reality in the remaining drizzle.

She sat on her plank, the wall wet and cold beneath her. But then, every part of her was also wet and cold. The braziers still burned, and she leaned closer to one for warmth. Her hands were aching from gripping—the muscles, and her skin—and she flexed her muscles, trying to relax them.

"They're coming again!" called Sam. "Prepare yourselves . . . Second-line archers get ready . . . fire!"

Chapter 42

Non lost count of the number of attacks. Repeated surges with the rain, wet and terrible; snarling and writhing under the darkness of the clouds; sudden leaping and grabbing.

But by the time the gray light of dawn arrived, there were demon bodies strewn all over the ground—so many between the moat and the wall that there was barely any remaining ground visible. The students were in a state of watchfulness that made moving from the wall feel impossible. Sore, stiff, but ready to jump at the slightest movement or sound. Non's body ached—every part of her—but she thrummed with adrenaline so that she could feel her blood pulsing inside her. Those wet, cold walls felt part of her being. Non could no longer tell where her body ended and where the stone began. When she touched her own skin check for scratches, it felt cold and clammy—no longer alive. But re was no broken skin. Nowhere they'd managed to reach her, o g, or any of those near her.

They sat uched or stood, shoulders sagging, staring at the dawn. The fir of the birds made them start, a squeaking in the portcullis le them shudder, the rippling wind through the trees made their weapons.

And the slow silence rang in their ears. The sky was white with a thin layer of dirty cloud that covered the valley, deadening everything. The wind had fallen toward dawn, and so the cloud drifted slowly across the sun, brightening occasionally as the wispier sections moved underneath, but never so the light broke through completely. It was cold, and the heavy rain of last night had left the plain boggy. Where the demons had run and fought or slid, there were streaks of mud cutting through the grass, but there were also puddles everywhere now, pools where only the taller tips of grass protruded, the rest sunken and waiting for the sun to dry.

There were no demons in the woods. No live ones anywhere.

It was Sam who spoke first, his voice creaky from shouting. "I make that forty-eight bodies. Can anyone else confirm?"

There was a moment's silence again as everybody counted, but it was tricky to tell, as without clothes, and slippery with blood, some of the demons were indistinguishable from each other, their corpses tangled together—legs intertwined with legs, arms under heads. Non felt her shoulders starting to relax, became aware of the pain everywhere. She moved her feet out from underneath her so that she was sitting, letting her legs dangle off the edge of the wall. For a split second, her heart jumped as she remembered the danger of those claws, but there was nothing moving down there. She was suddenly aware of how tired she was—exhausted beyond anything she'd ever felt before.

"Watchers, can you confirm sight of any of the enemy?" he called.

The two students holding their binoculars shook their heads, confirming what everybody could see.

"We need to send word to the citadel," said Sam. "Now, while the enemy are weak and retreating."

"The track looks clear," called a watcher.

"Who can still run?"

A few Castle Goch boys put up their hands.

"Go now, then. Quickly. Take weapons, but don't stop to fight if you can run round. We have to tell the citadel about their water being poisoned—just in case they don't know." His voice faltered on the last few words, and Non wondered about their guards and the missing commanders. It had been almost a week now. Something must have happened. But was it something on the way there before they'd given the message, or was it something on the way back? Or maybe the guards had stopped to help out with the plague, to make sure all the castles knew and that everybody was fine before they came back? She thought briefly about Daffy too—but he could wait.

Callie thrust some bread into each of the boys' hands. They jumped down and, looking anxiously toward the hillside, ran.

Sam turned to the rest of them. "We need to collect our weapons. Get those arrows back."

"Can't we wait a bit?" replied Paul.

"No," said Sam. "Collecting our weapons is the priority, and I want archers out on the plain to cover anybody who's doing it. Volunteers only."

Paul raised his hand, along with Becky, Jane, and a few of the other Castle Goch students.

"Those logs also need to go."

"No," interrupted Callie. "Bring them in. I can use them for something."

"Drawbridge down this time," said Sam. "So I need people ready to pull it up in a hurry. Just in case."

Paul and Jane didn't wait for the drawbridge and jumped down on the plain, picking their way between the bodies to get to the moat. Non caught Sam's eye, and he turned away to stop himself laughing.

"Can everybody else wait for the drawbridge?" he said. "In case you need to get back inside quickly."

Paul cleared the moat easily again, whereas Jane jumped straight into the middle. She took her ponytail out and ducked under for a moment, emerging with her hair wet and her top sticking even more tightly to her chest.

"Oh, for goodness' sake," muttered Meg, unfurling herself from her crouched position. Her face was very pale, and her lips were stretched thin. "Wouldn't she be much happier in a nice warm jumper?" Non started to laugh. "It is ridiculous to look like that straight after a battle."

The drawbridge was lowered with a juddering thump, and then the portcullis raised, the clanking of the chains reassuring and heavy today. Students started walking over, heads bowed with tiredness. Jane and Paul both clutched handfuls of arrows already.

"And we're going to need to get rid of those bodies too," said Sam, more quietly now.

Non nodded. There weren't many people left on the wall. Most of those still sitting were there, Non felt, because they were so tired they could no longer move.

"Me and Meg will do it."

"Don't even think of volunteering me for that," said Meg. She gave a laugh, but there were tears behind the laughter.

"It's clearly our specialty, Meg. And we know you can do it while still looking good."

"Glad you've offered," said Sam. "But I think we'll need more than just you two for this job."

Meg sighed. She shook out her hair and stood up. "I would *love* to get rid of those dead bodies," she said. She stretched, raising her arms above her head so that her stomach was partly exposed and her breasts protruded more obviously. She casually let her fingers brush over her breasts as she pulled her top back down.

Silently, several of the boys stood up.

"I'll go and get a cart," said Non.

———o———

With others helping, and a cart, it was much faster work. Non tried not to look too closely at the individual features of the dead, but she could see their faces were all different, even in death. She wondered if they'd had different personalities too.

Many of the bodies they loaded onto the cart and then placed in the pit were scarred, their muscles sagging or their color a deeper red. On some, their claws and feet were misshapen, twisted, like they had a form of demon arthritis. A part of Non would have liked to take one of the bodies to examine it more closely and dissect it, but a much, much bigger part of her just desperately wanted to get rid of them and never look at them again. She felt waves of revulsion and fear even as they covered the bodies in lime, clouds of powder rising as the sacks were poured in the pit. The dead demons remained terrifying—something about the fact that they looked humanoid was more threatening than if they were a four-legged predator, as though the recognition of their similarity to humans made them more relatedly awful.

As they stood at the pit, unloading the last of the bodies, somehow most of the students were there. The pit was now filled almost to the top, the smell of the forest emanating from it not unpleasant—musty, mushroomy, damp earth, fresh leaves. Not rotting vegetation yet—more an extra freshness to the air that you'd get as you walked into the woods in the autumn.

Most people just stared, silently, at the dead stacked on top of each other. There was an awe and a weirdness—a sadness—about the bodies, but it looked, even now, as though their eyes could suddenly swivel, and their claws suddenly grab at a leg to scratch and infect. Nobody stood too close.

"A prayer," said Mary. The Kintaborel Castle students led, but this time nobody laughed, and everybody held hands—they kept their eyes open, though, and trained on the pit. "We thank you for saving us from death and giving us the strength to make it through the night. Bless these creatures, Lord, and . . . whatever happens to them after their death, let it be good. Amen."

"Oh my God, I hope demons don't go to wherever we go after death," said Meg. "That would be the worst afterlife ever."

Non nodded and put her arm round her. Meg was still shaking—maybe just shivering this time, because it *was* cold this morning. There wasn't so much a breeze as just shifting patches of bitterly cold air. They were filled with moisture that clung to everything, coating Non's skin and hair in beads of cold.

But the plain felt empty and fresh, like it belonged to them—like they'd really earned it back.

"I think we should get those strings of lanterns," said Non, "and put them round the pit."

Meg nodded.

Some people started to walk back slowly, toward the castle and bed, but others remained, maybe praying, maybe just thinking. And when Meg and Non got back with the lanterns, Callie and Mary were already there to add more oil. They filled them and spaced them evenly around the pit. Non knew the glow would be seen from up in the hills.

It was only then that Non felt they could go back into the castle. She searched for Sam, and he was already back on the wall, standing guard over the plain. As she watched him, there were shouts from inside the castle—several voices. She couldn't make out what they were saying, but she didn't need to. She could tell from the tone and the timing. Commander Daffy had gone.

Chapter 43

The tunnel in Commander Daffy's cell was open, the flagstone slid to one side. There were ropes still hanging from the manacles, but they were shredded. Sam leaned down to examine the floor. "We need lights," he said. "Nobody's going down until we can see our way. There's daylight from somewhere, so my guess is it probably only goes as far as the banks of the moat." He peered at the stone. "But it looks like . . . this doesn't open from inside the castle. It opens from underneath. I don't think . . . yeah. There's a mechanism here. You'd have to have something to hook into the stone from inside the tunnel to move it."

"Would a demon claw work?" asked Non.

The whole room went silent. "Yeah," he said. "I think that would be perfect. A demon claw would be exactly the right shape for opening this tunnel."

"So the tunnel was designed to be opened from the outside," said Non.

"Yes." Sam nodded grimly.

"The ropes we used to tie him have either been bitten away or scratched apart," said Paul. "They haven't been cut."

Sam nodded again. "I don't suppose there's any blood, is there?"

"No," said Paul. "No. The demons attacked the ropes, not Commander Daffy."

"We'll get a load of stone to dump down the tunnel now," said Callie. "We can open it up again later, when this castle's definitely secure—but I don't want a surprise way in here. Look: Me, Cath, and Mary will sort this room out. You go and get everything else fixed."

<hr />

A lot of people had gone straight to bed, but Non was too wired. She did feel exhausted but also like she had too much energy, as though now was the time when she could run to the citadel and back. And she would need to do something like that to get to sleep. She knew that if she lay down, her head would become even more active, ideas and thoughts spinning round in her mind. She climbed back onto the wall where they'd fought the battle—now dry and cleared of any sign of action. She wondered how many other battles had been fought here on these stones without any evidence being left behind of those either. A few others were standing there too, looking out over the plain at nothing. Meg was there, a few of the Castle Goch students, and Sam.

She walked along to Meg and gave her a hug. They stayed like that for a few moments before Non let go.

"I want to go up there, back to the church," said Non. "Now's the best time, because the demons are injured or tired."

"Just like us," said Meg. "So now's the worst time."

"Please? I went out of the castle for you."

"That's when we were being idiots and didn't know what was out there. We do know now."

"I still don't think we do know, exactly. I think we need to figure out what's in that red book to be sure."

Sam came up behind and put his arms around her, leaning his head on hers. Both Becky and Jane looked over, open-mouthed in surprise. "Do you want to go to sleep?" he said. Becky started to giggle.

"Yes. But I want to go up there and look for Commander Daffy and the surviving demons first."

He groaned. "Really?"

"Please?"

"Right up to where the lights come from?"

He was no longer resting his chin on her head now but looking around the hillside, searching for routes. She knew he'd be interested.

"Yes. I reckon we can get there and back in a couple of hours. If you fancy a run?"

He laughed. "Non, even I don't fancy a run. But I would like to see what's going on up there. Does anybody else want to come? Back up to the church and maybe higher?"

"Yeah," said Jane, so Paul nodded too. Becky shrugged.

"We could try and capture Commander Daffy and bring him back," said Non. Paul smiled and stood up straighter.

"Or we could just leave him to hang out with the demons," said Meg. "If that's the sort of thing he wants to do."

"Don't you think they'll have killed him?" asked Becky.

"I honestly don't know," said Non.

"Fine," said Meg. "I'll come, then. But you owe me big-time."

"I always pay you back, though, don't I?"

Meg grinned. "Oh, you are going to owe me so many favors for this one."

Chapter 44

They set off across the boggy plain and headed straight for the path up the hill. It was much faster and easier this time, knowing exactly where they were going, and maybe it was the adrenaline, or maybe she really did need a run, but Non found it much easier going. She wasn't out of breath at all. This time she jogged next to Sam and Meg; it was Paul, Becky, and Jane who brought up the rear.

As they emerged from the trees, they stopped to look back at the castle. The drawbridge was still down, and there was a halo of dark brown mud around the castle wall, which gradually lightened and merged into the bright green of the plain. Here and there strange lumps moved, shaggy and misshapen—the red kites on the ground.

They looked in each of the rotting houses as they passed, more carefully than before now that they knew predators lived nearby, but there was no sign of animal habitation in any of them. When they reached the clearing with the rabbits, though, a demon was sitting, leaning against a tree.

"Stop!" Paul held his arm up, looked around carefully, and then edged forward. The demon turned its head slowly at their approach, but it could barely lift its chin and didn't try to get out of their way.

There was a large cut along its thigh and, even now, it was wet with blood, the grass next to it glistening with dark droplets.

Paul raised his spear.

"Don't kill it," said Non.

He nodded. "We'll just take out its venom though. Maybe de-claw and file the teeth later. Jane. Help and take its hand."

Jane bent down and grabbed one of its hands, holding the claws together so that they couldn't cut. The demon bared its teeth at her as though to bite, but she wagged her finger at it.

"No!" she said. "No!"

Holding its other hand, Paul took his knife and followed one of the claws to a point on the ridged skin beyond the demon's fingers on the back of its hand. Paul searched for a couple of seconds, then pressed the flat of his knife down firmly. A clear-white liquid started to ooze out, falling onto the ground beside the demon. Paul moved to another finger and did the same, and then again for all the fingers. He hadn't cut the skin, as far as Non could see—there was no blood mingled with the liquid, and the demon didn't seem to be in any pain.

"Swap, Jane," he said. And he did the same with the other hand. The whole process took less than five minutes. "I'm going to do the mouth now. They don't like that."

"Do you want any help?" asked Sam.

"Jane, can you manage both arms?"

She nodded.

"Then Sam—you can keep lookout. And could somebody do something with its leg?"

Non bent down to see. She really only knew about injuries from books—and those were about humans. But this cut did look deep—although clean. It had obviously been done with a spear. On a human she'd have assumed it needed stitches, and she'd seen skin being sewn back together before. But on a creature without skin? She peered in closer as Jane held back the arms and Paul pried open the mouth. There really was no obvious epidermis. The creature was just muscle and flesh and bones. There was nothing that appeared to be holding it together, yet now, here, only when it was injured did the blood spill out and the creature feel pain. She ripped away a strip from her shirt and bound the wound together as best she could, tying it up. She thought she'd managed to get the two sides of the flesh to join together again, and the blood did seem to have eased.

Paul was holding both sides of the jaw apart with just the fingers of his left hand. It was clearly a well-practiced move, but Non would not have been as confident as him, especially as the canines rested on his index finger. He already had his knife in the demon's mouth, but he was frowning in concentration, and it was a few moments before Non saw the clear-white liquid oozing. Paul moved his knife to the other side of the demon's jaw and pressed down again, so that more liquid came out.

"Done!" said Paul, standing back up and tucking his knife into his belt. Jane gave the demon a stroke under its chin, and it made a whimpering noise. Then she stood up too.

"If it's still there on the way down, can we take it back with us?"

"Yes, sweetheart," said Paul. "I'll bring it down for you."

"He's a lovely specimen."

"God," whispered Meg. "There are no words."

Sam grinned at Non.

"Let's go quickly," said Becky. "There's been nothing moving, but the sooner we get up there, the better."

They walked on past the dilapidated village houses and straight toward the church. Paul opened the gate to the graveyard, and they stepped in again.

"It's interesting that the gate is still on its hinges, isn't it?" said Sam.

Paul peered down at the hinges. "I think they've even been oiled," he said.

They each looked out for other signs—things they should have spotted before. But the situation in the church was so strange that it was easy to excuse them having missed the other things. Like why the church was in such good condition in the first place, or that clear pathway through the grass, or the animal droppings when there were no animals.

This time Non looked closely at the circular patterns around the door. They were definitely from stencils—and she could see this time that there were only three different ones, repeated over and over. Between the knots and decorations, the creature hiding in one of them was a monkey, on another a man, and on the third a demon. Concealed even more faintly and more difficult to see, she could just make out the figure of Death in all of them, his scythe part of that repeating knot pattern.

The door was still tightly shut. Now that she was more familiar with demon claws, Non could see that the creatures wouldn't have been able to turn the handle to go inside.

"Shall we look through the window first to check?" suggested Meg.

"No." Non shook her head.

"I'll go in first," said Sam. The thick, heavy handle did not turn easily, grating against the wood and something metal inside its workings, but it gave suddenly, and the door banged against the wall with a clatter that echoed throughout the church. For a moment they waited, but there was nothing moving inside. They walked in, and Becky shut the door tightly behind them. The church had been cleared, the benches pulled completely up against the wall so that the space felt very big and empty. The broken window had been boarded up, and the light felt different—some of the magic of the church had gone.

"I don't think they've been in here," said Sam.

"No. Let's go up the tower," said Non.

Looking down over the valley, the four castles stood out, just as they had before. Cirtop was noticeably neater now—not much bigger, but less ruined than it had been when they'd arrived, the walls straightened up a bit and perhaps a little higher. What Non hadn't noticed when she'd looked before was how small they all were in comparison to the valley itself—how cramped, how artificial, how enclosed. All the human world she knew was concentrated inside those four, squat, protected places, and, suddenly, looking at the miles of valley where she hadn't been, and the hills and the clouds and the world beyond, it felt difficult to tell the difference between protection and a prison. Just the thought of returning to the hard, opaque, rough walls of the citadel—they suddenly felt too high, too solid, too vast. The thought of it made her feel like she would be the one hiding, shrinking, becoming invisible.

Non turned and looked the other way. The rest of the valley curled down to the sea. The hills on either side were high and thickly wooded, blocking any view of the rest of the world, but there were glimpses of the river as it turned a corner, and perhaps a lake beyond.

"Let's go," she said.

Chapter 45

When they left the churchyard, they saw what they hadn't noticed before—a second track leading away from the church. This one went farther up the hill, and was well-worn, though not wide enough for a cart. At points it was overgrown with bushes or overhanging branches. But it was easily wide enough for a human to walk along. Or a demon.

Non took a deep breath and pointed. The others nodded.

Sam went first, then Paul, and everybody gripped their weapons, but the track was steep and so were the sides. Anything hiding along here would be having to cling onto the rock of the hillside or crouch behind impossibly angled clumps of ivy. There were no trees up here, but the canopy of the forest below was level with the track, concealing it from the castle and the village. It didn't feel like a secret passage—more a passage that they'd ignored, just hadn't noticed, because they'd been looking at different things.

It was the smell that she noticed first. That fungusy, ferny air—a forest smell, but more intense, sharper, and sudden. It felt deliberate, a marking of territory, and Sam slowed, holding up his hand to give a signal that wasn't necessary. They had all realized. Silently they crept forward, holding their weapons ready.

And the smell became even more focused. Meg put her hand over her mouth as they climbed higher, and when she turned every so often to scan the hillside, Non saw her nostrils flaring. There was still nowhere for demons to hide: The bushes were low, the hill steep on both sides of the track. But a red kite was circling the brow, flying slowly over and around something. Non wondered what it was. Whether it was already dead, or whether it was about to be. She hoped it wasn't them.

They crept along, single file, looking across the valley constantly to check if they were at the point where they'd seen the lights, but the moment came suddenly. It was just a gap in the trees below—not even a clearing, and nothing they'd have noticed before. But through it they could see the castle, now with its banners up and the watchers in their right places. And just ahead of them on the pathway, there was a dip, then a couple of large boulders to the side stood in front of a cut in the hillside—part of that whole cliff was missing, or perhaps curved suddenly back. From here Non couldn't see what it was, but the boulders felt deliberate, like they had been placed there at some time to mark something—maybe to hold up the mud on either side of that unnatural cut through the hill. Or perhaps as a gateway. Was it humans who had done it? Or was it demons?

They had slowed further and were now all crouching low, on high alert, looking round for movement. Because of that, they didn't notice the stillness.

Suddenly, Becky gave a muffled scream, and Paul stopped. She dropped to the ground, crouching and pointing at something just below them on the hillside. Paul and Jane tried to pull her back upright, but she sobbed silently and shook her head.

Non turned to see what they were looking at.

There, laid out on one of the bushes, was a staring, upside-down human head. She felt a jolt of panic as she saw it, but it was clearly dead. Stretched out above, pulled taut over the branches and leaves, was the skin to go with it. It was still recognizable as belonging to a person, and Non's stomach clenched as she forced herself to look and see if it was somebody she knew. In death, the features were twisted, without the animation that normally gave a face personality, but the eyes were open and glassy. The hair on this one was short, probably meaning it was male and military. The attached skin gave no clue. It was pale, curling up at the edges, and a few flies walked across it idly, but stretched out and misshapen without its flesh and bones, it gave no hint to the shape of the body it had once enclosed.

Becky knelt down on the pathway and gagged, tears in her eyes as she tried to stop herself from throwing up. Meg turned back to face Non, her eyes squeezed shut. It was then that Non realized there was more than one. On each of the nearest bushes, and maybe more beyond, there were the drying skins of humans. Some still fresh, some more leathery, but all recent. All from this year. And she looked along them, knowing that she was looking for a couple in particular. One was there. A few bushes along, there was a hanging face, the cheeks partly torn—maybe in battle. But its long hair was still tied up in what had been a tight ponytail. That hair dragged now over the face, obscuring the blotchy red patches Non knew would be there: Dog.

"Let's get out of here," whispered Meg.

"No!" Becky shook her head. She gagged again as she got to her feet. "No."

"I don't like it," whispered Sam, still scanning the hillside. "It feels like a trap. They have the advantage here. We can only go single file on this track."

"But they're mostly dead," said Paul. "We've seen them. Like that injured one near the church."

"Let's go down and get more people," said Meg. "Wait for reinforcements."

"No," said Sam. "More people would make it worse. Even if we had reinforcements, they'd have to go single file uphill on this path—which would be a massacre if demons attack. And the demons are at their weakest now."

He glanced at the skins in the bushes and then glanced away again.

"A vote, then," he whispered. "Who's happy to go on? Because I am." He twisted his spear round in his hands.

Becky raised her hand immediately, then Jane and Paul followed more slowly.

Meg looked at Non. Meg's face was pale, and her lips were pressed tightly together. Non took a deep breath. She felt shaky even thinking about those skins, but it also made her angry. "I'm sick of being scared," she said. "I'm sick of us keeping ourselves prisoner in the castles pretending we own this valley when really we're scared to go into it. So let's do this!"

"Fine." Meg laughed grimly, and there were tears in her eyes again. "But the favors you owe me now are so massive you'll be paying them back forever."

Non reached out and squeezed her hand.

"You stay in the middle," said Sam to Meg. "It'll be safest there." She nodded.

"OK?" mouthed Paul, raising his spear. Then he ran forward to the first boulder and crouched down, peering behind it. But slowly he stood up again and beckoned everybody forward.

Behind the boulders was an area of flat ground, and then, beyond that, a rectangular slit into the hillside. A doorway. Too neat and artificial to be a cave, but too rough to be a house. It also lined up, once more, with another gap in the trees. It wouldn't have been significant from down on the plain, or in the clearing beneath, but there was enough space between the branches so that anybody—or anything—leaving the door in the hillside would have been able to see the castle, yet the watchers on the battlements, even with their binoculars, would have struggled to see them.

Just to one side of the doorway sat several young demons. Two had their teeth bared and were scratching at each other with their claws, making high-pitched snarling noises. They made a grab for each other and rolled over in the dirt, but as quickly as they'd started, they were standing up again—one placing his teeth on the other's shoulder as though to bite. But no blood was drawn, and none of the other demons reacted. It looked more like play than a fight.

Two others were sitting on the dirt, much smaller ones—the size of human two-year-olds. They had no claws, only slightly pointed fingernails; they were both scraping at the dirt and emitting gentle wails.

Others were sitting in the partial shadow of the cliff itself. They still weren't fully grown—their claws not yet formed—but they were much larger. They weren't doing anything in particular—just stretching or staring out into the sky.

Jane gasped and covered her mouth with her hands. Non felt a stab of revulsion just looking at them, but their bodies were rounder, softer, and their heads disproportionately large. The little ones were clumsy and moved in a comical fashion, with none of the grace of the adults. They were almost . . . cute. Not in the way that a kitten is cuter than a cat, or a puppy even more lovable than a dog, but maybe in the way that a newborn snake is less repellent than a full-grown one, or a freshly hatched black widow less dangerous than the adult spider.

"Do you think there are any of the bigger demons in there, somebody to look after these?" whispered Meg.

"The one in the clearing was there to guard something, even if it was too injured to do it properly," pointed out Sam. "Probably these babies."

"There might be others, though, down in the cave. I can't tell how deep it is," said Non. "It must go back farther than we can see, because at night their lights only appear gradually—which I suppose is them getting brighter, because they start deeper in the cave."

"Should we kill them?" whispered Paul. "Isn't that what we should probably do?" He still clutched his spear, but as he said those words, he moved it farther back, away from the demons.

There was silence for a moment as everybody tried to figure out what to say. Finally, it was Sam who spoke. "Why would we kill them when they're not attacking us and they don't have any way of transmitting the parasite?"

"I'm not killing them unless they attack me," said Jane. "They're basically pacers. But even more gorgeous."

Meg pulled a face.

Sam looked around the hillside and up the cliff, but it was still all clear. Nothing moving.

"Can you wait here with them, Jane?" he said. "Keep them out of our way."

She nodded. "No problem."

One of the two wrestling demons let out a snarl again, high-pitched and playful. He jumped on the other one, play-scratching it, and they were on the floor again, rolling in the dirt and biting each other with teeth that didn't draw blood.

"Come on," whispered Sam, and they walked between the boulders.

The young demons immediately leaped back into the doorway, crouching down and making snarling noises—their little teeth bared. But Paul pushed them to one side and stepped into the darkness.

"Come here, babies," said Jane, herding them back outside with her spear.

Chapter 46

It was a passageway, roughly cut—but cut deliberately. It went back much deeper than Non could see, and much farther than she wanted to go into darkness. But they stood for a moment, tense, aware of the young demons snarling, and Jane's soothing noises, behind them. It only took that moment before Non could make out what looked like eyes staring at them in the darkness. And then, almost immediately, there was the awareness that they were flickering—not demon. Not real. Not moving toward them. But those lights lit up the darkness of the passage so that, slowly, as her eyes adjusted, Non could see a way down into the hillside.

The flickering lights were blue and cast strange shadows on the walls and ceiling, so that there was a feeling of strange, unearthly shapes moving, with those eyes watching them.

"Look!" whispered Meg.

On the walls there were odd patterns. Swirls, dots, animals. Non reached out to touch them but then stopped. Because what had they been painted with? Their reddish-brown color reminded her of dried blood. Was it? She followed the patterns up. They covered the ceiling, the walls, almost the entirety of the passageway. Farther down she saw images of figures with their arms raised. Other painted figures lay down beneath, maybe dead. She couldn't tell if the images were supposed to be demon or human. Or monkey. And she couldn't tell if they were dancing or in a battle.

"Don't look at the lanterns," gasped Becky. So they all looked at the lanterns and Non could see right then that they were skulls, the white of the bone smoky from the flames inside so that they were hard to make out against the gray of the stone walls. Some of them were demon, she thought, the teeth sharp and prominent. But she knew some of them would be human too.

It wasn't fear Non felt at all. It was definitely anger—and she knew it was at the demons. But it was also at them. At the humans. How had they not figured out about this place before? How had nobody managed to go here, observe the demons, and then come back to tell everybody else? Sitting in their increasingly fancy castles, behind their high walls, congratulating themselves on their military skills, people had stayed for centuries, ignoring the fact that they were trapping themselves. And they were choosing to stay trapped with their own ignorance.

"Commander Daffy," she called, and the others jumped. "We know you're in there. Come out!"

From somewhere along the passageway, there was an answering scrabbling sound. A shuffling. But nobody came.

"Commander Daffy. Come out—or we'll have to go in. And we're armed."

There was no reply. They waited, looking at each other.

"Nobody's coming out to attack us anyway," whispered Sam. "Come on. Let's go."

He strode down, picking up one of the skull lanterns on the way. Others picked up one too, and Non noticed each preferring the demon ones—the idea of touching a human skull feeling more wrong somehow. She held hers delicately, away from her, but high up so that the light would reach into each of the shadows in the ceiling. There were stalactites forming in places, thin, wet spikes of stone, like teeth—not yet those thick pillars she'd seen in the caves or the dungeons of the citadel back home. How long had this passageway been here?

In front, Meg's light shook as she held it up, and she looked around her as if expecting things to leap from the walls at any moment. Their footsteps were loud, the slightest tread an echo in the silence. The damp stone of the passageway confused and warped any sound, so that Non couldn't tell if it was her own breathing she was hearing or somebody else's. She kept turning round anyway, to check behind her, even though they'd already seen every crevice as they passed. But the shadows of the skulls seemed to project faces on the walls, faces that changed and disappeared as soon as you looked at them; crevices they'd passed, which had been clear and free of anything, seemed to become darker, as though they were endlessly deep, as soon as they'd moved on. And the light was fading behind them, the escape route of the entrance getting farther away.

Suddenly Sam stopped. Non tensed, getting ready to run, and Meg turned slightly toward her too. He held up his hand

and shone his skull at the wall. The light disappeared into another doorway.

"It's a room," he whispered, and his voice was overly loud, so that Non looked down the passageway in case anything had heard. "Shall we . . ." he said, but he walked slowly into the room before finishing his sentence. "Oh . . . wow."

Non pushed forward and into the room. It was small—not much larger than Commander Daffy's cell—and circular. The walls were smooth and unpainted, the ceiling also curving up so that it felt like the room was almost entirely spherical. The floor might once have been too, but any indentation in the stone was covered with layers of thick leaves. Much thicker than the forest floor outside, the surface felt soft and springy as Non stepped onto it. She did so slowly, because the leaves covered her ankles with each footstep, and she couldn't see to start off with what else they concealed. But the leaves were crispy and dry, decaying, and she could feel that beneath them it was mainly soil—soft, dry, rich, and dark. The room felt warmer than the passageway, drier, and the air in there smelled like the outside forest pathway.

"I'll guard the door," whispered Becky. "Be quick."

In among the leaves there were eggshells. Hundreds and hundreds of eggshells. The cracked pieces had been pushed toward the wall, so that there was a ring of white around the room, and it was that which Sam walked on as he paced round, bending to examine it. Non could see that there were layers of eggshell too. Sunk deep beneath the leaves, with other shells piled on top, there were lower jagged bits—far more than she could ever have imagined. It must have been the cracked eggs of all the hatched demons for centuries. That left a large space in the middle of the room, though, ready for more.

Sam stopped and prodded something. Then he pushed aside the leaves, exposing a cluster of round white eggs. They were sunken into the humus around them, and the grime and soil on top suggested that they'd been there for a while.

"Oh, look," said Paul. "Those eggs are still whole."

"Do you want to smash one?" asked Meg. "That might be funny. The noise!" She laughed, and then as Paul looked at her, she started to laugh even more at the confusion in his face. "It wouldn't be funny. It really wouldn't. Don't smash them."

"Definitely don't smash it," said Non. "I'll want to look at them."

"So you can smash them in a scientific way, in a laboratory?" said Meg, still laughing.

Non grinned, despite herself and the situation. "I'll collect them later. It's just I hadn't thought about it before, but the eggshells must be made from a combination of human and demon bodies. Which is interesting. And it's also interesting they need to be so thick and strong, because that suggests the demon babies need protecting from something inside the host body—which isn't how parasites normally work."

"Sorry, but why is that interesting right now?" asked Meg.

"Just—because it's maybe the beginning of looking for a cure. Looking at the eggshells and unhatched eggs might be a really good start."

Non caught Sam's eye for a moment, and she saw that he was restless, his body charged, ready to fight. For a moment she'd forgotten what they were doing and also what had happened last time they'd found a set of demon eggs. "Let's go," she whispered, and they crept back out again.

Becky was still standing facing out to the passageway, and she waved them forward. They passed another room, roughly cut, with long grooves on the floor. Sam bent down to touch them as he peered into the room.

"Train tracks? This must be a mine!" he whispered, and the others nodded. It felt inevitable, really. Commander Daffy being in charge of the maps must have been to give him the opportunity to erase lots of useful information. Whatever mineral had been the reason for digging into this hillside originally, it had long been abandoned, run by the demons for many, many years, and Non wondered what had happened to those ancient miners who'd tunneled into this rock, whether it was them who'd ended up being mined by the demons, their bodies growing those eggs.

"It's empty," said Sam, shining his lantern into the room, but they all stopped to peer in anyway; none of them felt they could walk past an expanse of darkness without checking what was in those shadows.

The floor was noticeably sloping downward now; as they went deeper into the mine, the air was cooler. Every so often there was a step cut into the floor or it had been left rough, to prevent slipping. As the passageway veered round a slight corner, they all raised their weapons, but there was no movement, and Non could see only darkness ahead. The blue lanterns were no longer placed at intervals in the walls, and the way seemed to stretch on deep into the hillside.

Then, suddenly, Sam stopped. In front of him, the darkness was shifting. Paul stepped so that he was next to him, and both of them raised their spears.

From the depths of the darkness, a figure emerged. Commander Daffy was also carrying a lantern, the blue of its light flickering brightly on his face. It made him look unearthly, a specter, the blue color twisting the shadows across his face so that his skin seemed blurred. He stopped and stared at the students, waiting for them to speak.

"What's written in the book?" asked Non.

Commander Daffy laughed, his smile slowly stretching that loose skin across his face again so that Non realized what it reminded her of: a plague mask. One of those masks the body carriers in the citadel used to protect themselves from infection—the hard, wooden shape of the masks twisted into exaggerated human faces, frozen in an expression that never represented the emotions of the person wearing it.

"We've won against the demons," she said. "So you might as well tell us."

Becky and Meg raised their spears, and Paul stepped forward.

"Oh, I'll tell you," he said. "But the knowledge has always been there for those who really wanted to look. Hardly anybody did, though. Mostly people don't want to know.

"I think you'll enjoy it," he continued. "It's largely a genealogy of the demons—our guardians of the valley. It just lists their provenance—their maker."

"It's a list of every demon, and every person who died to create them?" said Non.

"Well, it's a list of each of the people involved. The demons have proved a little complex to keep track of over the years. Not many distinguishing features unless you're prepared to get close up—and most of us aren't. We did name them, but they don't always answer to those names."

Non took a deep breath. "Why did you make it? And how?"

"Isn't it obvious?"

"It's obvious that nobody who was kept in Cirtop's dungeon was safe from the demons."

"No." He beamed. "That dungeon has proved very useful over the centuries. Almost everybody who's ever been held prisoner there was infected by the guardians. It's amazing how few people care, or notice, what happens to criminals."

"And you?" said Non—though she already knew the answer.

"Of course. I invited my friends in and let myself be infected several weeks ago, so I'm just starting to notice the changes in my body. I think the egg is starting to grow nicely." He placed his hands on his bulbous stomach again.

"What about the church?" asked Sam. "What happened there?"

"The church is a tomb. It marks one of the saddest moments for our order. Some fool had started questioning the disappearance of prisoners and followed those ones, locking them in before they could reach their home to deliver the precious babies. They were killed before the babies were born. We faked a massive uprising, of course, so that the villagers would be punished for their actions. And we left the whole church as a tomb to our blessed babies. We mourn both there—the people too, of course. But they both died together—demon and human as one, intertwined in death as they were in life. So it's a special place for us—beautiful."

"What about the lights?" asked Non. "What are they?"

He looked at her, his mouth working again as he debated ignoring the question. "I suppose it's all in the book anyway." He laughed, merry and loud, as though this was all a hilarious joke. "They're a signal from the demons; they're a signal that they'd like us to bring them offerings. So we do. We slaughter sheep or cattle and leave them out for the guardians."

"You've been feeding the demons?" said Sam. "Feeding the enemy!"

"Well, offerings," said Commander Daffy. "A tribute."

"Why?" asked Non. "Why a tribute?"

"Well, because we're interlinked, aren't we? God created man in his own image, we're told. But if we're in God's image, aren't demons also? And are monkeys a mockery of God's image—or a joke he made to show the world his humor?" He paused for dramatic effect. "But what we believe is that maybe humans are also the joke. God created woman out of man—so she is part of him. For humans or monkeys to reproduce, they need both those male and female sections, because they remain incomplete by themselves. But demons are pure. They are complete in themselves—and they are still the original males, the creatures that God made first in his own image. There are no female demons, because they don't need them."

The students stared at him for a couple of moments. But it was Meg who spoke first, and she spoke with awe. "That is absolute batshit. Wow."

"Look, my darling," said Commander Daffy, beaming at her and with his head tilted to one side. "Your life on this earth is very short. You're really rather insignificant—though I'm sure you feel like you're not." He laughed again. "We have worked—my order—over the centuries to ensure that this valley continues to function the way it always has. We need to help keep the number of demons high, because they're not just one of God's creatures—they're probably God's *most* precious of creatures. We don't care about the short time we're here on earth—that pathetic little dance we call life. We care about the beauty of our eternal life, in heaven."

"What?" said Meg. "Do monkeys even go to heaven? How do you still think you're going to go to heaven when you're wrong in so many ways, but you also don't even think you're created in God's image?"

He laughed. "You silly little girl," he said. "Silly little girl."

"Shall I kill him?" asked Paul. "I think it would be easy enough." He twisted his spear in his hands.

"No," said Non. "I'd like to bring him back to study him. Normally those infected are gone by this stage—so being able to observe and test Commander Daffy as the parasite changes in his system would be really useful. We can keep him—like those people in the church were kept."

Non remembered she had their names in her hand now. And somewhere inside that book would also be the information about what had happened to her mother. She grasped the book to her chest.

"We've got nothing to tie him up with," said Paul. "It might just be easier to kill him. If he's dead, surely it's easier to see what's happening to the egg inside him, because you can just cut him up to have a look?"

Commander Daffy smiled.

"You'll come with us, won't you?" said Becky to him. "Because if we kill you, your demon baby will die too."

"Oh, no. I won't be coming with you." Behind him, the darkness started to shift. Non took a step backward. Meg gasped. "Because you're going to be staying here."

Chapter 47

Immediately everybody raised their weapons. "Get ready!" shouted Sam.

Then something changed. Sam lowered his spear slightly, faltering, and from the darkness emerged a military uniform, and then another. And then beyond, more. Uncertain, Paul and Sam paused, as Commander Edwards stepped into the light.

"Well, good morning!" he drawled. "Didn't you do well in your battle? I am proud of you."

Paul glanced at Sam, frowning in confusion. They still had their spears raised, but their grips were loose, wavering.

"Come with us, sir," said Paul. "Can you help us arrest Commander Daffy?"

The spiderweb scars on Commander Edwards's face seemed to dance in the darkness as he turned to look at each of them, and there was an extra one now, deep, a claw mark, still scabbed over, running across his cheek. He moved his lips into that smile and now, in the shadow, it seemed more twisted, more like a leer than ever.

"They're infected!" gasped Meg. For a second, Non still didn't get it, and Meg pulled at her wrist. "Run!"

But they were too slow, too uncertain, and the guards grabbed Sam and Paul, pushing them up against the sides of the passageway. Paul's spear clattered uselessly to the ground, but Sam kept gripping onto his, as though that would achieve anything. Their lantern skulls fell too, the oil in each splattering against the floor but still burning.

Becky, Meg, and Non backed away, out of reach, still unsure of the situation.

"I need them unharmed," said Commander Daffy. "Or, not too harmed anyway."

"Let them go," said Non, but her voice sounded feeble, the echo in the passageway exaggerating her lack of conviction.

"Are you *not* infected?" asked Commander Edwards. "Did you really come here of your own free will?"

"Run, Meg," whispered Non.

"No, you," whispered Meg back. Her skull lantern was shaking in her hands, and slowly, she put it down on the floor.

Paul was still struggling, but Sam was peering into the darkness, and at the guards, frowning. There was no more movement in the passageway beyond, but it was too dark to see properly, and narrower too. There were five guards in total, plus Commander Daffy and Commander Edwards. Sam caught Non's eye, and she felt like she should be communicating some sort of message. But there was nothing. Nothing to say. She just felt frozen with panic.

Suddenly, next to her, Non felt the air shift, and Meg raised her arm. In one swift movement, Meg unhooked her bow, aimed an arrow, and shot it straight at Commander Edwards. There was a second of stillness when he turned, stared, and glanced down at the arrow in his chest. Then, suddenly, there was a spear flying too, and the corridor erupted.

"They don't have weapons," screamed Becky, lunging forward to pick up her spear. Meg fired another arrow at one of the guards, and Non threw her spear too, wildly, without aiming, into the middle of them. She couldn't see if it hit, but the guards leaped to one side, and somebody stumbled over Commander Edwards's body. There were shouts, yelps of pain, and weapons flying everywhere.

Non took a step back, paused, and picked up Paul's spear. In the shadows, the fighting was a mess, chaos. She couldn't see where to fire—it felt like the passageway was suddenly full of arms, legs, some she wanted to protect, others trying to kill, but all mixed together, and with noise and shouts echoing and confusing. Becky and Meg were both in the middle attacking.

She turned and stabbed her spear at the guard holding Sam. She felt it hitting, but then the guard leaped away, and Sam jumped into the fray. Non ran over to the other side and stabbed at the other guard, freeing Paul.

Then, suddenly, it was over. Commander Edwards lay on the floor dead, another three guards lay around him or up against the walls, injured or dead, and the running footsteps of the others faded away into the hillside. Non tried to listen over the loud panting of her own breath, but the sound disappeared rather than stopped. The mine was deep.

The flames in the remaining skulls were smoking, and Non could smell what was burning inside them now—it was some sort of animal fat. She didn't want to think too much about what animal it was made from, but she was also grateful for the light. For a moment they all looked at each other as they caught their breath. Then Meg stepped forward. "Just got to collect my arrows," she said with a laugh that was also half a sob, as she reached to pick up the arrows on the floor. She hesitated over the one sticking out of Commander Edwards's chest but then pulled it out, wiping the tip on his shirt.

"What shall we do?" asked Paul.

"There's only three of them left," said Sam. "And one of those is Commander Daffy—so that's only two real guards. We can take him on."

Non stepped over the bodies, peering into the darkness beyond.

"I can see a light ahead," she whispered.

"Do you want to go?" asked Sam.

Did she? It was very tempting to go back to the castle. But at the same time, that thought was mixed with a new anxiety—or maybe it was the old anxiety dressed up in a different way. She knew it would feel like running away, that it would feel like Commander Daffy and the demons were the ones who were free, while they were trapped. And that wasn't the way it should be! The castle felt stifling and cramped in comparison to the whole of the valley.

"What could be worse than what we've faced already today?" she said.

Meg started to laugh again. So much, this time, that she had to lean against the wall for support. She put her arrow between her fingers and held her bow ready, but as she stood up again and grinned grimly at Non, Non saw that her hands had stopped shaking. "Let's go, then," said Meg. "But just so you know, when we get back, I'm going to break into the stores and take all the alcohol out, because I'm going to need another party tonight. That's just the start of what you owe me, Non. Plus," she added, "Commander Daffy is the only person in charge who knew what was in those stores, and now that it turns out he's insane, we can always say he's making stuff up if anybody tells us off."

"Good plan," agreed Paul, looking into the darkness.

They continued down the passageway. They passed two other rooms on the way—rough, low-ceilinged places where the miners had followed seams in the stone. They each had the fungusy, forest stench of the demons, but it was faint, only a hint. There were leaves in them too, but both were otherwise empty.

It felt as though there were demons behind them, or in front of them, or above them. But it was almost worse that there weren't. The uncertainty, the expectation of there being something about to attack any second, meant that Non felt jumpy constantly. She felt like she could jump or start at every movement—if only she knew where was safe to jump to.

The passageway seemed to become even darker as they got closer to the light and, though it seemed almost pointless, they tried to creep along it quietly so that they were moving slowly—something Non felt she had to force, because every part of her wanted to run.

But as they crept closer to the light, there was another smell, a familiar one, acrid and herby. Smoke from a fire—but also, other things cooking. The light was different too. It was blue and flickering, but it was brighter than just that. There was also daylight.

They paused as they reached the room and, slowly, Sam peered in. Then he stepped inside.

"Oh, lovely, you're here. Lovely!" said Commander Daffy. "Unharmed? Or only a bit harmed?"

"Unharmed," said Becky. "And we've come to take you back to the castle."

"Or we could kill you if that's too much hassle," interjected Paul.

The room was roughly cut from the stone, and there were uneven indentations on the walls where ancient miners had searched for veins of copper, or whatever metal it was they were following. At the back of the room, there was a vent through the ceiling—cut perhaps for air, or maybe as an old entrance. Through it now there was sunlight—distant and weak but making this the brightest of the rooms so far. Beneath the vent, there was a lit stove on which a pot was bubbling, containing some sort of mixture. There was a table to one side of it, which was set up with various bottles, test tubes, and apparatuses. Non went over to it immediately.

"Oh, dear," said Commander Daffy. "You don't mean to tell me that you won that little fight, did you?"

"We've won everything," said Sam. "It's over."

"Of course it's not, you silly boy." He smiled.

There were several books on the table, thin but full of tiny, handwritten notes. Non grabbed them and held them to her chest, looking round quickly for more. There were no others that she could see, but the walls were lined with shelves, containing bottles labeled in that same handwriting.

"Let's get out of here," said Sam. "We can come back when we've got reinforcements."

"It's fine. I'll come. I know Non here will let my demon live," said Commander Daffy.

Non looked at him.

"Oh, of course you will. You're not going to miss that opportunity, are you?"

Non was going to disagree on the principle that she didn't want to agree with him about anything, but it was also true. Nobody had recorded the demon birthing process, and the opportunity to examine the changes it made in the human body—as well as the demon bodies—would help them understand more about the life cycle. Commander Daffy was worth far more to humanity alive than he was dead. Plus, judging by the size of his stomach, he was going to be dead soon anyway.

"What have you been doing here?" she said, looking around the room once more in case there was anything else valuable she needed there that could be carried.

"Oh, I know you'll be interested. It's taken years, and we went down a number of wrong turns. A lot of trial and error! But we've been searching for ways to boost the parasite so that the host body can take more than one. Although there's something beautifully balanced about needing the death of one human to make the life of one demon, it's also an inefficient process. I'm proud to say, though, that it looks like our guards have successfully been infected twice. Hopefully, they should, then, be able to produce two demons each."

"Trial and error?" said Non. She held the books more carefully now. What did that mean? Was all knowledge good? What was the error! She thought about those skins outside, and the animal fat inside the lanterns, and then wished she hadn't.

Suddenly there was a *boom*, and the ground shook—the ceiling too. Dust and small stones fell down so that for a moment they all raised their hands to cover their heads. But then, as the air cleared, there was a duller, longer rumbling. It was unmistakably the sound of rock falling farther down the passageway.

Commander Daffy smiled again. "Ah, excellent," he said. "I see you didn't kill everybody, then. Yes, now we can certainly go."

"What was that?" asked Sam. His eyes were narrowed, and his weapons were raised again.

"We've made it into another valley. Good old Commander Edwards managed that after he got infected. Cut through the last remaining foot of rock—what a hard worker! There are other valleys, you know. Other people. The Southerners, the Northerners, all our many enemies. But they're not the demons' enemies, because they're human too. They have bodies that the valley guardians can use just as well as ours. And there are more of them. So our brave band has gone off to see who else they can find out in the world. Yes, we're spreading God's work to the rest of the world."

They all stared, open-mouthed.

Commander Daffy laughed again. "Or, if you like, you can see it as being somebody else's problem now. That rock fall was them just closing off the way to the other valleys again, so that you can't follow."

"We can follow," said Sam. "We'll just cut through the rock."

"Yes, well, you're not going to be able to do that particularly quickly, are you? The point is, you're not going to be able to stop them infecting people in the other valleys. So you might as well see it as being that the door to this valley is shut now."

They all just looked at him in horror.

Non was the first to speak. "OK. Everything," she said. "I'm going to need absolutely everything from this room. All of those little bottles—whatever's in them." She wrinkled her nose. "There's some really weird science here—but some of it might give us some useful information. Because, Commander Daffy, just shifting the problem somewhere else doesn't get rid of it. Also, I don't know if we even want to get rid of it. I think it might be much better if we studied and managed it instead."

Meg grinned at Non. "It's going to be you studying it, is it?"

Non shrugged.

Meg shook her head. "Oh, you're in so much trouble with your dad."

"It's sort of like medicine. And if I can help find a cure for the demon parasite, then that would be amazing medicine." She clutched the books tightly and smiled. "Also, he's not my only parent. I'm guessing my mum would have been OK with it."

———o———

Becky led the way up the passageway again—which seemed much shorter now that they weren't creeping along it expecting to be attacked at any moment. Paul tapped Commander Daffy lightly with his spear every so often, but the commander walked with his hands in his pockets, as though they were out for a jolly stroll. He seemed happy enough to be going back to the castle, and Non wondered how much of his brain had now been taken over by the parasite.

As they stepped out from between the two boulders and onto the track, they could see Cirtop clearly through the trees. People moved along the battlements, and as they watched, a supply cart trundled out of the woods, the driver clearly alive—and surrounded by a unit of soldiers. The sky was clearing too, the clouds shifting higher up the valley and the sun brightening.

Chapter 48

Non sat on the wall, her legs dangling off the edge. The portcullis was up, and the drawbridge down. Nobody was manning it, and behind her, Non could already hear laughter and a few people starting to sing. There was a group by the kitchen sitting on logs of wood, cooking, preparing vegetables, but also just chatting.

"Drink?" said Meg, handing her a bottle.

Non took a tiny sip.

"Right. No pressure, but you're going to have to do better than that. We've probably only got tonight for partying, so you've got to make it count, Non. Now that we're in contact with the citadel again, we're sure to have somebody sent in to supervise us tomorrow, so I expect you to put some proper work into partying tonight."

Non smiled. "I'm a bit tired, to be honest."

"Pathetic. When we were leaving the mine, I also felt pretty tired. But, amazingly, now that we're back, I feel like I have enough energy for the best party ever." Meg stretched. "Actually, I might go for a quick nap first, maybe, just to make sure I can party until dawn." She climbed down and walked toward the guard tower. "But I'm taking that nap in Dog's bed," she called over her shoulder.

Down on the plain, Jane was surrounded by a small herd of young demons, each with a lead around their neck. A few of them were sitting down, and she rewarded those ones with treats. A couple of them were leaping around, however, yowling and play fighting with each other. She tapped one on the nose and wagged her finger at it. "No!" she called. "Naughty!" It leaped away from her and snarled.

A few moments later, Sam climbed up and sat next to her. They both sat watching Jane's demons, but Sam drummed his fingers on the wall, picking at the mortar, still restless.

"What's the matter?" asked Non.

"Nothing," he said, then pulled a face. "Do you think we made a mistake not clearing away that rock in the tunnel today?"

"No. I don't think that was an option. Commander Edwards knew what he was doing, and we wouldn't have been able to cut through that rock in time to do anything. I think, this time, it's better to sit and look at all of the information—to actually collect information—so that when we go into the other valley, we've got something to really tell them. Rather than just advising them to build castles and go and hide inside them like we've been doing forever. Hunting demons, and hiding from demons, is the pattern we've been following for too long. It's time to try something different." Non stretched. Her arms were still aching from the battle last night, and it felt like only now was she starting to relax.

"Do you think you'll be able to find a cure?"

"Not quickly, no, because I'm starting from scratch. Commander Daffy certainly wasn't trying to find one."

"It sounds like that's the exact opposite of what he was doing."

"Yeah." She shuddered at the memory of his laboratory. But it was also an exciting thought. She felt a thrill at searching through his notes and studies, at examining the extra information he must have. "We've got a starting point, though, if we can look at the different stages of the parasite's life cycle—and I think that must, at least partly, have been what he was doing. That would help give us a clue as to what might kill the parasite, at least, and I think that's the sort of information the people in other valleys would find useful."

"If we're able to find the infected ones."

"But we will, won't we?" Non turned to him. "Surely that'll be the easy bit? Because they'll just make their way to the mine and enter it from the other side?"

He turned to her, eyes wide.

"Did you not think of that?" Non smiled. "I think it'll be exactly where they'll be going back to, to wait until their demon eggs are ready to hatch. And when they're there, we can try to help them." She paused, making it sound casual, like she'd only just thought of it. "And so maybe we could make the mine into a sort of demon infection recovery center."

"A hospital for the infected!" Sam laughed and shook his head. "So, are you going to stay here, then, or are you going to go home? When quarantine's ended, that is?"

"I don't know," said Non, though she knew exactly what she wanted. "What about you?"

"I don't know either," he said. Then he looked at her. "I might stay here for a bit, actually. They might need some new guards.

Somebody to dig out rubble from mines so that infected people can get back into them. Or maybe somebody to hunt escaped demons in other valleys."

"I might stay here for a bit too," she said.

"That would be good," he said. He grinned, reached out, and took her hand. They sat, watching the young demons for a few moments, then Non leaned over and kissed him.

A red kite circled low over the plain, gliding on a pillar of air. But then something in the woods caught its eye and it flapped its wings, flying up the valley away from Cirtop. There were no other birds in the sky.